SNAKE EYES & STORM SHADOW

Written by **Chuck Dixon**
Art by **Robert Atkins** and **Atilio Rojo**
Inks by **Juan Castro**, **Brian Shearer**, and **Atilio Rojo**
Colors by **Simon Gough**, **Juan Fernandez**, **Joana Lafuente**, **J. Aburtov**, and **Graphikslava**
Letters by **Neil Uyetake**
Series Edits by **John Barber** and **Carlos Guzman**

Cover by **Andrea Di Vito**
Cover Colors by **Laura Villari**
Collection Edits by **Justin Eisinger** and **Alonzo Simon**
Collection Design by **Shawn Lee**

Special thanks to Hasbro's Aaron Archer, Derryl DePriest, Joe Del Regno, Ed Lane, Joe Furfaro, Jos Huxley, Heather Hopkins, and Michael Kelly for their invaluable assistance.

IDW founded by Ted Adams, Alex Garner, Kris Oprisko, and Robbie Robbins |

ISBN: 978-1-61377-419-9

15 14 13 12   1 2 3 4

Ted Adams, CEO & Publisher
Greg Goldstein, President & COO
Robbie Robbins, EVP/Sr. Graphic Artist
Chris Ryall, Chief Creative Officer/Editor-in-Chief
Matthew Ruzicka, CPA, Chief Financial Officer
Alan Payne, VP of Sales
Dirk Wood, VP of Marketing
Lorelei Bunjes, VP of Digital Services

Become our fan on Facebook **facebook.com/idwpublishing**
Follow us on Twitter **@idwpublishing**
Check us out on YouTube **youtube.com/idwpublishing**
www.IDWPUBLISHING.com

After Cobra's invasion of the Southeast Asian nation of Nanzhao, the G.I. JOE team thinks Snake Eyes is dead, but he's agreed to join the ninja clan of his sword-brother, Storm Shadow. Before heading to Tokyo, though, he visits the Hard Master in New York. He reassures him that he has not given in to the Arashikage: he is infiltrating the clan in order to destroy it from within. When Snake Eyes arrives in Tokyo, Storm Shadow greets him enthusiastically and reveals their first target: Zartan!

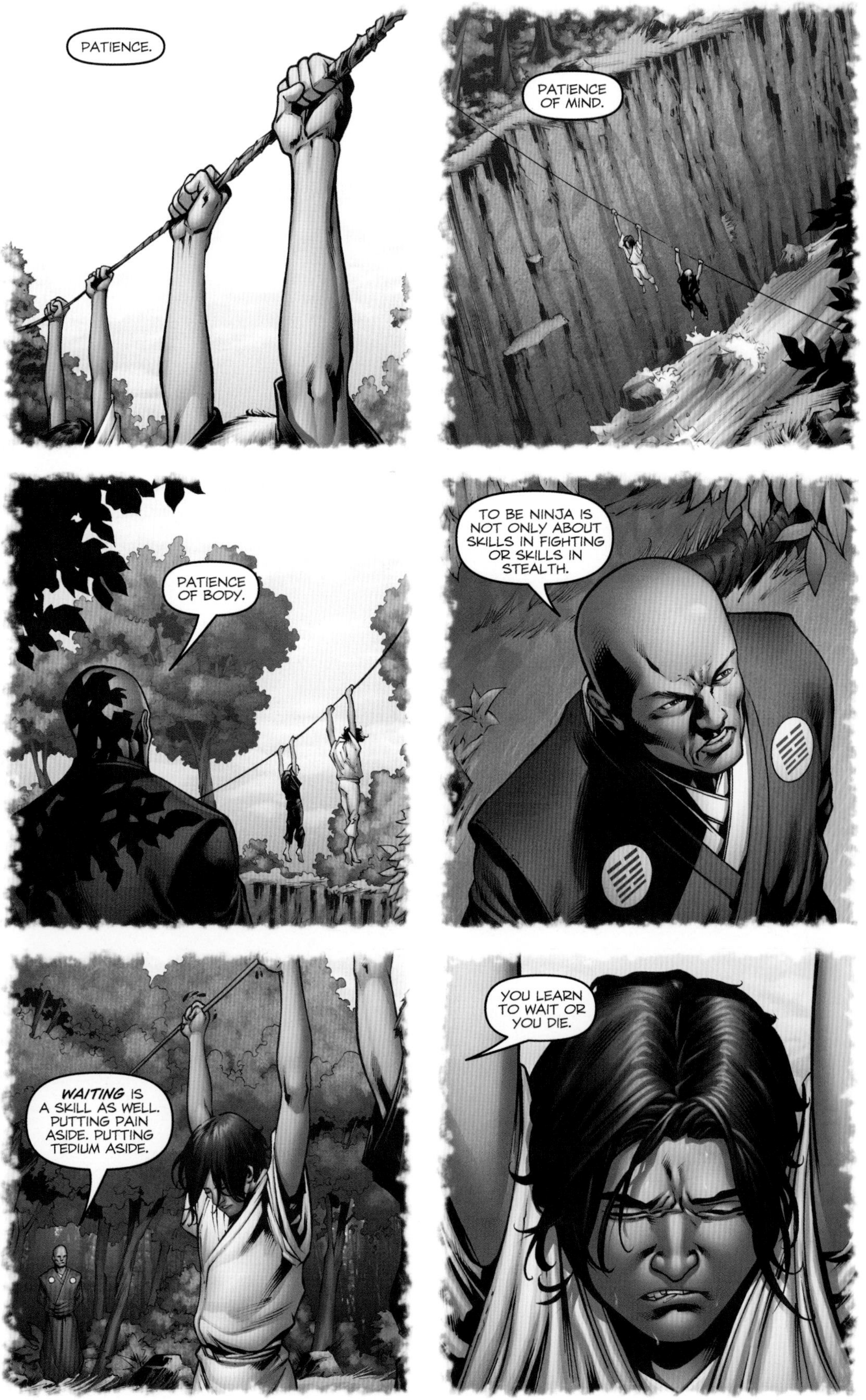
PATIENCE.
PATIENCE OF MIND.
PATIENCE OF BODY.
TO BE NINJA IS NOT ONLY ABOUT SKILLS IN FIGHTING OR SKILLS IN STEALTH.
WAITING IS A SKILL AS WELL. PUTTING PAIN ASIDE. PUTTING TEDIUM ASIDE.
YOU LEARN TO WAIT OR YOU DIE.

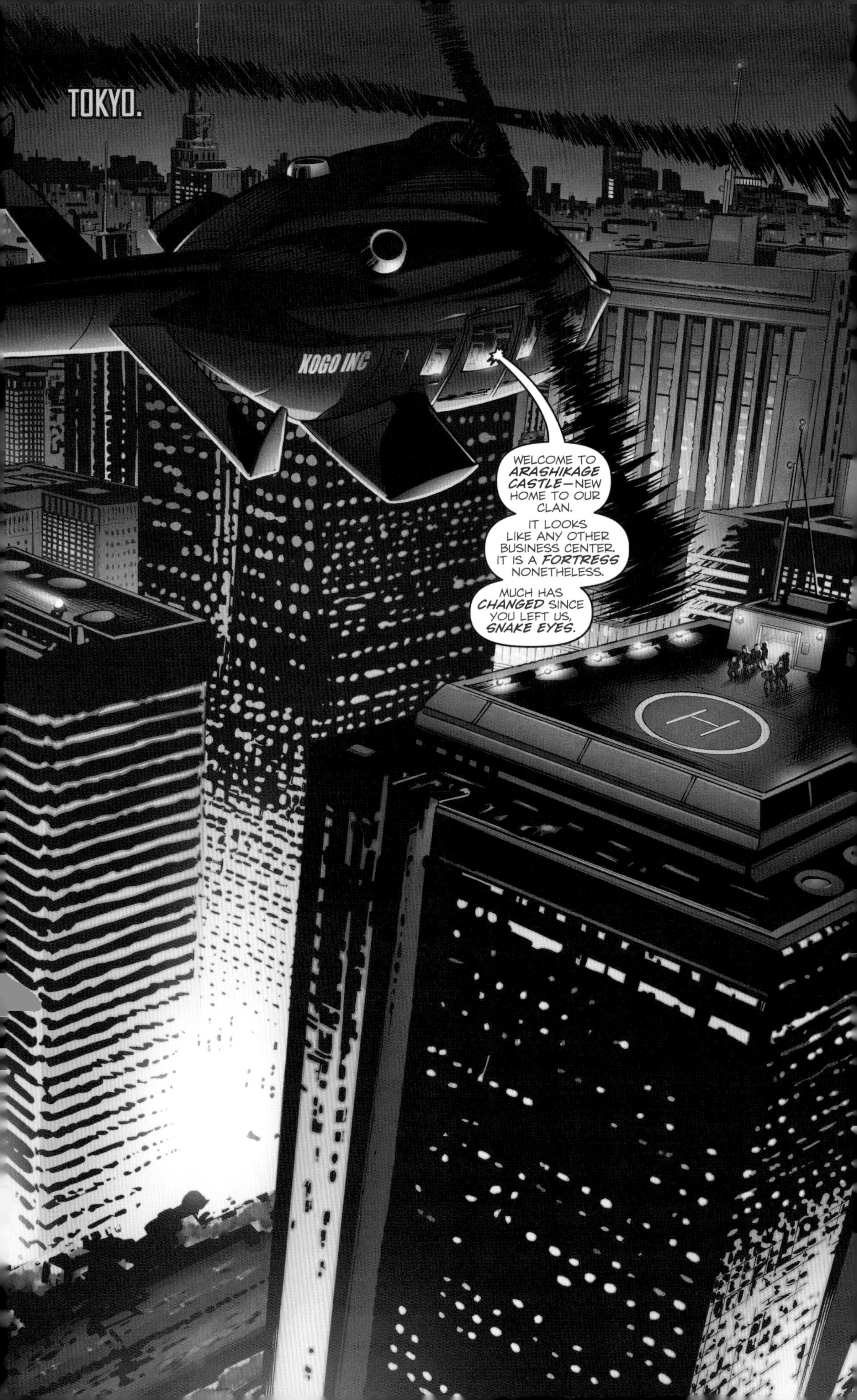
TOKYO.
KOGO INC
WELCOME TO ARASHIKAGE CASTLE—NEW HOME TO OUR CLAN.
IT LOOKS LIKE ANY OTHER BUSINESS CENTER. IT IS A FORTRESS NONETHELESS.
MUCH HAS CHANGED SINCE YOU LEFT US, SNAKE EYES.

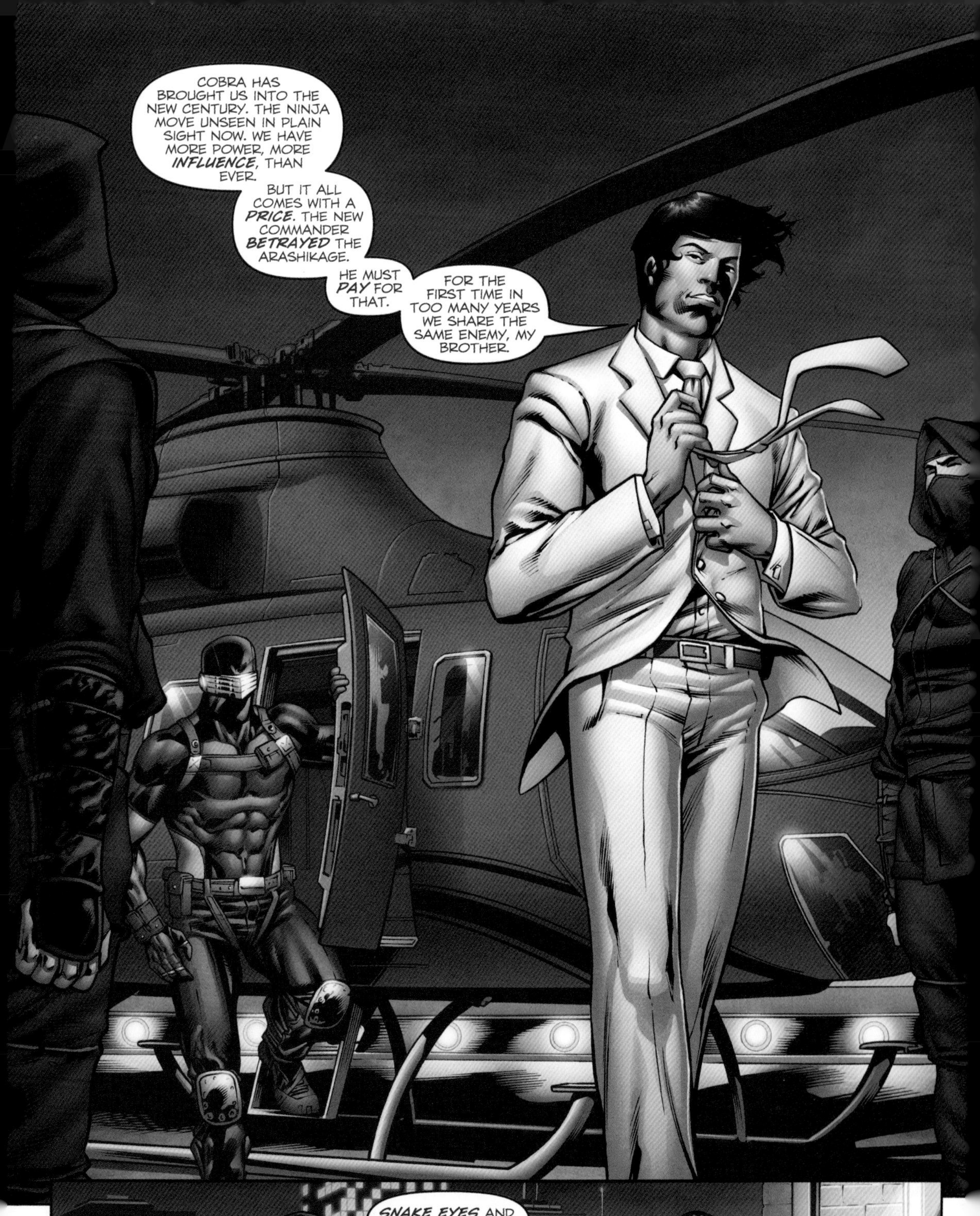
COBRA HAS BROUGHT US INTO THE NEW CENTURY. THE NINJA MOVE UNSEEN IN PLAIN SIGHT NOW. WE HAVE MORE POWER, MORE INFLUENCE, THAN EVER.
BUT IT ALL COMES WITH A PRICE. THE NEW COMMANDER BETRAYED THE ARASHIKAGE.
HE MUST PAY FOR THAT.
FOR THE FIRST TIME IN TOO MANY YEARS WE SHARE THE SAME ENEMY, MY BROTHER.

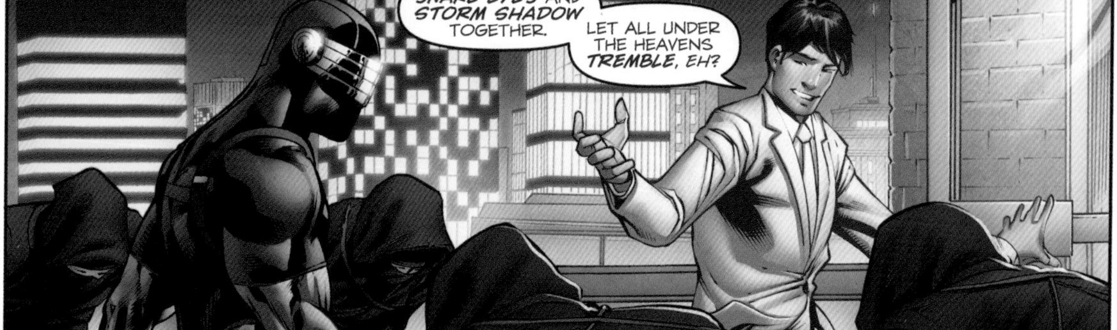
SNAKE EYES AND STORM SHADOW TOGETHER.
LET ALL UNDER THE HEAVENS TREMBLE, EH?

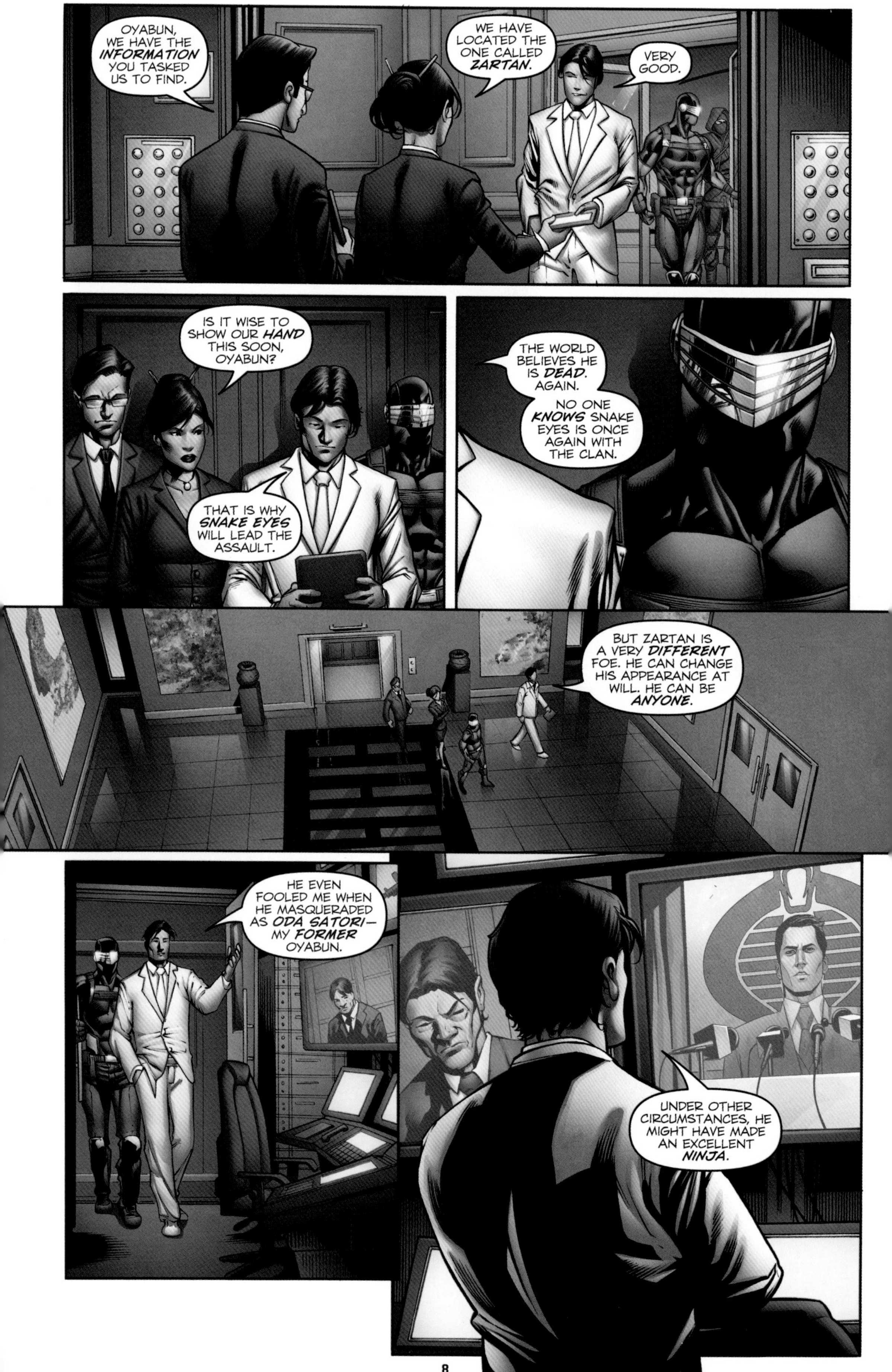

OYABUN, WE HAVE THE INFORMATION YOU TASKED US TO FIND.
WE HAVE LOCATED THE ONE CALLED ZARTAN.
VERY GOOD.
IS IT WISE TO SHOW OUR HAND THIS SOON, OYABUN?
THAT IS WHY SNAKE EYES WILL LEAD THE ASSAULT.
THE WORLD BELIEVES HE IS DEAD. AGAIN.
NO ONE KNOWS SNAKE EYES IS ONCE AGAIN WITH THE CLAN.
BUT ZARTAN IS A VERY DIFFERENT FOE. HE CAN CHANGE HIS APPEARANCE AT WILL. HE CAN BE ANYONE.
HE EVEN FOOLED ME WHEN HE MASQUERADED AS ODA SATORI— MY FORMER OYABUN.
UNDER OTHER CIRCUMSTANCES, HE MIGHT HAVE MADE AN EXCELLENT NINJA.

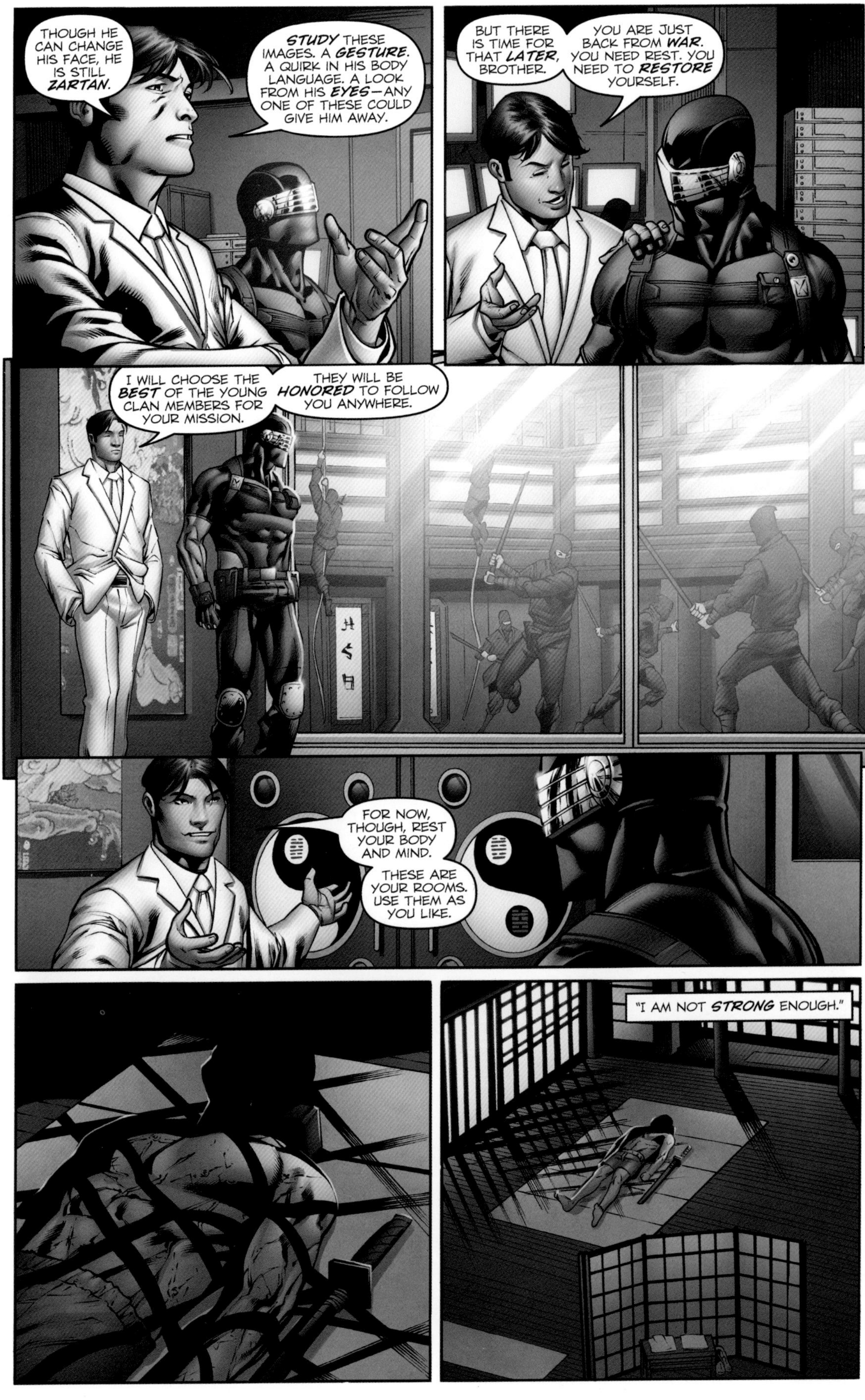

THOUGH HE CAN CHANGE HIS FACE, HE IS STILL ZARTAN.
STUDY THESE IMAGES. A GESTURE. A QUIRK IN HIS BODY LANGUAGE. A LOOK FROM HIS EYES—ANY ONE OF THESE COULD GIVE HIM AWAY.
BUT THERE IS TIME FOR THAT LATER, BROTHER.
YOU ARE JUST BACK FROM WAR. YOU NEED REST. YOU NEED TO RESTORE YOURSELF.
I WILL CHOOSE THE BEST OF THE YOUNG CLAN MEMBERS FOR YOUR MISSION.
THEY WILL BE HONORED TO FOLLOW YOU ANYWHERE.
FOR NOW, THOUGH, REST YOUR BODY AND MIND.
THESE ARE YOUR ROOMS. USE THEM AS YOU LIKE.
"I AM NOT STRONG ENOUGH."

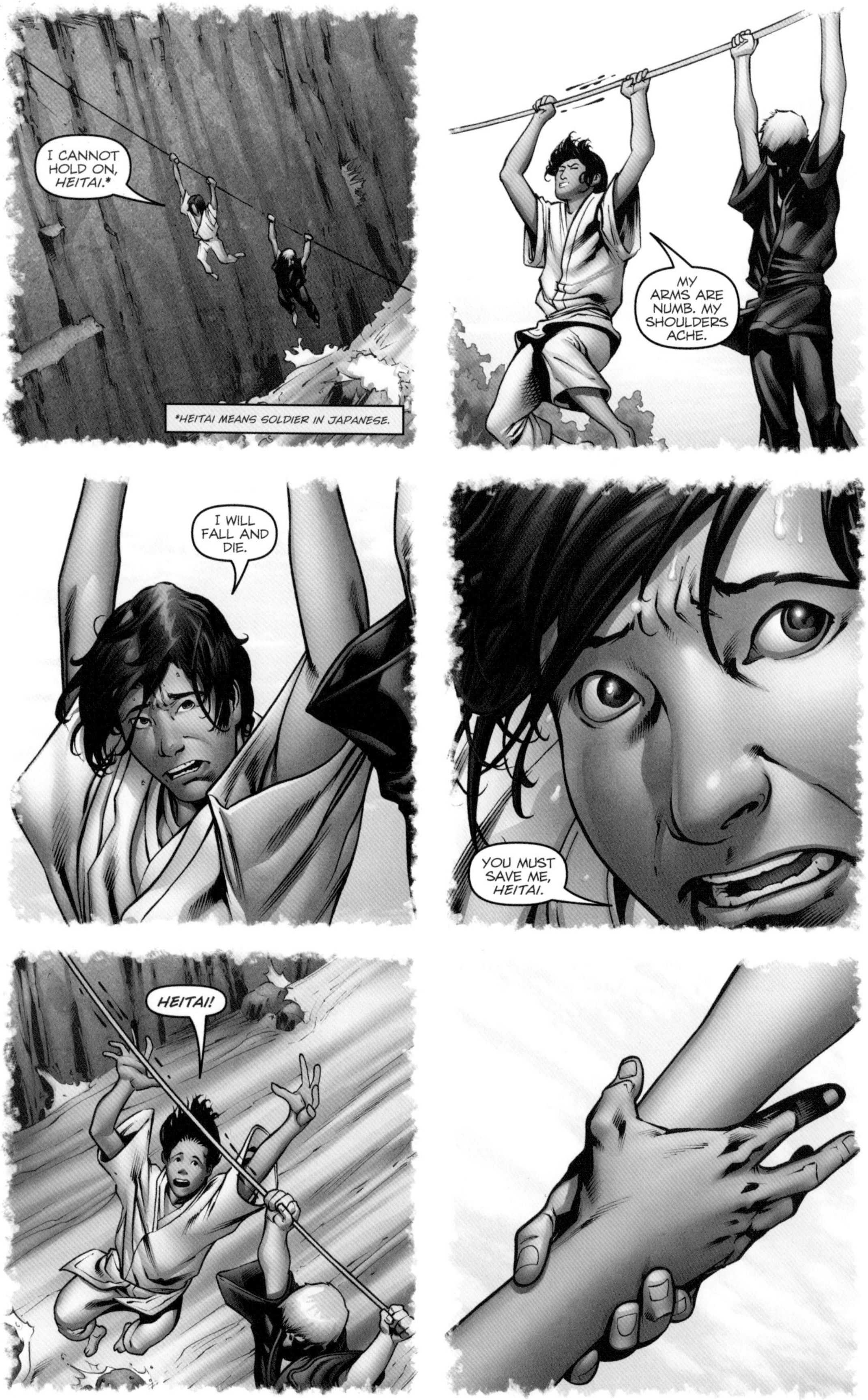
I CANNOT HOLD ON, *HEITAI*.*
**HEITAI* MEANS SOLDIER IN JAPANESE.
MY ARMS ARE NUMB. MY SHOULDERS ACHE.
I WILL FALL AND DIE.
YOU MUST SAVE ME, *HEITAI*.
HEITAI!

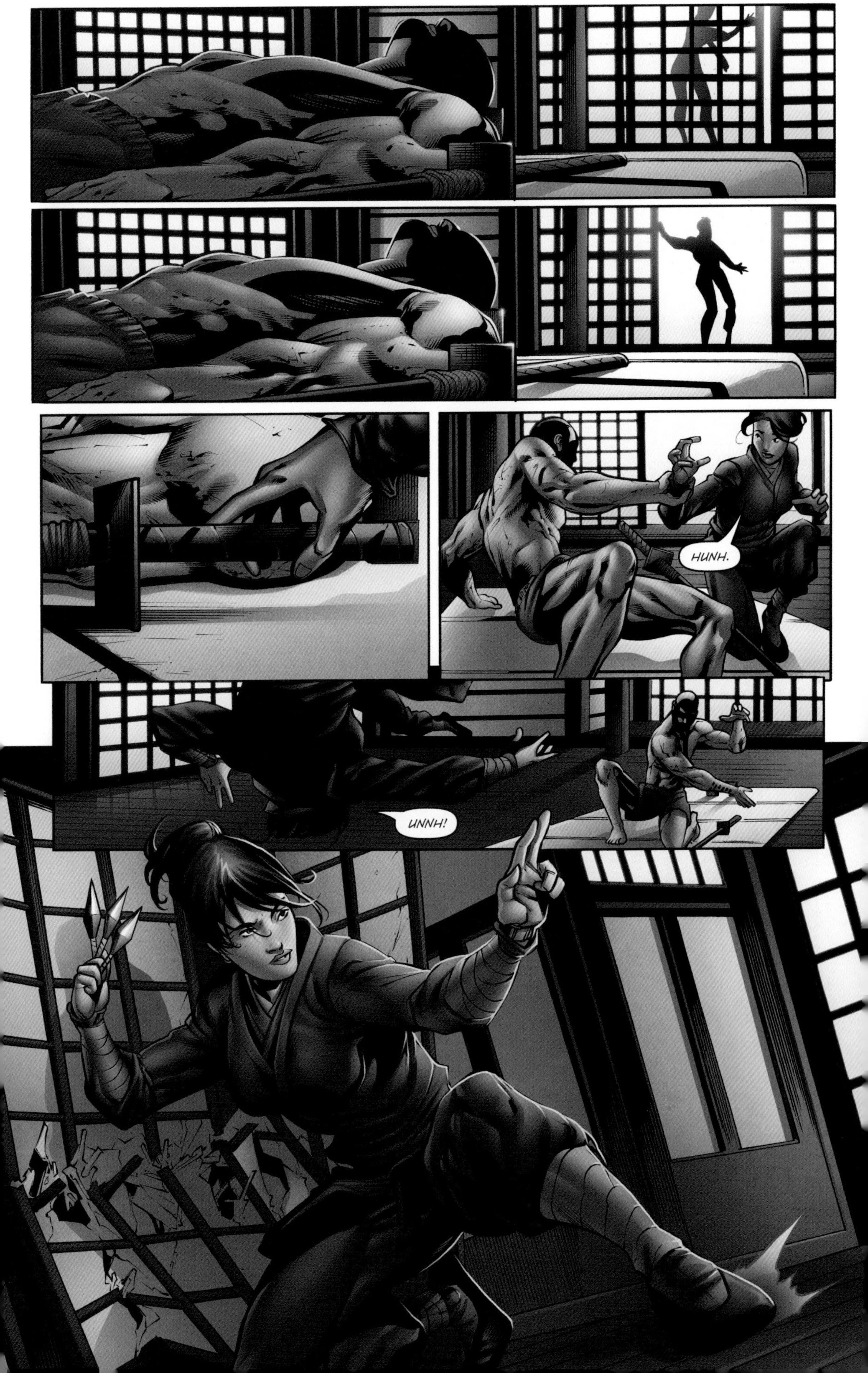
HUNH.
UNNH!

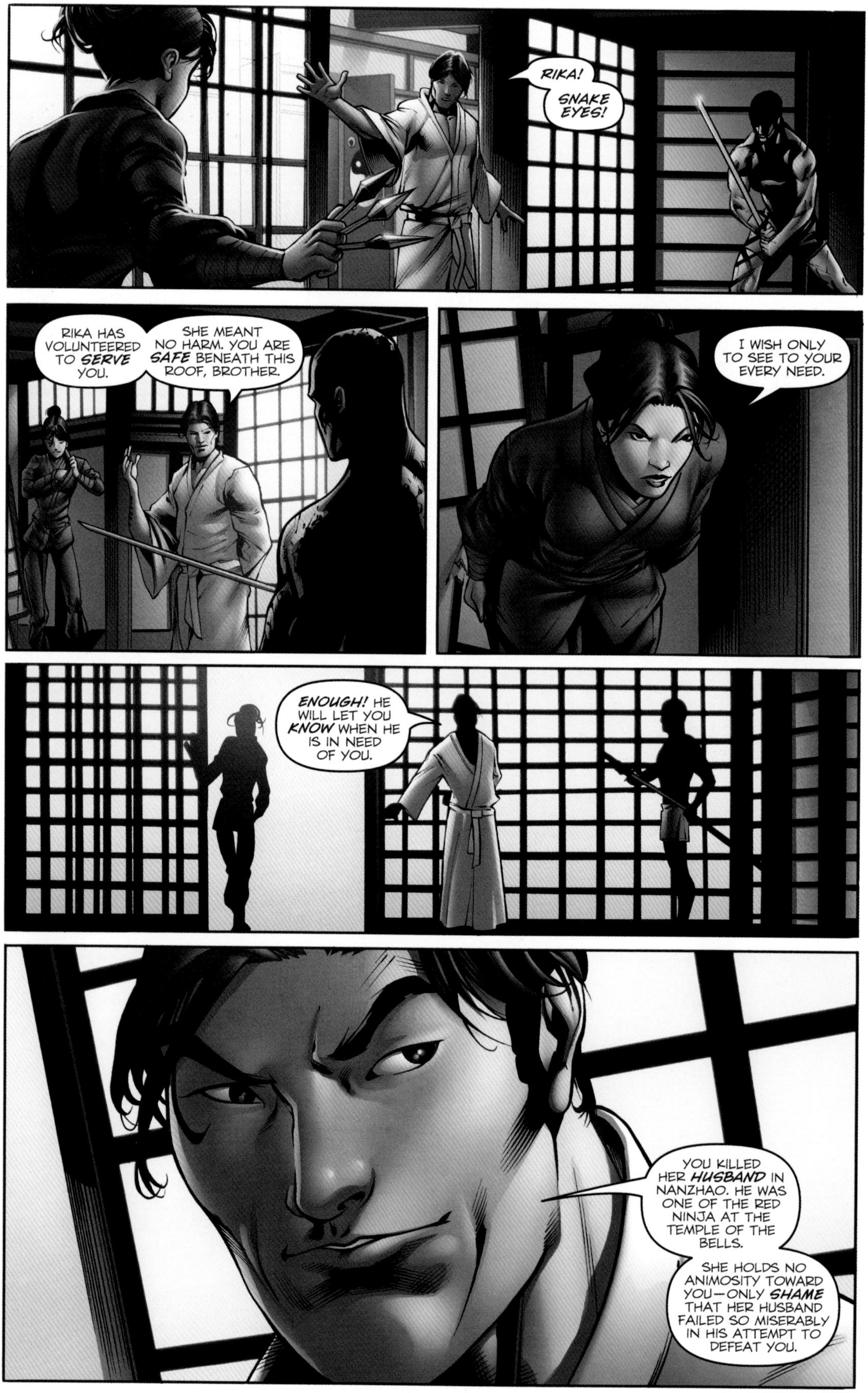
RIKA! SNAKE EYES!
RIKA HAS VOLUNTEERED TO SERVE YOU.
SHE MEANT NO HARM. YOU ARE SAFE BENEATH THIS ROOF, BROTHER.
I WISH ONLY TO SEE TO YOUR EVERY NEED.
ENOUGH! HE WILL LET YOU KNOW WHEN HE IS IN NEED OF YOU.
YOU KILLED HER HUSBAND IN NANZHAO. HE WAS ONE OF THE RED NINJA AT THE TEMPLE OF THE BELLS.
SHE HOLDS NO ANIMOSITY TOWARD YOU—ONLY SHAME THAT HER HUSBAND FAILED SO MISERABLY IN HIS ATTEMPT TO DEFEAT YOU.

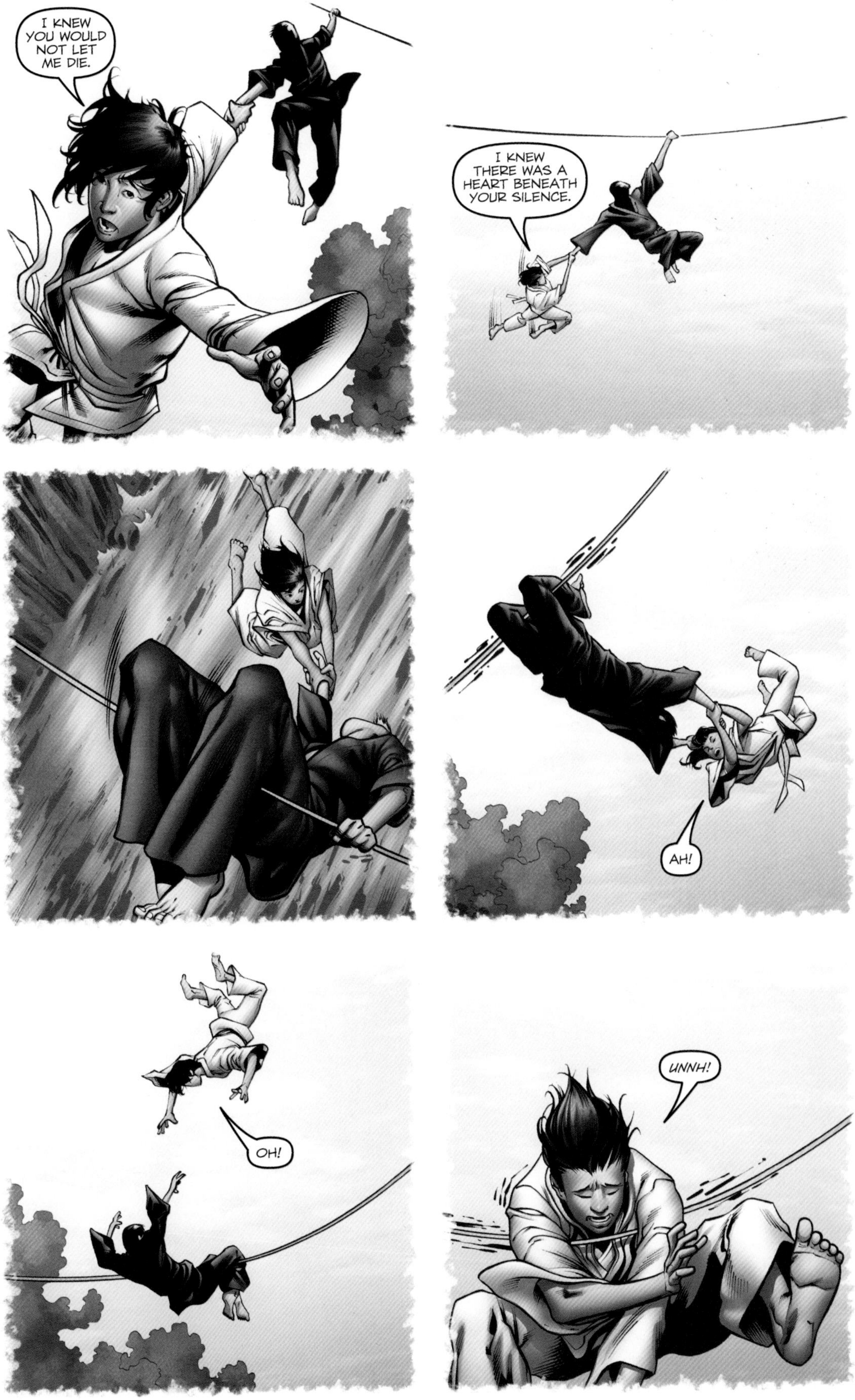
I KNEW YOU WOULD NOT LET ME DIE.
I KNEW THERE WAS A HEART BENEATH YOUR SILENCE.
AH!
OH!
UNNH!

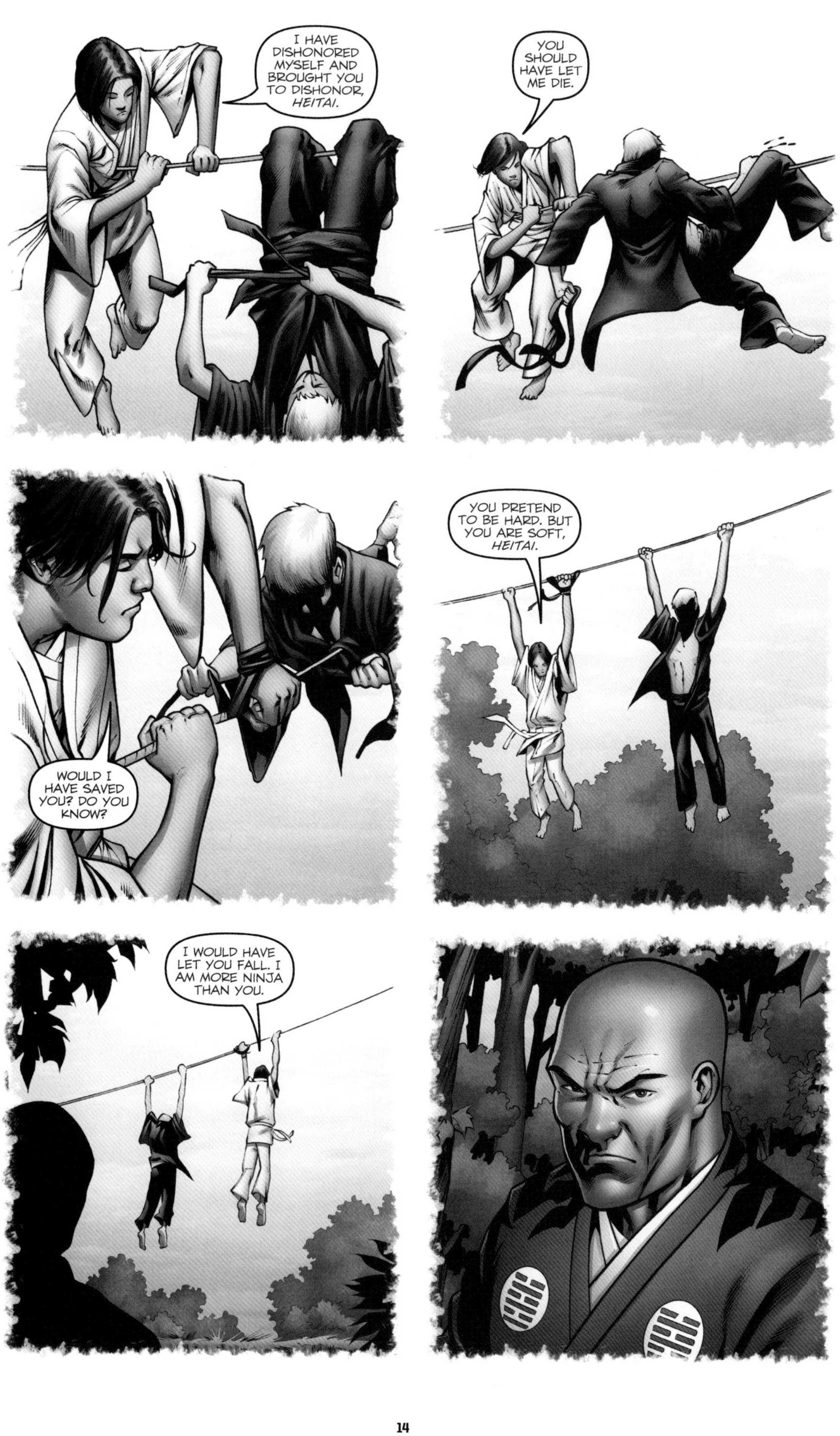
I HAVE DISHONORED MYSELF AND BROUGHT YOU TO DISHONOR, *HEITAI*.
YOU SHOULD HAVE LET ME DIE.
WOULD I HAVE SAVED YOU? DO YOU KNOW?
YOU PRETEND TO BE HARD. BUT YOU ARE SOFT, *HEITAI*.
I WOULD HAVE LET YOU FALL. I AM MORE NINJA THAN YOU.

SHANGHAI.

I UNDERSTAND YOUR *CONCERNS*, GENTLEMEN. BUT COBRA *HONORS* ITS PROMISES.

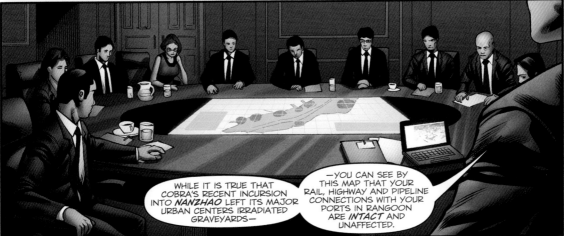

WHILE IT IS TRUE THAT COBRA'S RECENT INCURSION INTO *NANZHAO* LEFT ITS MAJOR URBAN CENTERS IRRADIATED GRAVEYARDS—

—YOU CAN SEE BY THIS MAP THAT YOUR RAIL, HIGHWAY AND PIPELINE CONNECTIONS WITH YOUR PORTS IN RANGOON ARE *INTACT* AND UNAFFECTED.

WE SEE THAT THIS BENEFITS THE PEOPLE'S REPUBLIC BUT FAIL TO SEE HOW *COBRA* PROFITS FROM THIS, MR. ZARTAN.

LIKE CHINA, COBRA PLAYS A *GENERATIONAL* GAME. IT WAS IN OUR INTERESTS TO SEE THE DRUG FIELDS OF THE GOLDEN TRIANGLE *ELIMINATED*.

AND NO NEED FOR AN HONORIFIC. IT'S JUST *ZARTAN*.

WELL, GENTLEMEN, IF THERE ARE NO OTHER ISSUES, I BELIEVE THAT *CONCLUDES* OUR BUSINESS. I HAVE TO CATCH ONE OF YOUR MARVELOUS HIGH SPEED *TRAINS* TO BEIJING.

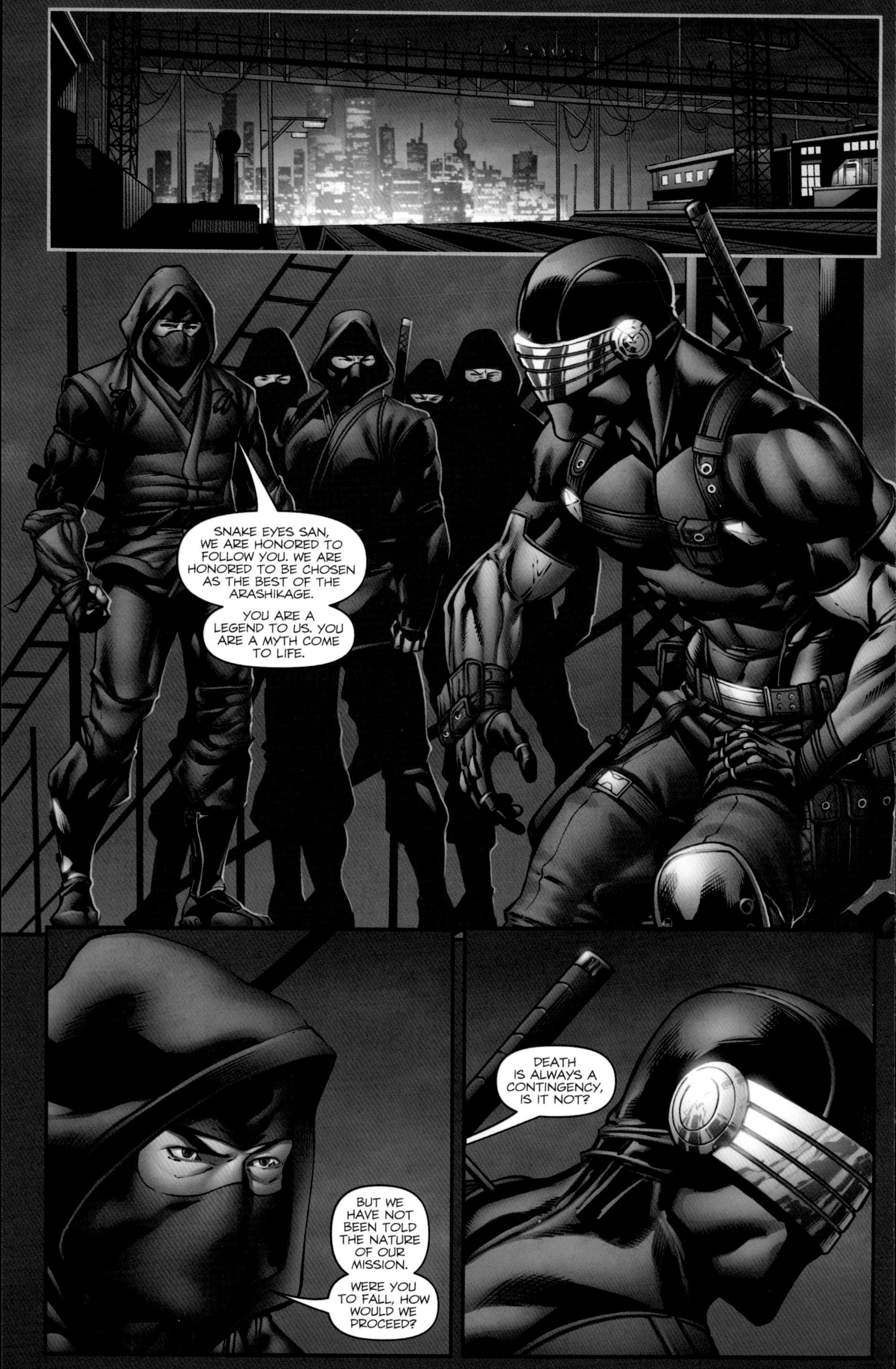

SNAKE EYES SAN, WE ARE HONORED TO FOLLOW YOU. WE ARE HONORED TO BE CHOSEN AS THE BEST OF THE ARASHIKAGE.
YOU ARE A LEGEND TO US. YOU ARE A MYTH COME TO LIFE.
BUT WE HAVE NOT BEEN TOLD THE NATURE OF OUR MISSION.
WERE YOU TO FALL, HOW WOULD WE PROCEED?
DEATH IS ALWAYS A CONTINGENCY, IS IT NOT?

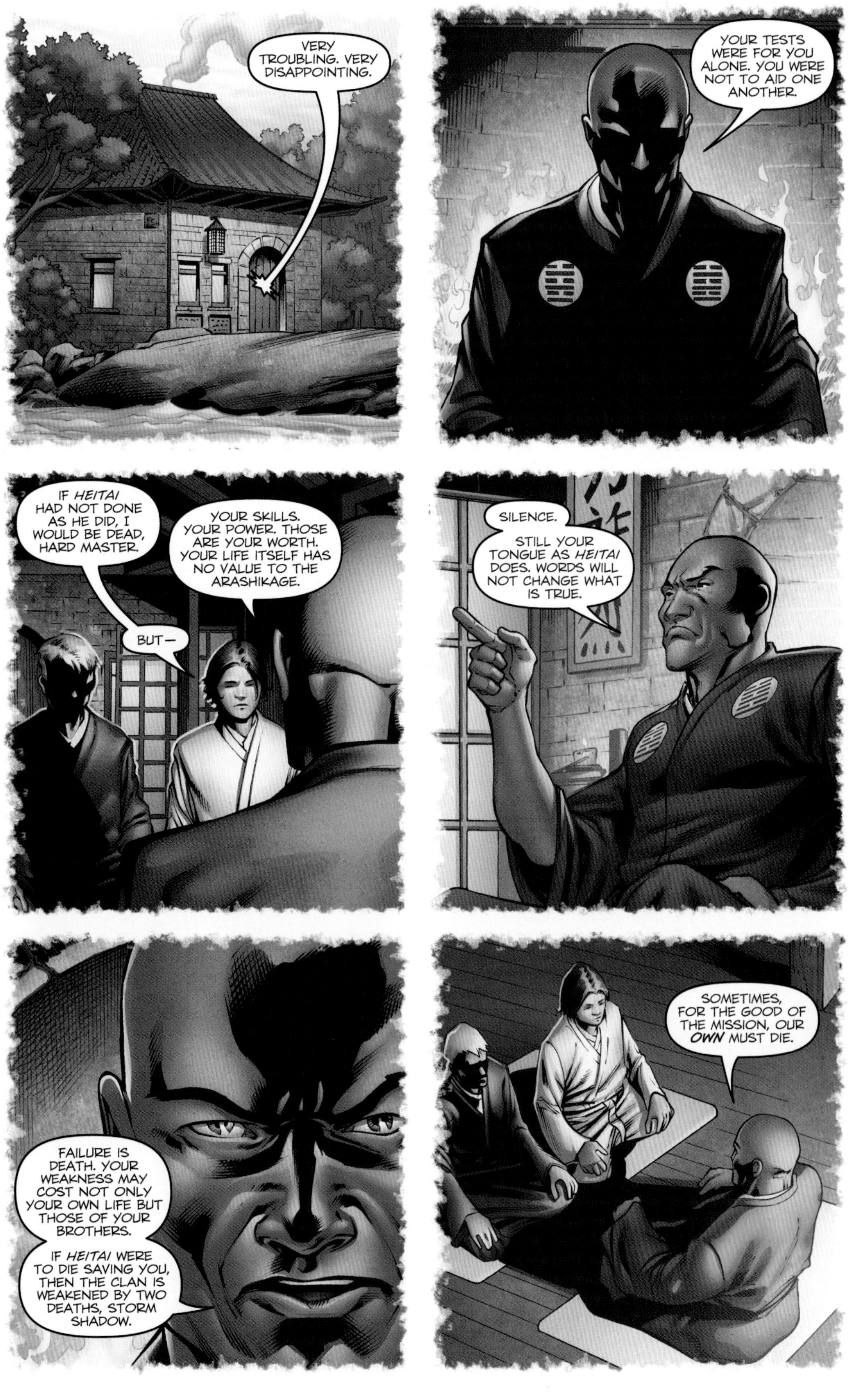
VERY TROUBLING. VERY DISAPPOINTING.
YOUR TESTS WERE FOR YOU ALONE. YOU WERE NOT TO AID ONE ANOTHER.
IF HEITAI HAD NOT DONE AS HE DID, I WOULD BE DEAD, HARD MASTER.
YOUR SKILLS. YOUR POWER. THOSE ARE YOUR WORTH. YOUR LIFE ITSELF HAS NO VALUE TO THE ARASHIKAGE.
BUT—
SILENCE.
STILL YOUR TONGUE AS HEITAI DOES. WORDS WILL NOT CHANGE WHAT IS TRUE.
FAILURE IS DEATH. YOUR WEAKNESS MAY COST NOT ONLY YOUR OWN LIFE BUT THOSE OF YOUR BROTHERS.
IF HEITAI WERE TO DIE SAVING YOU, THEN THE CLAN IS WEAKENED BY TWO DEATHS, STORM SHADOW.
SOMETIMES, FOR THE GOOD OF THE MISSION, OUR OWN MUST DIE.

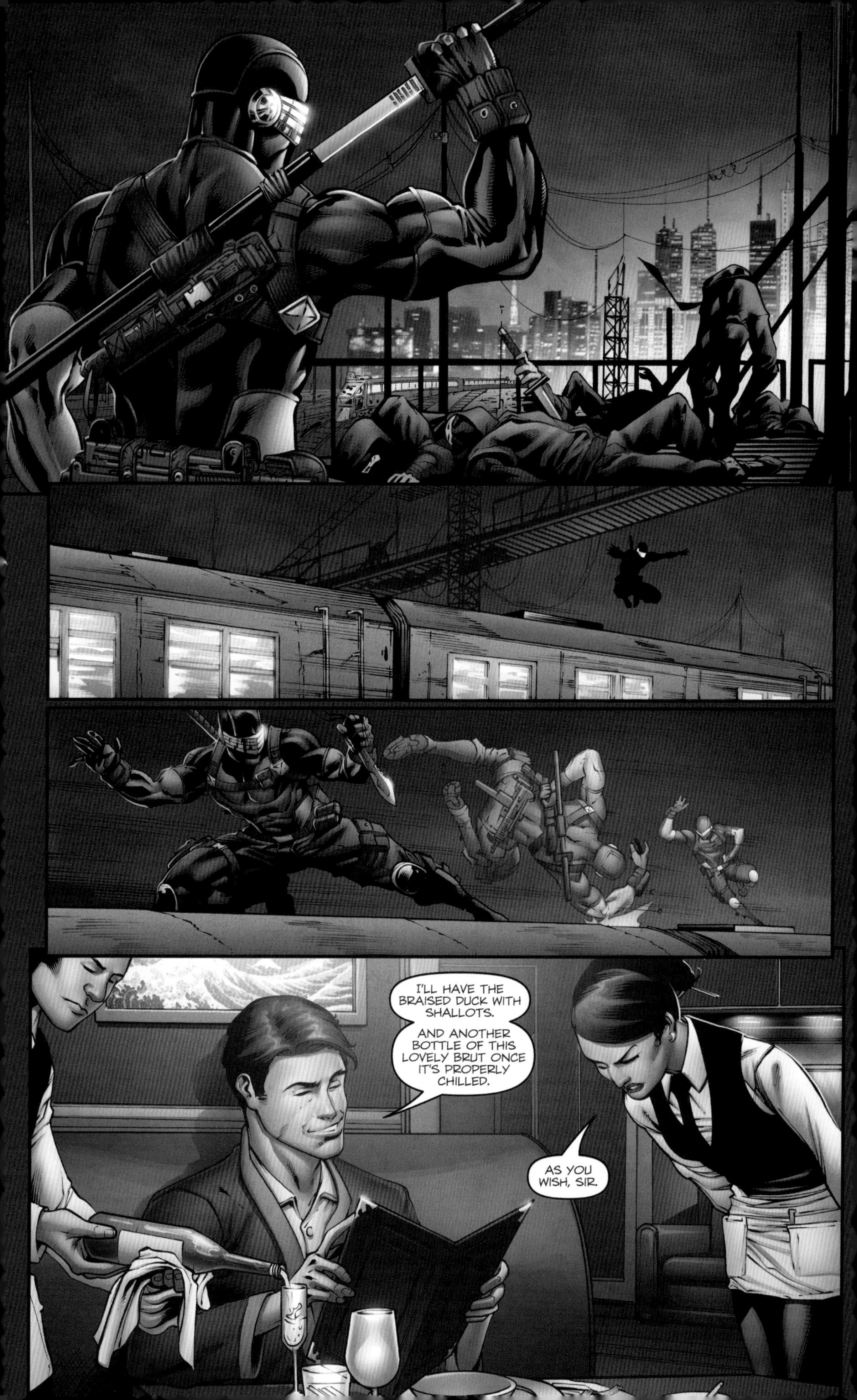
I'LL HAVE THE BRAISED DUCK WITH SHALLOTS.
AND ANOTHER BOTTLE OF THIS LOVELY BRUT ONCE IT'S PROPERLY CHILLED.
AS YOU WISH, SIR.

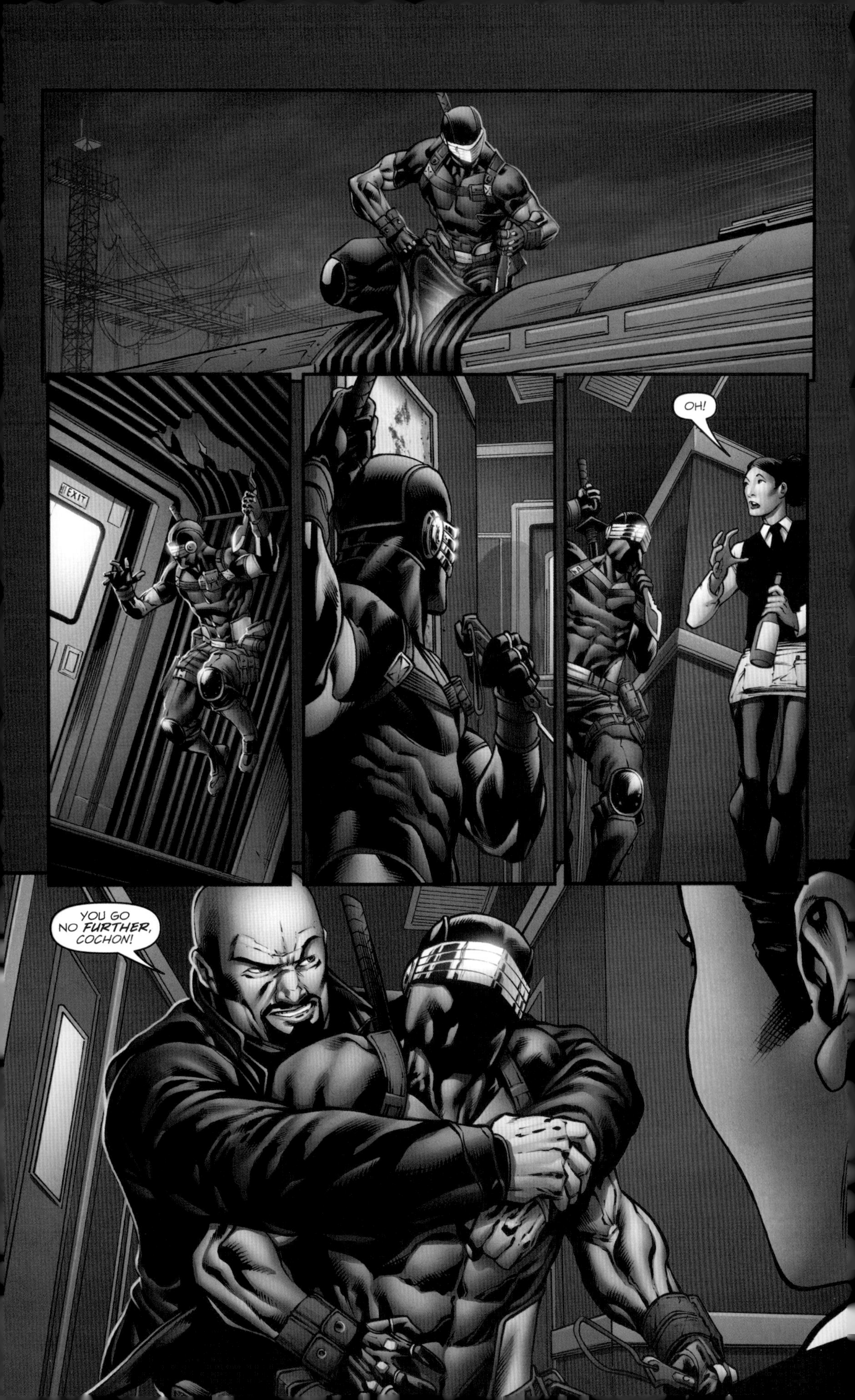
OH!
YOU GO NO FURTHER, COCHON!

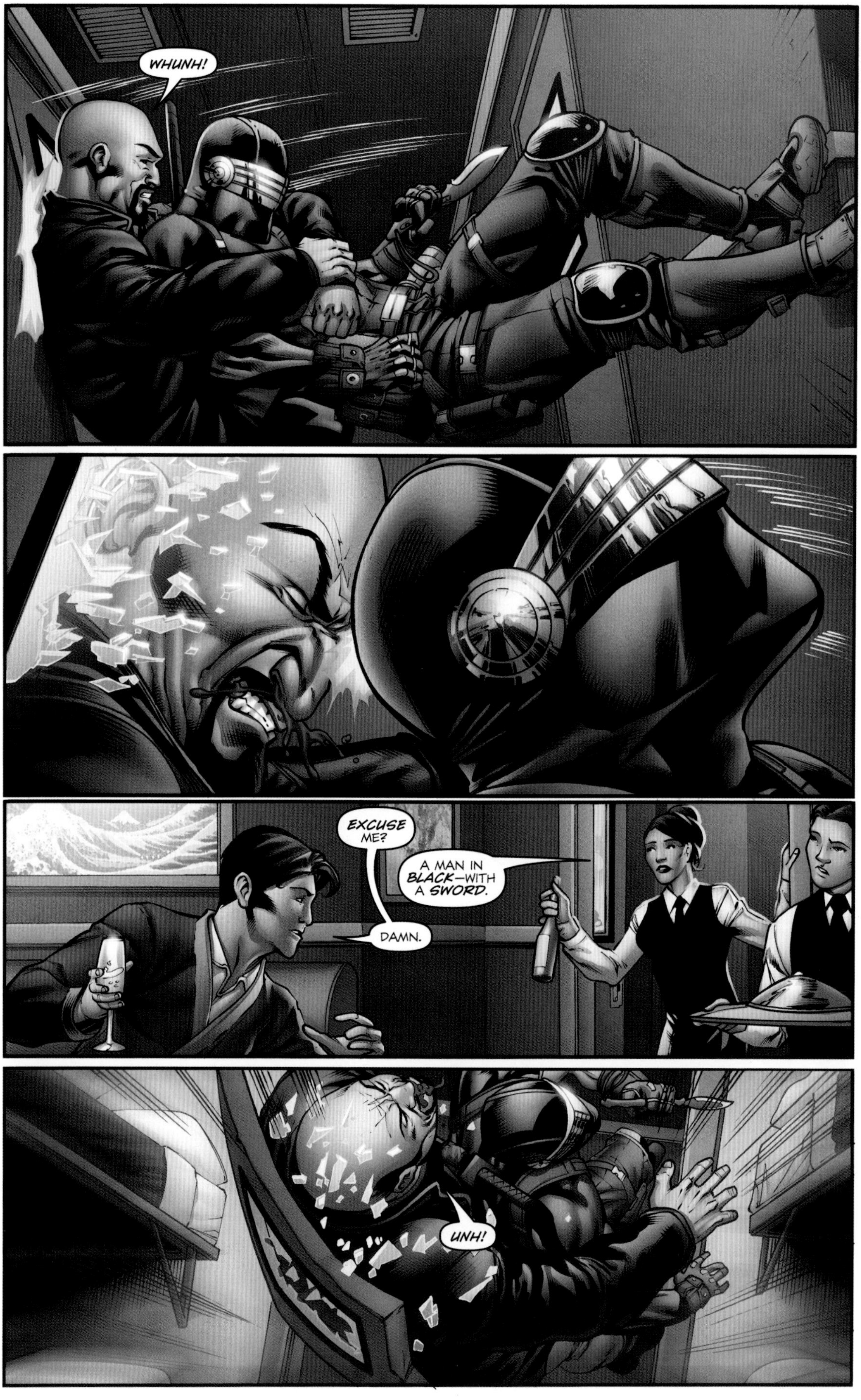
WHUNH!
EXCUSE ME?
A MAN IN BLACK—WITH A SWORD.
DAMN.
UNH!

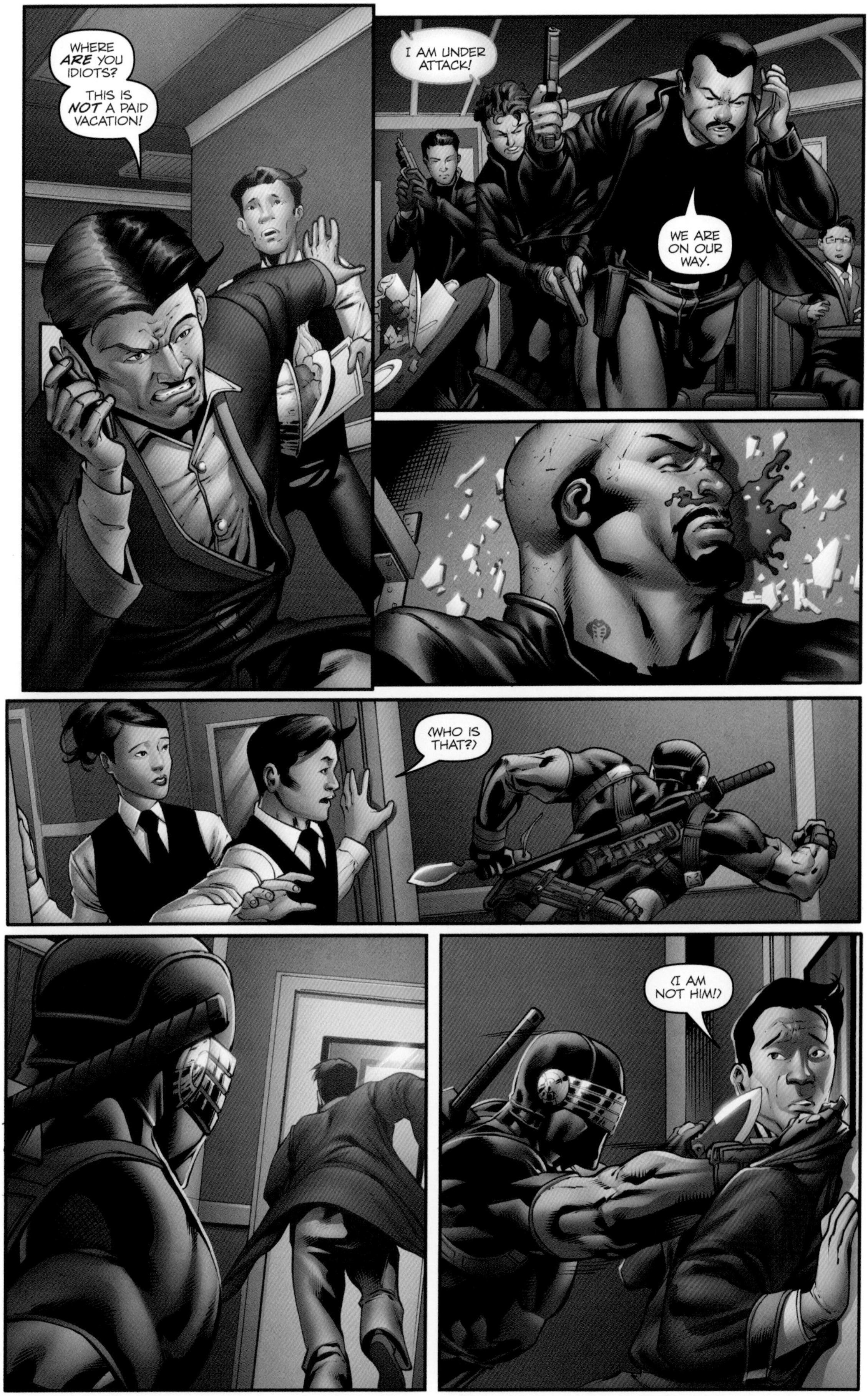

WHERE *ARE* YOU IDIOTS?
THIS IS *NOT* A PAID VACATION!
I AM UNDER ATTACK!
WE ARE ON OUR WAY.
‹WHO IS THAT?›
‹I AM NOT HIM!›

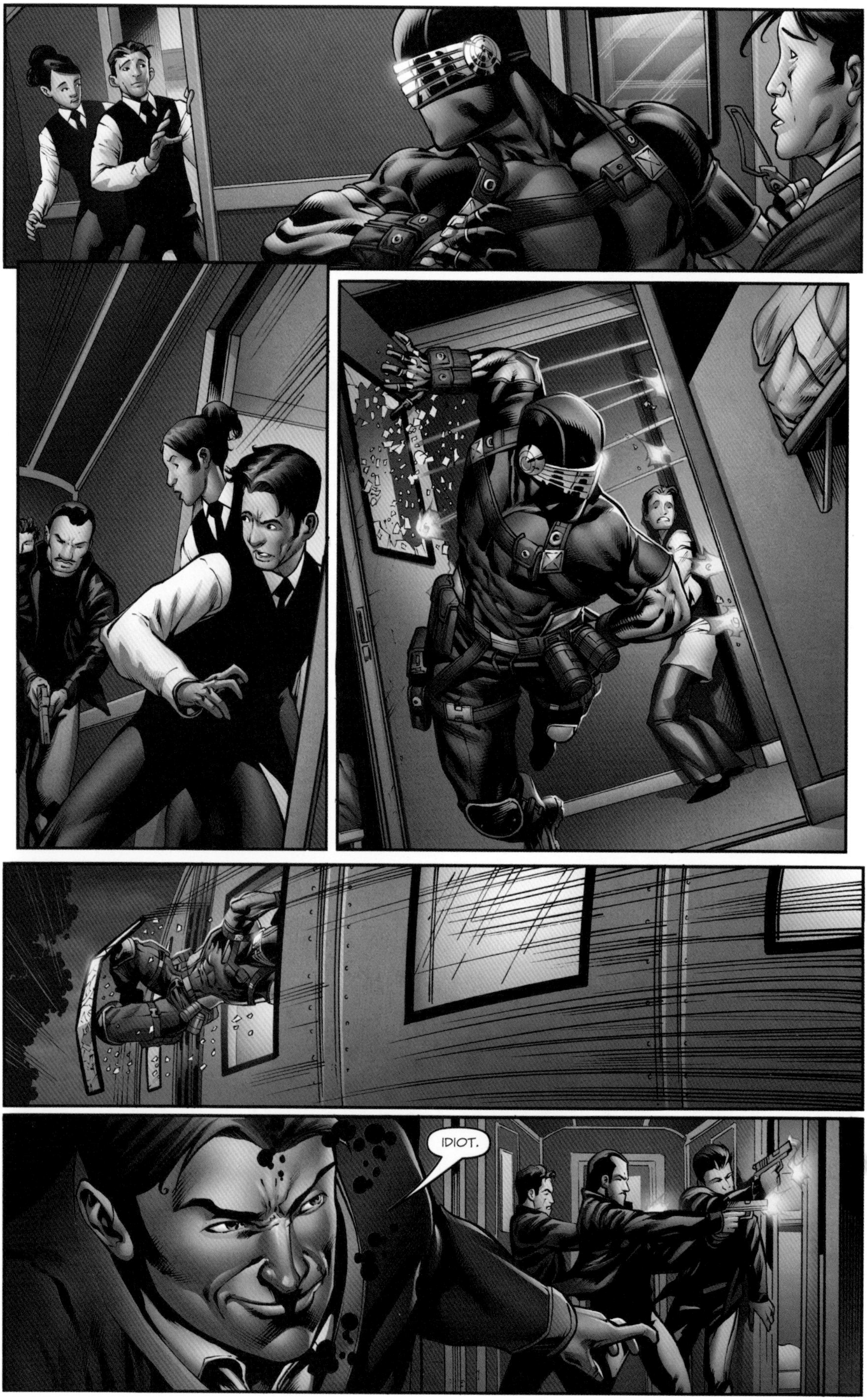
IDIOT.

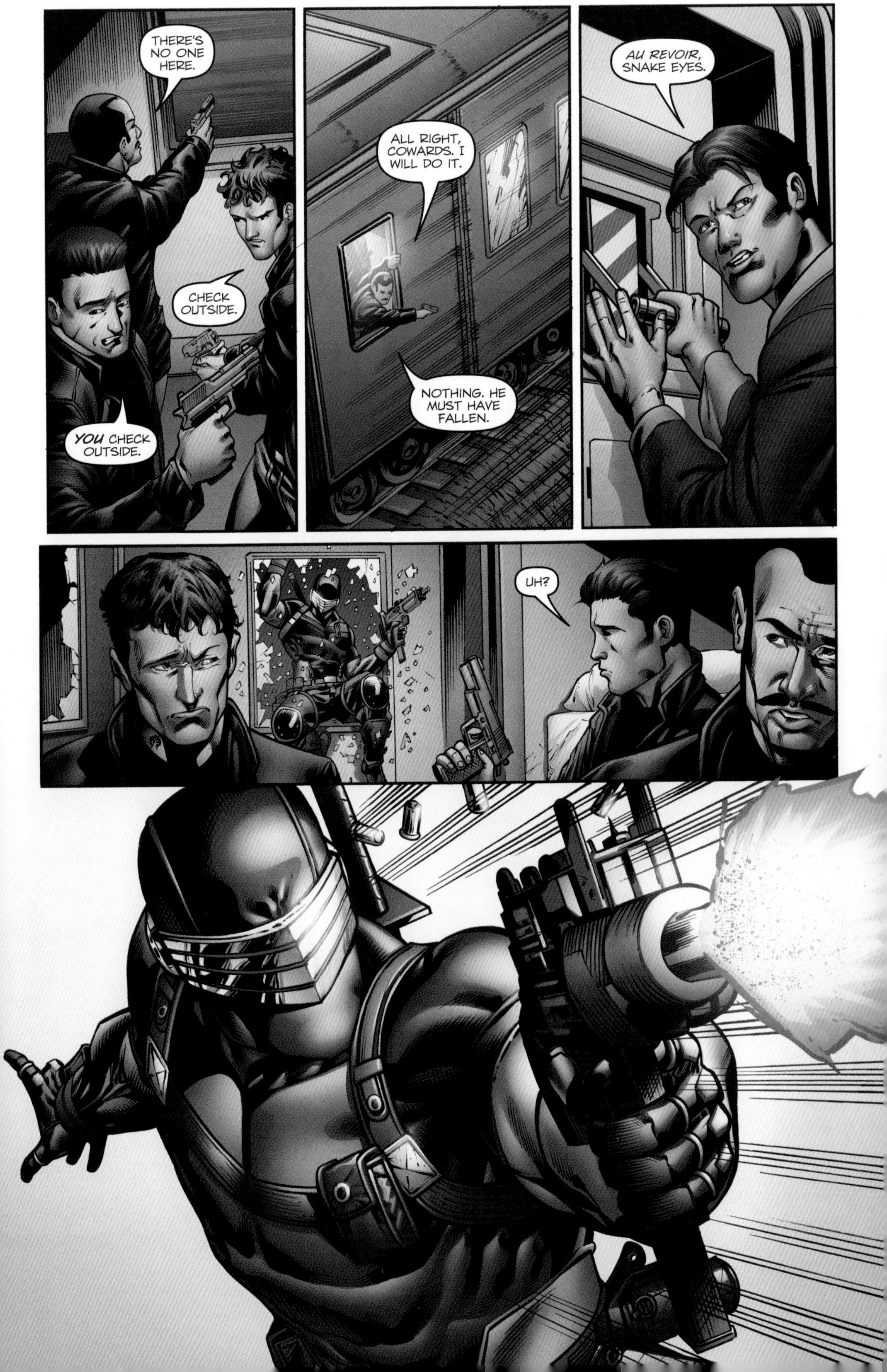
THERE'S NO ONE HERE.
CHECK OUTSIDE.
YOU CHECK OUTSIDE.
ALL RIGHT, COWARDS. I WILL DO IT.
NOTHING. HE MUST HAVE FALLEN.
AU REVOIR, SNAKE EYES.
UH?

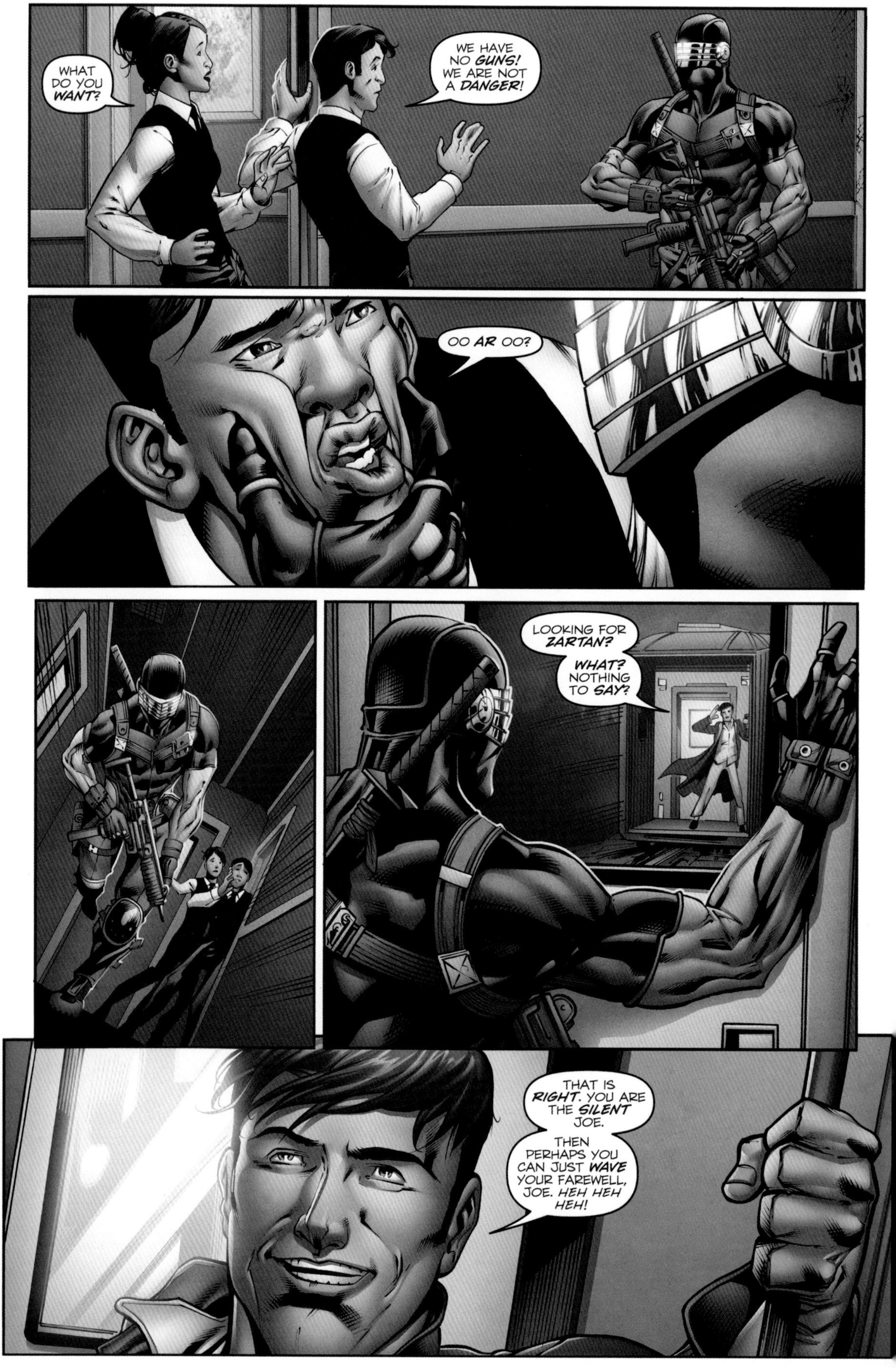
WHAT DO YOU WANT?
WE HAVE NO GUNS! WE ARE NOT A DANGER!
OO AR OO?
LOOKING FOR ZARTAN?
WHAT? NOTHING TO SAY?
THAT IS RIGHT. YOU ARE THE SILENT JOE.
THEN PERHAPS YOU CAN JUST WAVE YOUR FAREWELL, JOE. HEH HEH HEH!

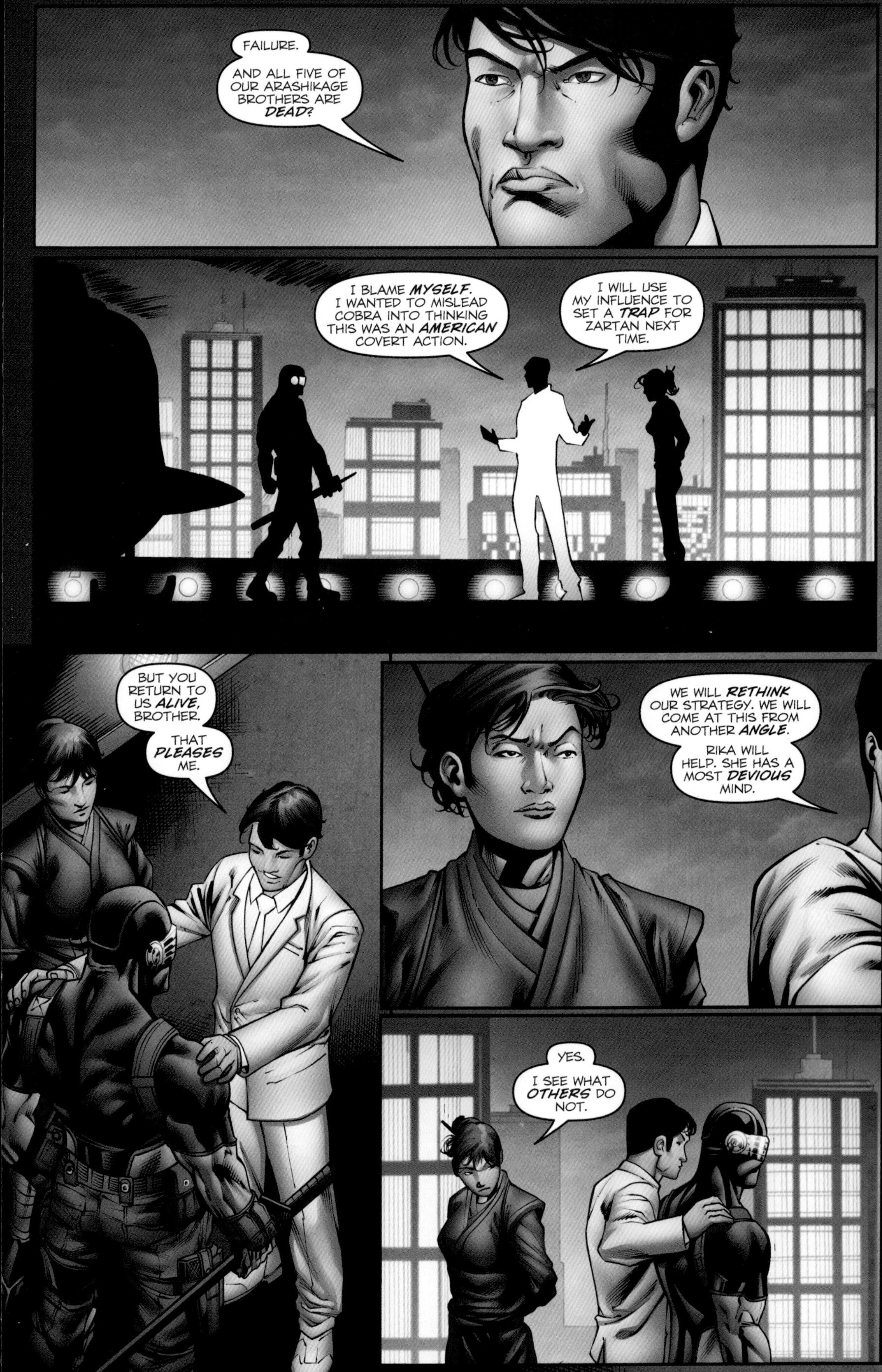
FAILURE.
AND ALL FIVE OF OUR ARASHIKAGE BROTHERS ARE DEAD?
I BLAME MYSELF. I WANTED TO MISLEAD COBRA INTO THINKING THIS WAS AN AMERICAN COVERT ACTION.
I WILL USE MY INFLUENCE TO SET A TRAP FOR ZARTAN NEXT TIME.
BUT YOU RETURN TO US ALIVE, BROTHER.
THAT PLEASES ME.
WE WILL RETHINK OUR STRATEGY. WE WILL COME AT THIS FROM ANOTHER ANGLE.
RIKA WILL HELP. SHE HAS A MOST DEVIOUS MIND.
YES.
I SEE WHAT OTHERS DO NOT.

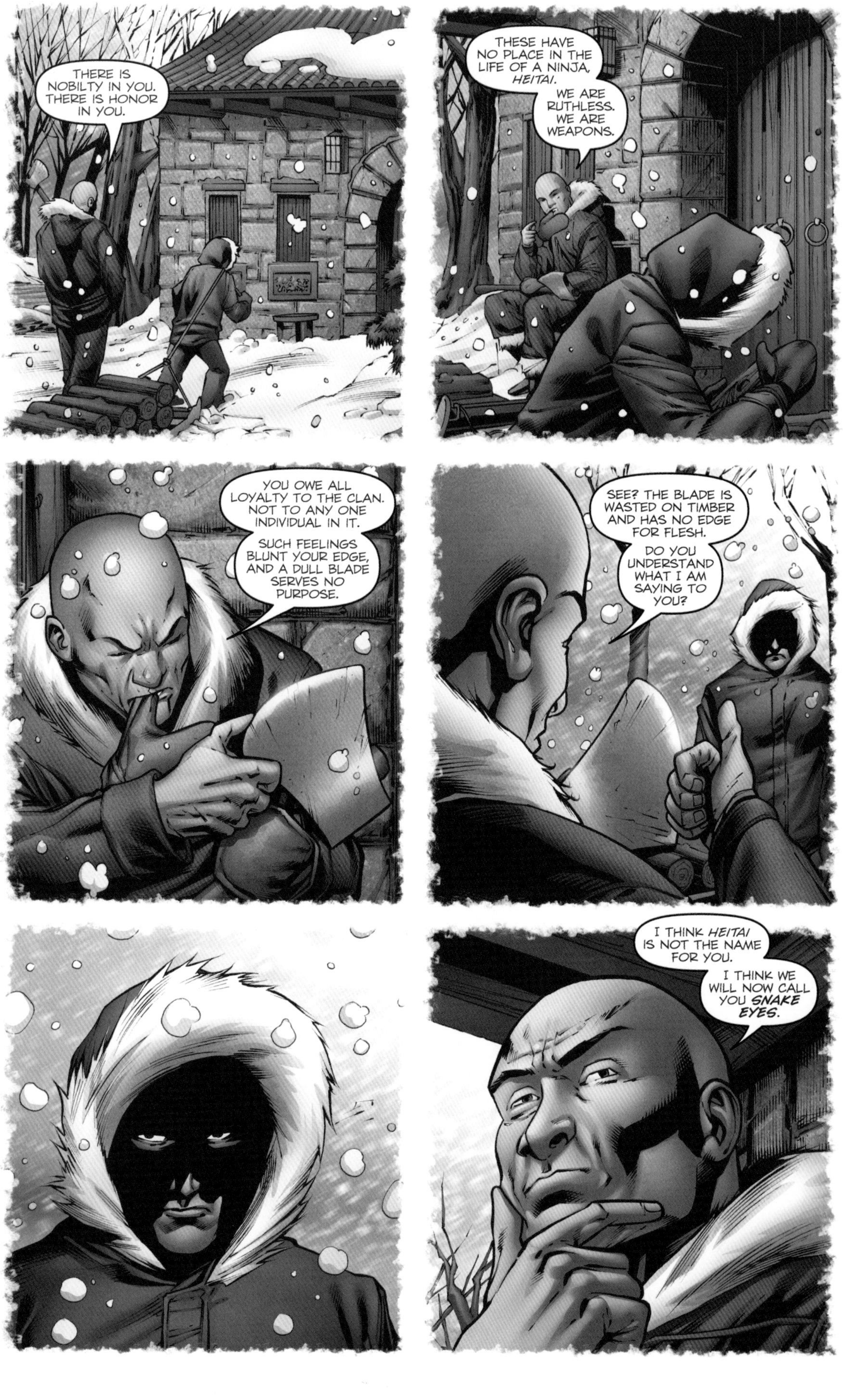
THERE IS NOBILTY IN YOU. THERE IS HONOR IN YOU.
THESE HAVE NO PLACE IN THE LIFE OF A NINJA, *HEITAI*.
WE ARE RUTHLESS. WE ARE WEAPONS.
YOU OWE ALL LOYALTY TO THE CLAN. NOT TO ANY ONE INDIVIDUAL IN IT.
SUCH FEELINGS BLUNT YOUR EDGE, AND A DULL BLADE SERVES NO PURPOSE.
SEE? THE BLADE IS WASTED ON TIMBER AND HAS NO EDGE FOR FLESH.
DO YOU UNDERSTAND WHAT I AM SAYING TO YOU?
I THINK *HEITAI* IS NOT THE NAME FOR YOU.
I THINK WE WILL NOW CALL YOU ***SNAKE EYES***.

Chapter Two

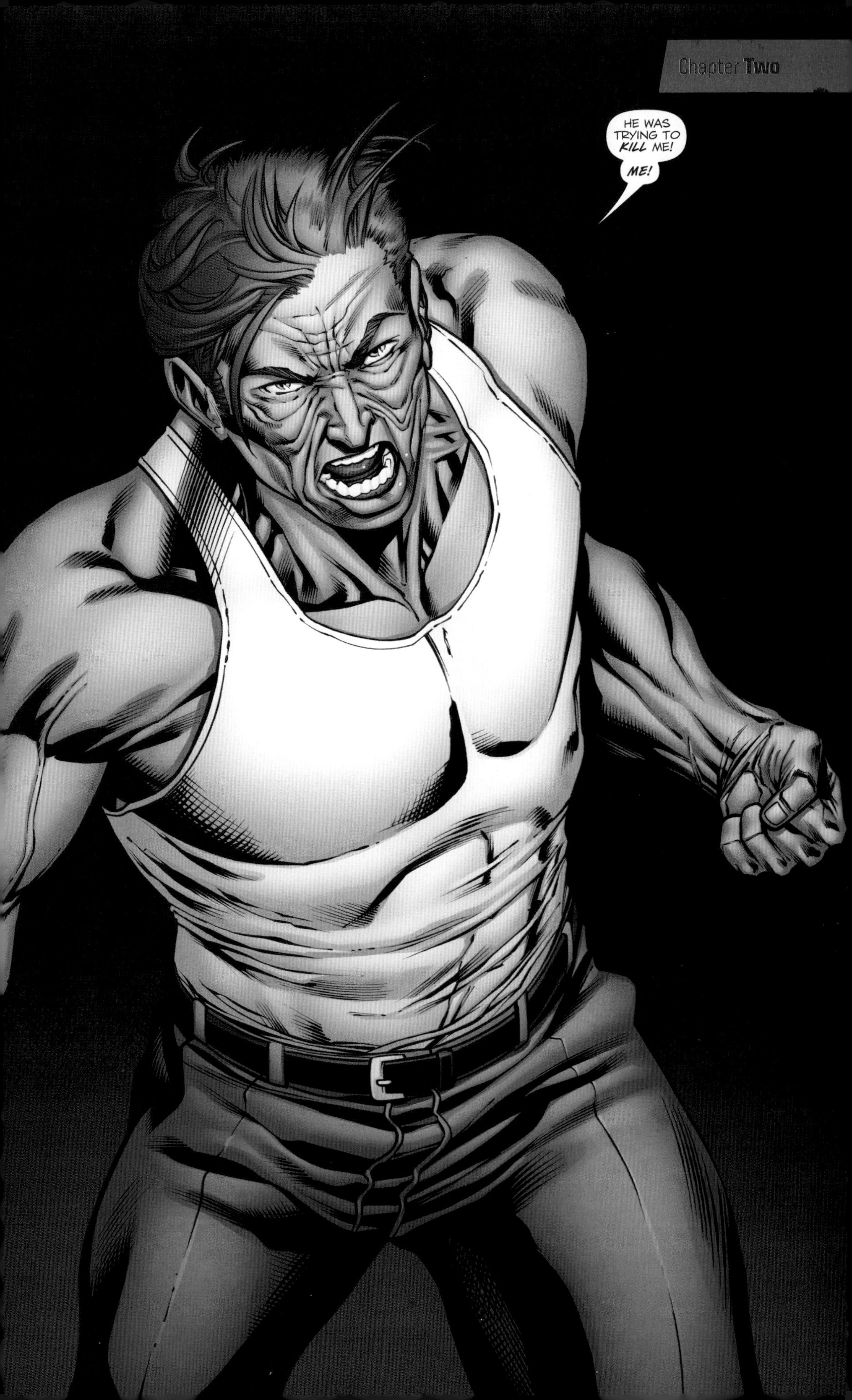
HE WAS TRYING TO KILL ME! ME!

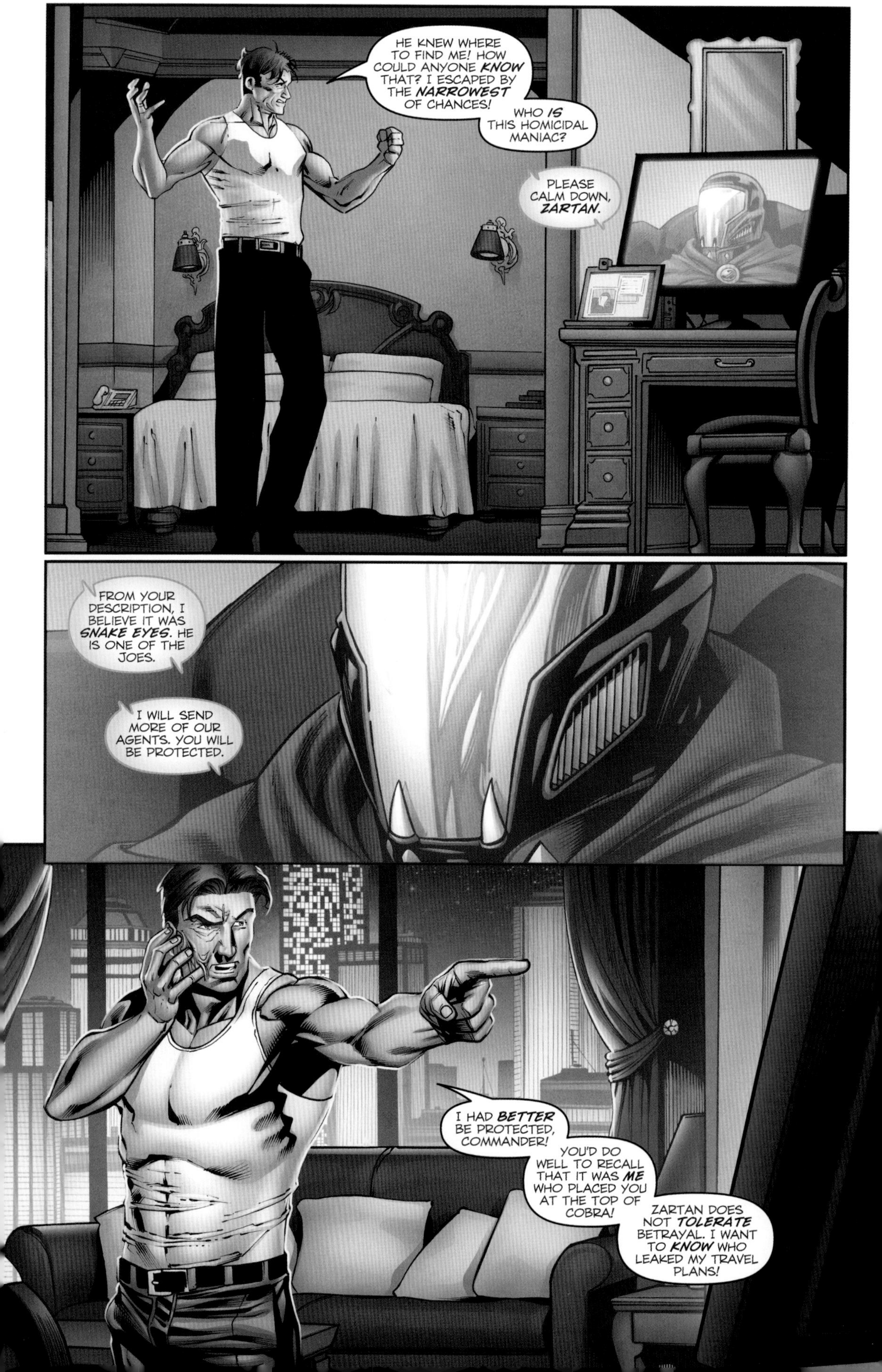

HE KNEW WHERE TO FIND ME! HOW COULD ANYONE KNOW THAT? I ESCAPED BY THE NARROWEST OF CHANCES!
WHO IS THIS HOMICIDAL MANIAC?
PLEASE CALM DOWN, ZARTAN.
FROM YOUR DESCRIPTION, I BELIEVE IT WAS SNAKE EYES. HE IS ONE OF THE JOES.
I WILL SEND MORE OF OUR AGENTS. YOU WILL BE PROTECTED.
I HAD BETTER BE PROTECTED, COMMANDER!
YOU'D DO WELL TO RECALL THAT IT WAS ME WHO PLACED YOU AT THE TOP OF COBRA!
ZARTAN DOES NOT TOLERATE BETRAYAL. I WANT TO KNOW WHO LEAKED MY TRAVEL PLANS!

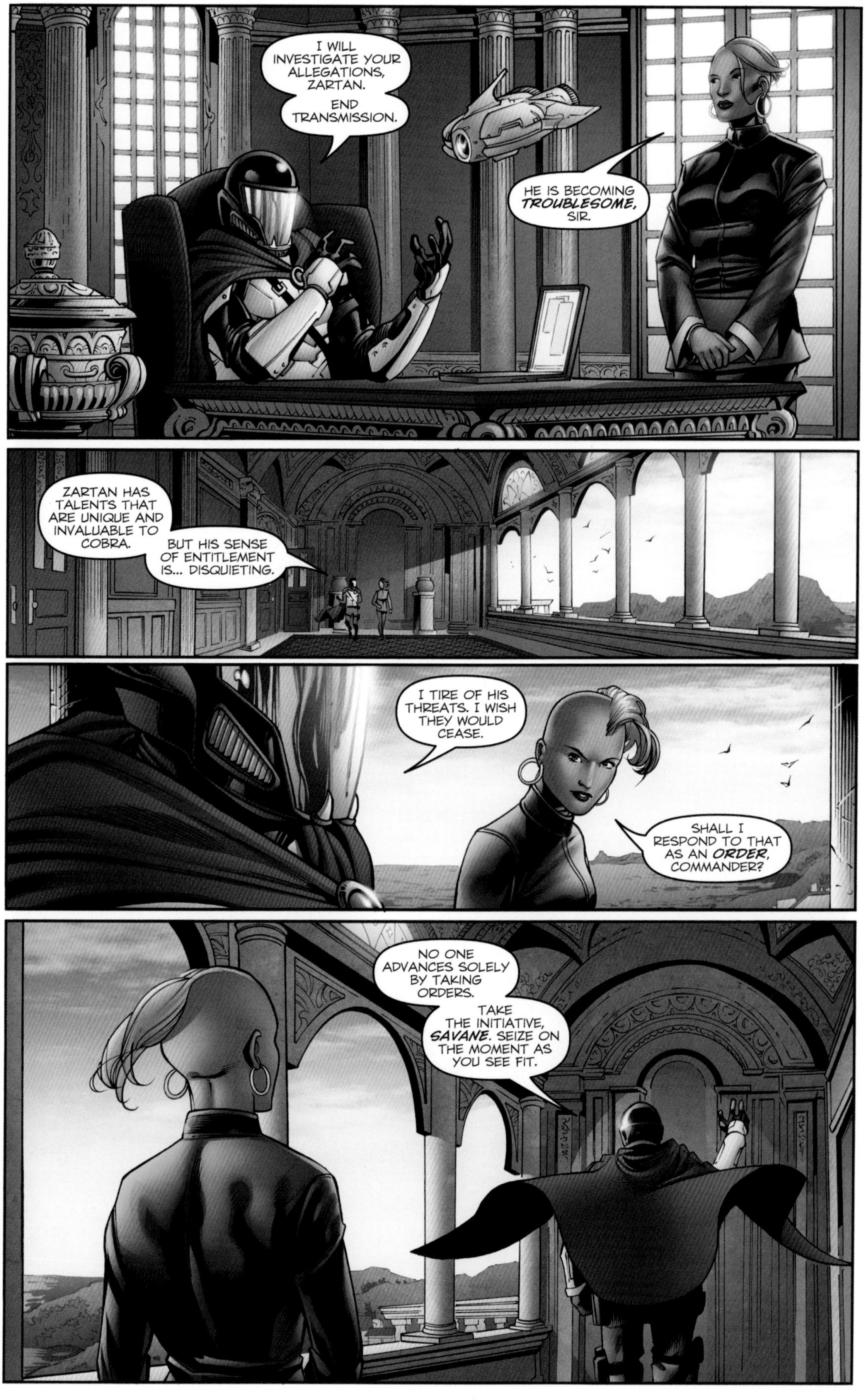
I WILL INVESTIGATE YOUR ALLEGATIONS, ZARTAN.
END TRANSMISSION.
HE IS BECOMING TROUBLESOME, SIR.
ZARTAN HAS TALENTS THAT ARE UNIQUE AND INVALUABLE TO COBRA.
BUT HIS SENSE OF ENTITLEMENT IS... DISQUIETING.
I TIRE OF HIS THREATS. I WISH THEY WOULD CEASE.
SHALL I RESPOND TO THAT AS AN ORDER, COMMANDER?
NO ONE ADVANCES SOLELY BY TAKING ORDERS.
TAKE THE INITIATIVE, SAVANE. SEIZE ON THE MOMENT AS YOU SEE FIT.

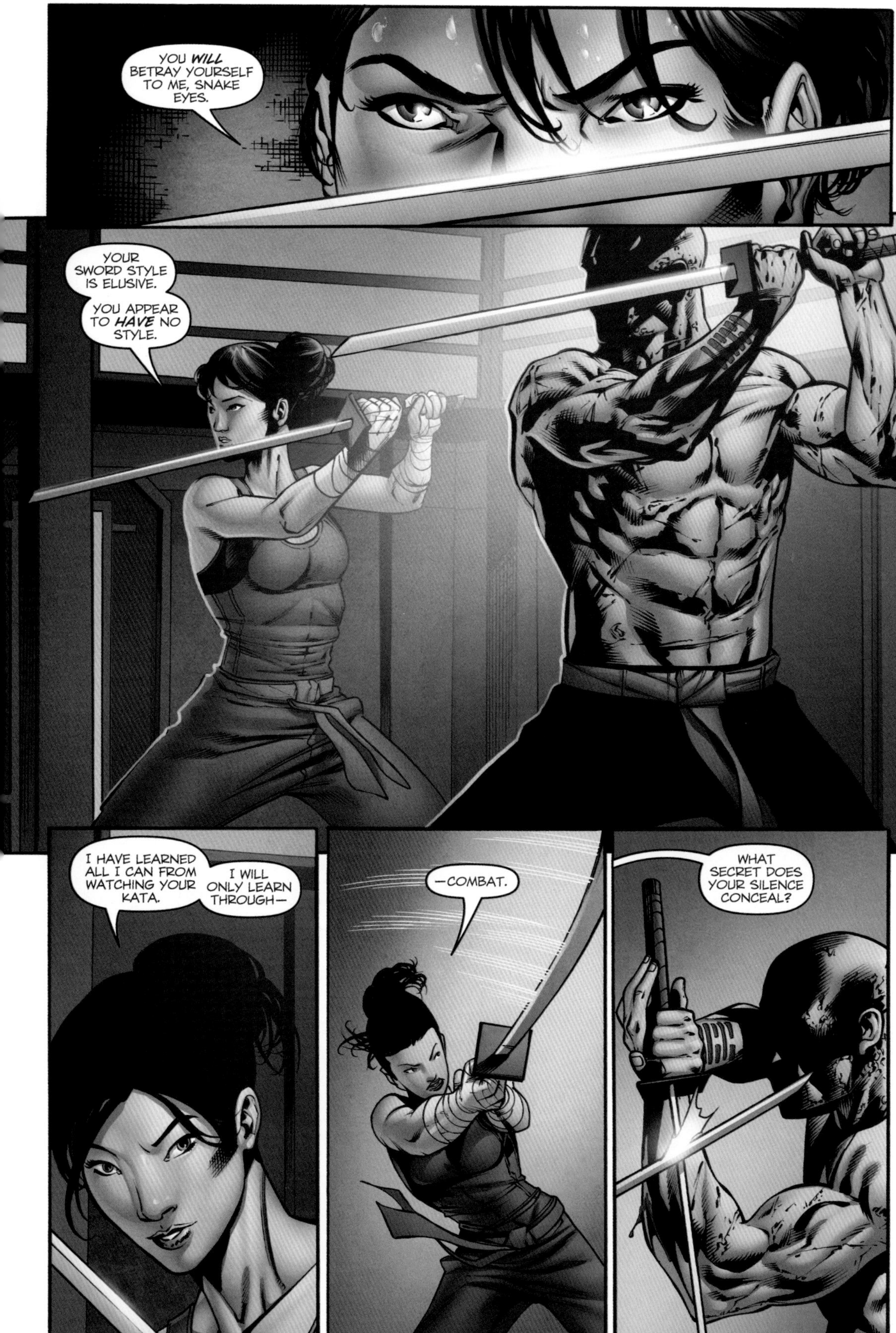
YOU WILL BETRAY YOURSELF TO ME, SNAKE EYES.
YOUR SWORD STYLE IS ELUSIVE.
YOU APPEAR TO HAVE NO STYLE.
I HAVE LEARNED ALL I CAN FROM WATCHING YOUR KATA.
I WILL ONLY LEARN THROUGH—
—COMBAT.
WHAT SECRET DOES YOUR SILENCE CONCEAL?

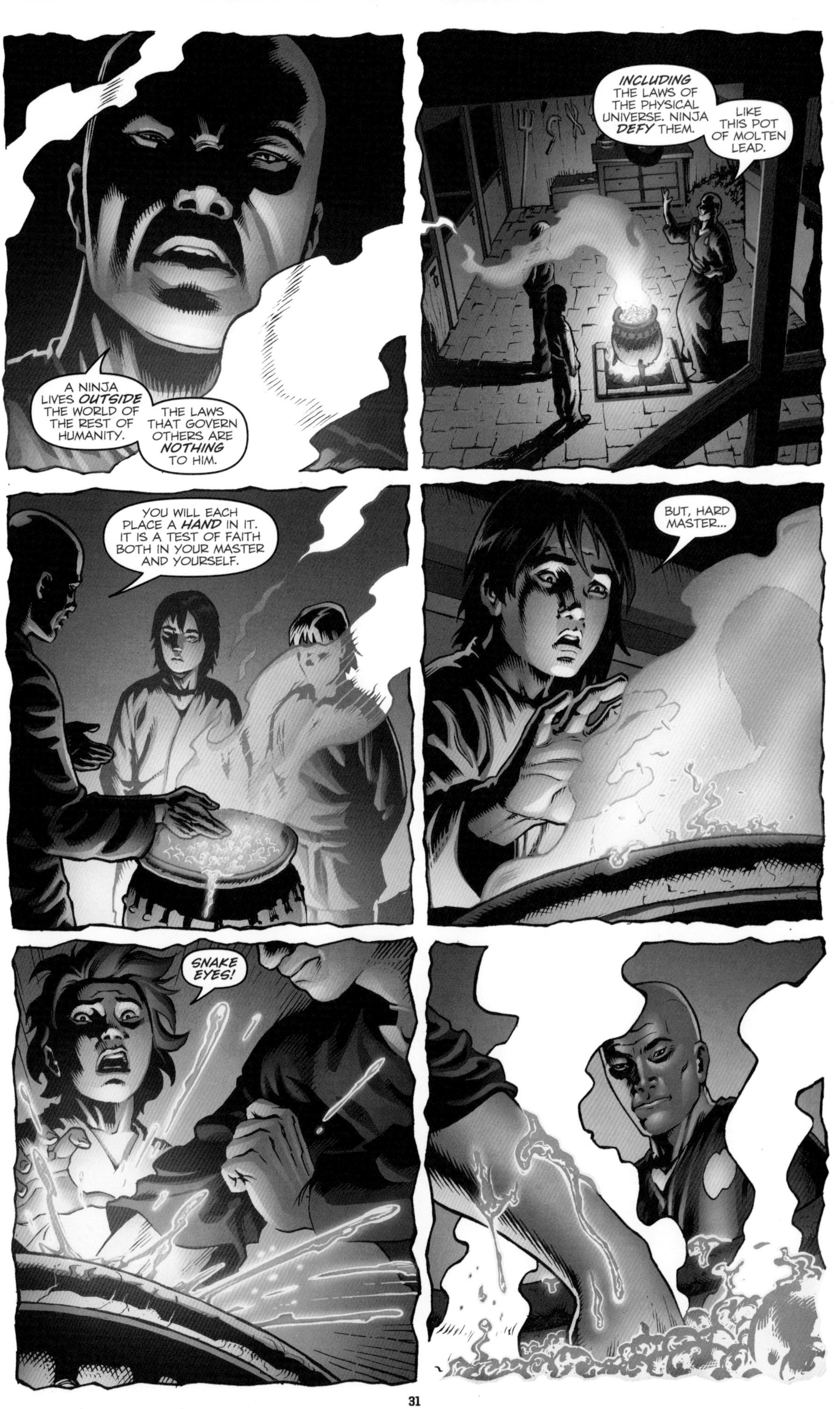
A NINJA LIVES OUTSIDE THE WORLD OF THE REST OF HUMANITY.
THE LAWS THAT GOVERN OTHERS ARE NOTHING TO HIM.
INCLUDING THE LAWS OF THE PHYSICAL UNIVERSE. NINJA DEFY THEM.
LIKE THIS POT OF MOLTEN LEAD.
YOU WILL EACH PLACE A HAND IN IT. IT IS A TEST OF FAITH BOTH IN YOUR MASTER AND YOURSELF.
BUT, HARD MASTER...
SNAKE EYES!

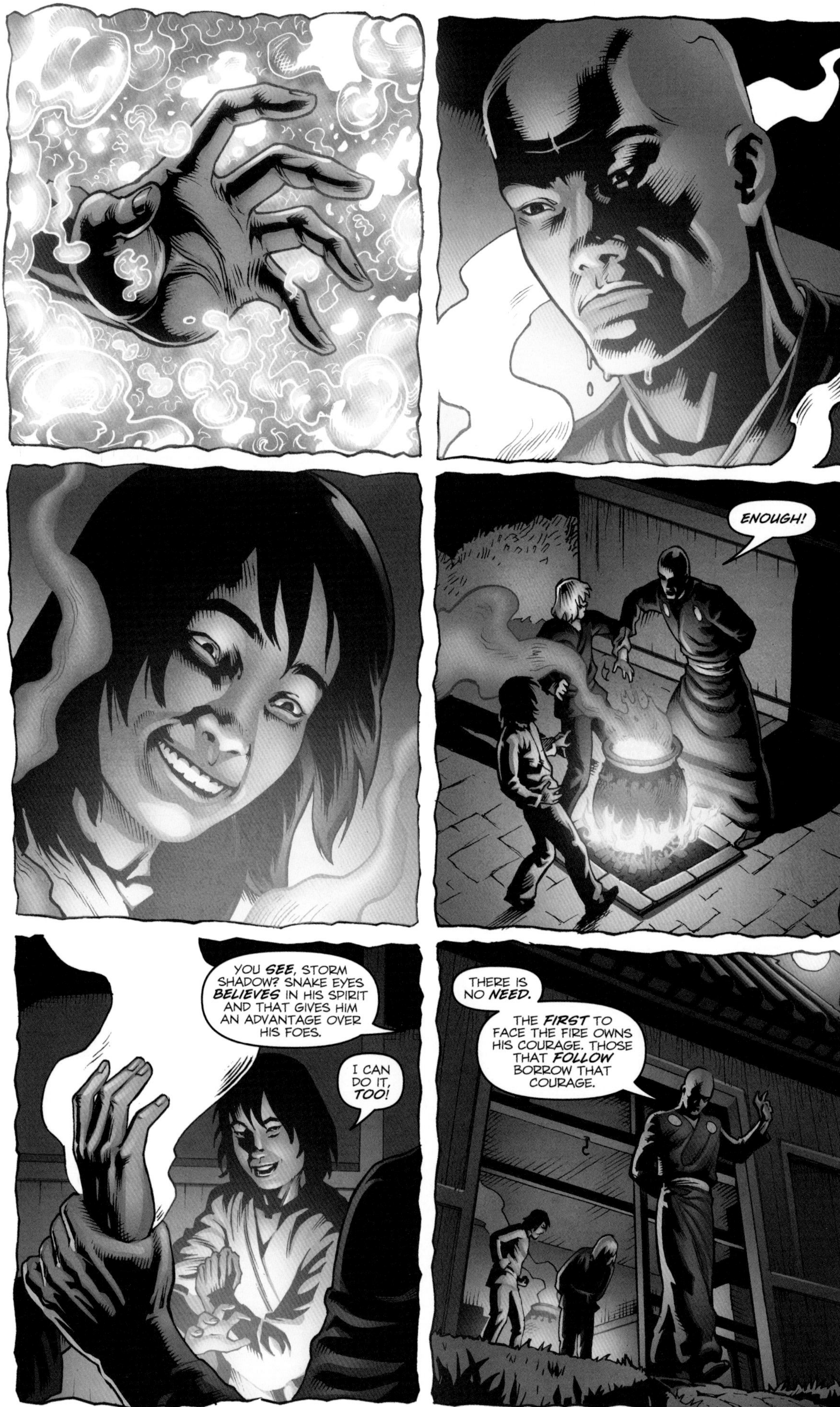
ENOUGH!
YOU SEE, STORM SHADOW? SNAKE EYES BELIEVES IN HIS SPIRIT AND THAT GIVES HIM AN ADVANTAGE OVER HIS FOES.
I CAN DO IT, TOO!
THERE IS NO NEED.
THE FIRST TO FACE THE FIRE OWNS HIS COURAGE. THOSE THAT FOLLOW BORROW THAT COURAGE.

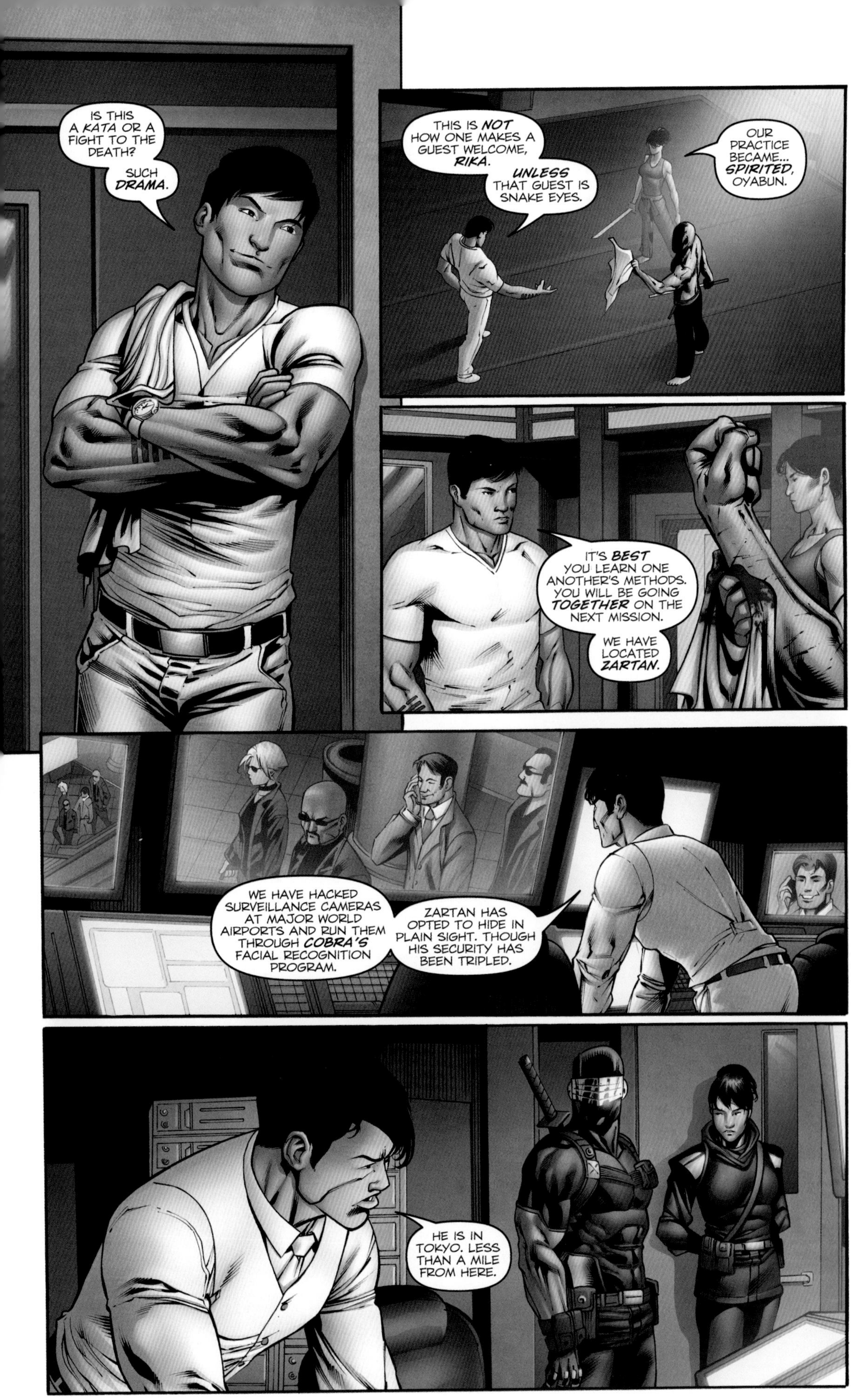
IS THIS A *KATA* OR A FIGHT TO THE DEATH?
SUCH ***DRAMA***.
THIS IS ***NOT*** HOW ONE MAKES A GUEST WELCOME, ***RIKA***.
UNLESS THAT GUEST IS SNAKE EYES.
OUR PRACTICE BECAME... ***SPIRITED***, OYABUN.
IT'S ***BEST*** YOU LEARN ONE ANOTHER'S METHODS. YOU WILL BE GOING ***TOGETHER*** ON THE NEXT MISSION.
WE HAVE LOCATED ***ZARTAN***.
WE HAVE HACKED SURVEILLANCE CAMERAS AT MAJOR WORLD AIRPORTS AND RUN THEM THROUGH ***COBRA'S*** FACIAL RECOGNITION PROGRAM.
ZARTAN HAS OPTED TO HIDE IN PLAIN SIGHT. THOUGH HIS SECURITY HAS BEEN TRIPLED.
HE IS IN TOKYO. LESS THAN A MILE FROM HERE.

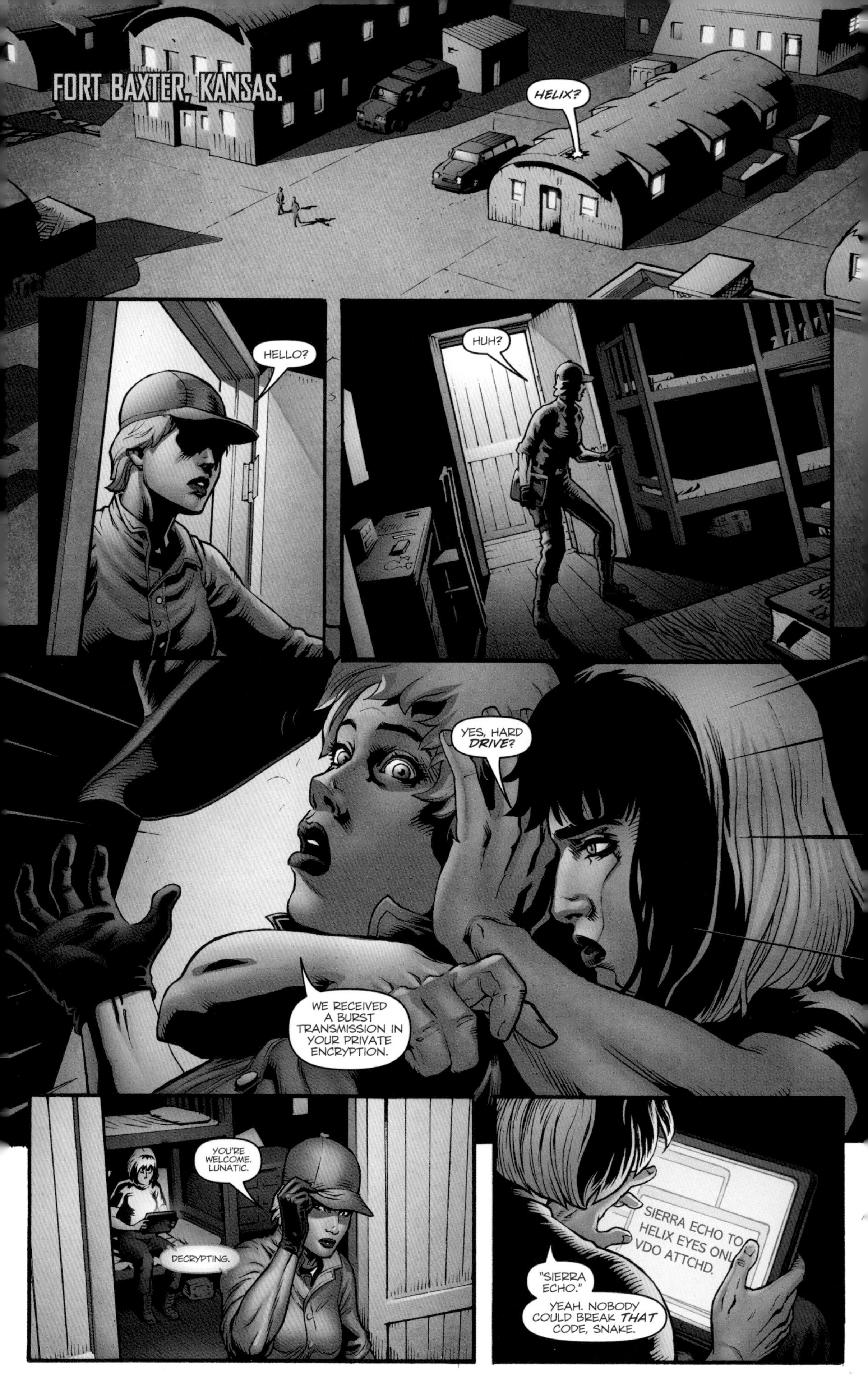
FORT BAXTER, KANSAS.
HELIX?
HELLO?
HUH?
YES, HARD DRIVE?
WE RECEIVED A BURST TRANSMISSION IN YOUR PRIVATE ENCRYPTION.
YOU'RE WELCOME. LUNATIC.
DECRYPTING.
SIERRA ECHO TO HELIX EYES ONL VDO ATTCHD.
"SIERRA ECHO."
YEAH. NOBODY COULD BREAK THAT CODE, SNAKE.

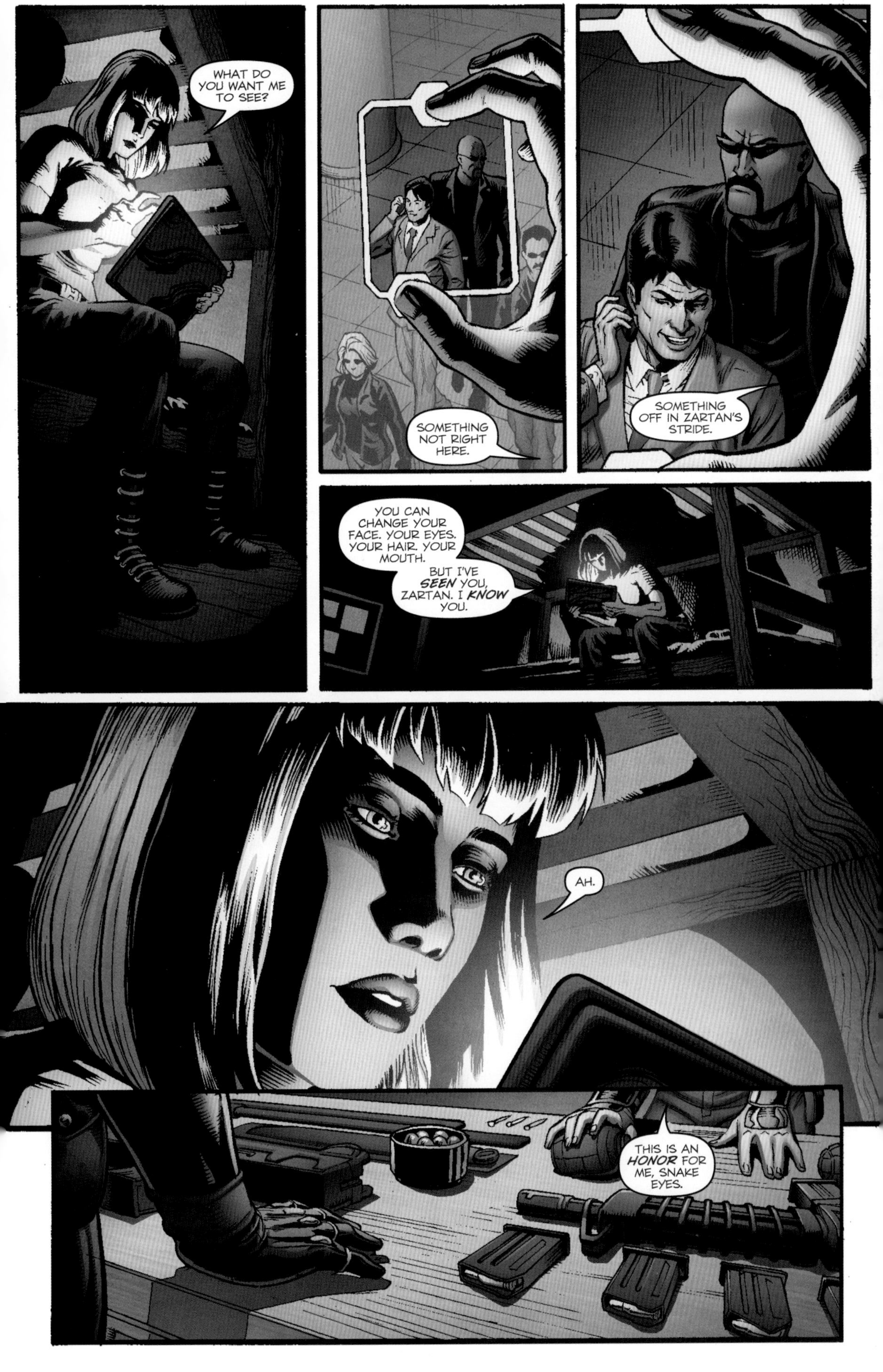
WHAT DO YOU WANT ME TO SEE?
SOMETHING NOT RIGHT HERE.
SOMETHING OFF IN ZARTAN'S STRIDE.
YOU CAN CHANGE YOUR FACE. YOUR EYES. YOUR HAIR. YOUR MOUTH.
BUT I'VE *SEEN* YOU, ZARTAN. I *KNOW* YOU.
AH.
THIS IS AN *HONOR* FOR ME, SNAKE EYES.

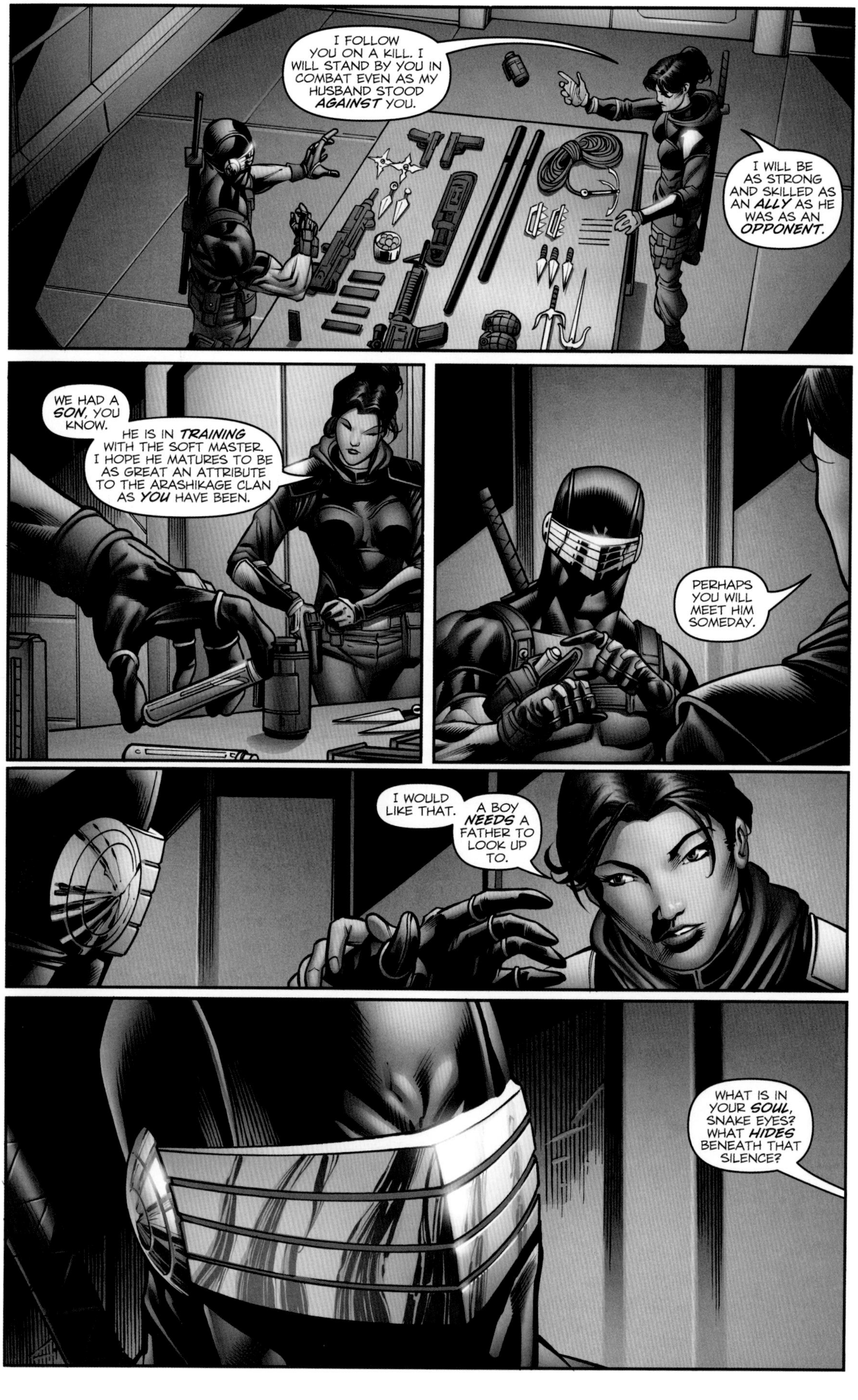

I FOLLOW YOU ON A KILL. I WILL STAND BY YOU IN COMBAT EVEN AS MY HUSBAND STOOD AGAINST YOU.
I WILL BE AS STRONG AND SKILLED AS AN ALLY AS HE WAS AS AN OPPONENT.
WE HAD A SON, YOU KNOW.
HE IS IN TRAINING WITH THE SOFT MASTER. I HOPE HE MATURES TO BE AS GREAT AN ATTRIBUTE TO THE ARASHIKAGE CLAN AS YOU HAVE BEEN.
PERHAPS YOU WILL MEET HIM SOMEDAY.
I WOULD LIKE THAT.
A BOY NEEDS A FATHER TO LOOK UP TO.
WHAT IS IN YOUR SOUL, SNAKE EYES? WHAT HIDES BENEATH THAT SILENCE?

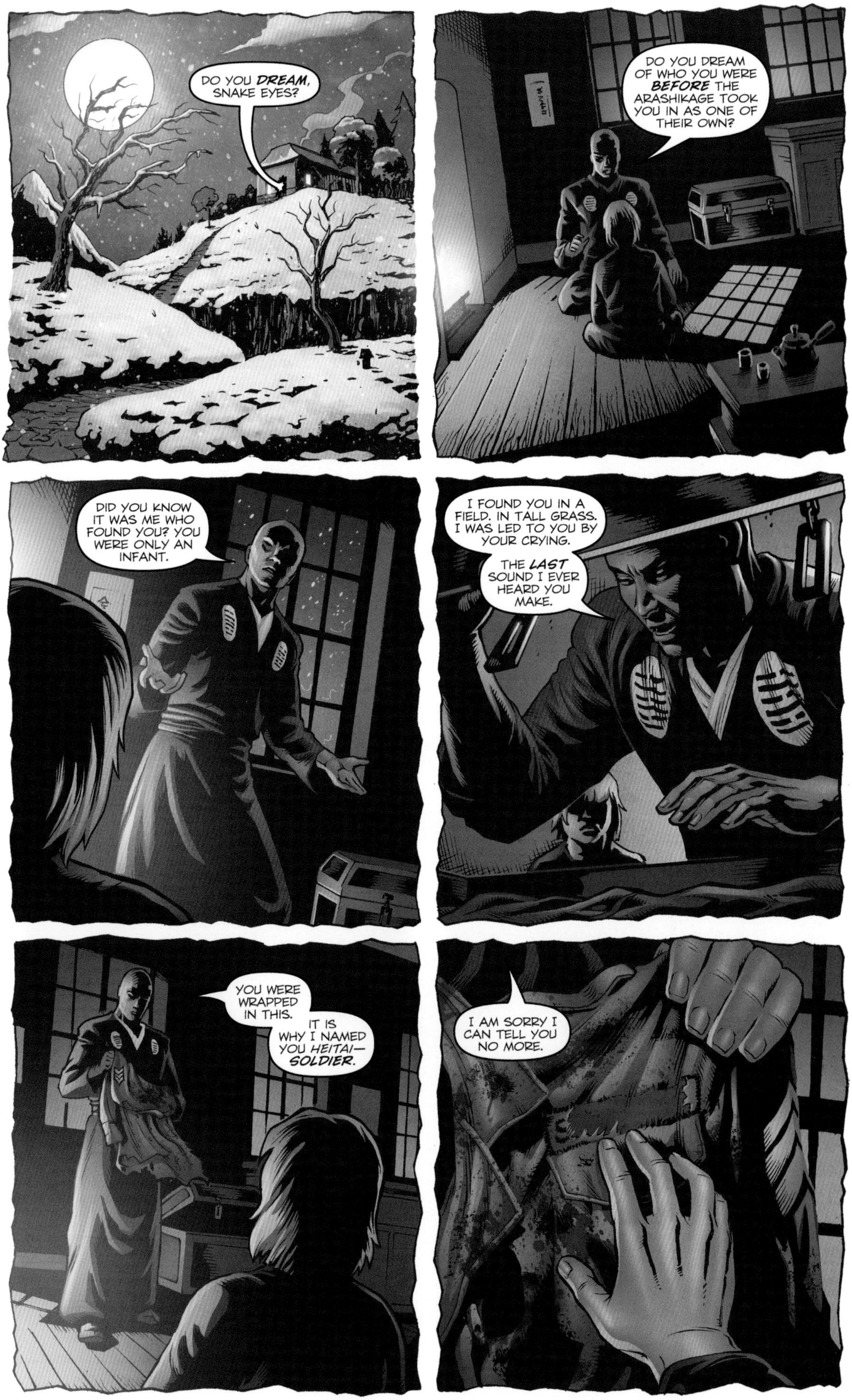
DO YOU DREAM, SNAKE EYES?
DO YOU DREAM OF WHO YOU WERE BEFORE THE ARASHIKAGE TOOK YOU IN AS ONE OF THEIR OWN?
DID YOU KNOW IT WAS ME WHO FOUND YOU? YOU WERE ONLY AN INFANT.
I FOUND YOU IN A FIELD. IN TALL GRASS. I WAS LED TO YOU BY YOUR CRYING.
THE LAST SOUND I EVER HEARD YOU MAKE.
YOU WERE WRAPPED IN THIS.
IT IS WHY I NAMED YOU HEITAI— SOLDIER.
I AM SORRY I CAN TELL YOU NO MORE.

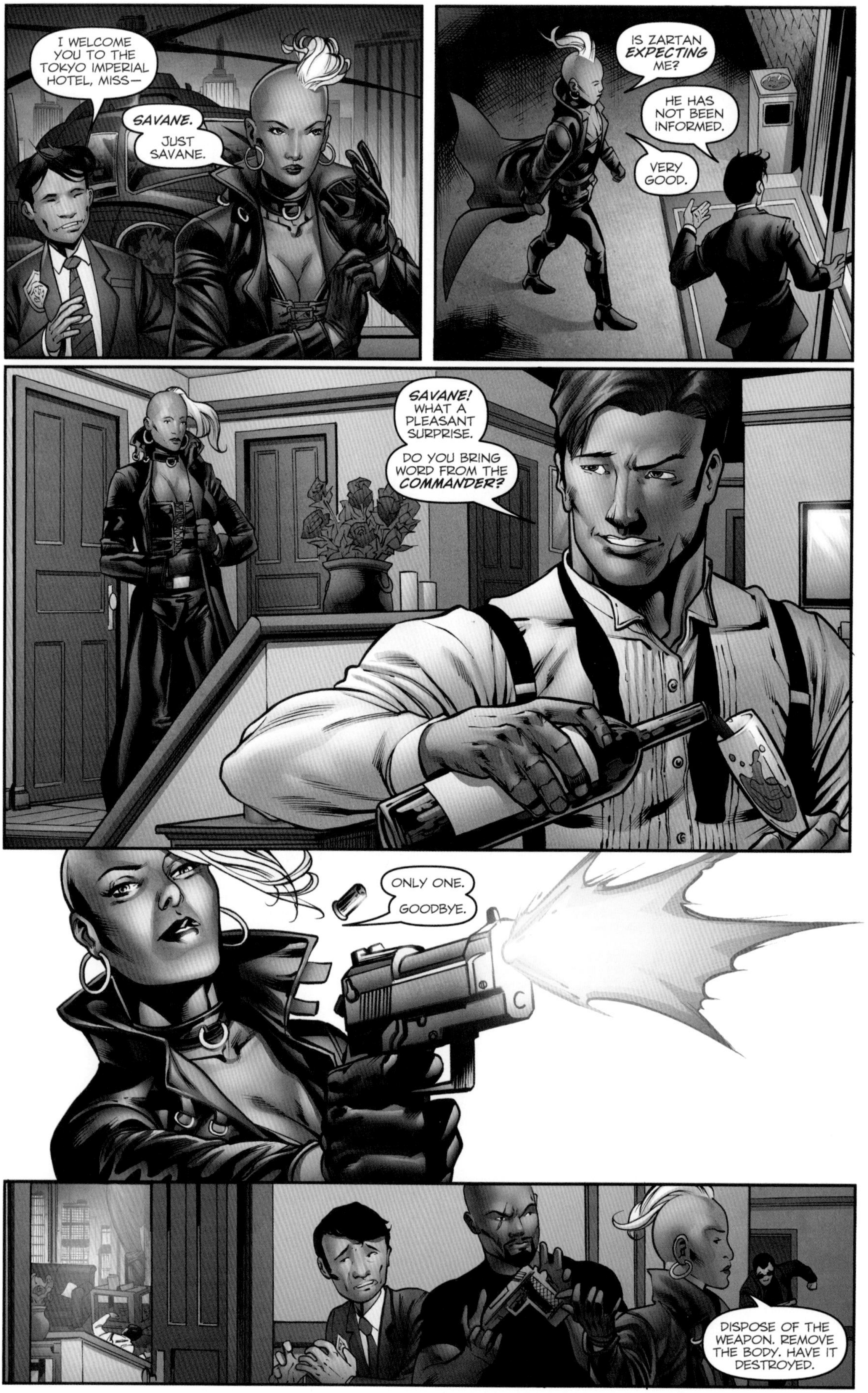
I WELCOME YOU TO THE TOKYO IMPERIAL HOTEL, MISS—
SAVANE.
JUST SAVANE.
IS ZARTAN EXPECTING ME?
HE HAS NOT BEEN INFORMED.
VERY GOOD.
SAVANE! WHAT A PLEASANT SURPRISE.
DO YOU BRING WORD FROM THE COMMANDER?
ONLY ONE.
GOODBYE.
DISPOSE OF THE WEAPON. REMOVE THE BODY. HAVE IT DESTROYED.

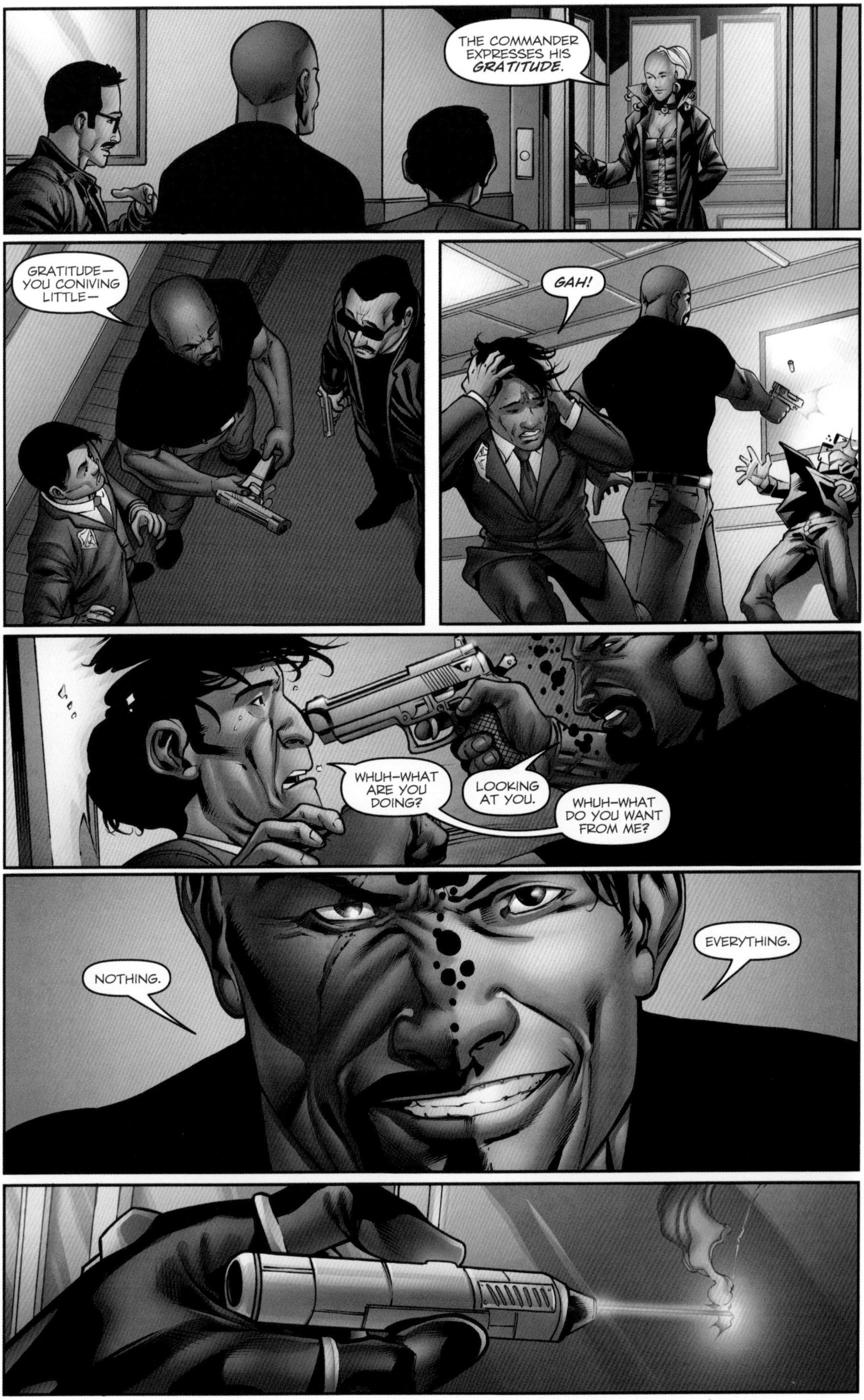
THE COMMANDER EXPRESSES HIS GRATITUDE.
GRATITUDE— YOU CONIVING LITTLE—
GAH!
WHUH-WHAT ARE YOU DOING?
LOOKING AT YOU.
WHUH-WHAT DO YOU WANT FROM ME?
NOTHING.
EVERYTHING.

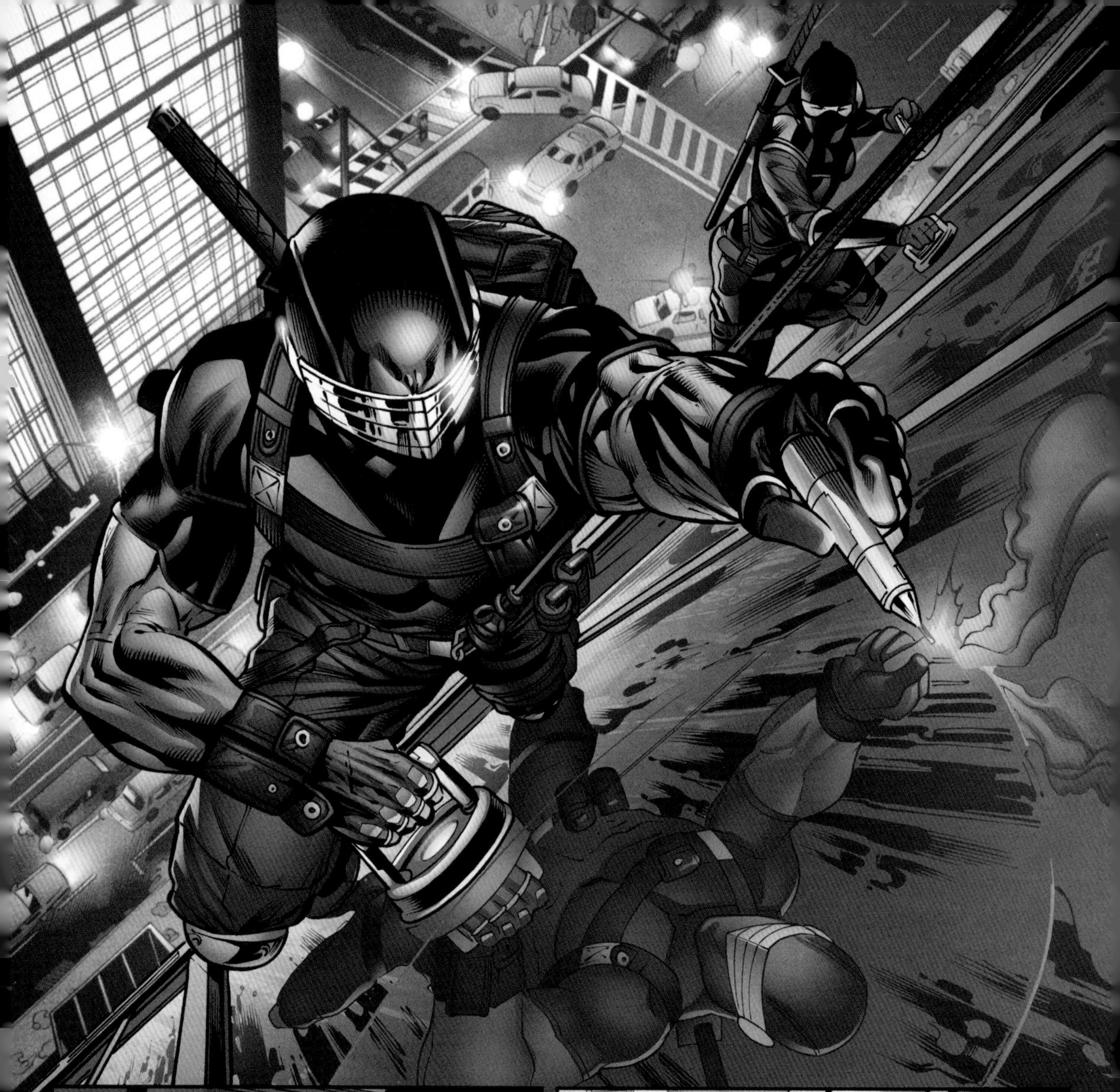

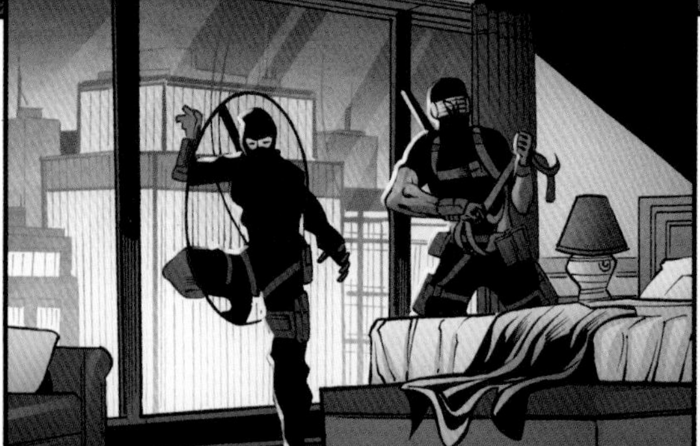

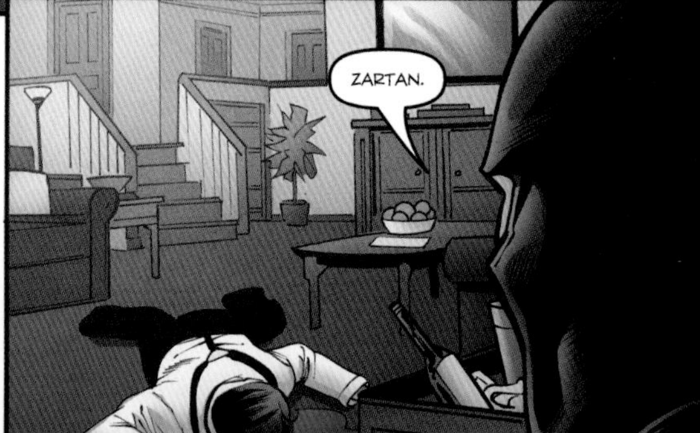
ZARTAN.

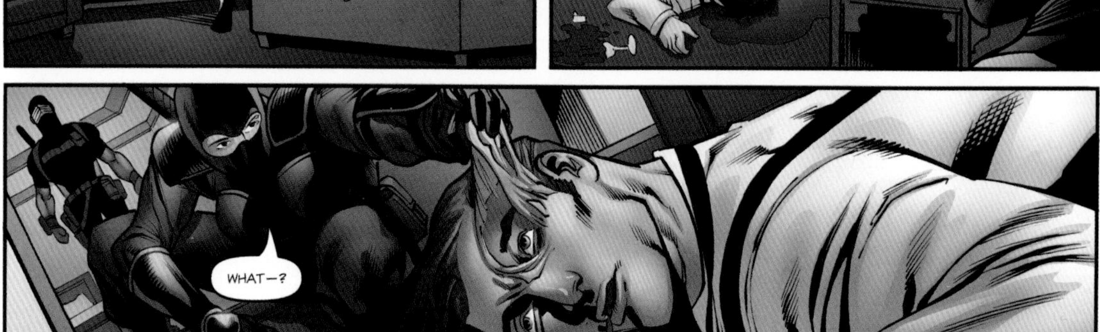
WHAT—?

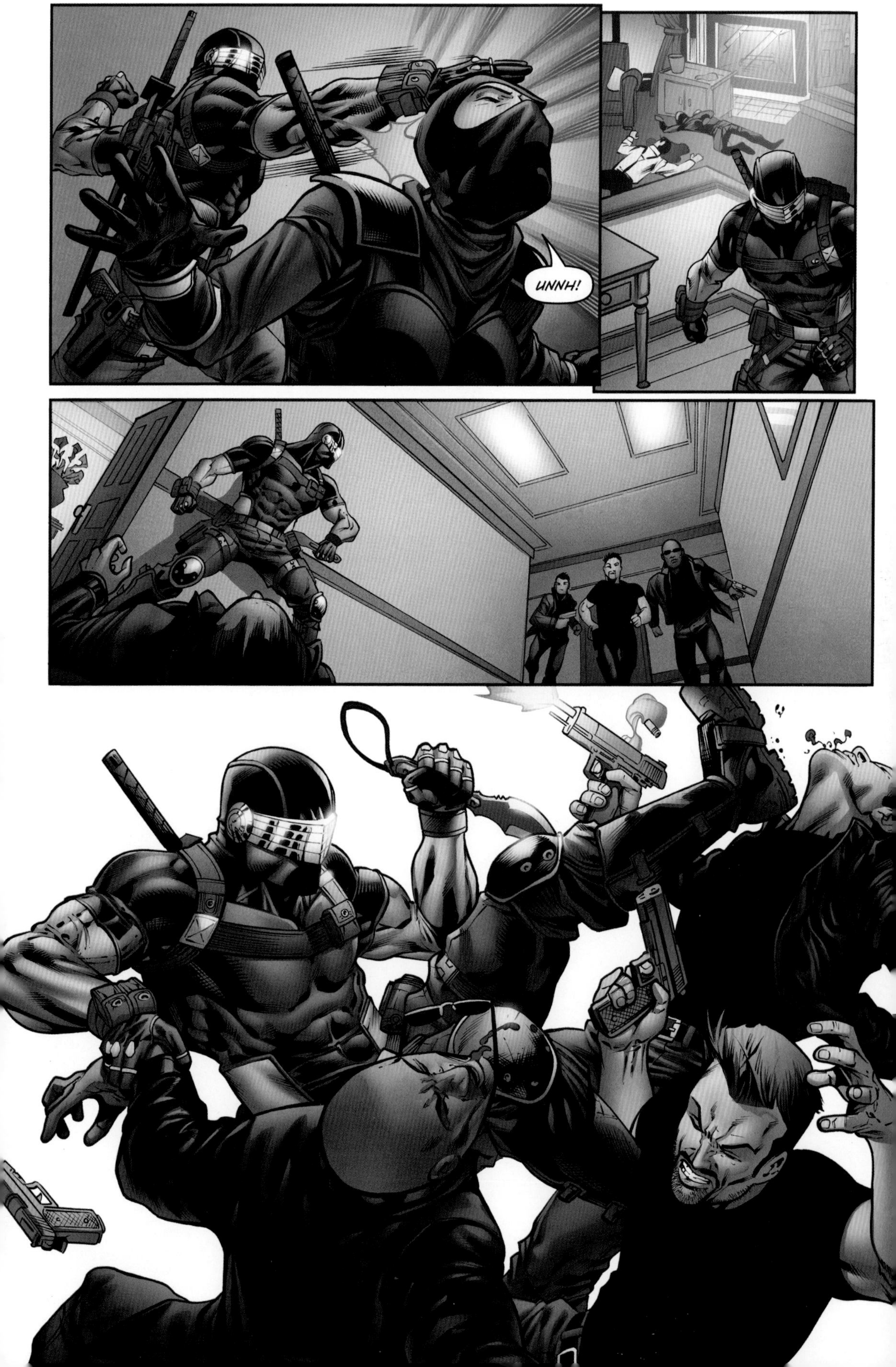
UNNH!

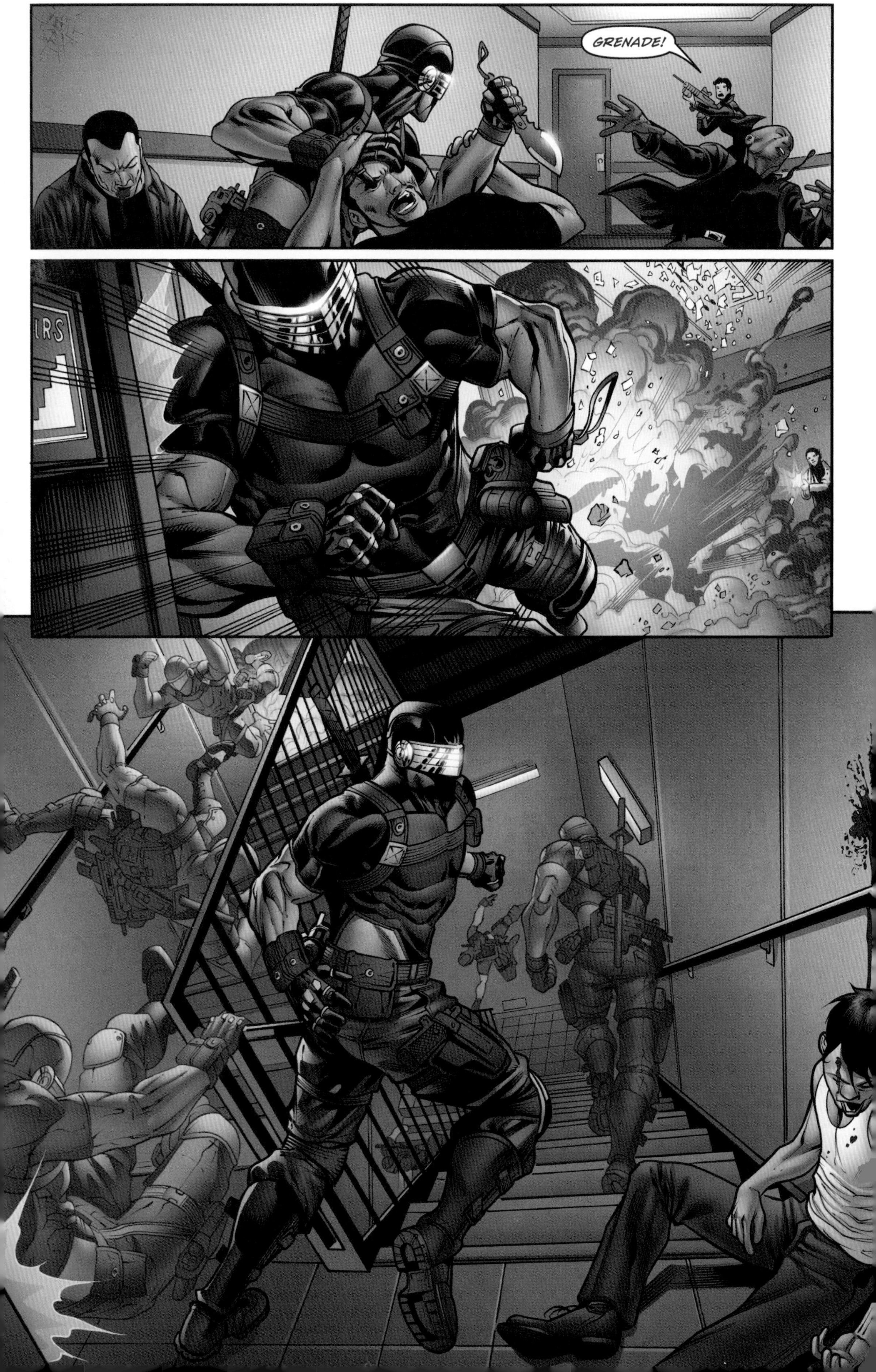
GRENADE!

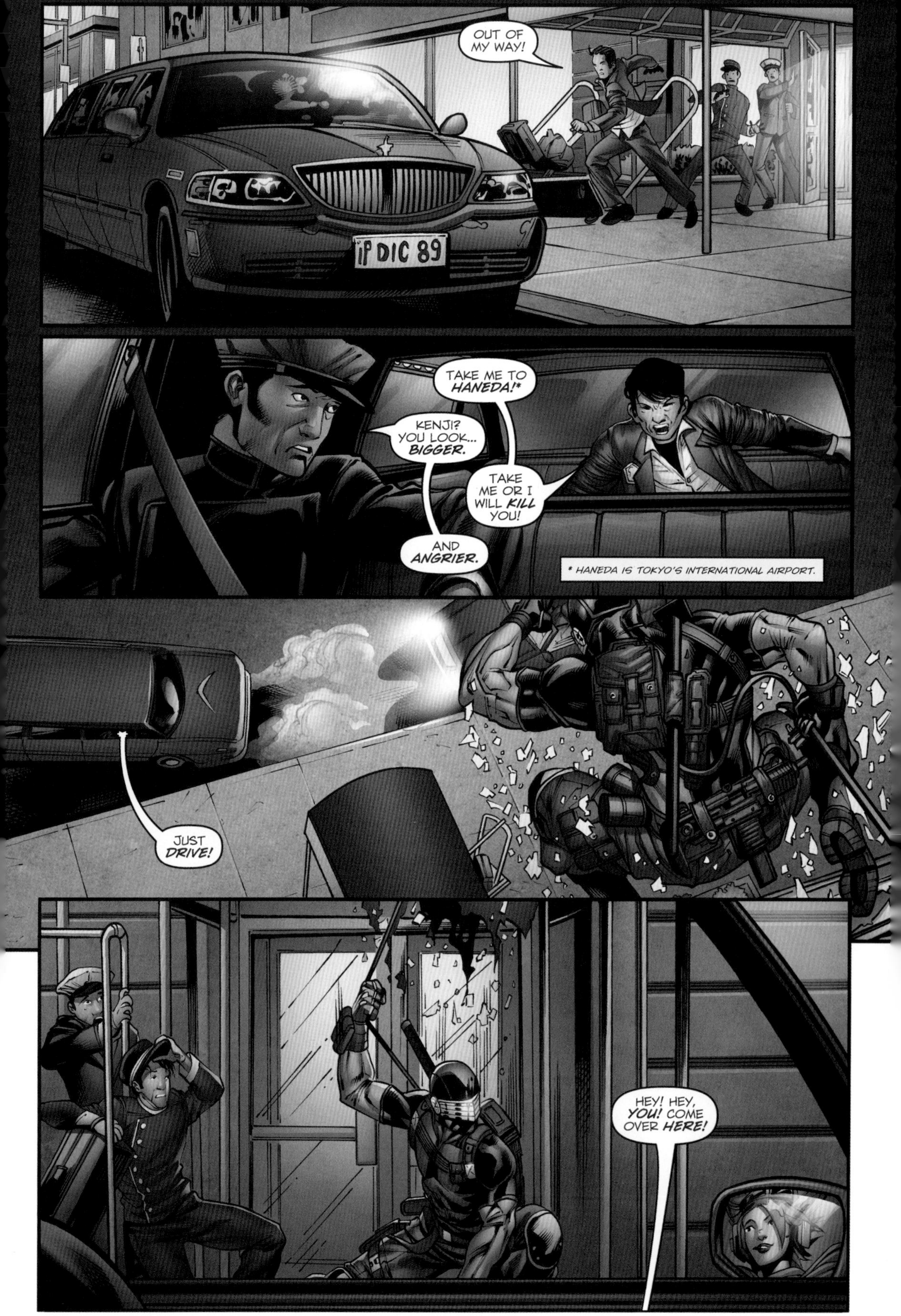

OUT OF MY WAY!
IP DIC 89
TAKE ME TO HANEDA!*
KENJI? YOU LOOK... BIGGER.
TAKE ME OR I WILL KILL YOU!
AND ANGRIER.
* HANEDA IS TOKYO'S INTERNATIONAL AIRPORT.
JUST DRIVE!
HEY! HEY, YOU! COME OVER HERE!

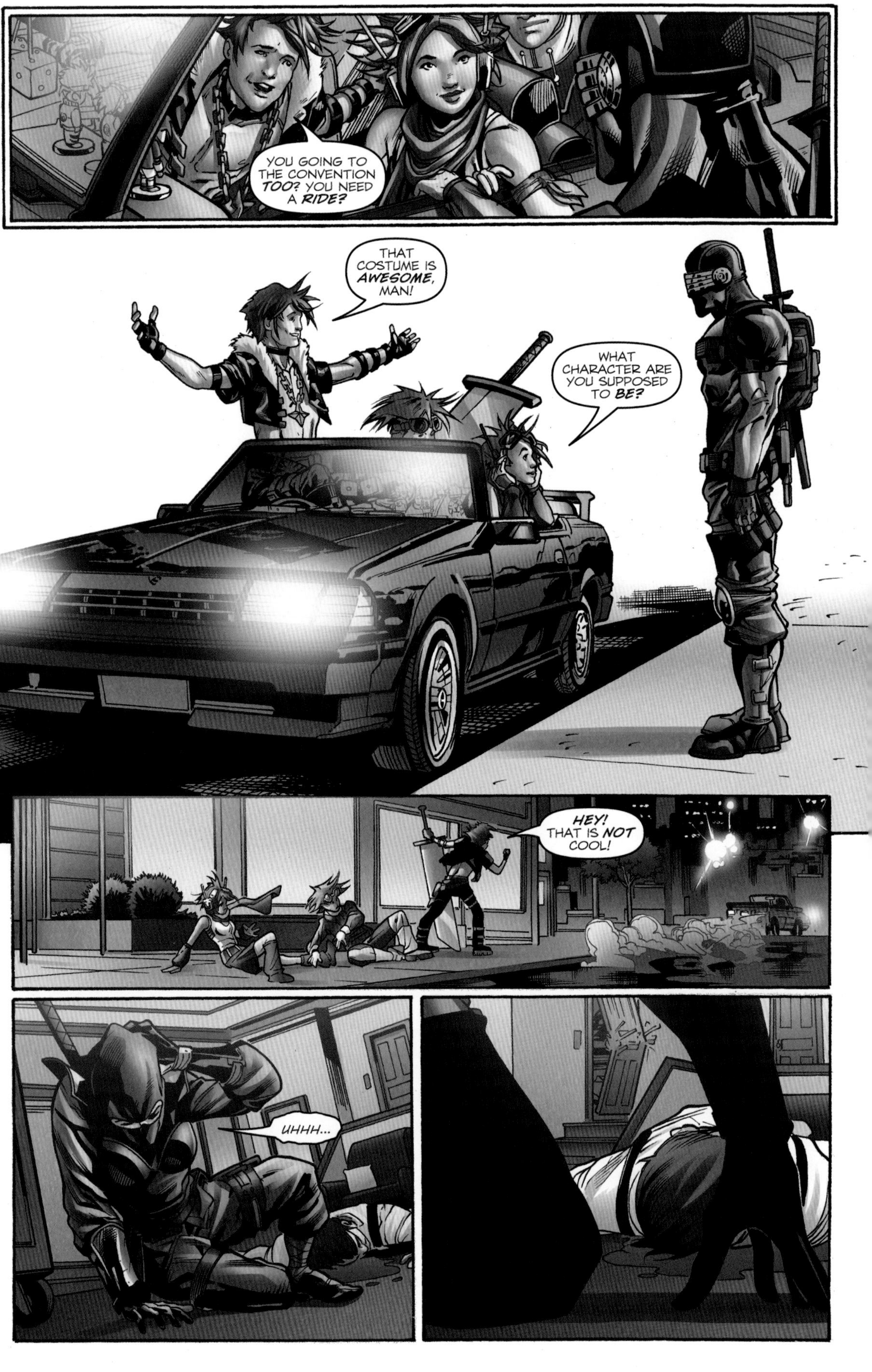
YOU GOING TO THE CONVENTION TOO? YOU NEED A RIDE?
THAT COSTUME IS AWESOME, MAN!
WHAT CHARACTER ARE YOU SUPPOSED TO BE?
HEY! THAT IS NOT COOL!
UHHH...

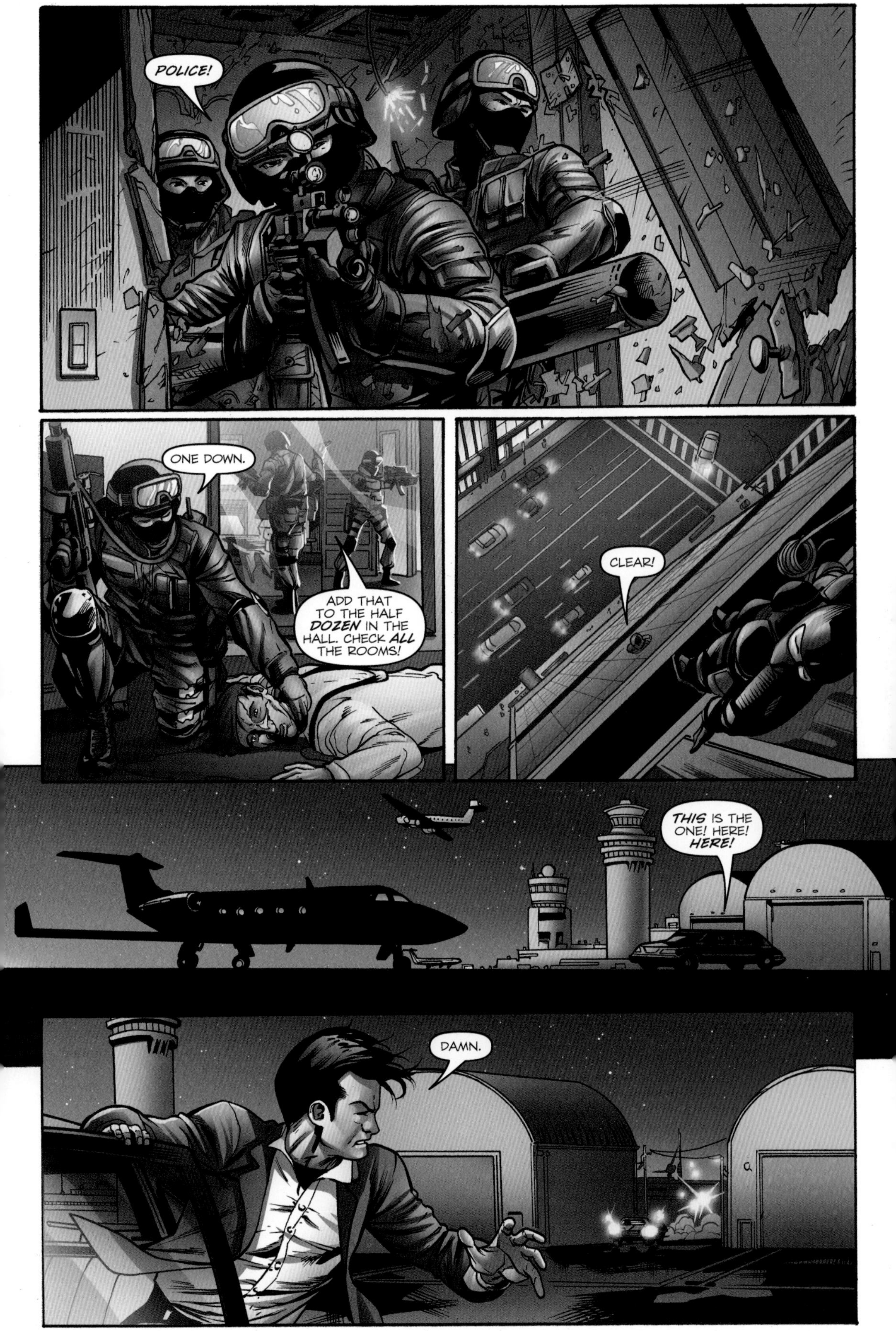
POLICE!
ONE DOWN.
ADD THAT TO THE HALF DOZEN IN THE HALL. CHECK ALL THE ROOMS!
CLEAR!
THIS IS THE ONE! HERE! HERE!
DAMN.

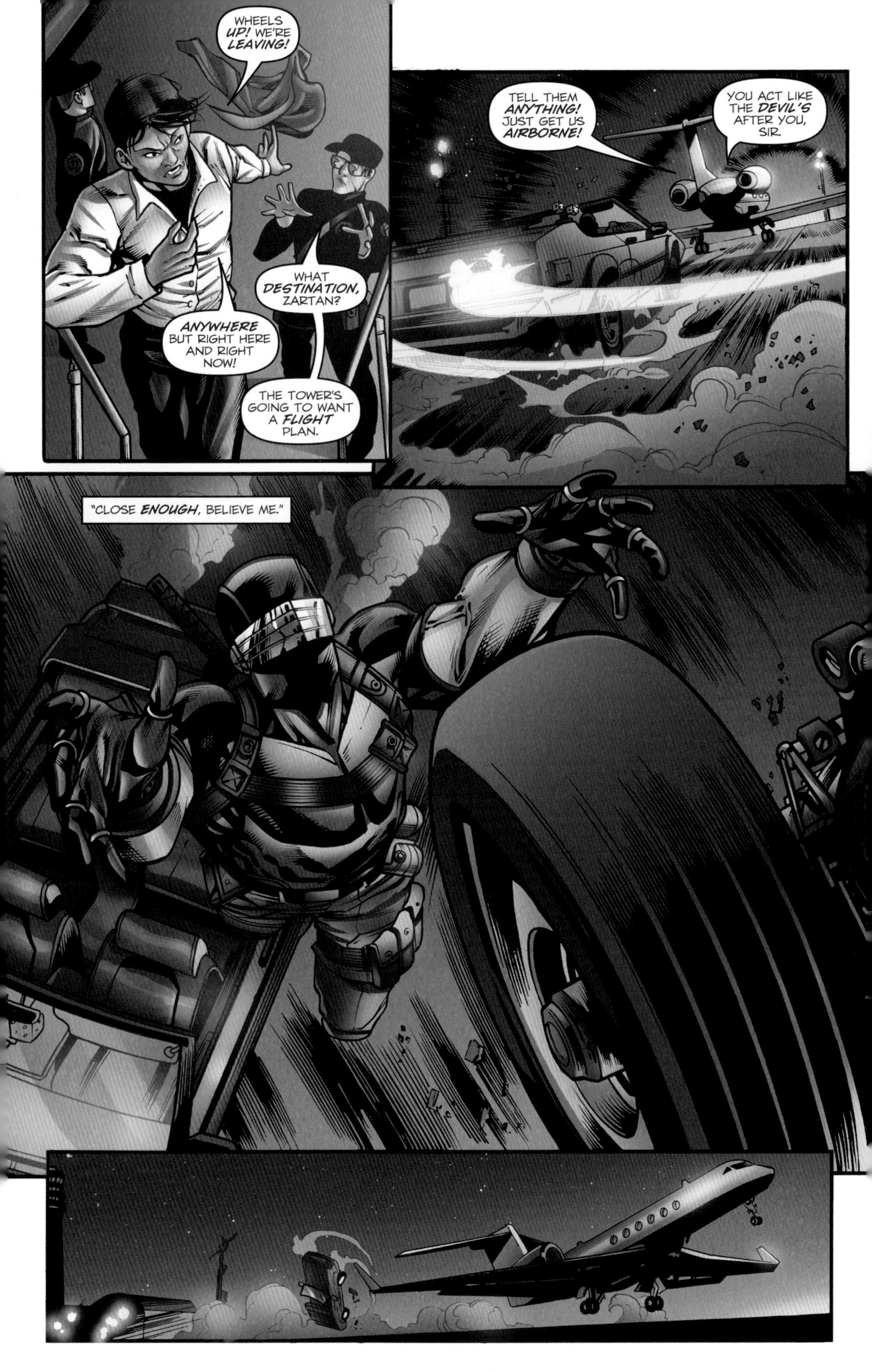
WHEELS UP! WE'RE LEAVING!
WHAT DESTINATION, ZARTAN?
ANYWHERE BUT RIGHT HERE AND RIGHT NOW!
THE TOWER'S GOING TO WANT A FLIGHT PLAN.
TELL THEM ANYTHING! JUST GET US AIRBORNE!
YOU ACT LIKE THE DEVIL'S AFTER YOU, SIR.
"CLOSE ENOUGH, BELIEVE ME."

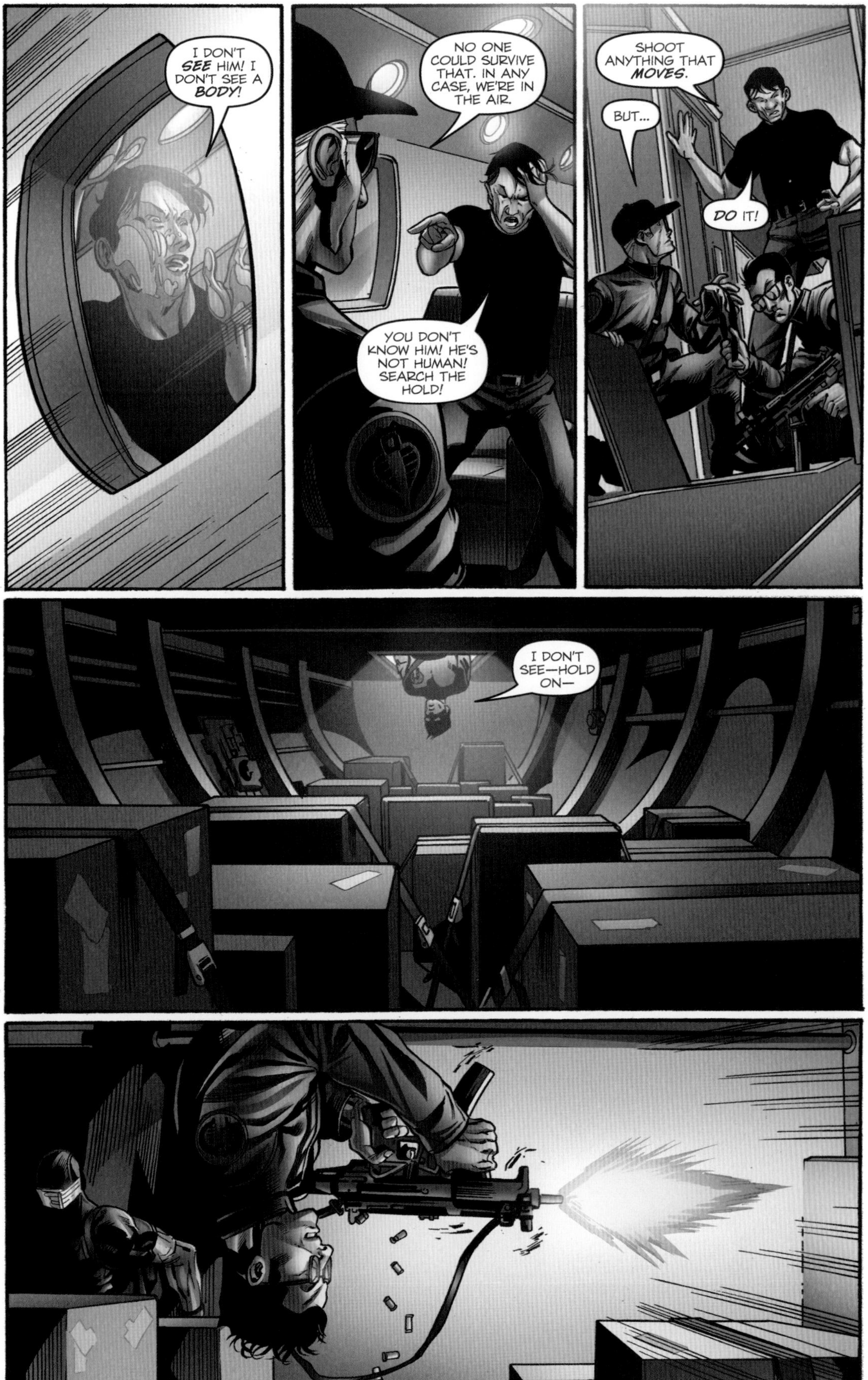
I DON'T *SEE* HIM! I DON'T SEE A *BODY*!
NO ONE COULD SURVIVE THAT. IN ANY CASE, WE'RE IN THE AIR.
YOU DON'T KNOW HIM! HE'S NOT HUMAN! SEARCH THE HOLD!
SHOOT ANYTHING THAT *MOVES*.
BUT...
DO IT!
I DON'T SEE—HOLD ON—

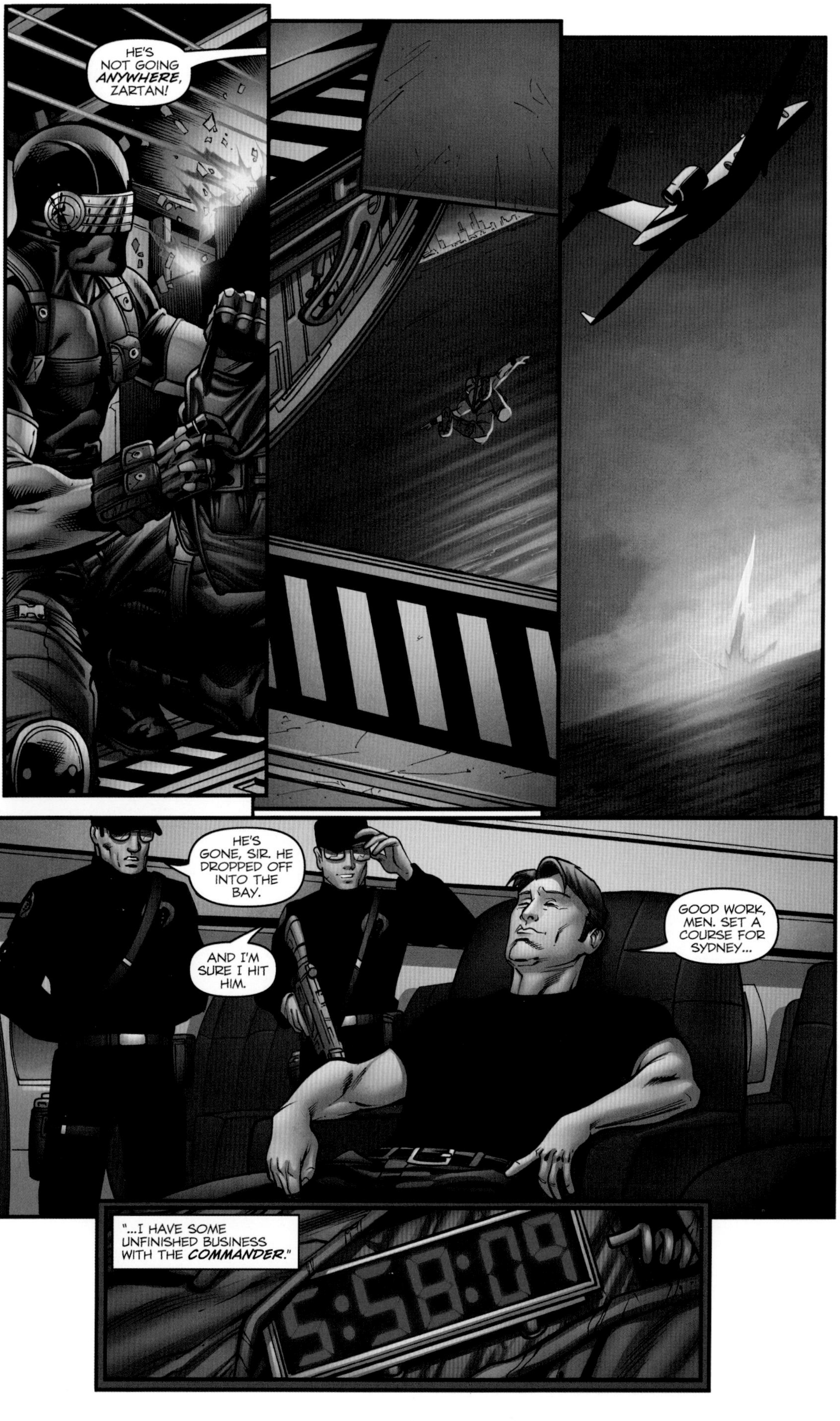

HE'S NOT GOING *ANYWHERE,* ZARTAN!
HE'S GONE, SIR. HE DROPPED OFF INTO THE BAY.
AND I'M SURE I HIT HIM.
GOOD WORK, MEN. SET A COURSE FOR SYDNEY...
"...I HAVE SOME UNFINISHED BUSINESS WITH THE *COMMANDER.*"
5:58:09

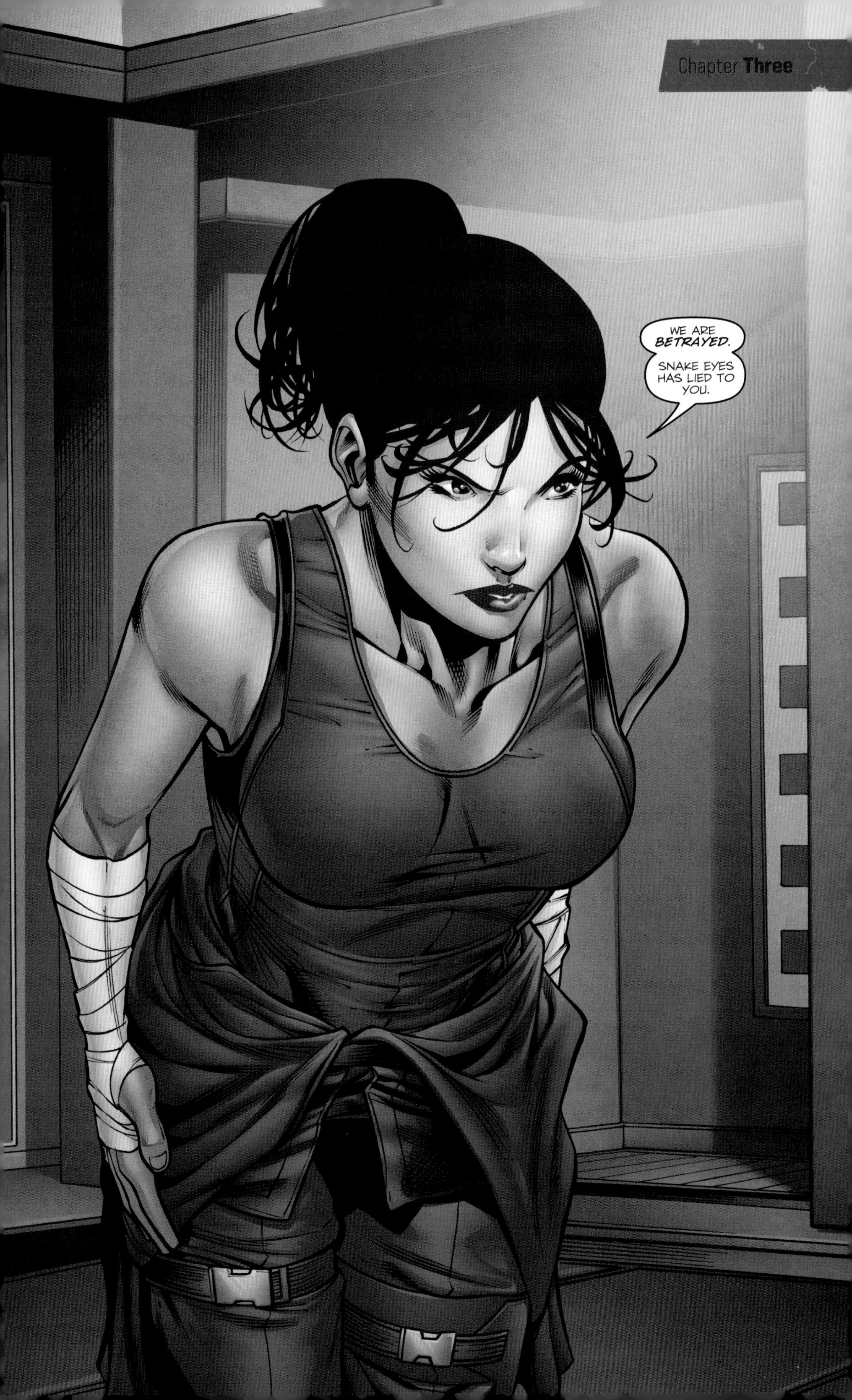
WE ARE *BETRAYED*.
SNAKE EYES HAS LIED TO YOU.

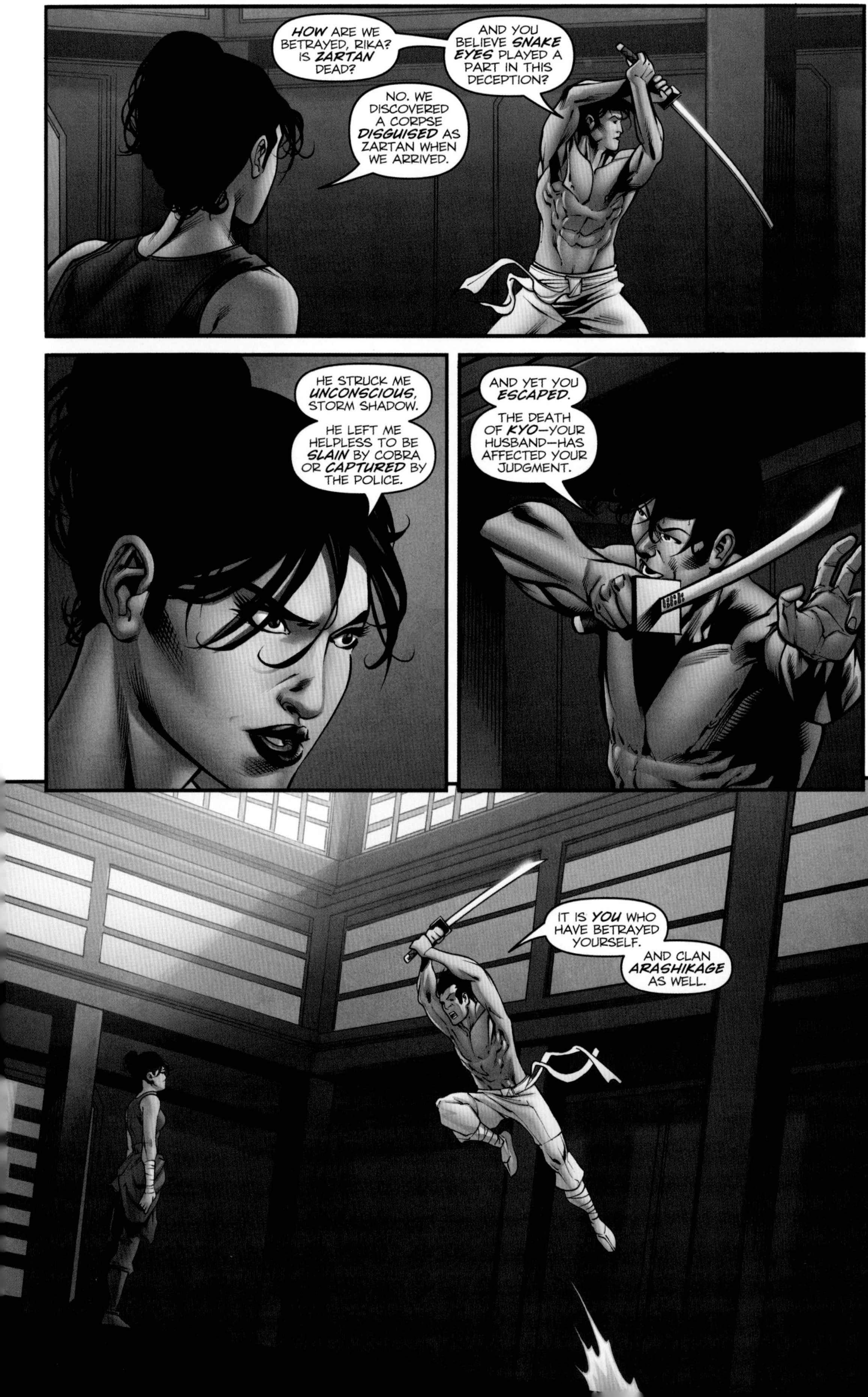
HOW ARE WE BETRAYED, RIKA? IS ZARTAN DEAD?
AND YOU BELIEVE SNAKE EYES PLAYED A PART IN THIS DECEPTION?
NO. WE DISCOVERED A CORPSE DISGUISED AS ZARTAN WHEN WE ARRIVED.
HE STRUCK ME UNCONSCIOUS, STORM SHADOW.
HE LEFT ME HELPLESS TO BE SLAIN BY COBRA OR CAPTURED BY THE POLICE.
AND YET YOU ESCAPED.
THE DEATH OF KYO—YOUR HUSBAND—HAS AFFECTED YOUR JUDGMENT.
IT IS YOU WHO HAVE BETRAYED YOURSELF.
AND CLAN ARASHIKAGE AS WELL.

I KNOW WHAT I KNOW.

I SPEAK THE TRUTH.

SNAKE EYES AND I ARE LIKE BROTHERS.

HIS RETURN TO THE CLAN PLEASES ME.

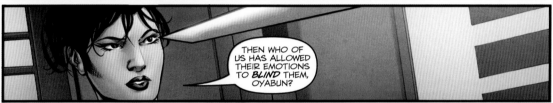

THEN WHO OF US HAS ALLOWED THEIR EMOTIONS TO *BLIND* THEM, OYABUN?

SNAKE EYES IS USING YOUR TRUST *AGAINST* YOU.

YOU HAVE *NO* UNDERSTANDING OF WHAT YOU ARE SAYING.

I DO NOT SPEAK FROM MEMORIES OF A *CHILD'S* AFFECTIONS.

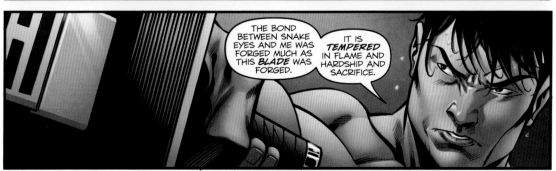

THE BOND BETWEEN SNAKE EYES AND ME WAS FORGED MUCH AS THIS *BLADE* WAS FORGED.

IT IS *TEMPERED* IN FLAME AND HARDSHIP AND SACRIFICE.

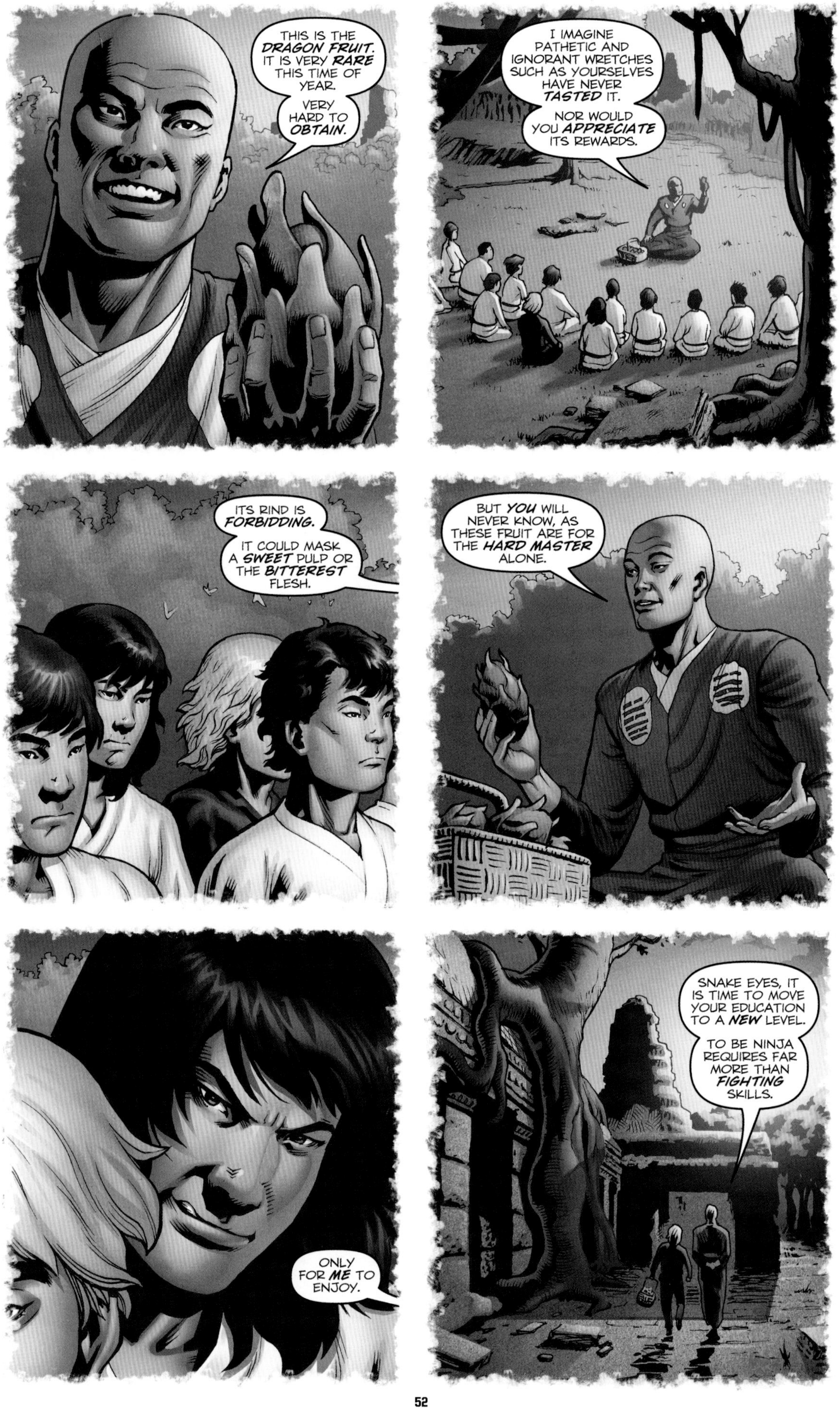
THIS IS THE DRAGON FRUIT. IT IS VERY RARE THIS TIME OF YEAR.
VERY HARD TO OBTAIN.
I IMAGINE PATHETIC AND IGNORANT WRETCHES SUCH AS YOURSELVES HAVE NEVER TASTED IT.
NOR WOULD YOU APPRECIATE ITS REWARDS.
ITS RIND IS FORBIDDING.
IT COULD MASK A SWEET PULP OR THE BITTEREST FLESH.
BUT YOU WILL NEVER KNOW, AS THESE FRUIT ARE FOR THE HARD MASTER ALONE.
ONLY FOR ME TO ENJOY.
SNAKE EYES, IT IS TIME TO MOVE YOUR EDUCATION TO A NEW LEVEL.
TO BE NINJA REQUIRES FAR MORE THAN FIGHTING SKILLS.

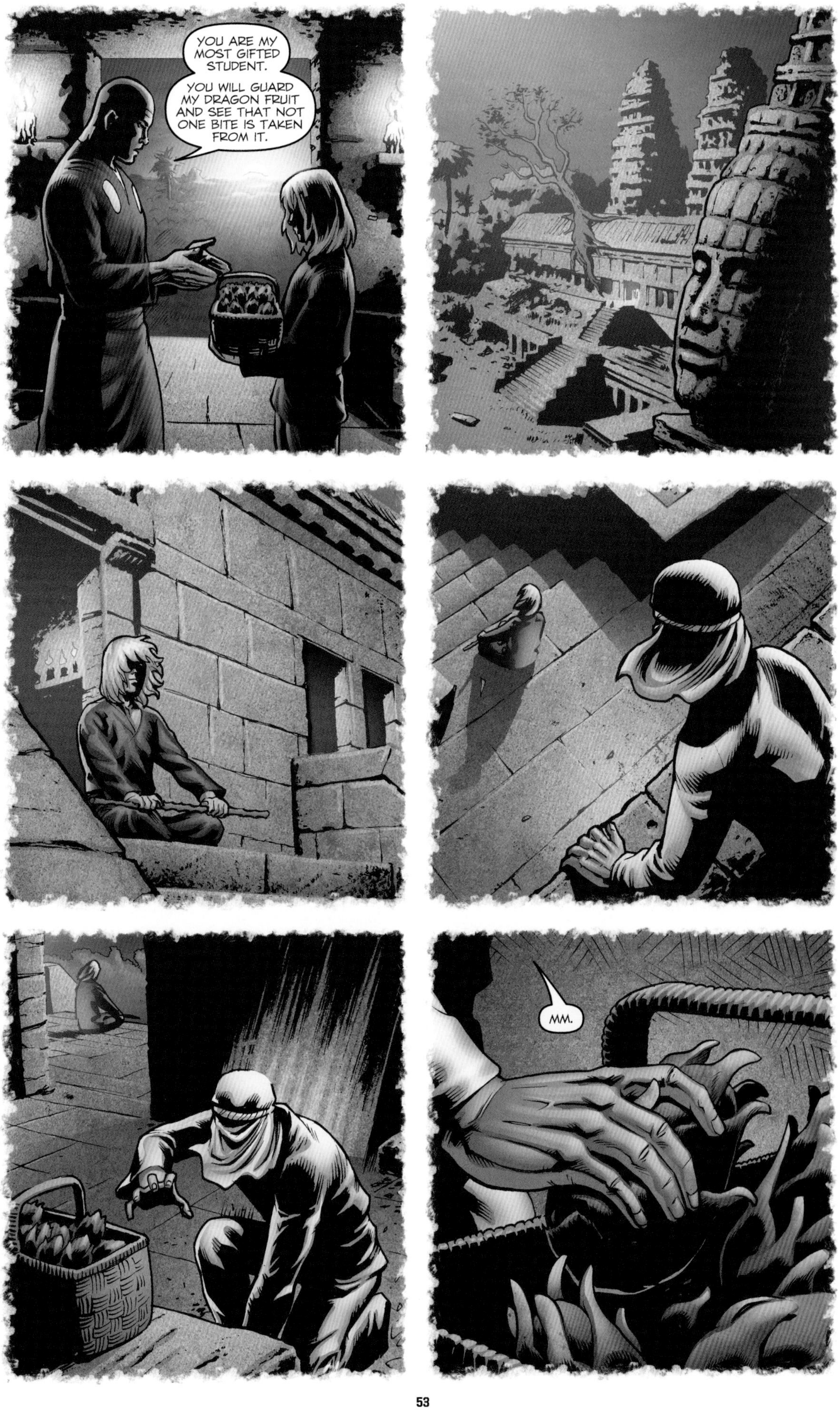
YOU ARE MY MOST GIFTED STUDENT.
YOU WILL GUARD MY DRAGON FRUIT AND SEE THAT NOT ONE BITE IS TAKEN FROM IT.
MM.

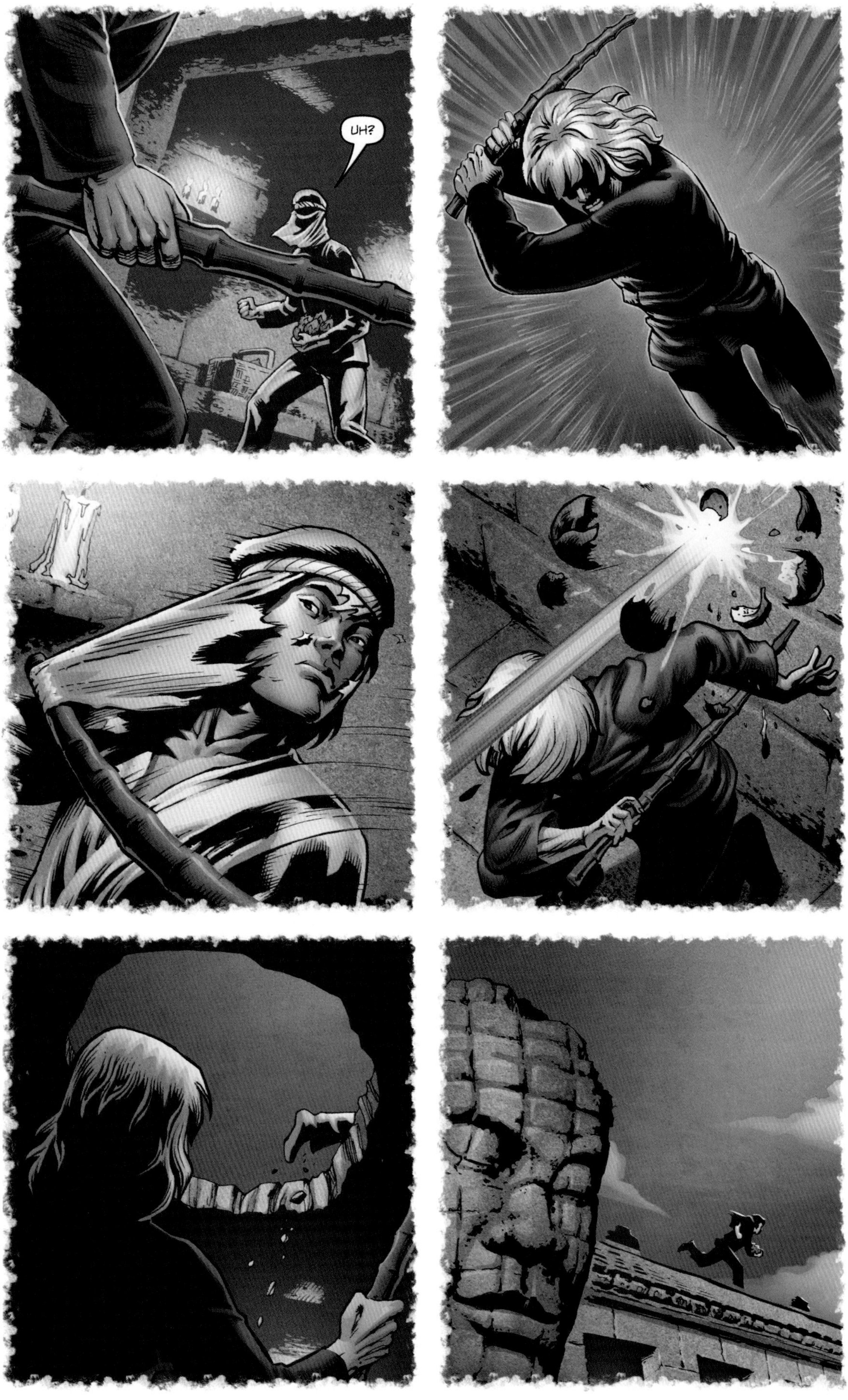
UH?

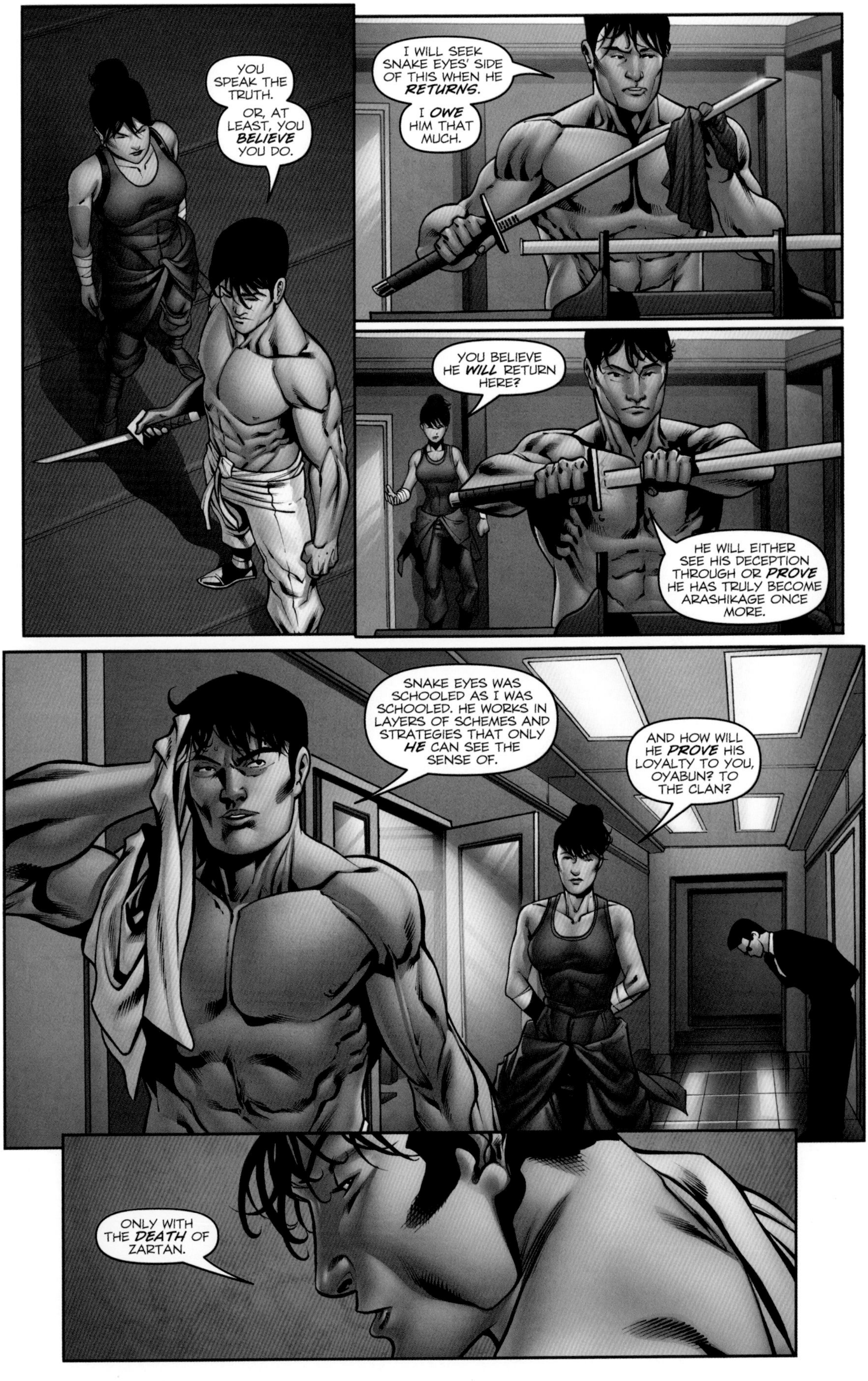
YOU SPEAK THE TRUTH.
OR, AT LEAST, YOU BELIEVE YOU DO.
I WILL SEEK SNAKE EYES' SIDE OF THIS WHEN HE RETURNS.
I OWE HIM THAT MUCH.
YOU BELIEVE HE WILL RETURN HERE?
HE WILL EITHER SEE HIS DECEPTION THROUGH OR PROVE HE HAS TRULY BECOME ARASHIKAGE ONCE MORE.
SNAKE EYES WAS SCHOOLED AS I WAS SCHOOLED. HE WORKS IN LAYERS OF SCHEMES AND STRATEGIES THAT ONLY HE CAN SEE THE SENSE OF.
AND HOW WILL HE PROVE HIS LOYALTY TO YOU, OYABUN? TO THE CLAN?
ONLY WITH THE DEATH OF ZARTAN.

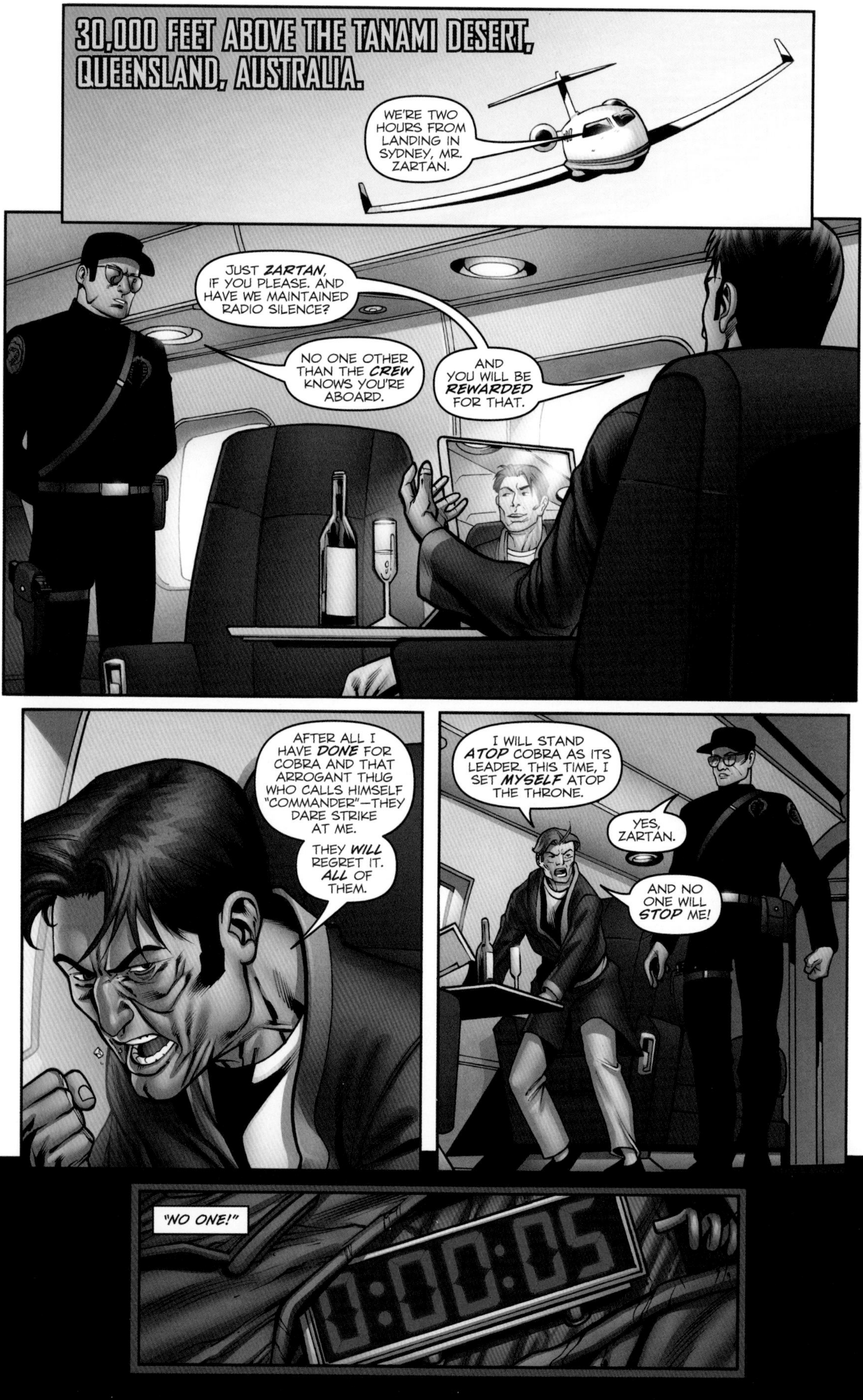

30,000 FEET ABOVE THE TANAMI DESERT, QUEENSLAND, AUSTRALIA.
WE'RE TWO HOURS FROM LANDING IN SYDNEY, MR. ZARTAN.
JUST ZARTAN, IF YOU PLEASE. AND HAVE WE MAINTAINED RADIO SILENCE?
NO ONE OTHER THAN THE CREW KNOWS YOU'RE ABOARD.
AND YOU WILL BE REWARDED FOR THAT.
AFTER ALL I HAVE DONE FOR COBRA AND THAT ARROGANT THUG WHO CALLS HIMSELF "COMMANDER"—THEY DARE STRIKE AT ME.
THEY WILL REGRET IT. ALL OF THEM.
I WILL STAND ATOP COBRA AS ITS LEADER. THIS TIME, I SET MYSELF ATOP THE THRONE.
YES, ZARTAN.
AND NO ONE WILL STOP ME!
"NO ONE!"
0:00:05

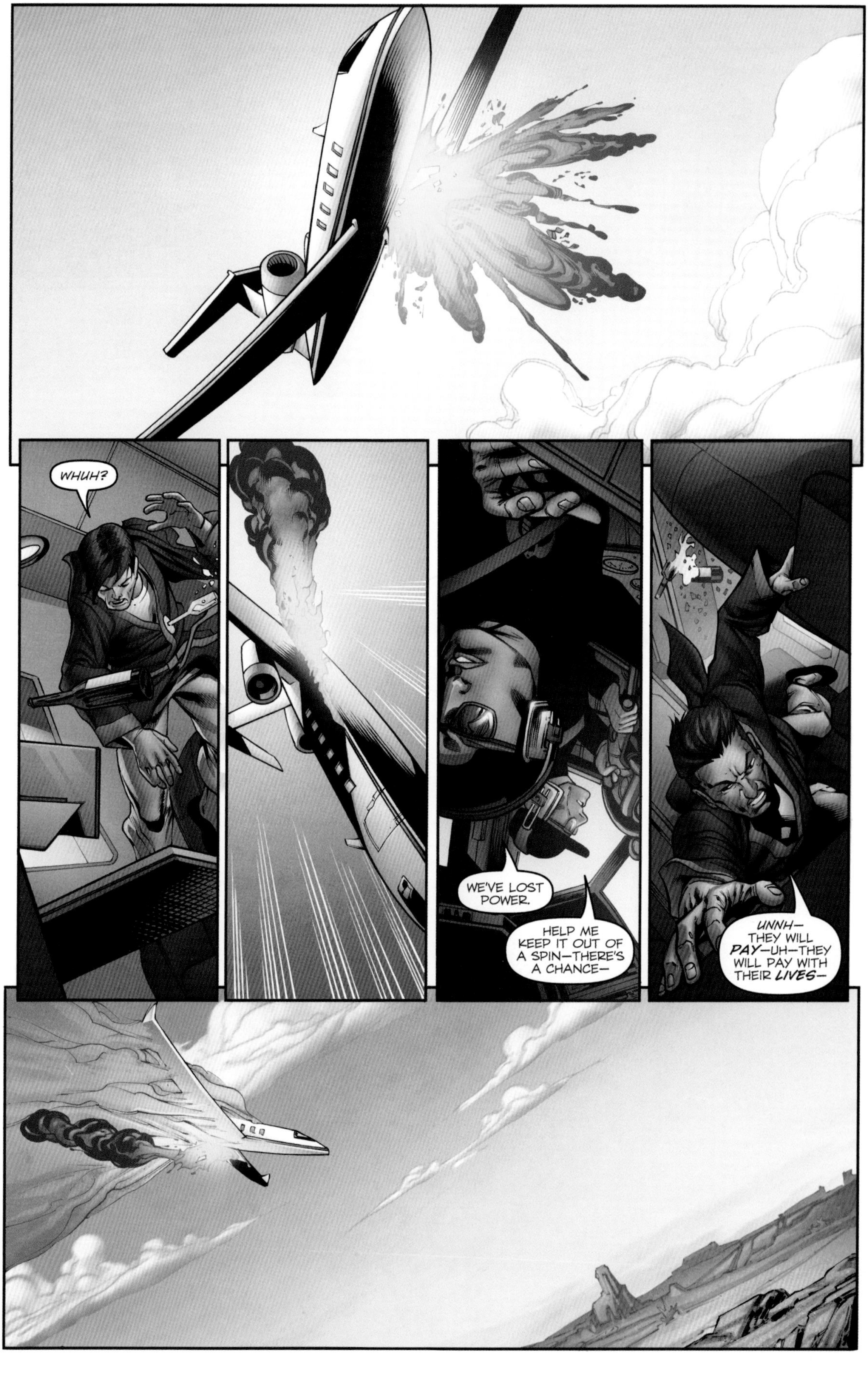
WHUH?
WE'VE LOST POWER.
HELP ME KEEP IT OUT OF A SPIN—THERE'S A CHANCE—
UNNH— THEY WILL PAY—UH—THEY WILL PAY WITH THEIR LIVES—

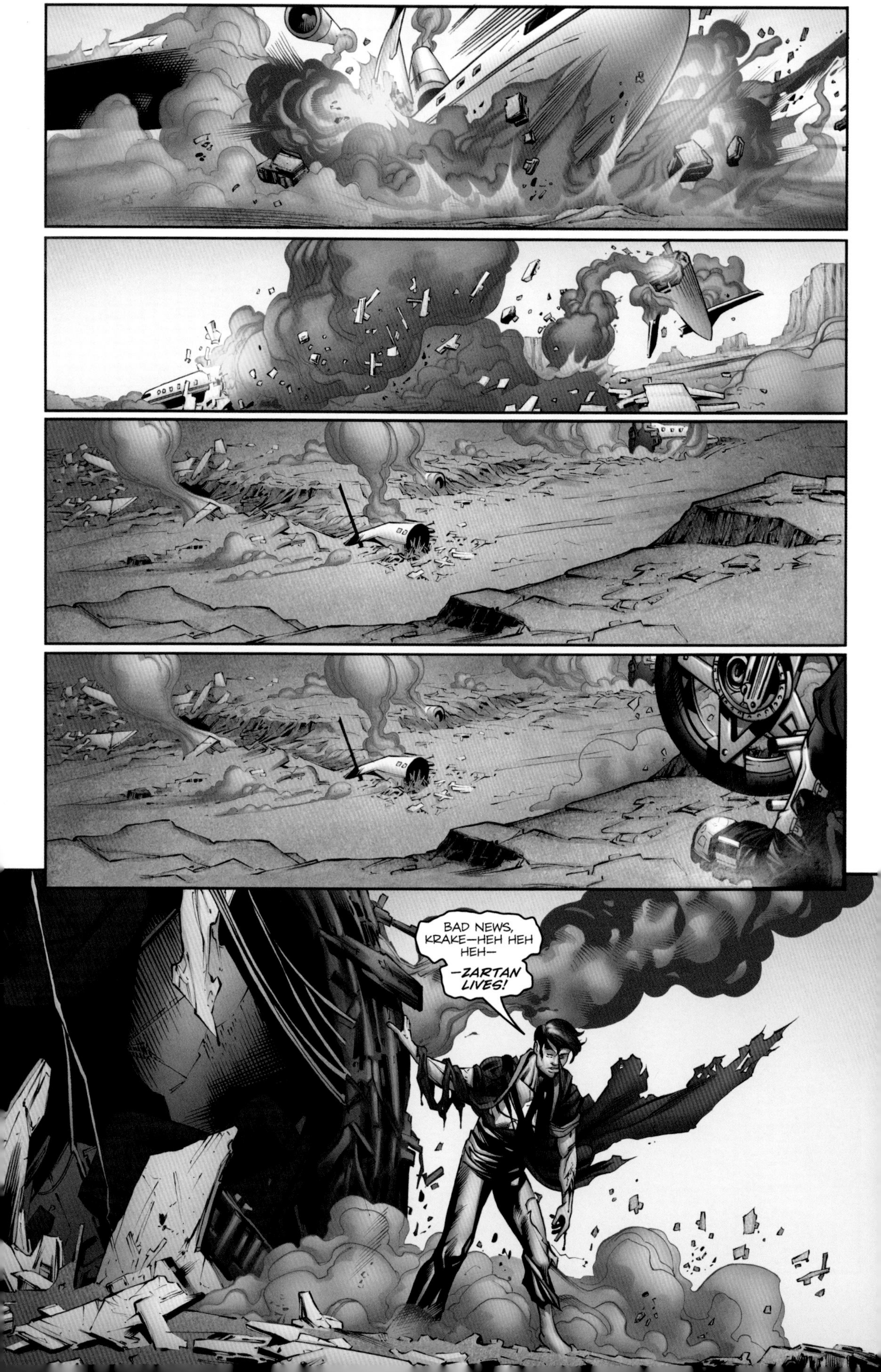
BAD NEWS, KRAKE—HEH HEH HEH—
—ZARTAN LIVES!

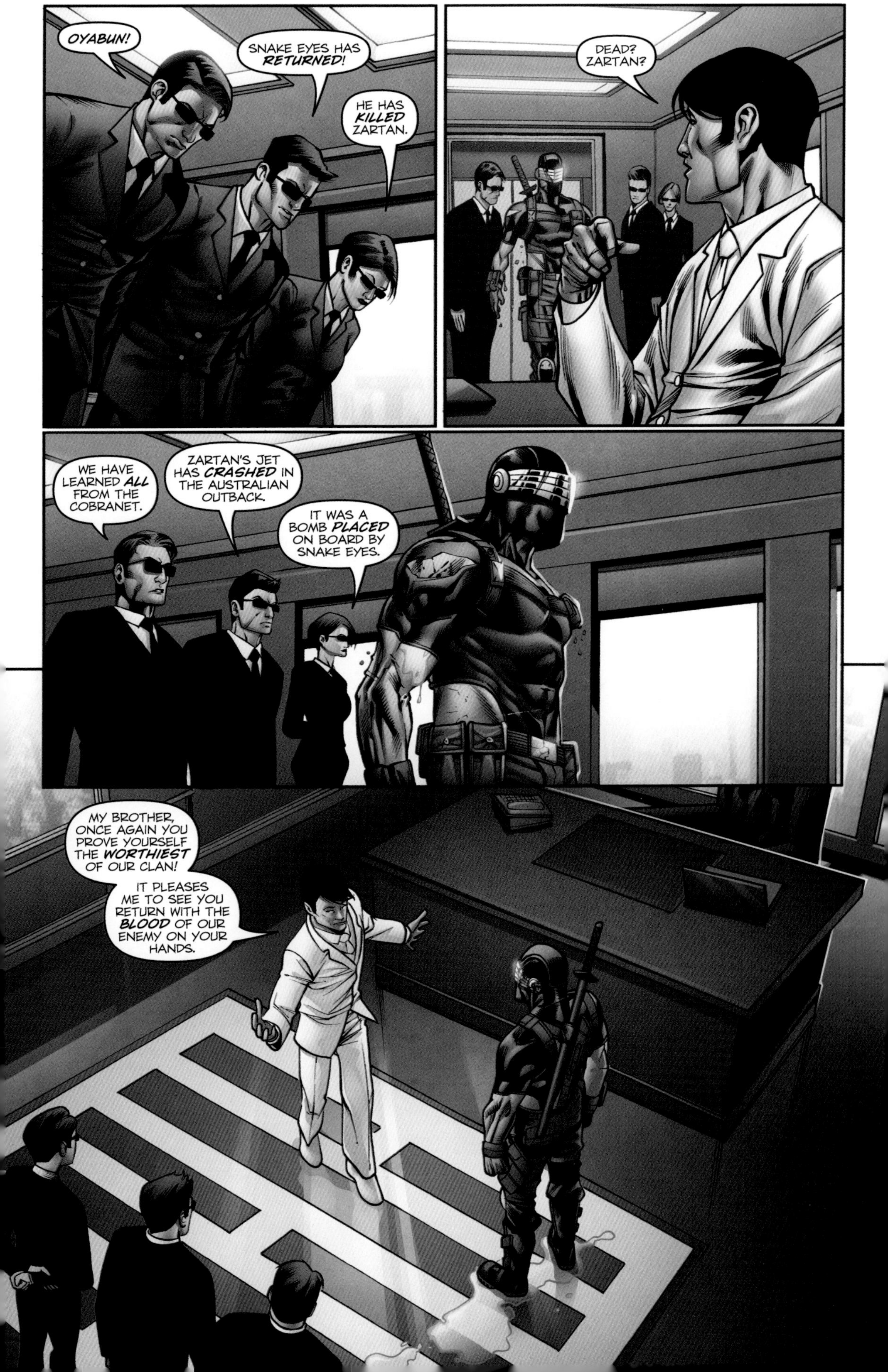
OYABUN!
SNAKE EYES HAS RETURNED!
HE HAS KILLED ZARTAN.
DEAD? ZARTAN?
WE HAVE LEARNED ALL FROM THE COBRANET.
ZARTAN'S JET HAS CRASHED IN THE AUSTRALIAN OUTBACK.
IT WAS A BOMB PLACED ON BOARD BY SNAKE EYES.
MY BROTHER, ONCE AGAIN YOU PROVE YOURSELF THE WORTHIEST OF OUR CLAN!
IT PLEASES ME TO SEE YOU RETURN WITH THE BLOOD OF OUR ENEMY ON YOUR HANDS.

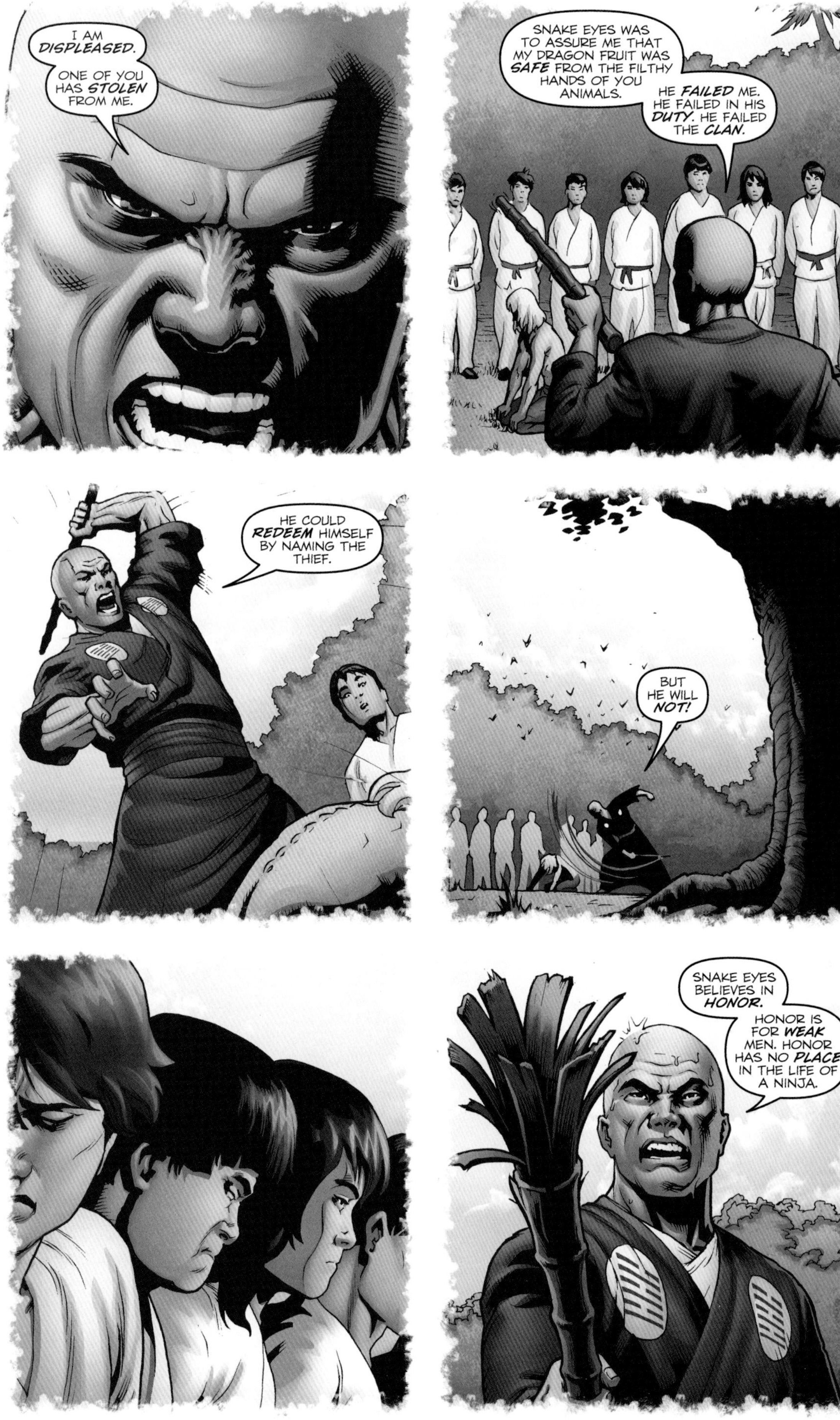
I AM DISPLEASED.
ONE OF YOU HAS STOLEN FROM ME.
SNAKE EYES WAS TO ASSURE ME THAT MY DRAGON FRUIT WAS SAFE FROM THE FILTHY HANDS OF YOU ANIMALS.
HE FAILED ME. HE FAILED IN HIS DUTY. HE FAILED THE CLAN.
HE COULD REDEEM HIMSELF BY NAMING THE THIEF.
BUT HE WILL NOT!
SNAKE EYES BELIEVES IN HONOR.
HONOR IS FOR WEAK MEN. HONOR HAS NO PLACE IN THE LIFE OF A NINJA.

HE HOLDS HIS LOYALTY TO ONE OF YOU *ABOVE* HIS LOYALTY TO HIS SENSEI.

HE SUFFERS TO PROTECT ONE OF YOU IN DEFIANCE TO HIS OATH TO THE *CLAN!*

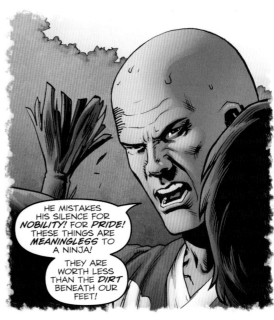

HE MISTAKES HIS SILENCE FOR *NOBILITY!* FOR *PRIDE!* THESE THINGS ARE *MEANINGLESS* TO A NINJA!

THEY ARE WORTH LESS THAN THE *DIRT* BENEATH OUR FEET!

A NINJA HOLDS *NOTHING* DEAR BUT THE CLAN. A NINJA IS A *LOW* CREATURE AND DOES WHAT OTHER MEN *FEAR* TO DO AND GOES WHERE OTHER MEN *FEAR* TO GO.

HE *EMBRACES* DECEIT! HE *REVELS* IN BETRAYAL! HE *LIVES* TO TRICK AND TO KILL AND TO CAUSE SUFFERING.

BUT SNAKE EYES HOLDS HIMSELF *ABOVE* ALL OF THAT. HE SEES HIMSELF AS SUPERIOR AND BY DOING SO *REDUCES* HIMSELF IN MY EYES.

AND ALL FOR NOTHING, AS THE JUICE OF THE DRAGON FRUIT STAINS THE TEETH OF ANY WHO EAT IT. THE THIEF BETRAYS *HIMSELF* BY OPENING HIS MOUTH.

AND SO IT IS THE THIEF WHO HAS LEARNED THE LESSON OF THE NINJA WELL AND SURRENDERED HIS SOUL TO SECRECY AND GUILE.

HE HAS NO CAUSE TO HIDE HIS IDENTITY ANY LONGER.

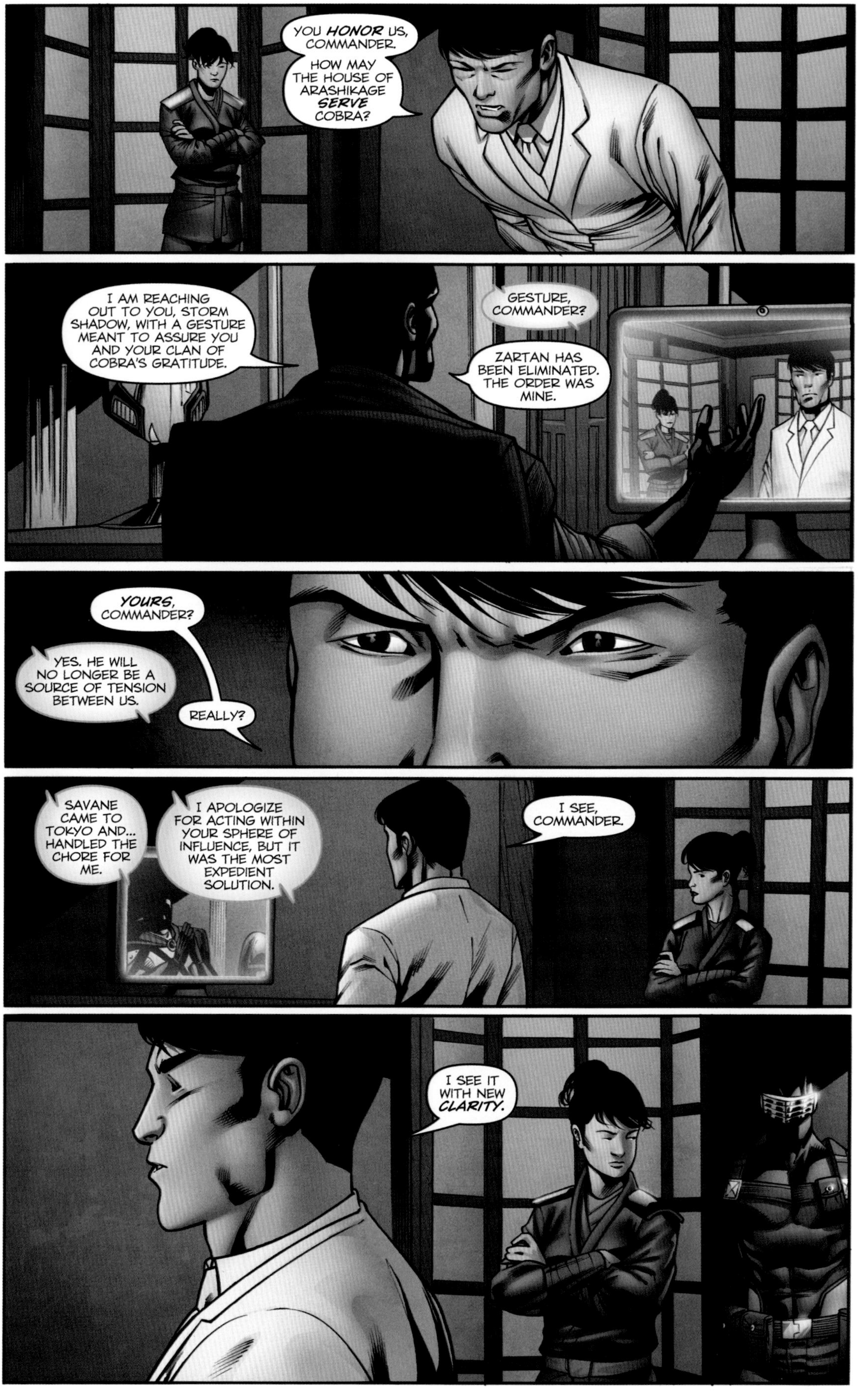

YOU HONOR US, COMMANDER.
HOW MAY THE HOUSE OF ARASHIKAGE SERVE COBRA?
I AM REACHING OUT TO YOU, STORM SHADOW, WITH A GESTURE MEANT TO ASSURE YOU AND YOUR CLAN OF COBRA'S GRATITUDE.
GESTURE, COMMANDER?
ZARTAN HAS BEEN ELIMINATED. THE ORDER WAS MINE.
YOURS, COMMANDER?
YES. HE WILL NO LONGER BE A SOURCE OF TENSION BETWEEN US.
REALLY?
SAVANE CAME TO TOKYO AND... HANDLED THE CHORE FOR ME.
I APOLOGIZE FOR ACTING WITHIN YOUR SPHERE OF INFLUENCE, BUT IT WAS THE MOST EXPEDIENT SOLUTION.
I SEE, COMMANDER.
I SEE IT WITH NEW CLARITY.

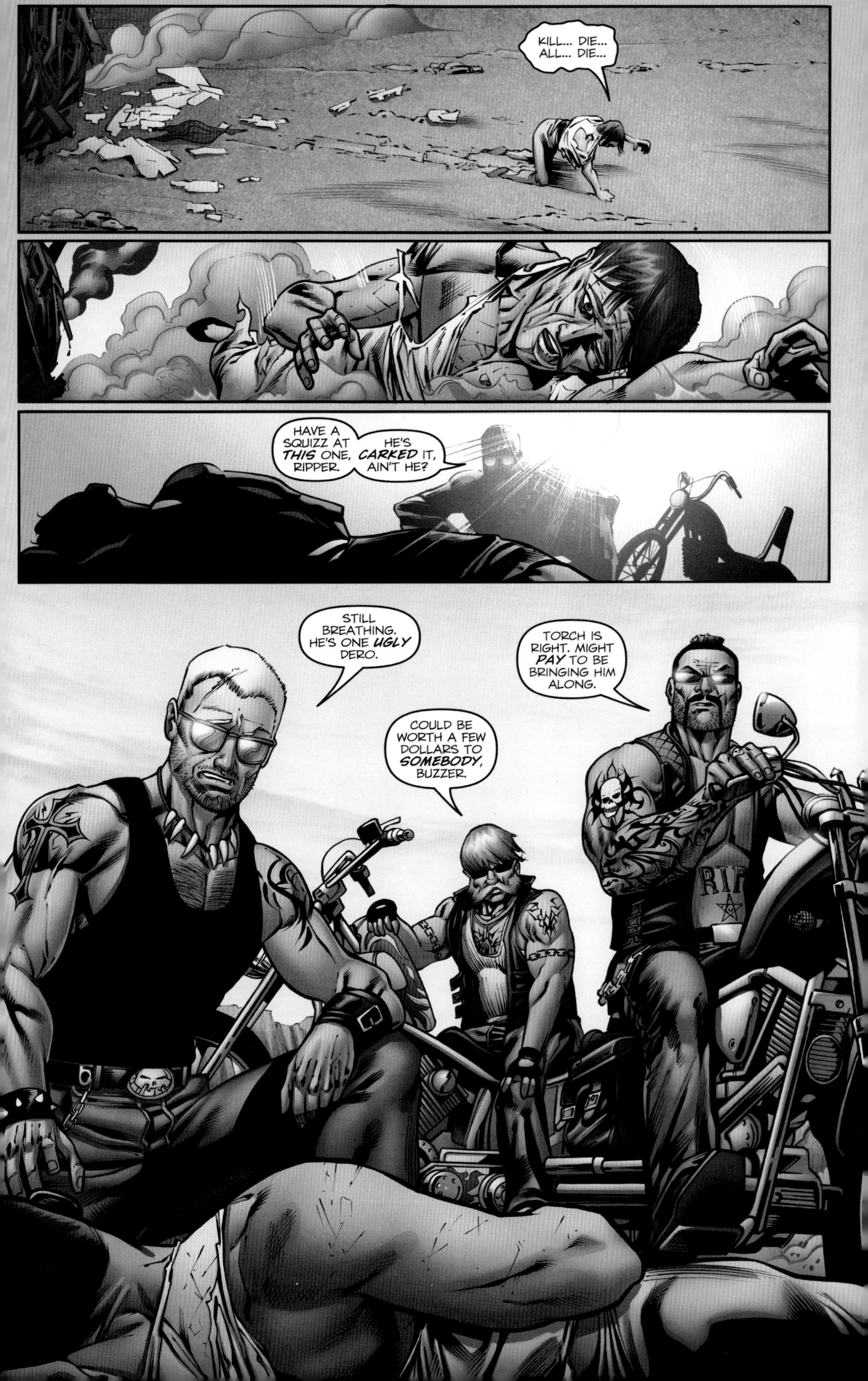
KILL... DIE... ALL... DIE...
HAVE A SQUIZZ AT THIS ONE, RIPPER.
HE'S CARKED IT, AIN'T HE?
STILL BREATHING. HE'S ONE UGLY DERO.
TORCH IS RIGHT. MIGHT PAY TO BE BRINGING HIM ALONG.
COULD BE WORTH A FEW DOLLARS TO SOMEBODY, BUZZER.
RIP

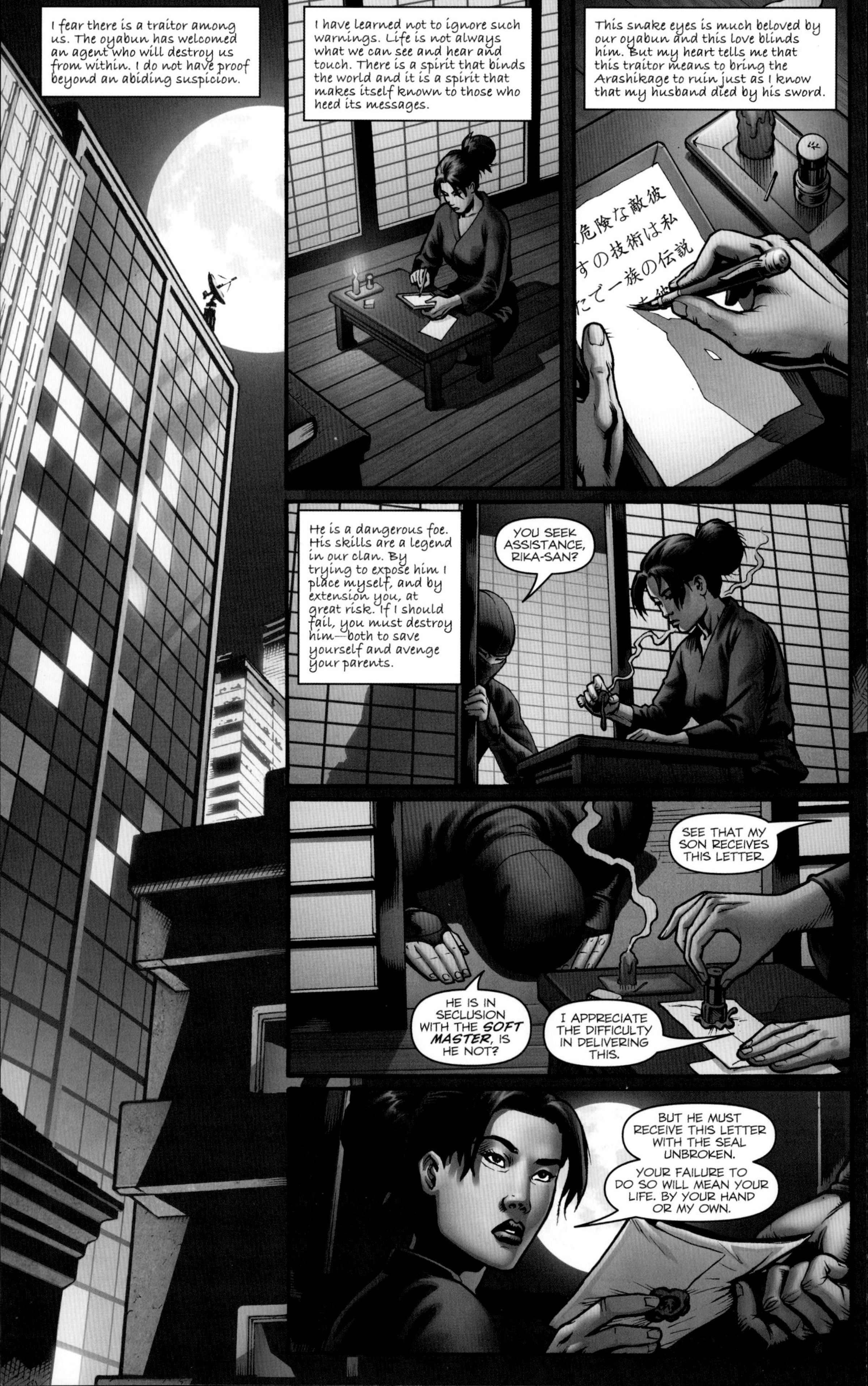
I fear there is a traitor among us. The oyabun has welcomed an agent who will destroy us from within. I do not have proof beyond an abiding suspicion.
I have learned not to ignore such warnings. Life is not always what we can see and hear and touch. There is a spirit that binds the world and it is a spirit that makes itself known to those who heed its messages.
This snake eyes is much beloved by our oyabun and this love blinds him. But my heart tells me that this traitor means to bring the Arashikage to ruin just as I know that my husband died by his sword.
He is a dangerous foe. His skills are a legend in our clan. By trying to expose him I place myself, and by extension you, at great risk. If I should fail, you must destroy him—both to save yourself and avenge your parents.
YOU SEEK ASSISTANCE, RIKA-SAN?
SEE THAT MY SON RECEIVES THIS LETTER.
HE IS IN SECLUSION WITH THE SOFT MASTER, IS HE NOT?
I APPRECIATE THE DIFFICULTY IN DELIVERING THIS.
BUT HE MUST RECEIVE THIS LETTER WITH THE SEAL UNBROKEN.
YOUR FAILURE TO DO SO WILL MEAN YOUR LIFE. BY YOUR HAND OR MY OWN.

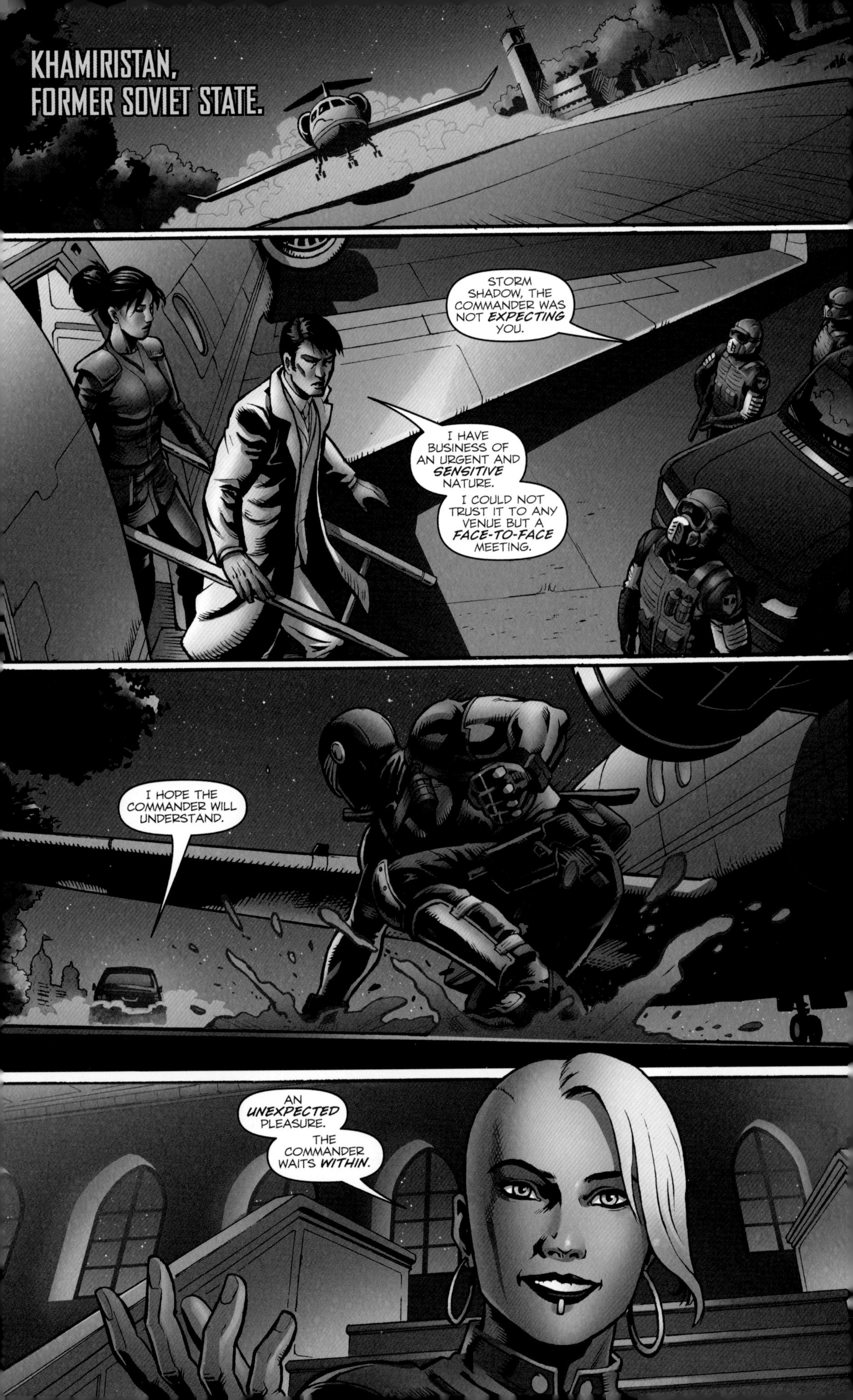
KHAMIRISTAN, FORMER SOVIET STATE.
STORM SHADOW, THE COMMANDER WAS NOT EXPECTING YOU.
I HAVE BUSINESS OF AN URGENT AND SENSITIVE NATURE.
I COULD NOT TRUST IT TO ANY VENUE BUT A FACE-TO-FACE MEETING.
I HOPE THE COMMANDER WILL UNDERSTAND.
AN UNEXPECTED PLEASURE.
THE COMMANDER WAITS WITHIN.

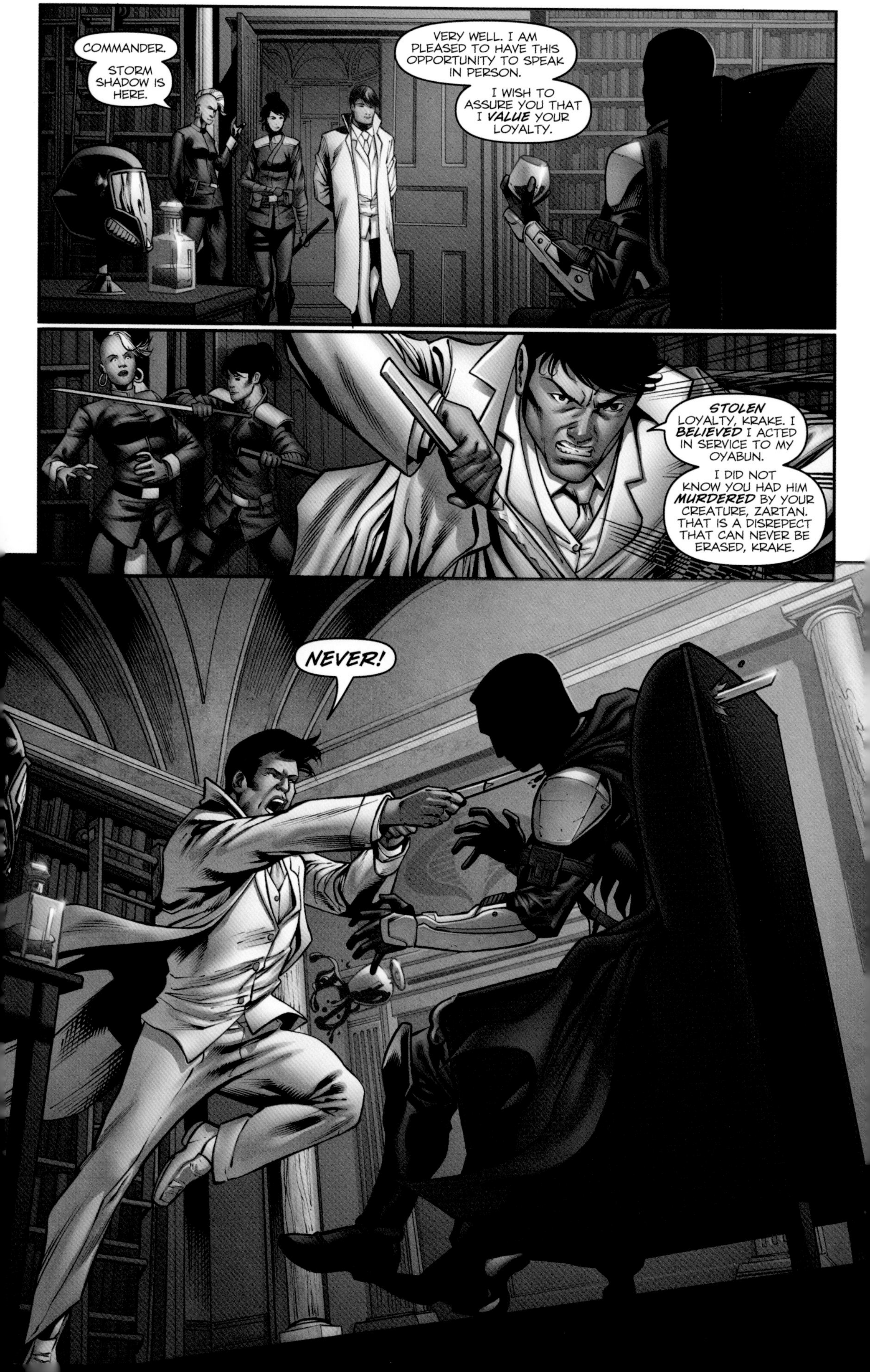

COMMANDER.
STORM SHADOW IS HERE.
VERY WELL. I AM PLEASED TO HAVE THIS OPPORTUNITY TO SPEAK IN PERSON.
I WISH TO ASSURE YOU THAT I VALUE YOUR LOYALTY.
STOLEN LOYALTY, KRAKE. I BELIEVED I ACTED IN SERVICE TO MY OYABUN.
I DID NOT KNOW YOU HAD HIM MURDERED BY YOUR CREATURE, ZARTAN. THAT IS A DISREPECT THAT CAN NEVER BE ERASED, KRAKE.
NEVER!

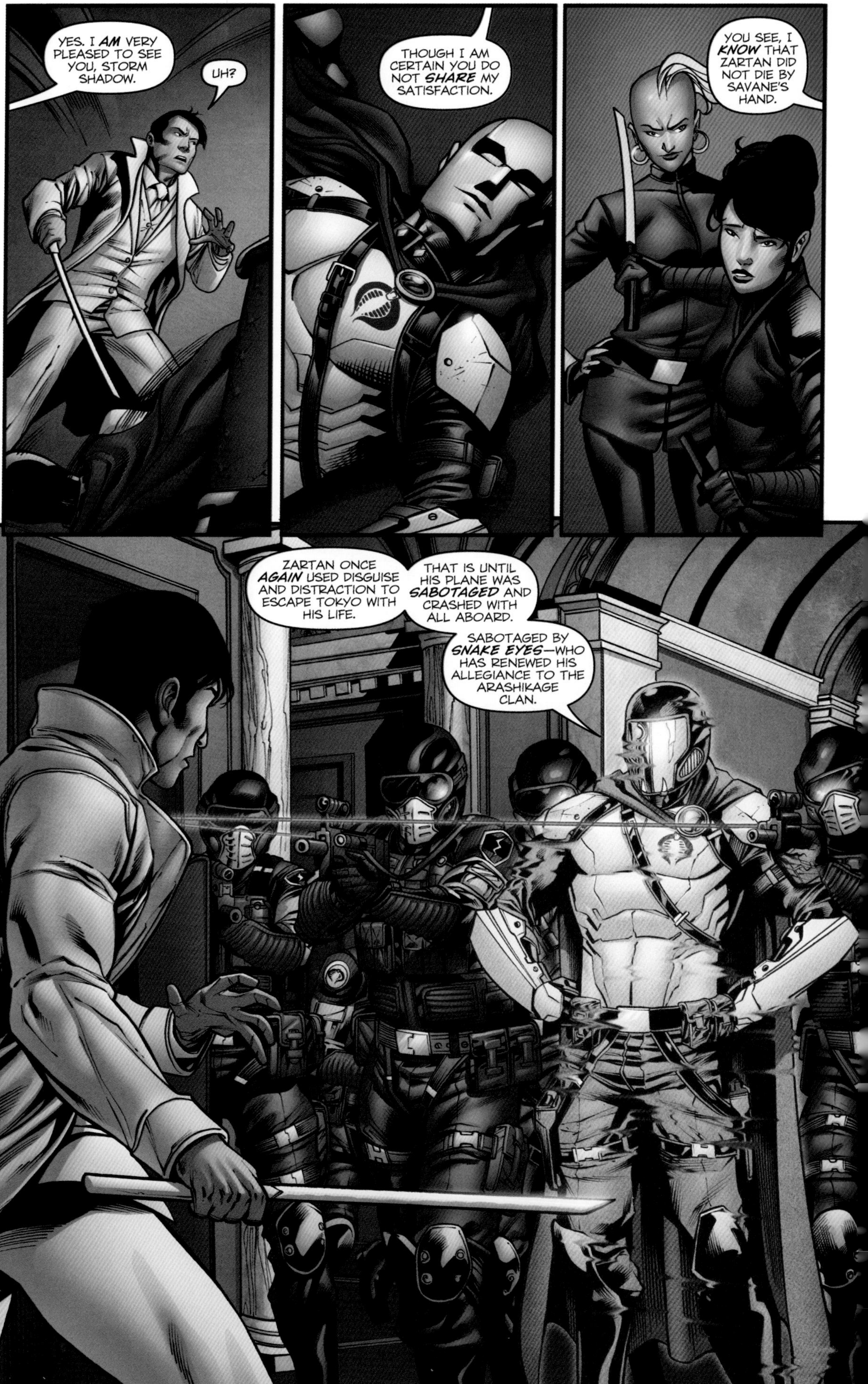
YES. I AM VERY PLEASED TO SEE YOU, STORM SHADOW.
UH?
THOUGH I AM CERTAIN YOU DO NOT SHARE MY SATISFACTION.
YOU SEE, I KNOW THAT ZARTAN DID NOT DIE BY SAVANE'S HAND.
ZARTAN ONCE AGAIN USED DISGUISE AND DISTRACTION TO ESCAPE TOKYO WITH HIS LIFE.
THAT IS UNTIL HIS PLANE WAS SABOTAGED AND CRASHED WITH ALL ABOARD.
SABOTAGED BY SNAKE EYES—WHO HAS RENEWED HIS ALLEGIANCE TO THE ARASHIKAGE CLAN.

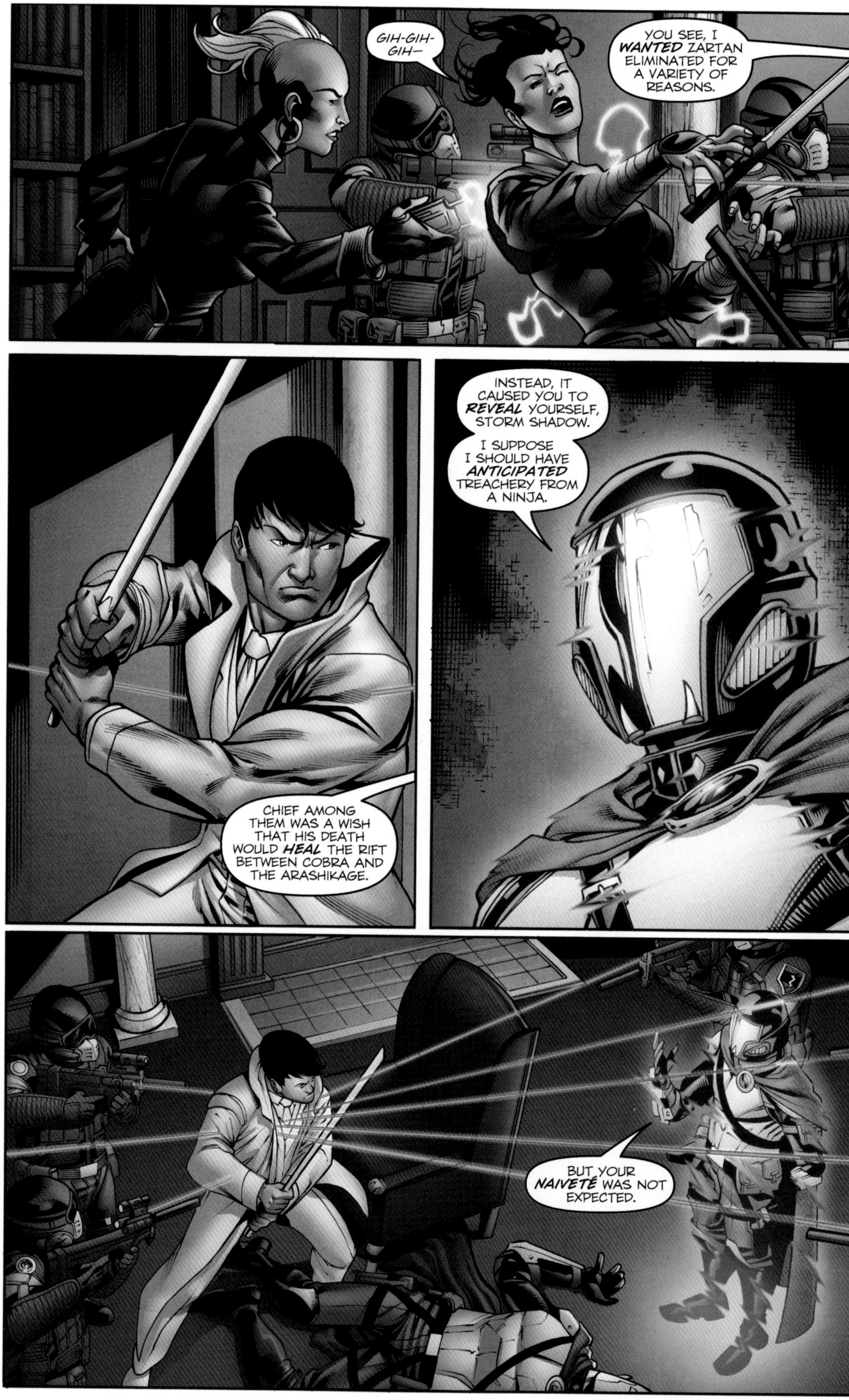
GIH-GIH-GIH—
YOU SEE, I WANTED ZARTAN ELIMINATED FOR A VARIETY OF REASONS.
CHIEF AMONG THEM WAS A WISH THAT HIS DEATH WOULD HEAL THE RIFT BETWEEN COBRA AND THE ARASHIKAGE.
INSTEAD, IT CAUSED YOU TO REVEAL YOURSELF, STORM SHADOW.
I SUPPOSE I SHOULD HAVE ANTICIPATED TREACHERY FROM A NINJA.
BUT YOUR NAIVETÉ WAS NOT EXPECTED.

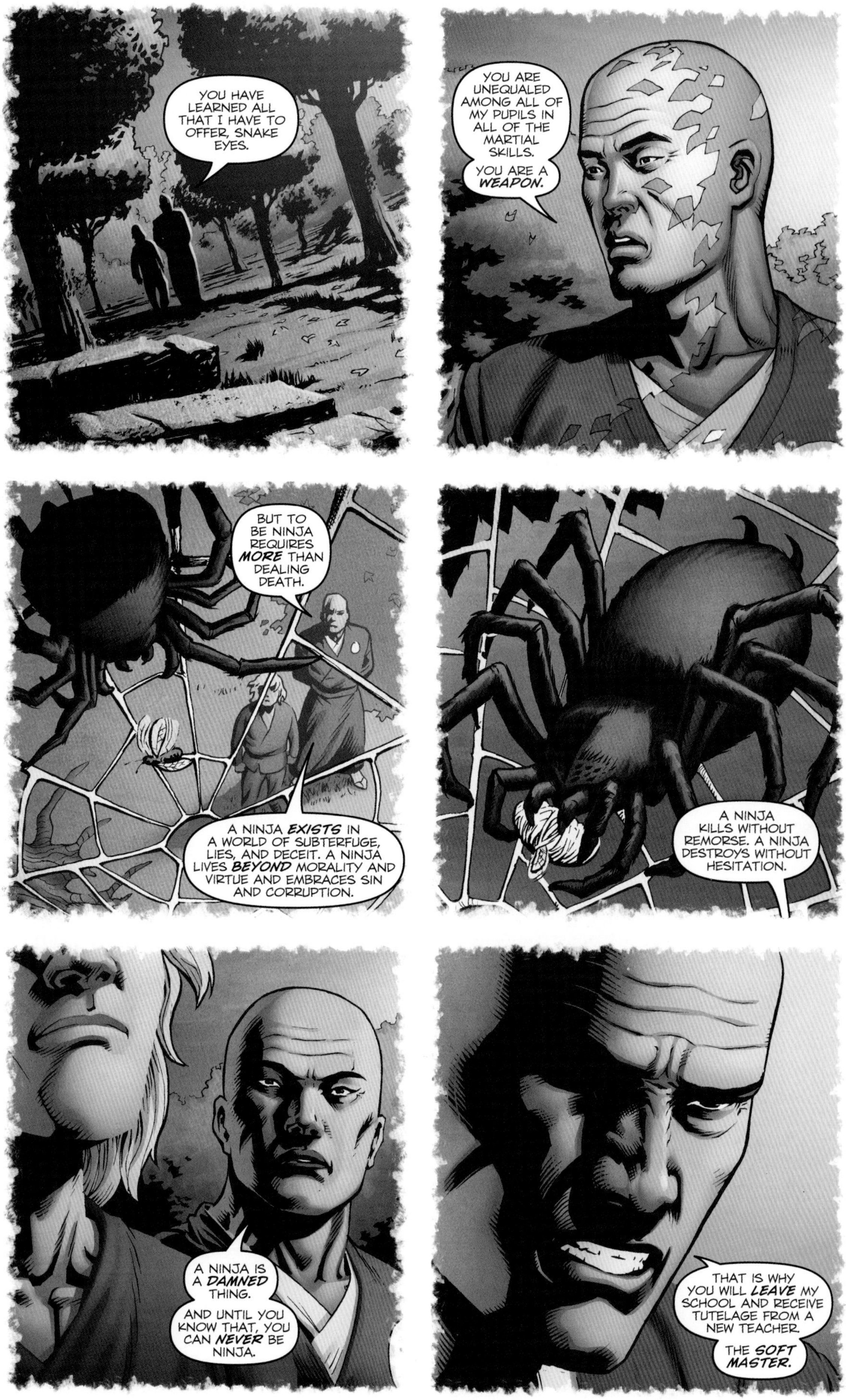
YOU HAVE LEARNED ALL THAT I HAVE TO OFFER, SNAKE EYES.
YOU ARE UNEQUALED AMONG ALL OF MY PUPILS IN ALL OF THE MARTIAL SKILLS.
YOU ARE A WEAPON.
BUT TO BE NINJA REQUIRES MORE THAN DEALING DEATH.
A NINJA EXISTS IN A WORLD OF SUBTERFUGE, LIES, AND DECEIT. A NINJA LIVES BEYOND MORALITY AND VIRTUE AND EMBRACES SIN AND CORRUPTION.
A NINJA KILLS WITHOUT REMORSE. A NINJA DESTROYS WITHOUT HESITATION.
A NINJA IS A DAMNED THING.
AND UNTIL YOU KNOW THAT, YOU CAN NEVER BE NINJA.
THAT IS WHY YOU WILL LEAVE MY SCHOOL AND RECEIVE TUTELAGE FROM A NEW TEACHER.
THE SOFT MASTER.

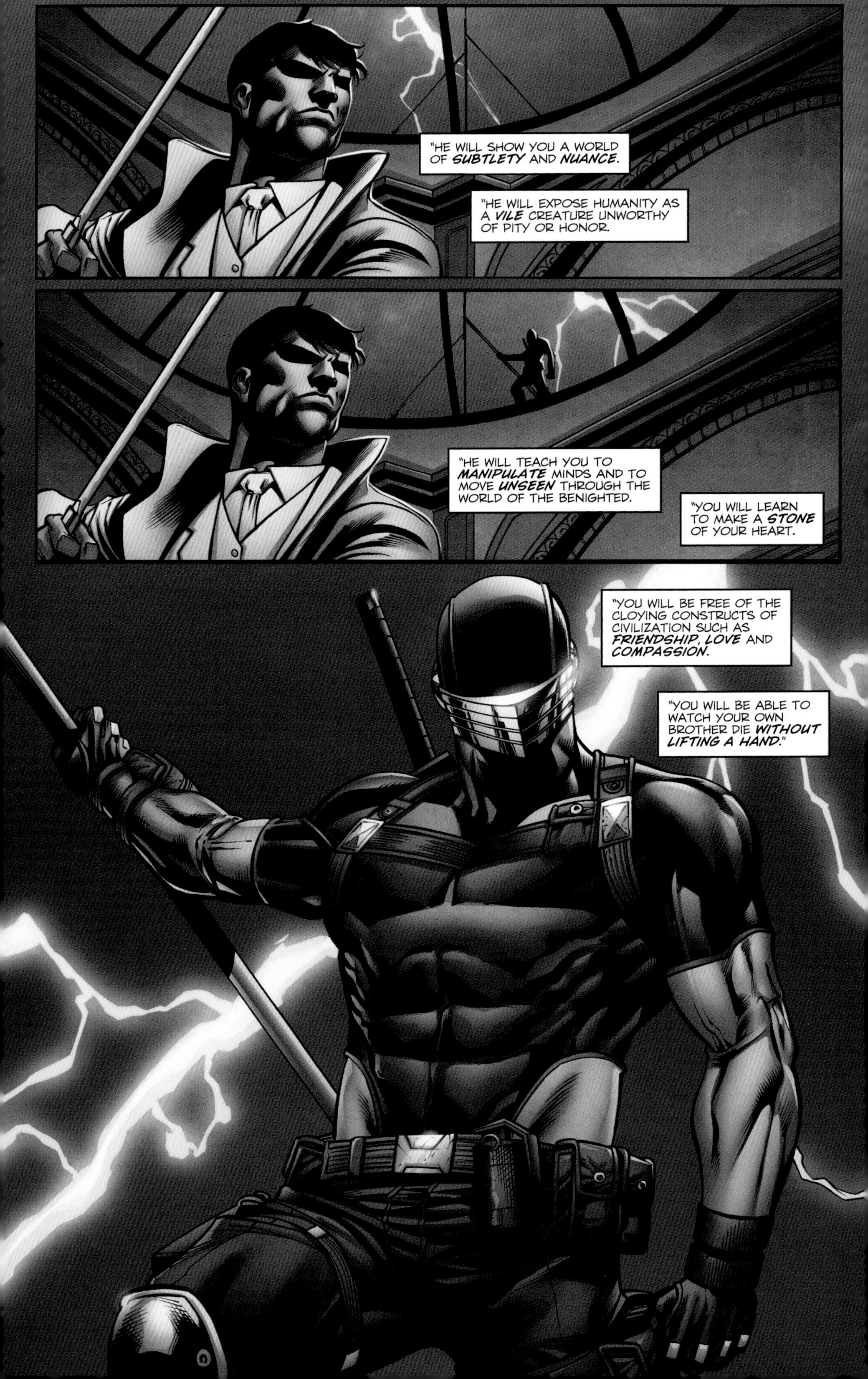
"HE WILL SHOW YOU A WORLD OF SUBTLETY AND NUANCE.
"HE WILL EXPOSE HUMANITY AS A VILE CREATURE UNWORTHY OF PITY OR HONOR.
"HE WILL TEACH YOU TO MANIPULATE MINDS AND TO MOVE UNSEEN THROUGH THE WORLD OF THE BENIGHTED.
"YOU WILL LEARN TO MAKE A STONE OF YOUR HEART.
"YOU WILL BE FREE OF THE CLOYING CONSTRUCTS OF CIVILIZATION SUCH AS FRIENDSHIP, LOVE AND COMPASSION.
"YOU WILL BE ABLE TO WATCH YOUR OWN BROTHER DIE WITHOUT LIFTING A HAND."

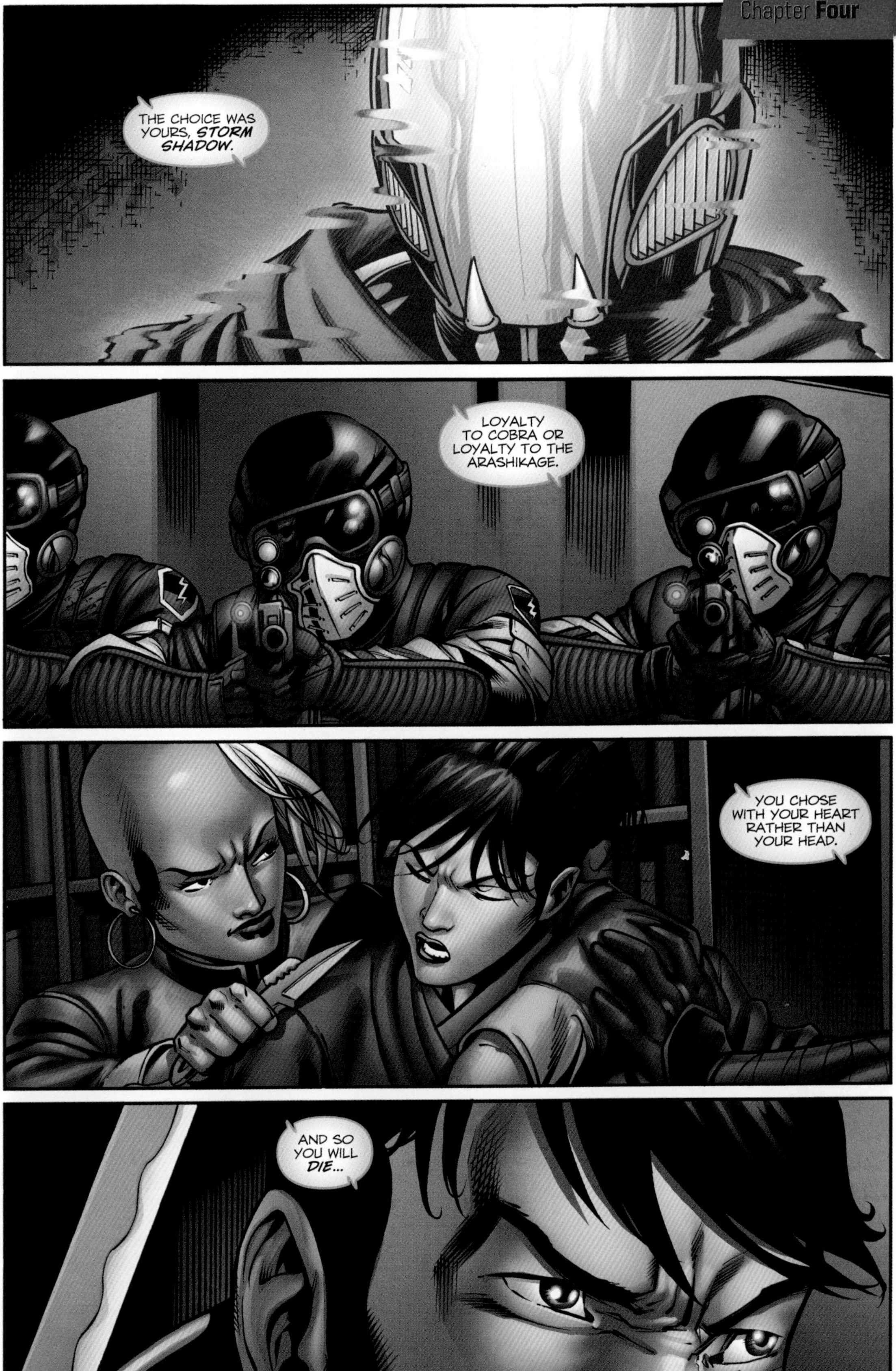
THE CHOICE WAS YOURS, *STORM SHADOW*.
LOYALTY TO COBRA OR LOYALTY TO THE ARASHIKAGE.
YOU CHOSE WITH YOUR HEART RATHER THAN YOUR HEAD.
AND SO YOU WILL *DIE*...

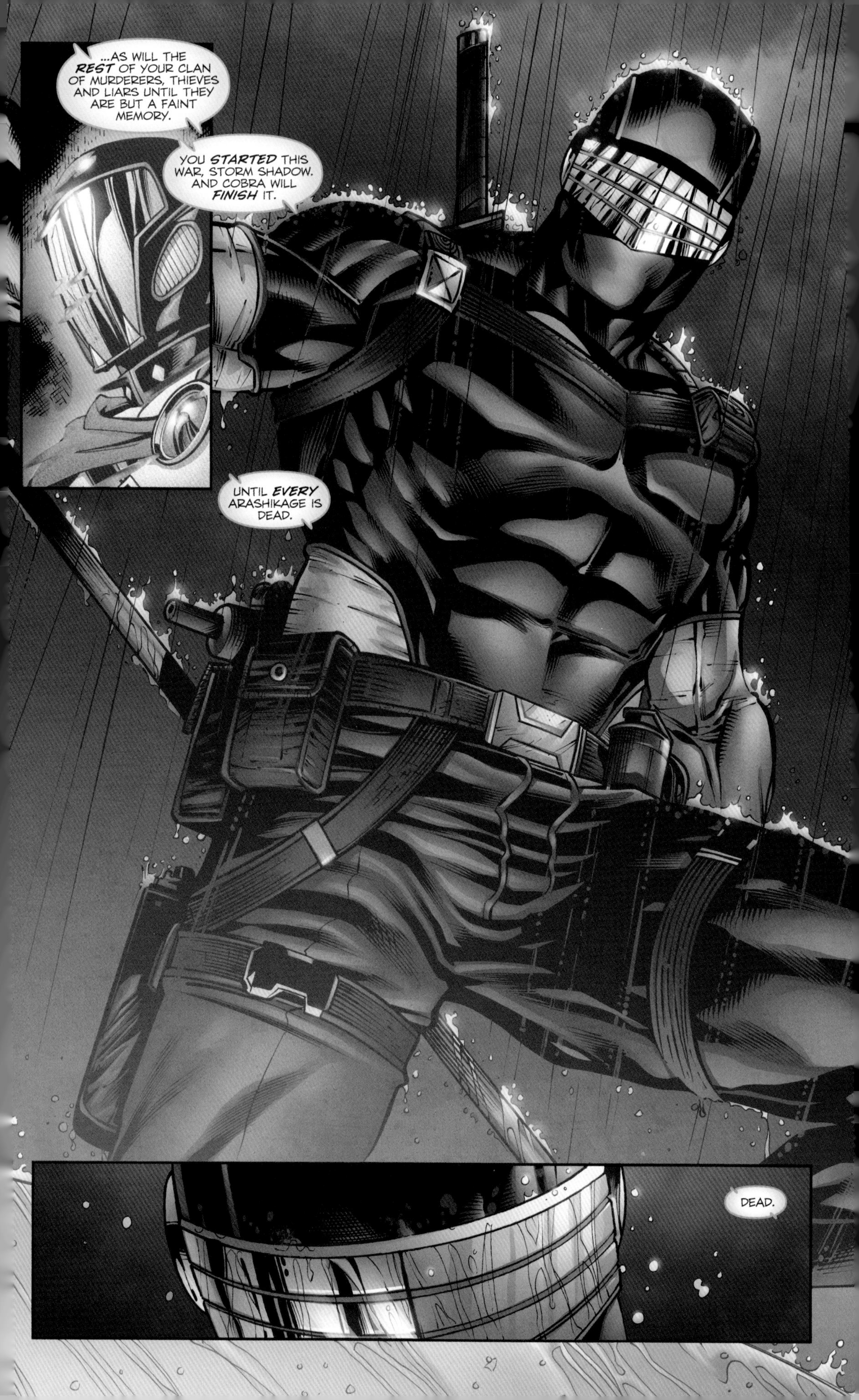
...AS WILL THE REST OF YOUR CLAN OF MURDERERS, THIEVES AND LIARS UNTIL THEY ARE BUT A FAINT MEMORY.
YOU STARTED THIS WAR, STORM SHADOW. AND COBRA WILL FINISH IT.
UNTIL EVERY ARASHIKAGE IS DEAD.
DEAD.

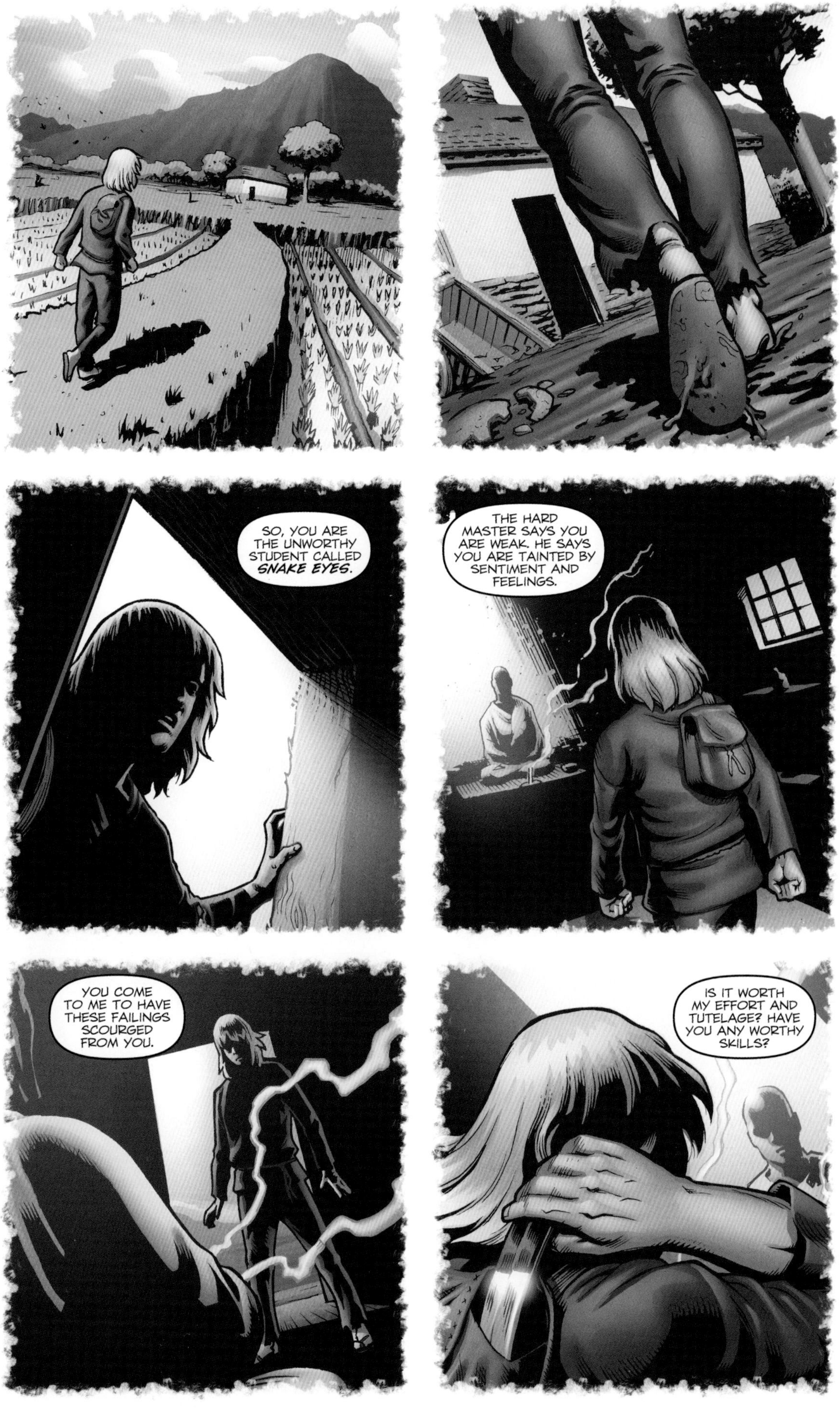
SO, YOU ARE THE UNWORTHY STUDENT CALLED SNAKE EYES.
THE HARD MASTER SAYS YOU ARE WEAK. HE SAYS YOU ARE TAINTED BY SENTIMENT AND FEELINGS.
YOU COME TO ME TO HAVE THESE FAILINGS SCOURGED FROM YOU.
IS IT WORTH MY EFFORT AND TUTELAGE? HAVE YOU ANY WORTHY SKILLS?

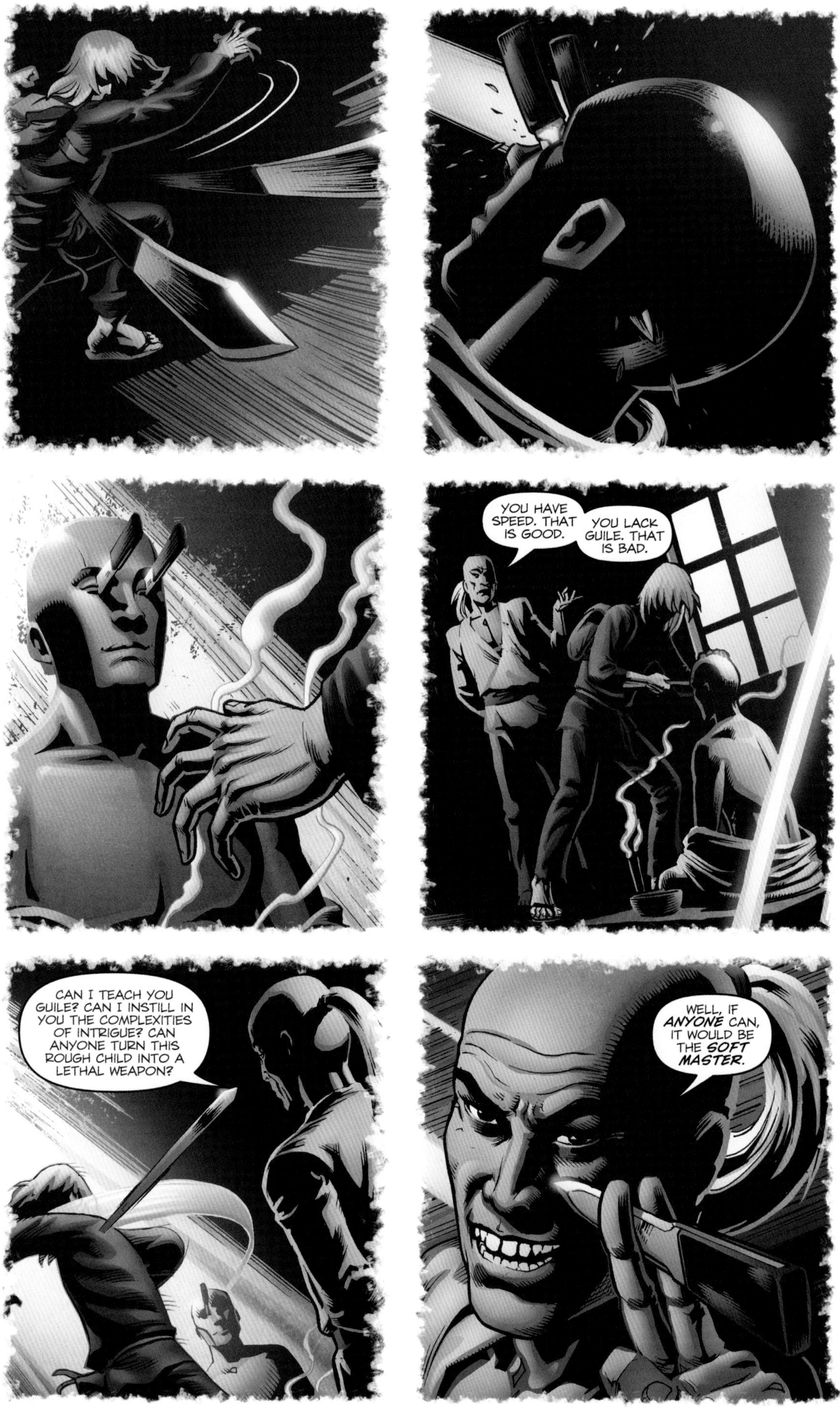
YOU HAVE SPEED. THAT IS GOOD.
YOU LACK GUILE. THAT IS BAD.
CAN I TEACH YOU GUILE? CAN I INSTILL IN YOU THE COMPLEXITIES OF INTRIGUE? CAN ANYONE TURN THIS ROUGH CHILD INTO A LETHAL WEAPON?
WELL, IF ANYONE CAN, IT WOULD BE THE SOFT MASTER.

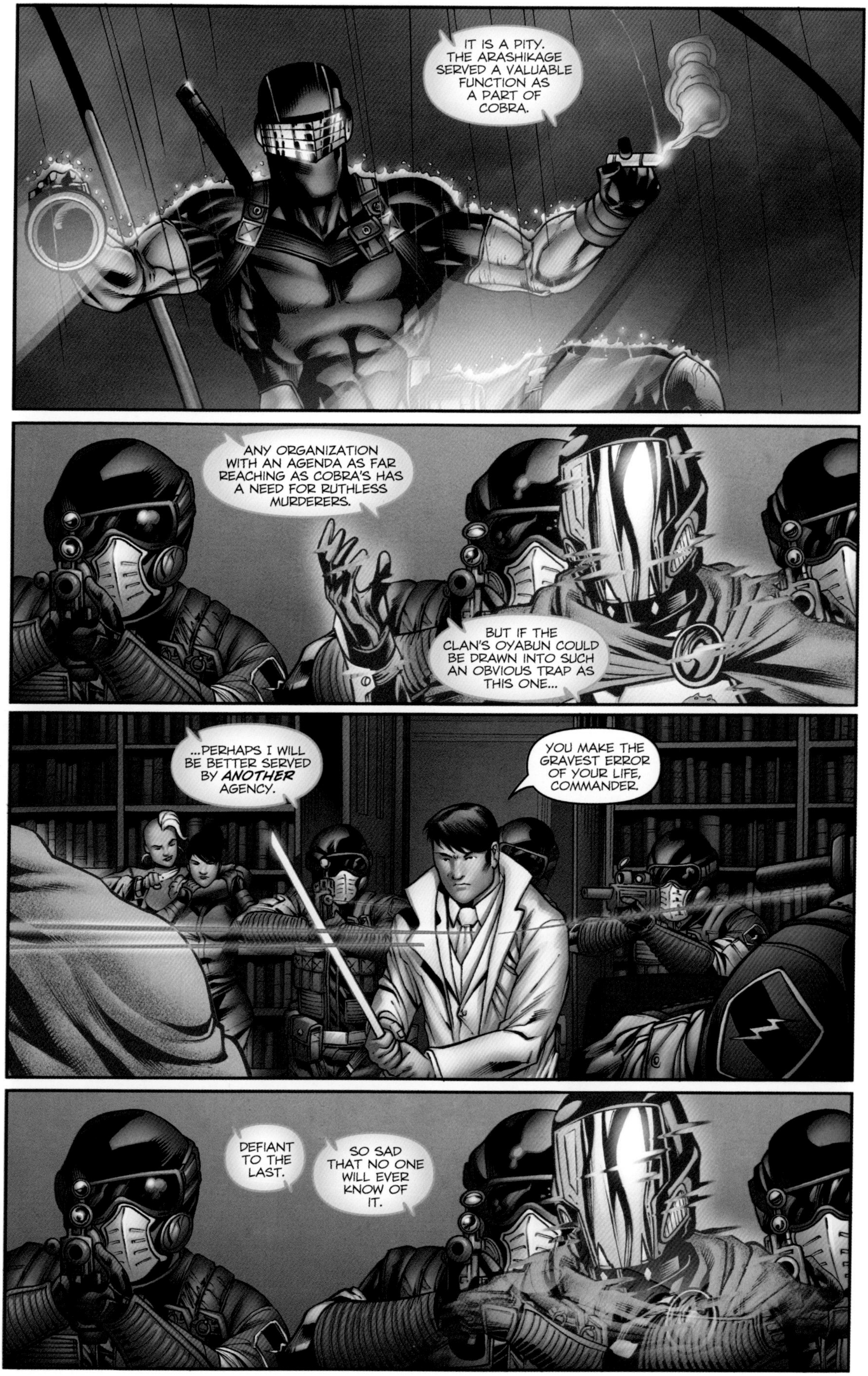
IT IS A PITY. THE ARASHIKAGE SERVED A VALUABLE FUNCTION AS A PART OF COBRA.
ANY ORGANIZATION WITH AN AGENDA AS FAR REACHING AS COBRA'S HAS A NEED FOR RUTHLESS MURDERERS.
BUT IF THE CLAN'S OYABUN COULD BE DRAWN INTO SUCH AN OBVIOUS TRAP AS THIS ONE...
...PERHAPS I WILL BE BETTER SERVED BY *ANOTHER* AGENCY.
YOU MAKE THE GRAVEST ERROR OF YOUR LIFE, COMMANDER.
DEFIANT TO THE LAST.
SO SAD THAT NO ONE WILL EVER KNOW OF IT.

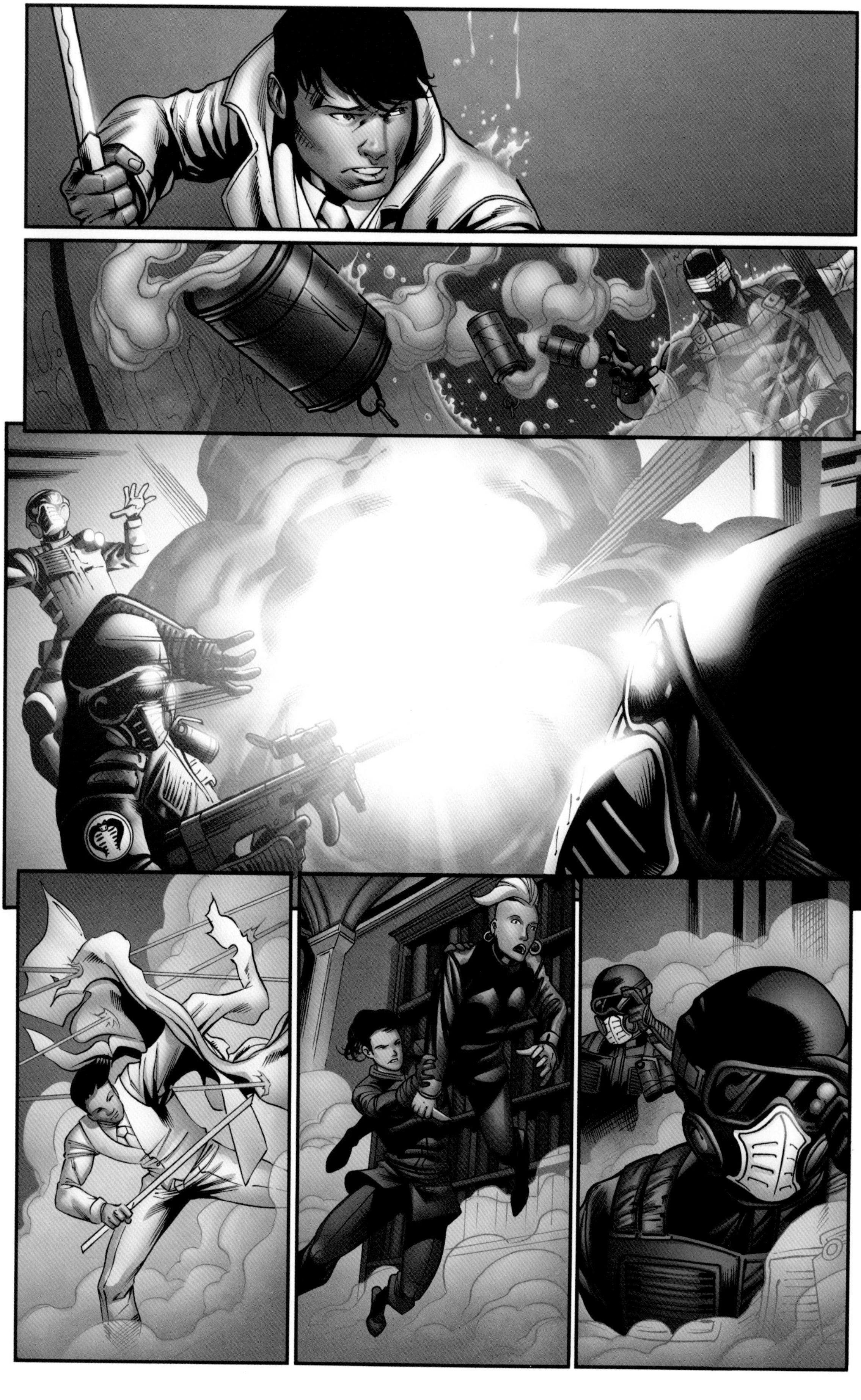

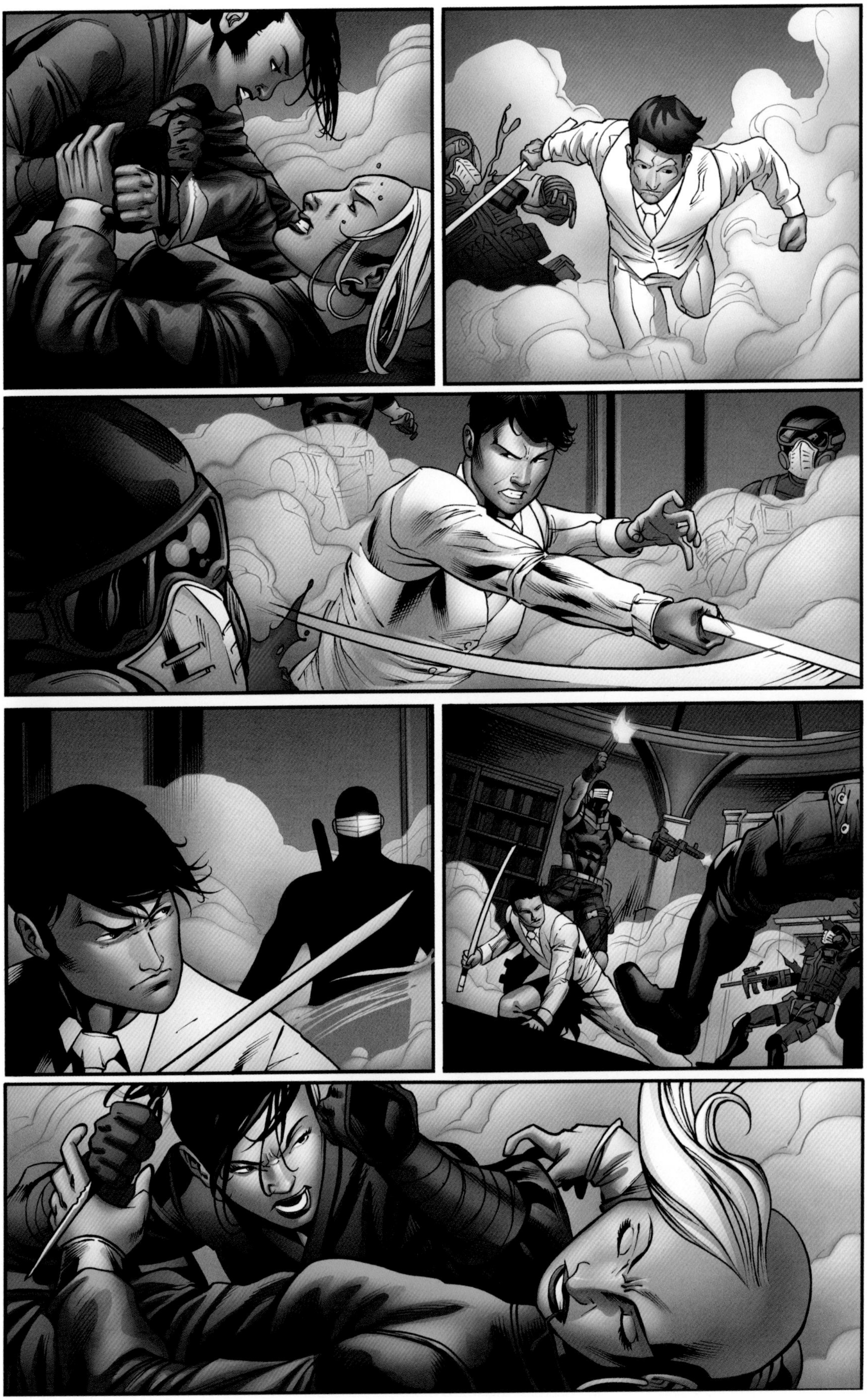

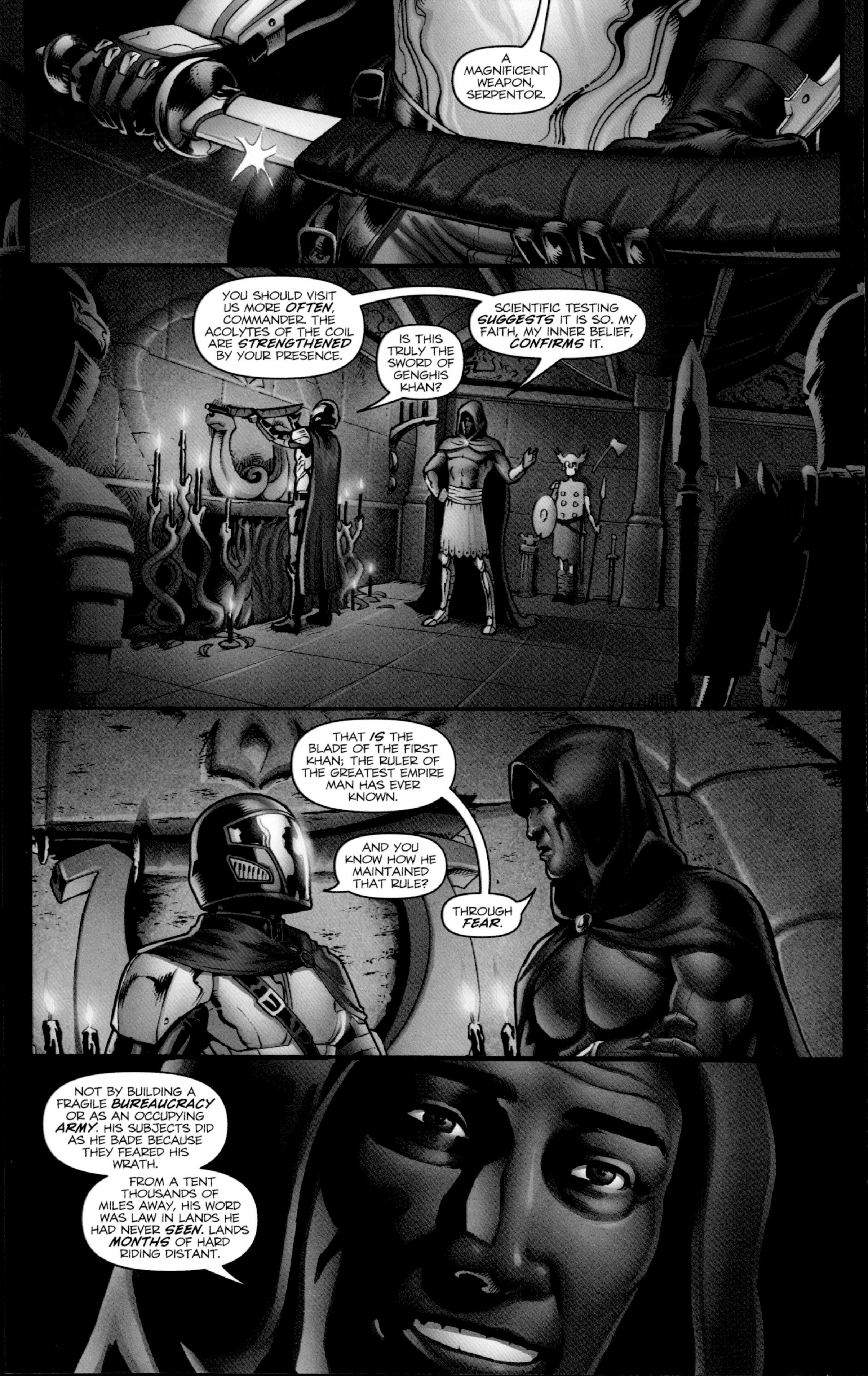
A MAGNIFICENT WEAPON, SERPENTOR.
YOU SHOULD VISIT US MORE OFTEN, COMMANDER. THE ACOLYTES OF THE COIL ARE STRENGTHENED BY YOUR PRESENCE.
IS THIS TRULY THE SWORD OF GENGHIS KHAN?
SCIENTIFIC TESTING SUGGESTS IT IS SO. MY FAITH, MY INNER BELIEF, CONFIRMS IT.
THAT IS THE BLADE OF THE FIRST KHAN; THE RULER OF THE GREATEST EMPIRE MAN HAS EVER KNOWN.
AND YOU KNOW HOW HE MAINTAINED THAT RULE?
THROUGH FEAR.
NOT BY BUILDING A FRAGILE BUREAUCRACY OR AS AN OCCUPYING ARMY. HIS SUBJECTS DID AS HE BADE BECAUSE THEY FEARED HIS WRATH.
FROM A TENT THOUSANDS OF MILES AWAY, HIS WORD WAS LAW IN LANDS HE HAD NEVER SEEN. LANDS MONTHS OF HARD RIDING DISTANT.

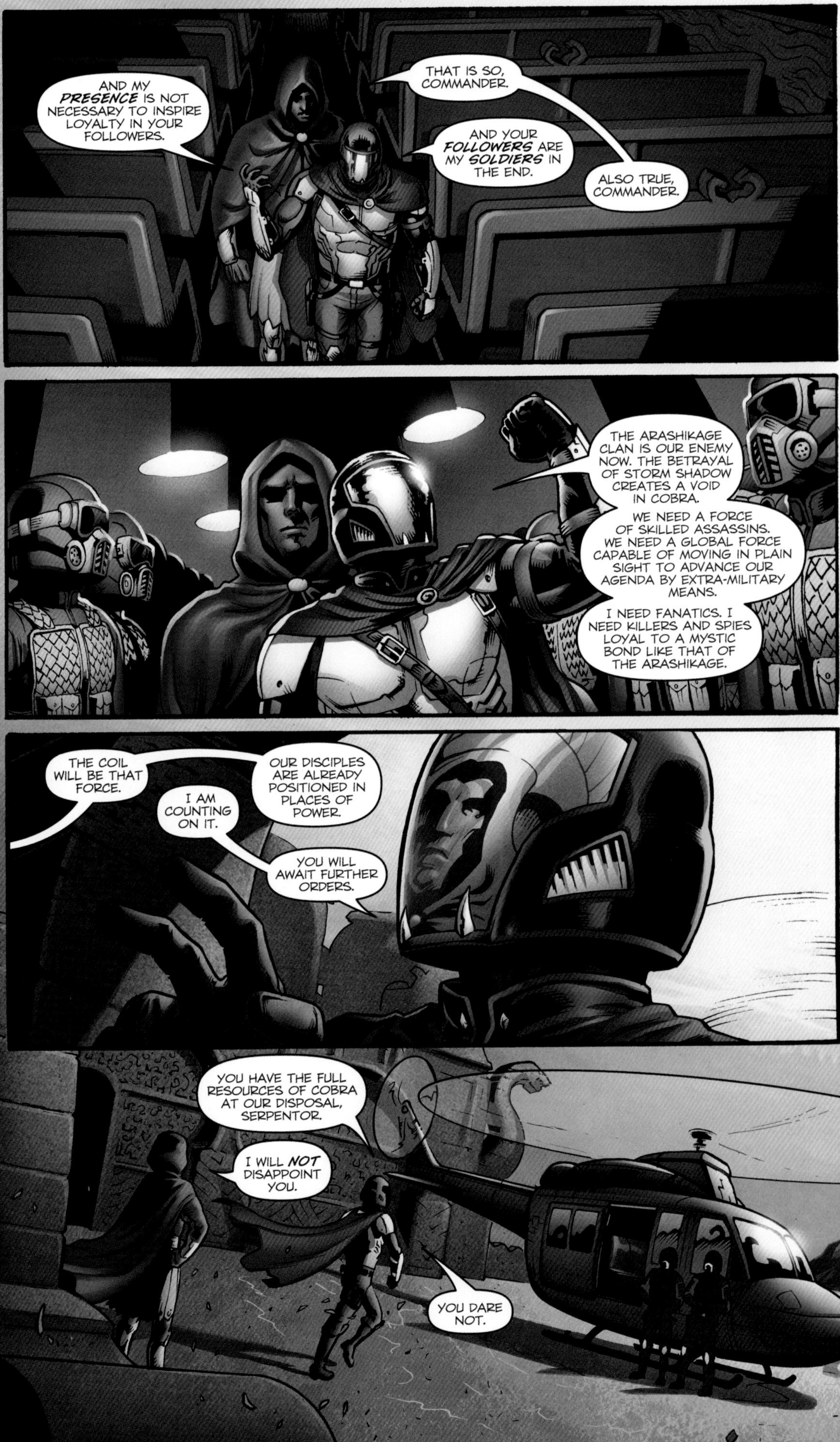
AND MY PRESENCE IS NOT NECESSARY TO INSPIRE LOYALTY IN YOUR FOLLOWERS.
THAT IS SO, COMMANDER.
AND YOUR FOLLOWERS ARE MY SOLDIERS IN THE END.
ALSO TRUE, COMMANDER.
THE ARASHIKAGE CLAN IS OUR ENEMY NOW. THE BETRAYAL OF STORM SHADOW CREATES A VOID IN COBRA.
WE NEED A FORCE OF SKILLED ASSASSINS. WE NEED A GLOBAL FORCE CAPABLE OF MOVING IN PLAIN SIGHT TO ADVANCE OUR AGENDA BY EXTRA-MILITARY MEANS.
I NEED FANATICS. I NEED KILLERS AND SPIES LOYAL TO A MYSTIC BOND LIKE THAT OF THE ARASHIKAGE.
THE COIL WILL BE THAT FORCE.
OUR DISCIPLES ARE ALREADY POSITIONED IN PLACES OF POWER.
I AM COUNTING ON IT.
YOU WILL AWAIT FURTHER ORDERS.
YOU HAVE THE FULL RESOURCES OF COBRA AT OUR DISPOSAL, SERPENTOR.
I WILL NOT DISAPPOINT YOU.
YOU DARE NOT.

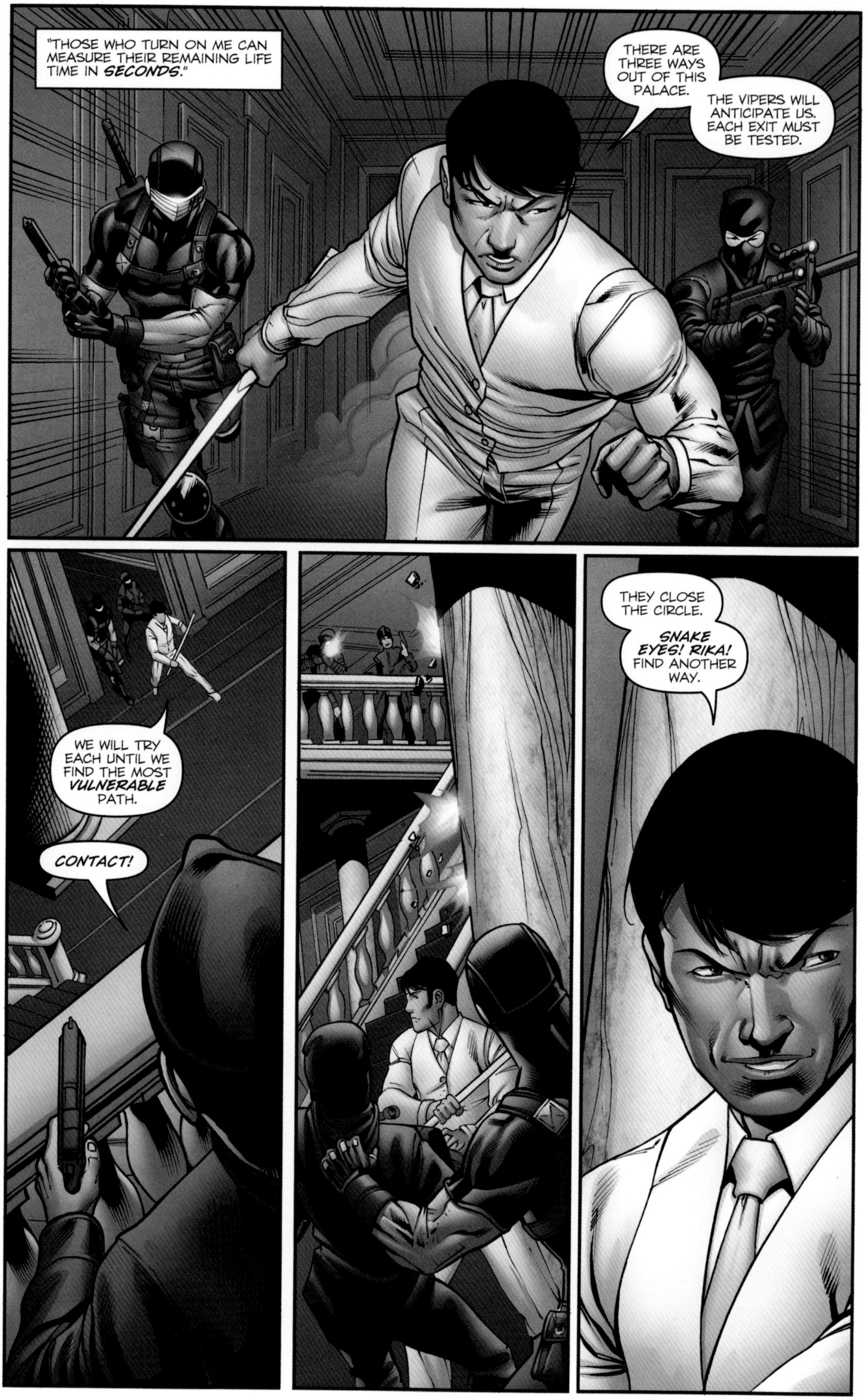
"THOSE WHO TURN ON ME CAN MEASURE THEIR REMAINING LIFE TIME IN SECONDS."
THERE ARE THREE WAYS OUT OF THIS PALACE.
THE VIPERS WILL ANTICIPATE US. EACH EXIT MUST BE TESTED.
WE WILL TRY EACH UNTIL WE FIND THE MOST VULNERABLE PATH.
CONTACT!
THEY CLOSE THE CIRCLE.
SNAKE EYES! RIKA! FIND ANOTHER WAY.

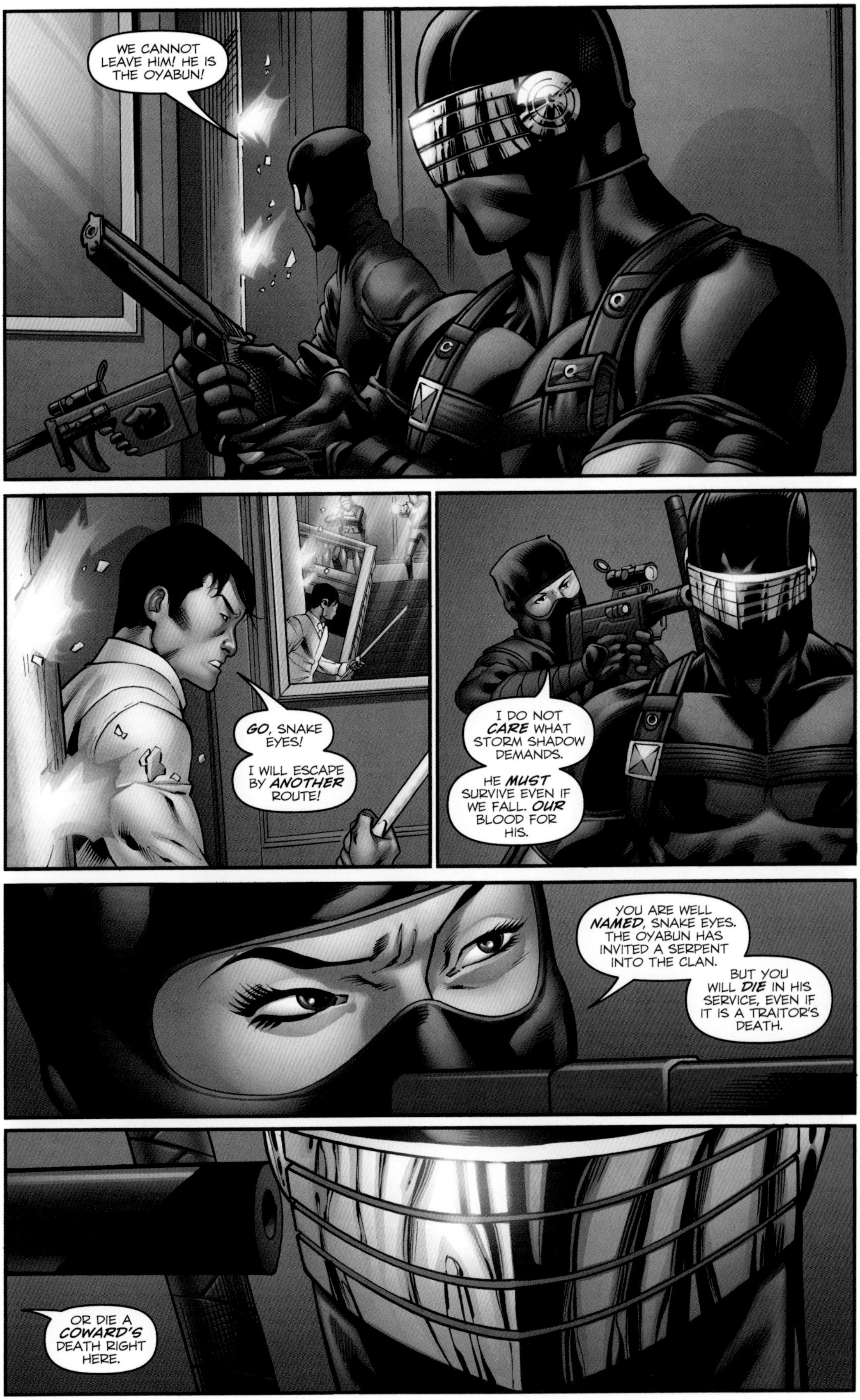
WE CANNOT LEAVE HIM! HE IS THE OYABUN!
GO, SNAKE EYES!
I WILL ESCAPE BY ANOTHER ROUTE!
I DO NOT CARE WHAT STORM SHADOW DEMANDS.
HE MUST SURVIVE EVEN IF WE FALL. OUR BLOOD FOR HIS.
YOU ARE WELL NAMED, SNAKE EYES. THE OYABUN HAS INVITED A SERPENT INTO THE CLAN.
BUT YOU WILL DIE IN HIS SERVICE, EVEN IF IT IS A TRAITOR'S DEATH.
OR DIE A COWARD'S DEATH RIGHT HERE.

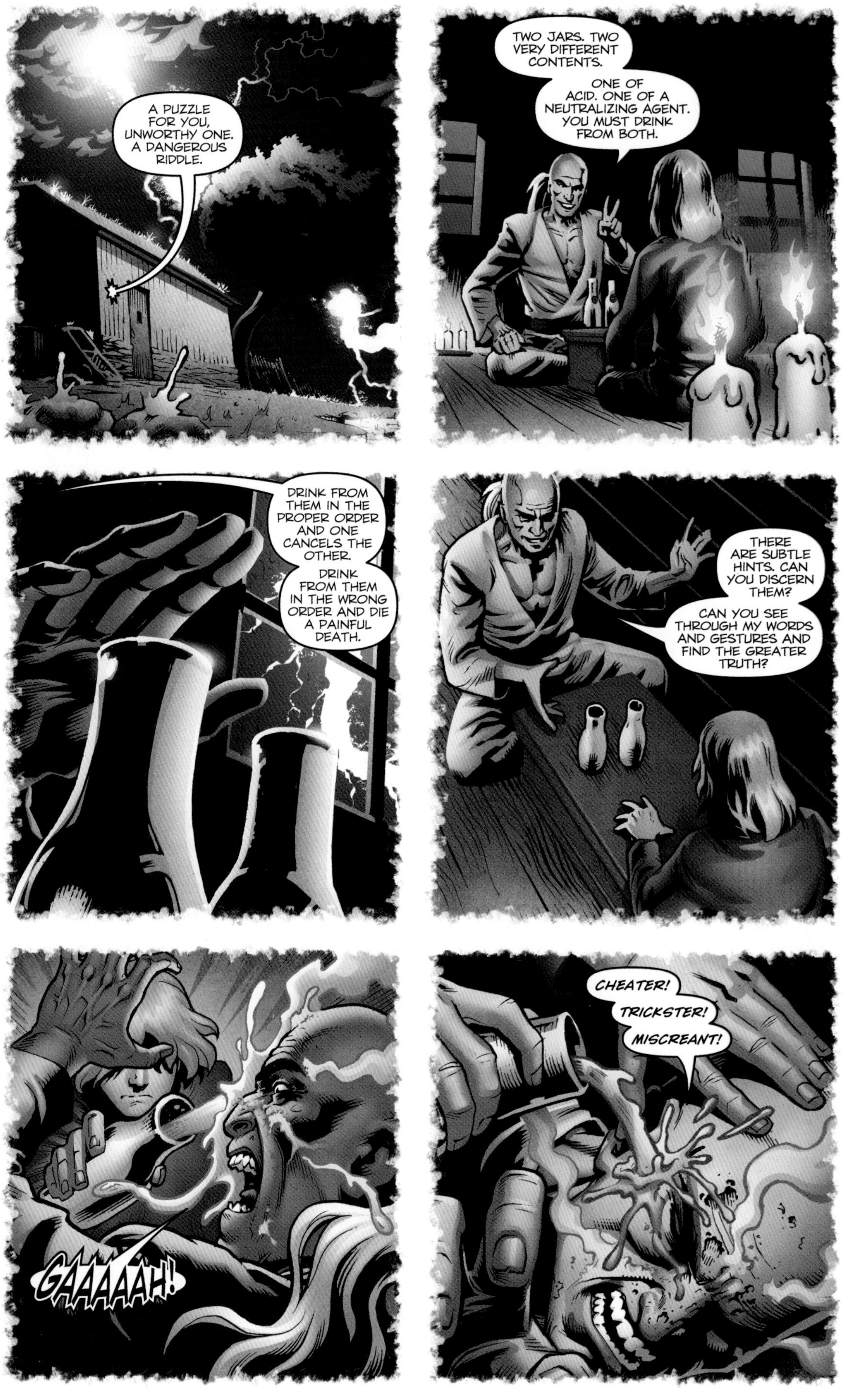
A PUZZLE FOR YOU, UNWORTHY ONE. A DANGEROUS RIDDLE.
TWO JARS. TWO VERY DIFFERENT CONTENTS.
ONE OF ACID. ONE OF A NEUTRALIZING AGENT. YOU MUST DRINK FROM BOTH.
DRINK FROM THEM IN THE PROPER ORDER AND ONE CANCELS THE OTHER.
DRINK FROM THEM IN THE WRONG ORDER AND DIE A PAINFUL DEATH.
THERE ARE SUBTLE HINTS. CAN YOU DISCERN THEM?
CAN YOU SEE THROUGH MY WORDS AND GESTURES AND FIND THE GREATER TRUTH?
GAAAAAH!
CHEATER!
TRICKSTER!
MISCREANT!

DECEIVER!

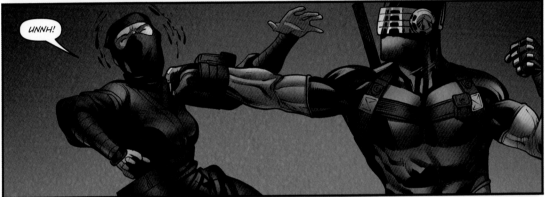

UNNH!

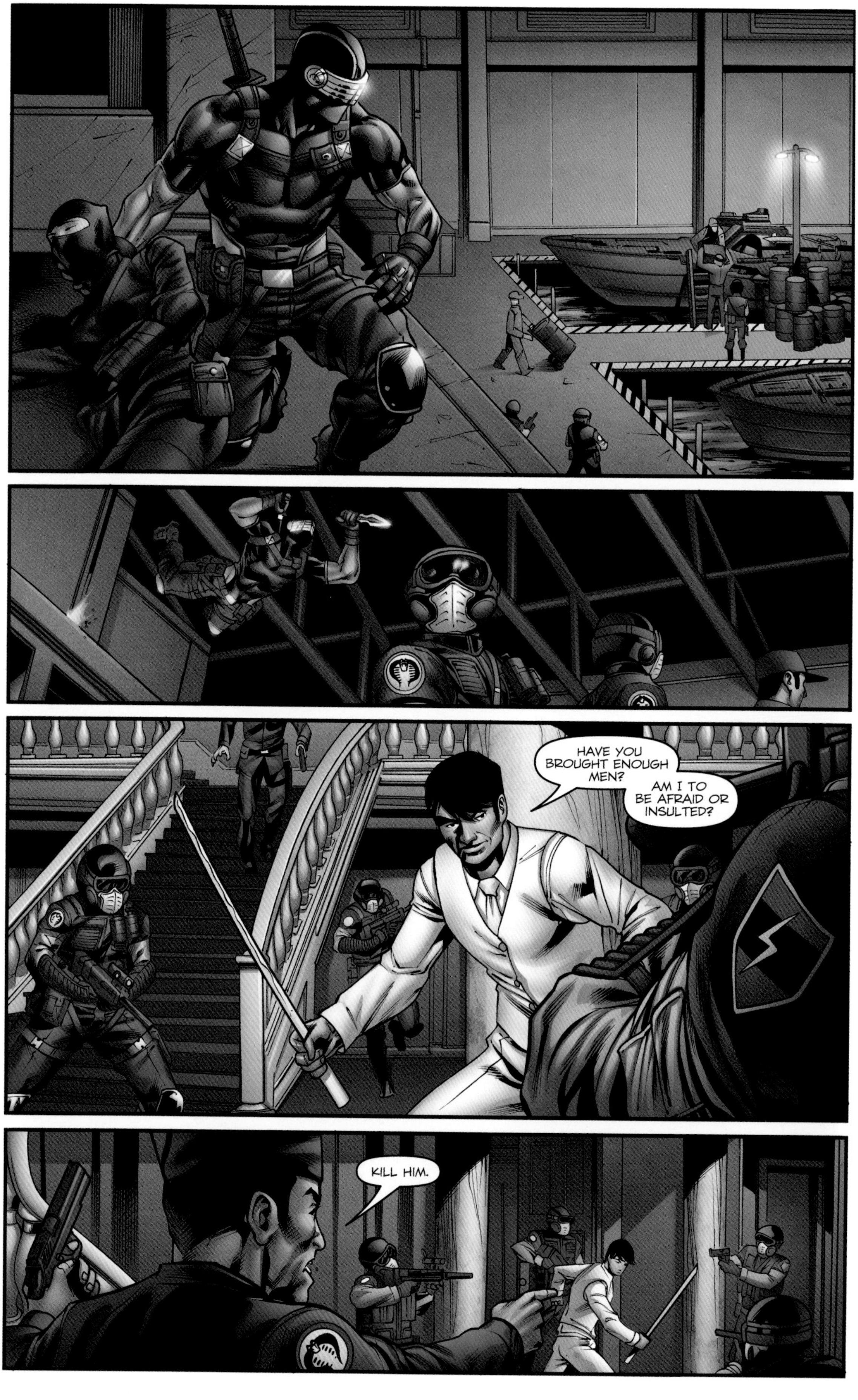
HAVE YOU BROUGHT ENOUGH MEN?
AM I TO BE AFRAID OR INSULTED?
KILL HIM.

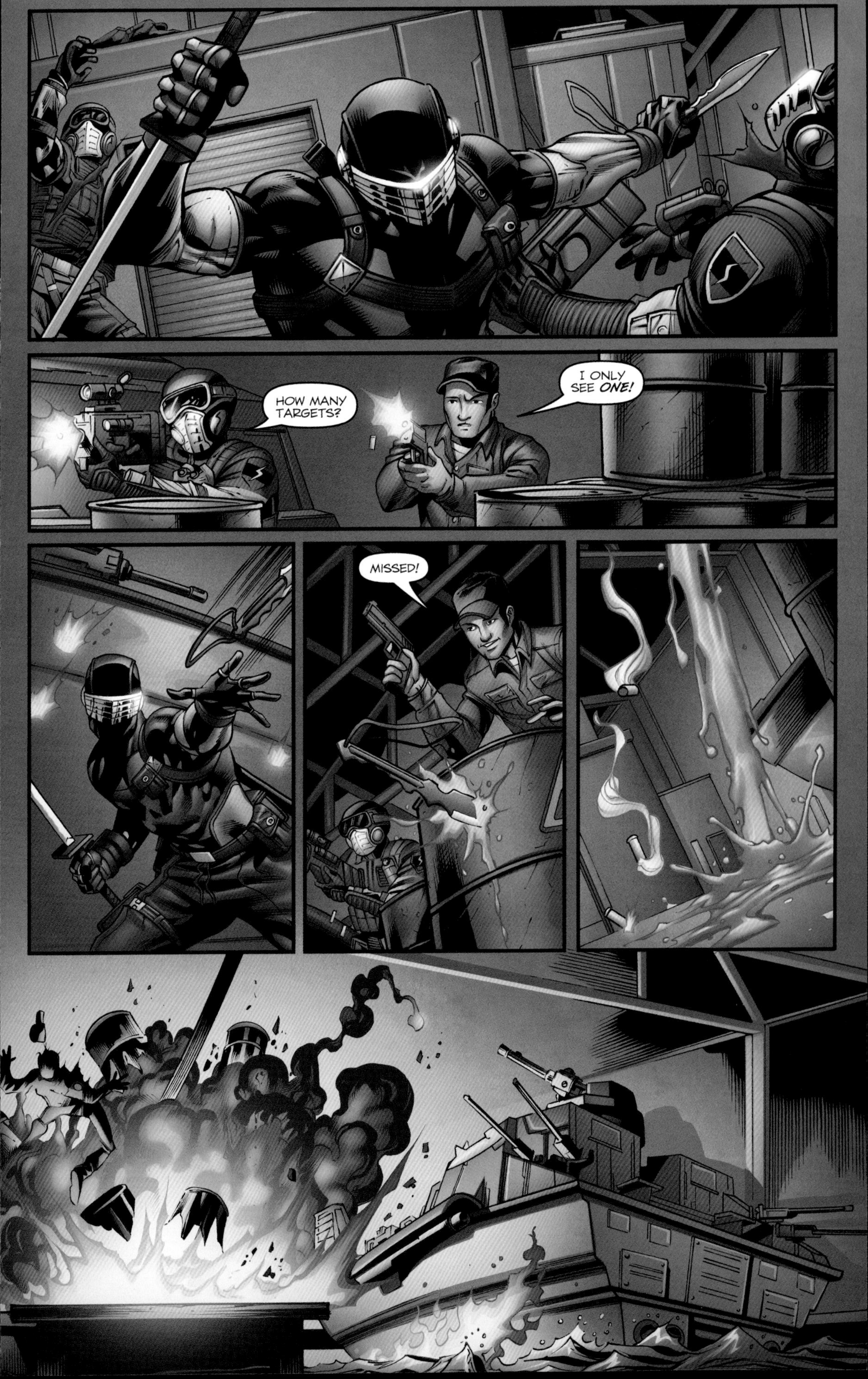
HOW MANY TARGETS?
I ONLY SEE ONE!
MISSED!

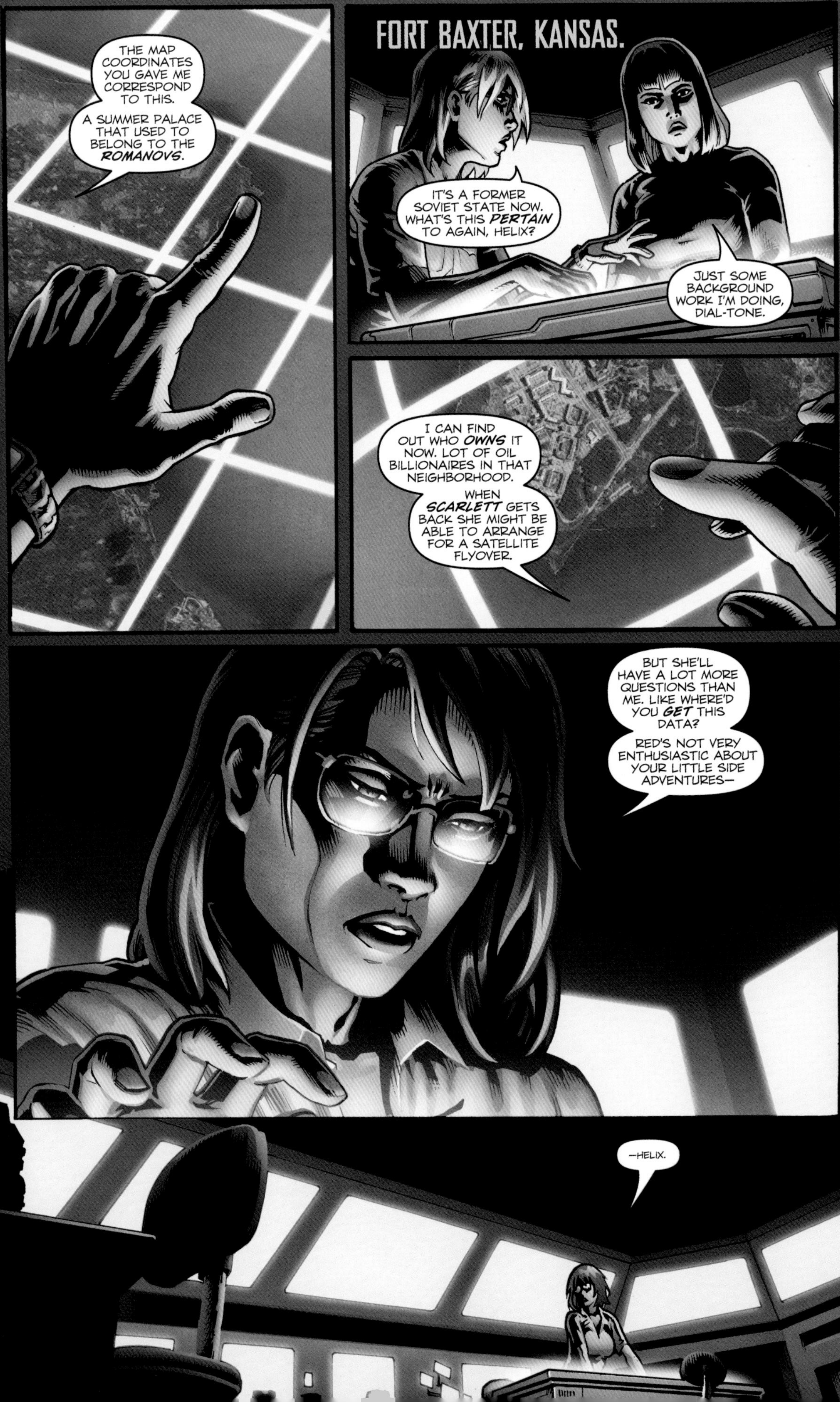

THE MAP COORDINATES YOU GAVE ME CORRESPOND TO THIS.
A SUMMER PALACE THAT USED TO BELONG TO THE ROMANOVS.
FORT BAXTER, KANSAS.
IT'S A FORMER SOVIET STATE NOW. WHAT'S THIS PERTAIN TO AGAIN, HELIX?
JUST SOME BACKGROUND WORK I'M DOING, DIAL-TONE.
I CAN FIND OUT WHO OWNS IT NOW. LOT OF OIL BILLIONAIRES IN THAT NEIGHBORHOOD.
WHEN SCARLETT GETS BACK SHE MIGHT BE ABLE TO ARRANGE FOR A SATELLITE FLYOVER.
BUT SHE'LL HAVE A LOT MORE QUESTIONS THAN ME. LIKE WHERE'D YOU GET THIS DATA?
RED'S NOT VERY ENTHUSIASTIC ABOUT YOUR LITTLE SIDE ADVENTURES—
—HELIX.

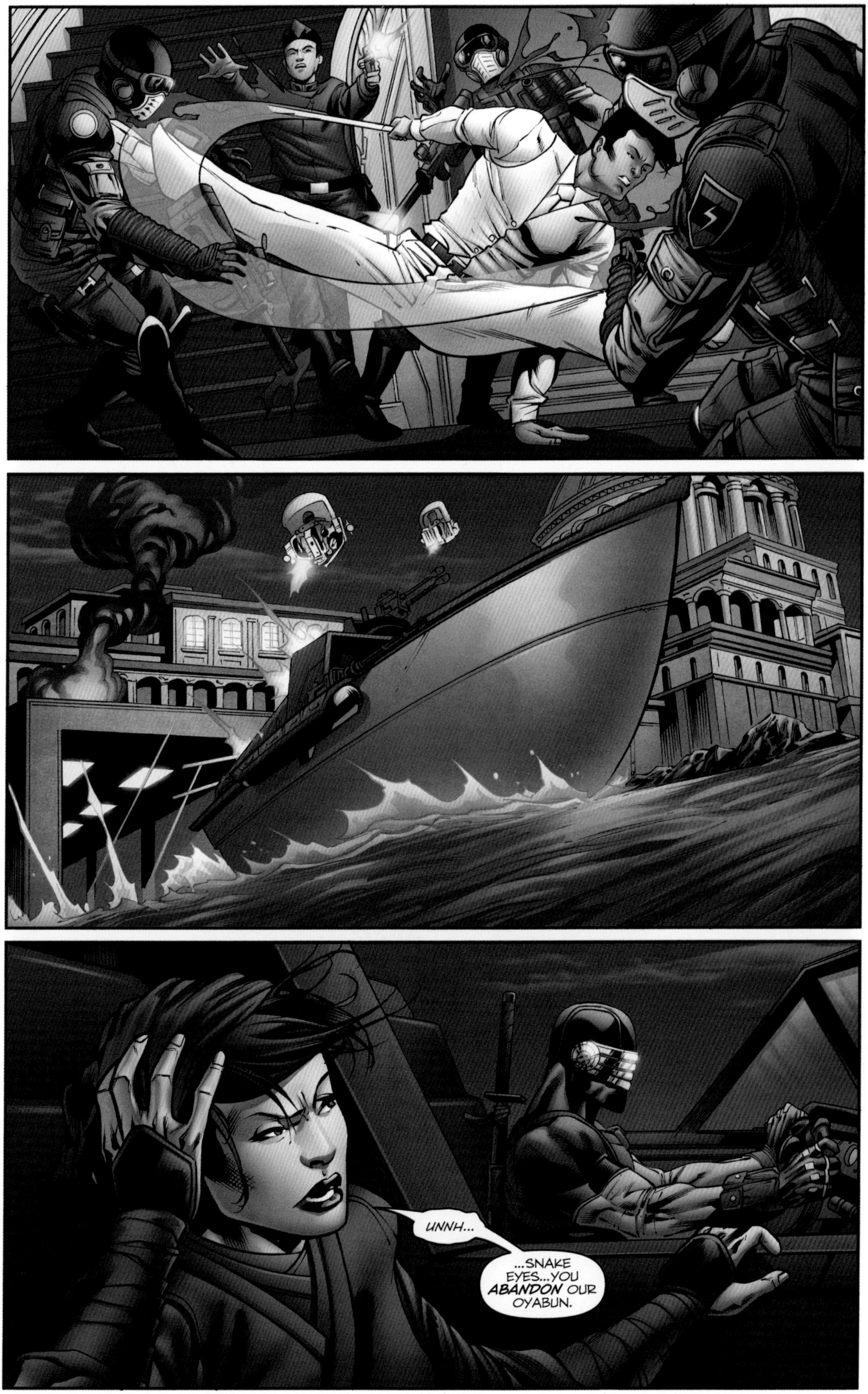
UNNH...
...SNAKE EYES...YOU ABANDON OUR OYABUN.

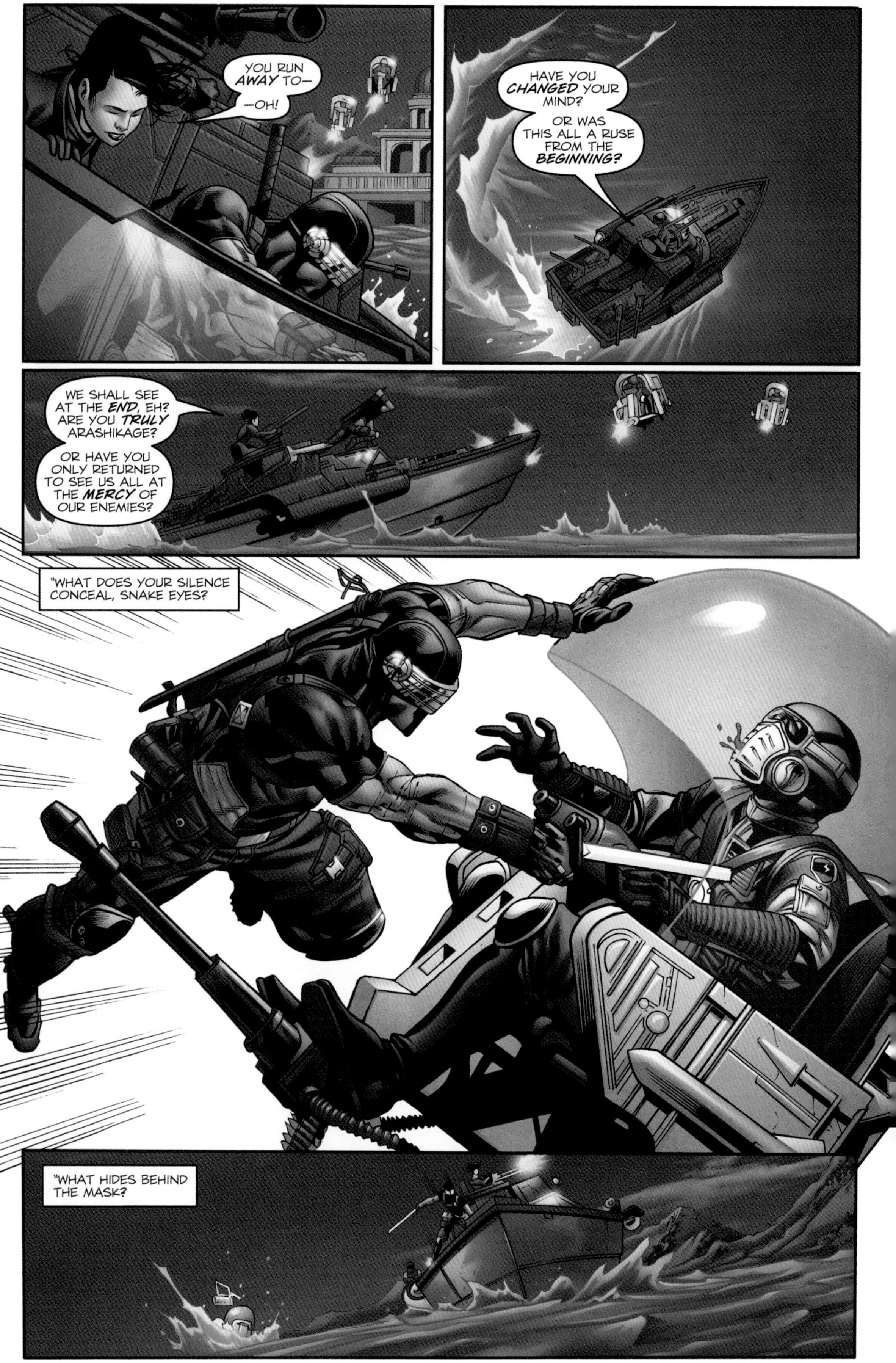
YOU RUN AWAY TO—
—OH!
HAVE YOU CHANGED YOUR MIND?
OR WAS THIS ALL A RUSE FROM THE BEGINNING?
WE SHALL SEE AT THE END, EH? ARE YOU TRULY ARASHIKAGE?
OR HAVE YOU ONLY RETURNED TO SEE US ALL AT THE MERCY OF OUR ENEMIES?
"WHAT DOES YOUR SILENCE CONCEAL, SNAKE EYES?
"WHAT HIDES BEHIND THE MASK?

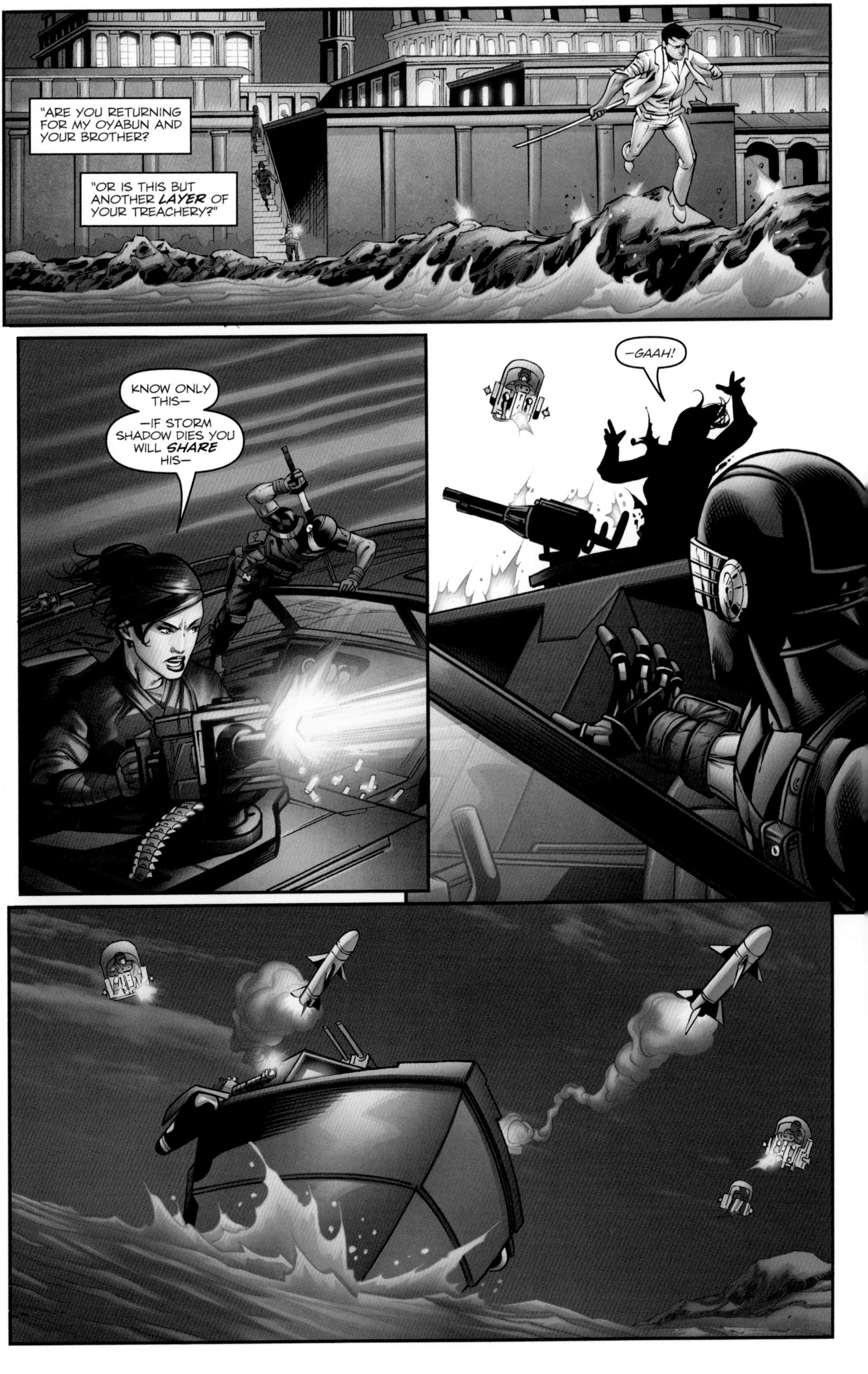
"ARE YOU RETURNING FOR MY OYABUN AND YOUR BROTHER?
"OR IS THIS BUT ANOTHER LAYER OF YOUR TREACHERY?"
KNOW ONLY THIS—
—IF STORM SHADOW DIES YOU WILL SHARE HIS—
—GAAH!

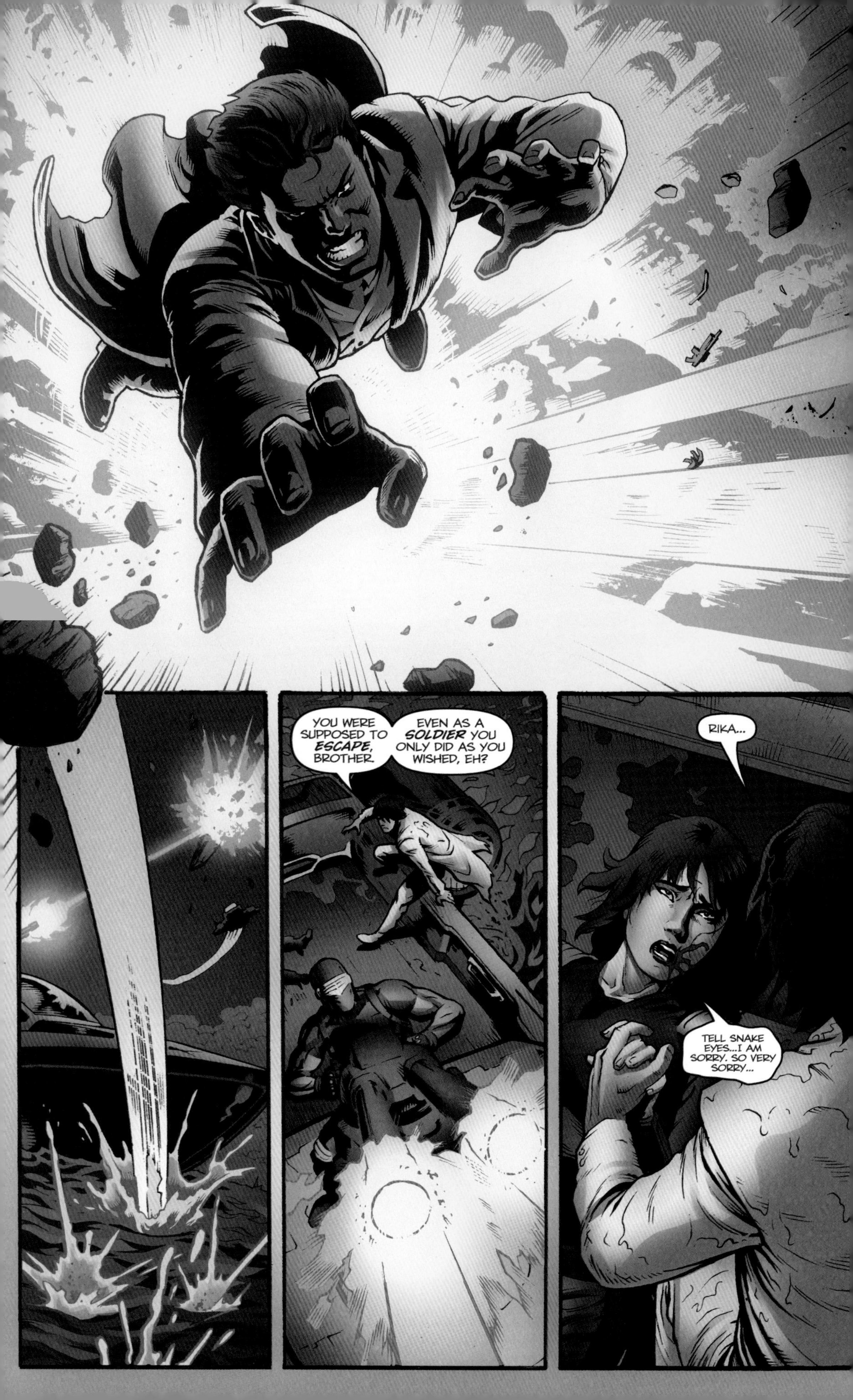
YOU WERE SUPPOSED TO ESCAPE, BROTHER.
EVEN AS A SOLDIER YOU ONLY DID AS YOU WISHED, EH?
RIKA...
TELL SNAKE EYES...I AM SORRY. SO VERY SORRY...

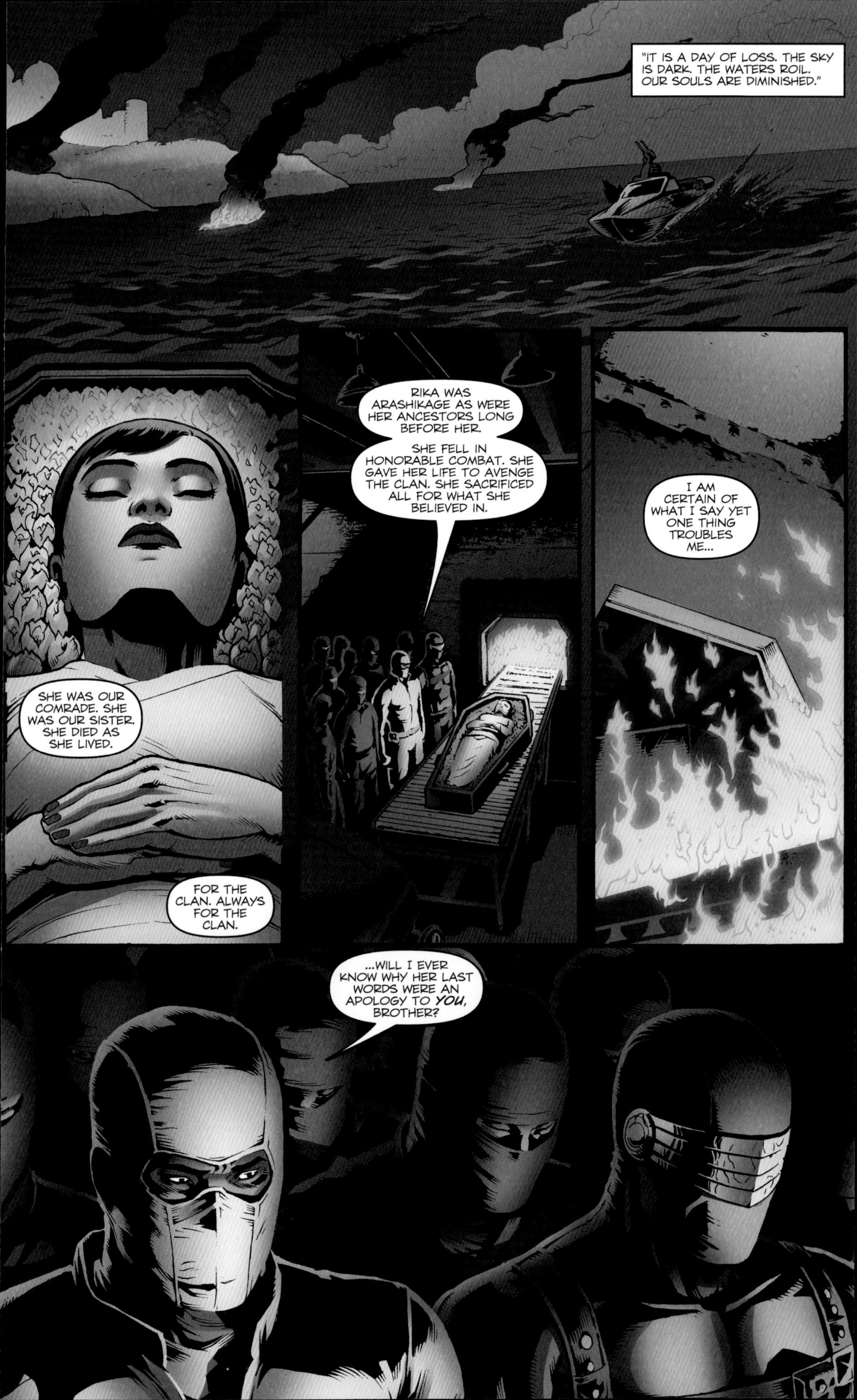
"IT IS A DAY OF LOSS. THE SKY IS DARK. THE WATERS ROIL. OUR SOULS ARE DIMINISHED."
SHE WAS OUR COMRADE. SHE WAS OUR SISTER. SHE DIED AS SHE LIVED.
FOR THE CLAN. ALWAYS FOR THE CLAN.
RIKA WAS ARASHIKAGE AS WERE HER ANCESTORS LONG BEFORE HER.
SHE FELL IN HONORABLE COMBAT. SHE GAVE HER LIFE TO AVENGE THE CLAN. SHE SACRIFICED ALL FOR WHAT SHE BELIEVED IN.
I AM CERTAIN OF WHAT I SAY YET ONE THING TROUBLES ME...
...WILL I EVER KNOW WHY HER LAST WORDS WERE AN APOLOGY TO *YOU*, BROTHER?

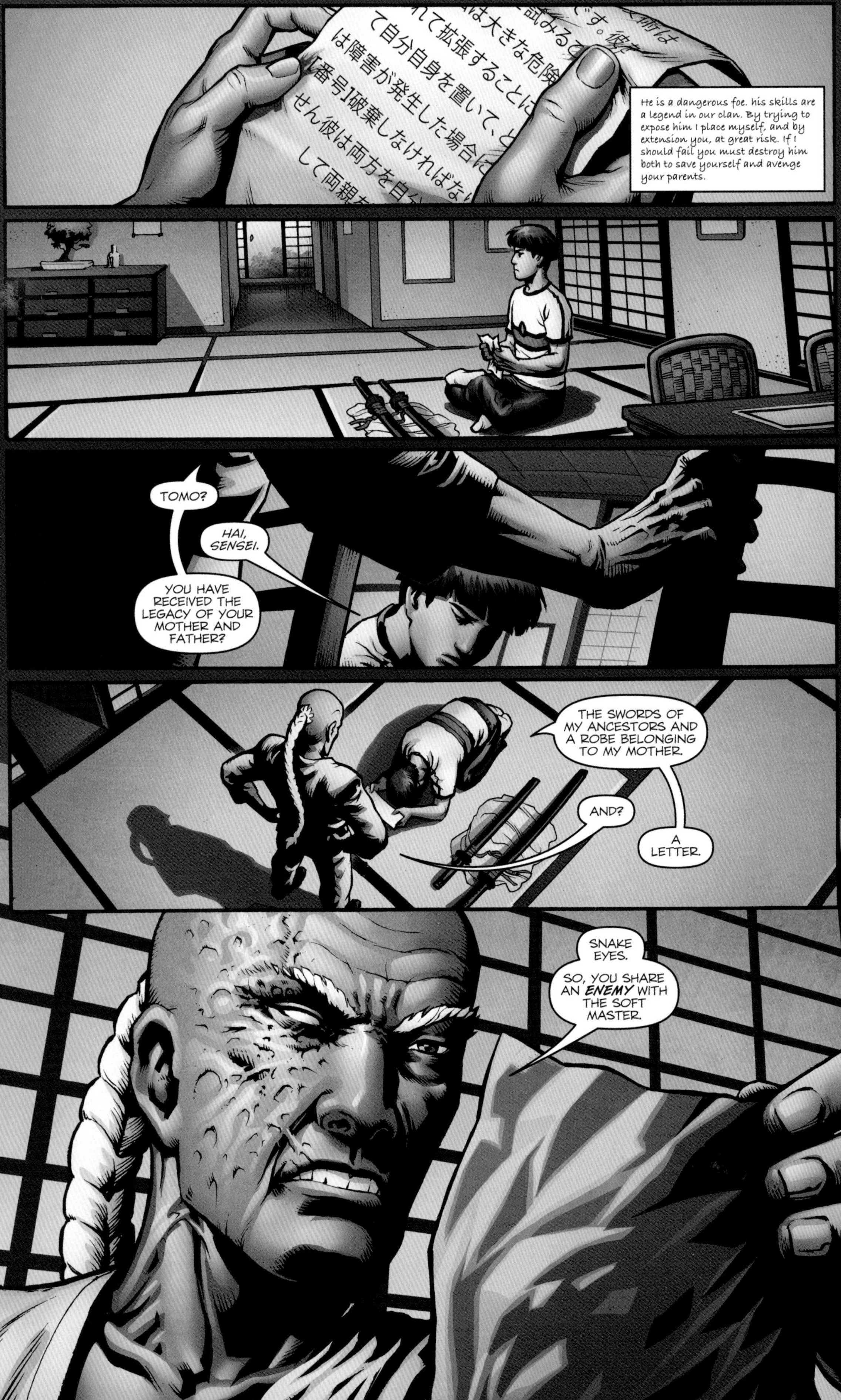
He is a dangerous foe. his skills are a legend in our clan. By trying to expose him I place myself, and by extension you, at great risk. If I should fail you must destroy him both to save yourself and avenge your parents.
TOMO?
HAI, SENSEI.
YOU HAVE RECEIVED THE LEGACY OF YOUR MOTHER AND FATHER?
THE SWORDS OF MY ANCESTORS AND A ROBE BELONGING TO MY MOTHER.
AND?
A LETTER.
SNAKE EYES.
SO, YOU SHARE AN *ENEMY* WITH THE SOFT MASTER.

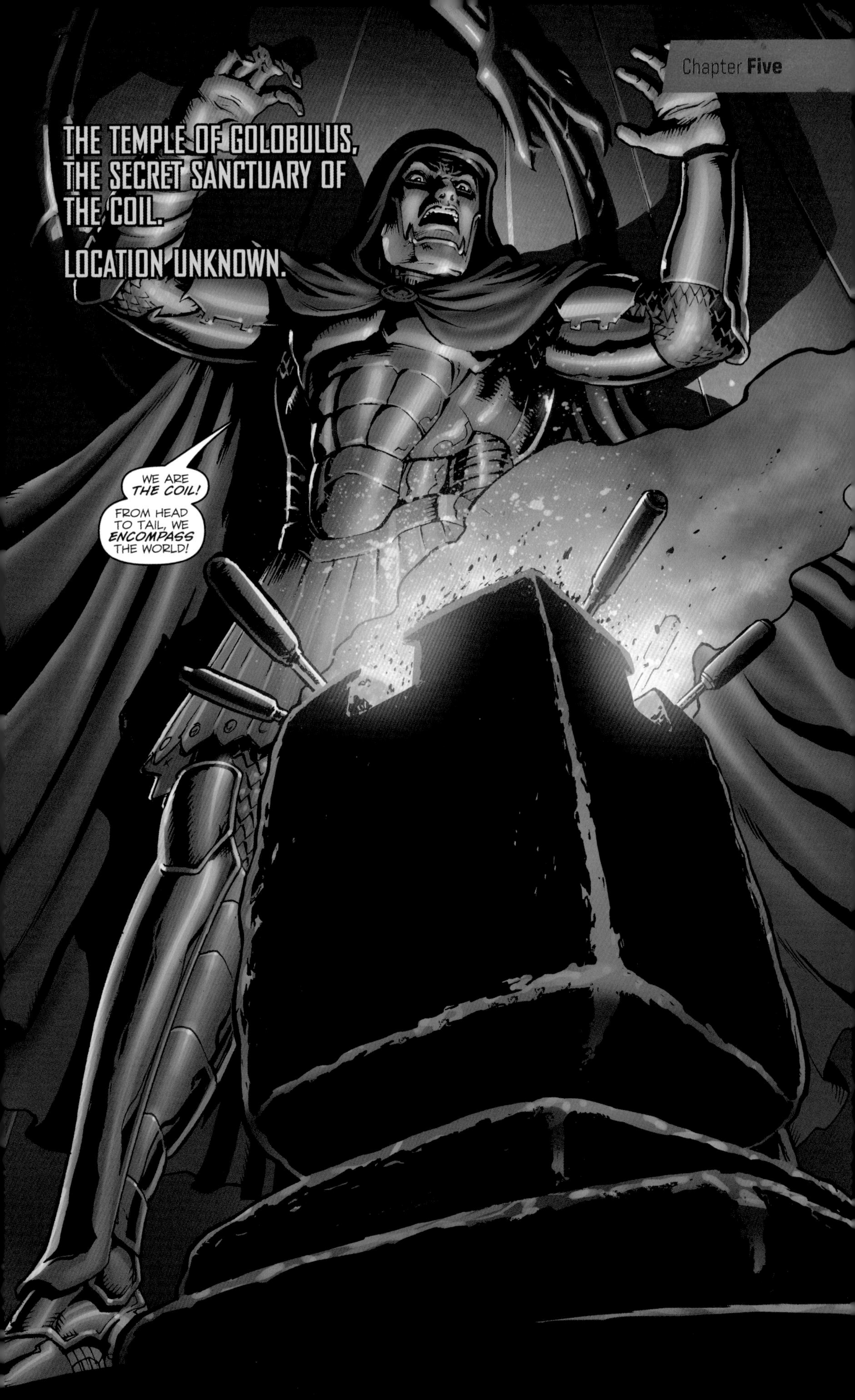
Chapter Five
THE TEMPLE OF GOLOBULUS, THE SECRET SANCTUARY OF THE COIL.
LOCATION UNKNOWN.
WE ARE THE COIL!
FROM HEAD TO TAIL, WE ENCOMPASS THE WORLD!

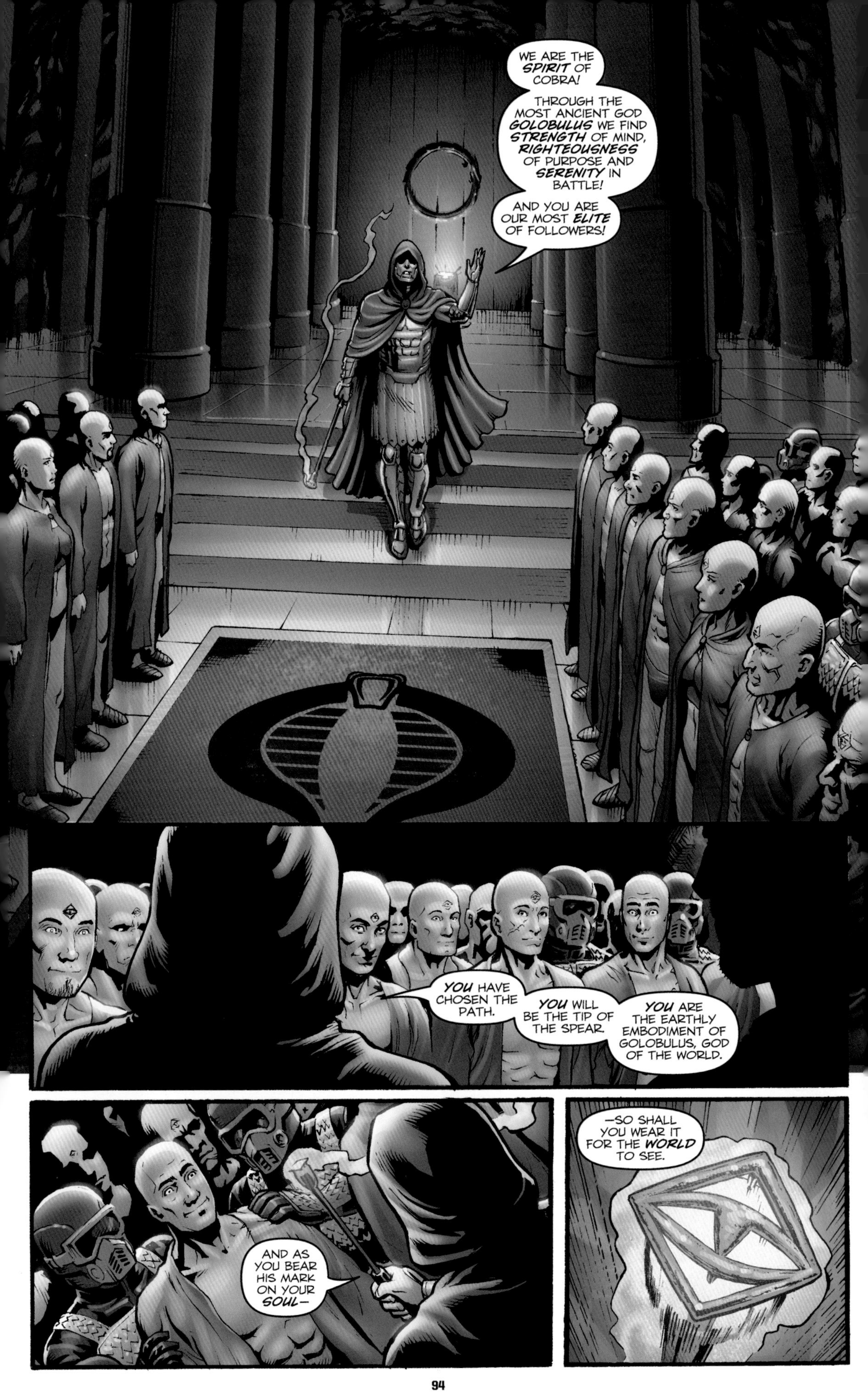
WE ARE THE SPIRIT OF COBRA!
THROUGH THE MOST ANCIENT GOD GOLOBULUS WE FIND STRENGTH OF MIND, RIGHTEOUSNESS OF PURPOSE AND SERENITY IN BATTLE!
AND YOU ARE OUR MOST ELITE OF FOLLOWERS!
YOU HAVE CHOSEN THE PATH.
YOU WILL BE THE TIP OF THE SPEAR.
YOU ARE THE EARTHLY EMBODIMENT OF GOLOBULUS, GOD OF THE WORLD.
AND AS YOU BEAR HIS MARK ON YOUR SOUL—
—SO SHALL YOU WEAR IT FOR THE WORLD TO SEE.

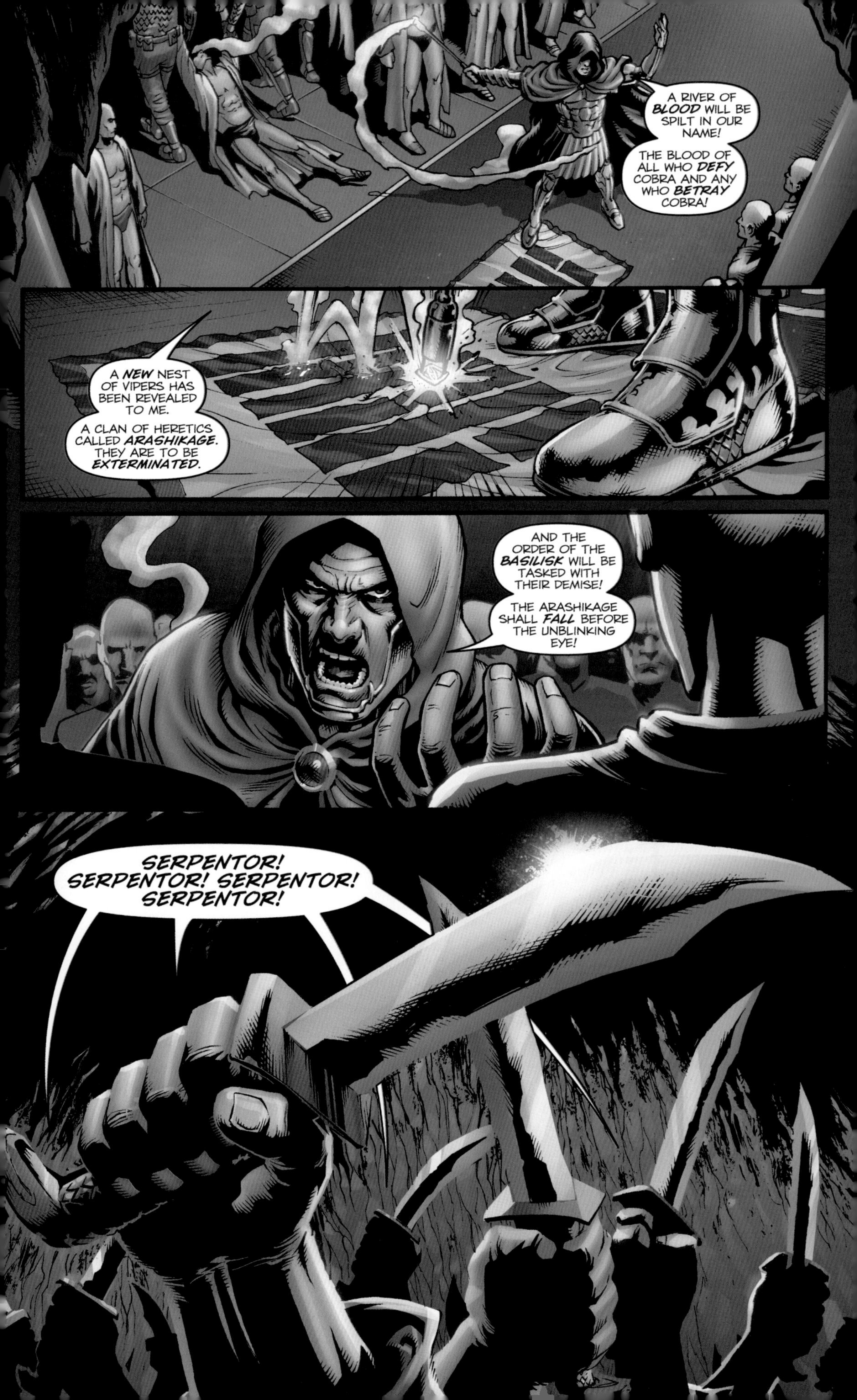

A RIVER OF BLOOD WILL BE SPILT IN OUR NAME!
THE BLOOD OF ALL WHO DEFY COBRA AND ANY WHO BETRAY COBRA!
A NEW NEST OF VIPERS HAS BEEN REVEALED TO ME.
A CLAN OF HERETICS CALLED ARASHIKAGE. THEY ARE TO BE EXTERMINATED.
AND THE ORDER OF THE BASILISK WILL BE TASKED WITH THEIR DEMISE!
THE ARASHIKAGE SHALL FALL BEFORE THE UNBLINKING EYE!
SERPENTOR! SERPENTOR! SERPENTOR! SERPENTOR!

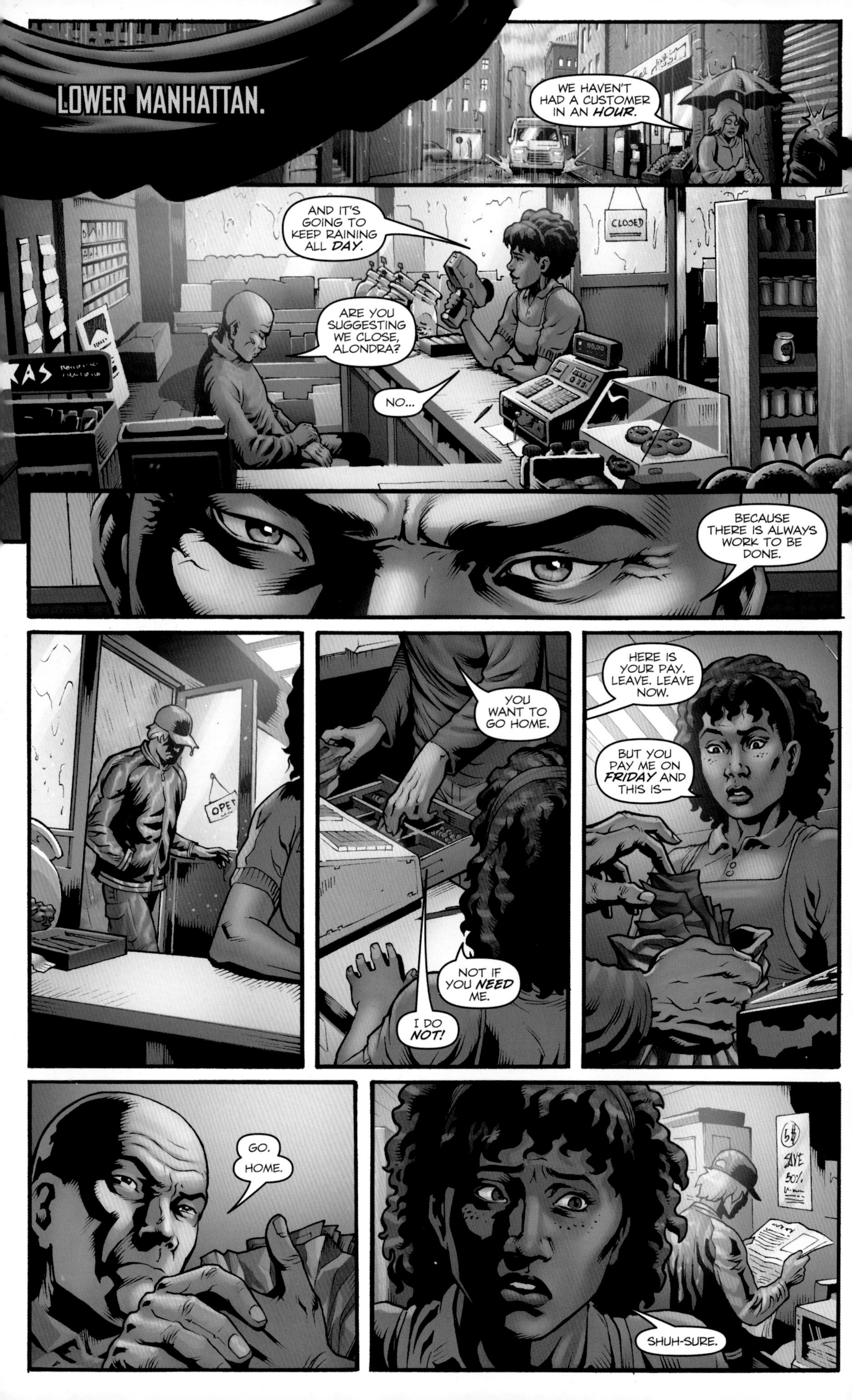

LOWER MANHATTAN.
WE HAVEN'T HAD A CUSTOMER IN AN HOUR.
AND IT'S GOING TO KEEP RAINING ALL DAY.
ARE YOU SUGGESTING WE CLOSE, ALONDRA?
NO...
CLOSED
BECAUSE THERE IS ALWAYS WORK TO BE DONE.
OPEN
YOU WANT TO GO HOME.
NOT IF YOU NEED ME.
I DO NOT!
HERE IS YOUR PAY. LEAVE. LEAVE NOW.
BUT YOU PAY ME ON FRIDAY AND THIS IS—
GO.
HOME.
SAVE 50%
SHUH-SURE.

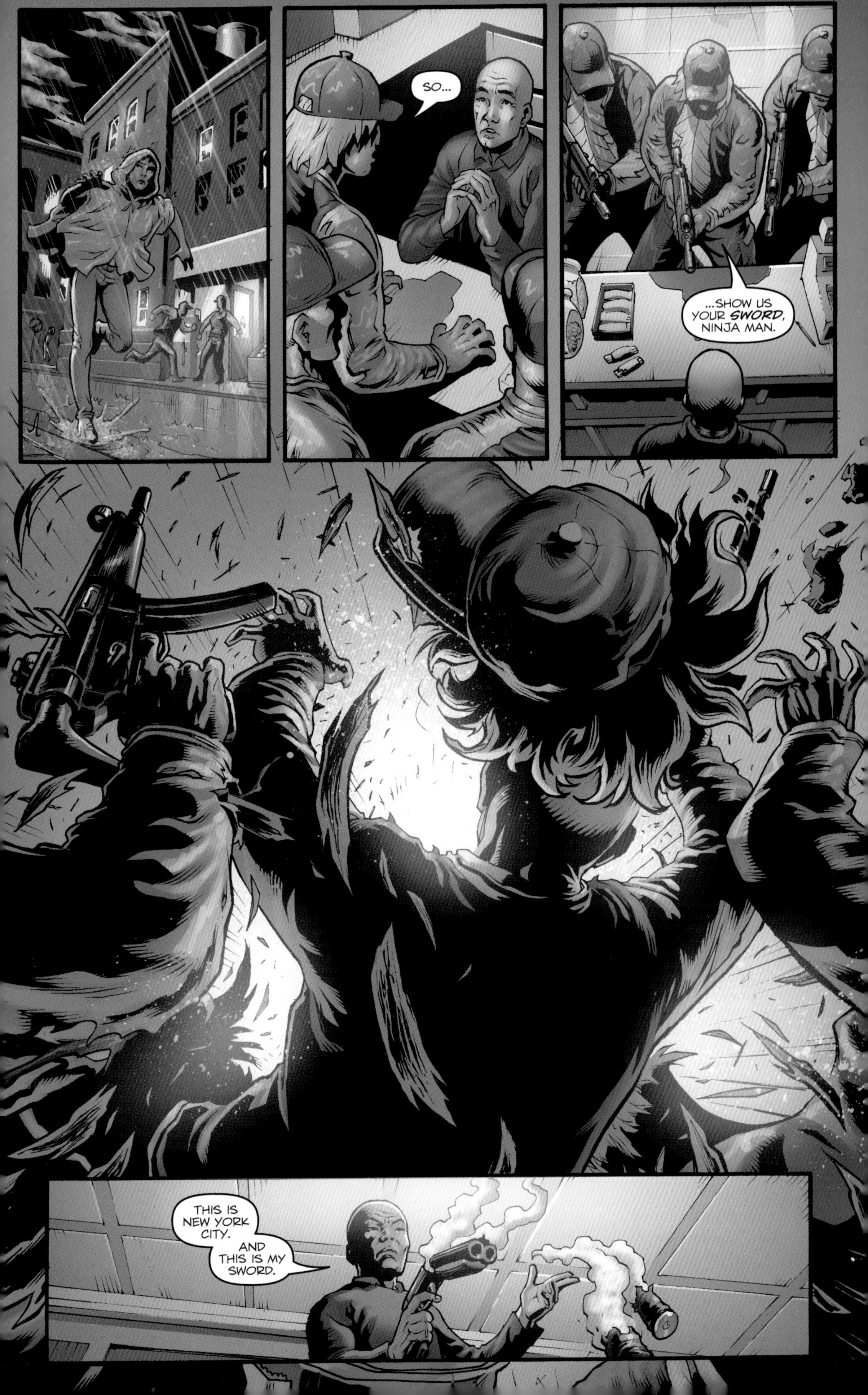

SO...
...SHOW US YOUR **SWORD**, NINJA MAN.
THIS IS NEW YORK CITY.
AND THIS IS MY SWORD.

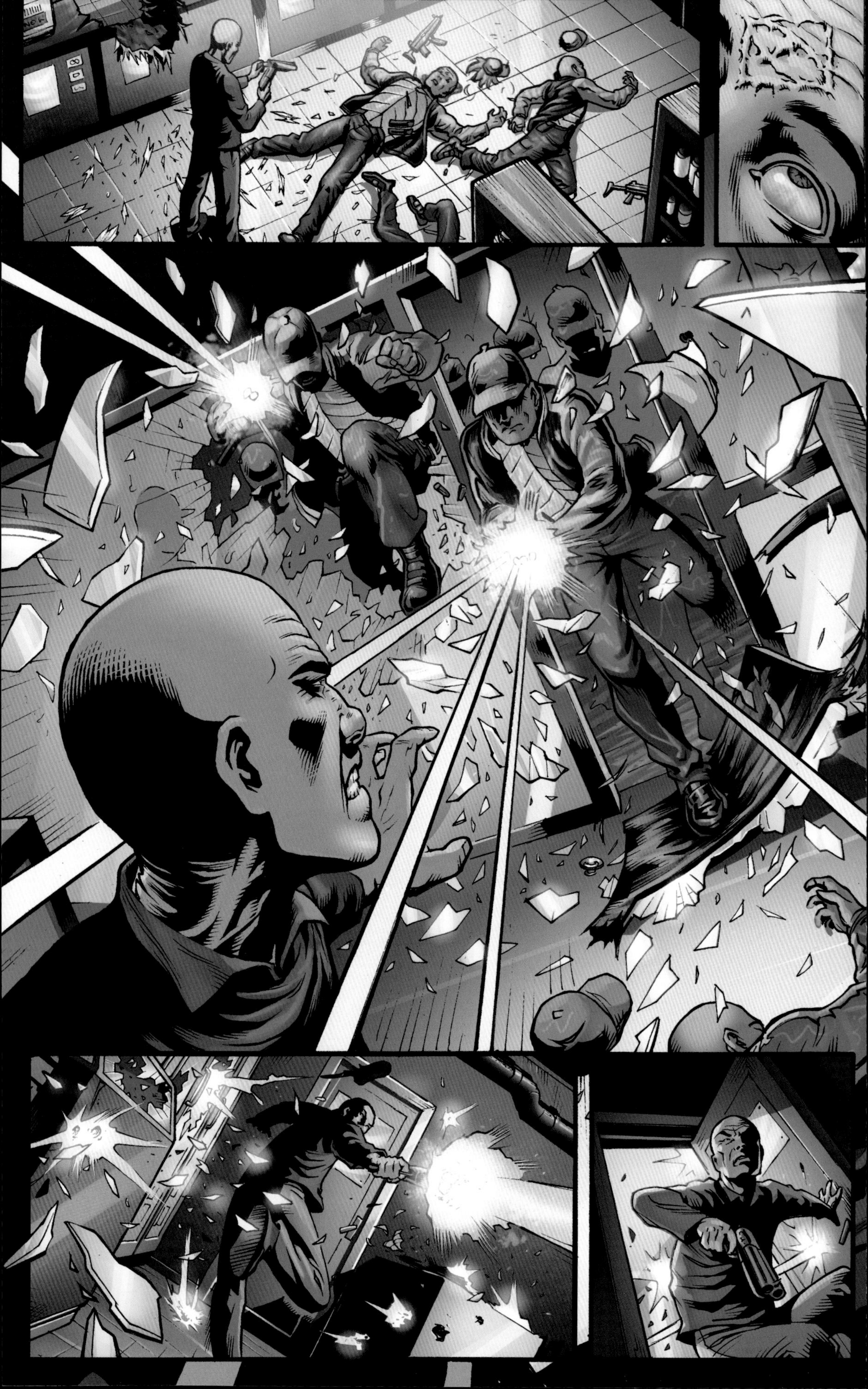

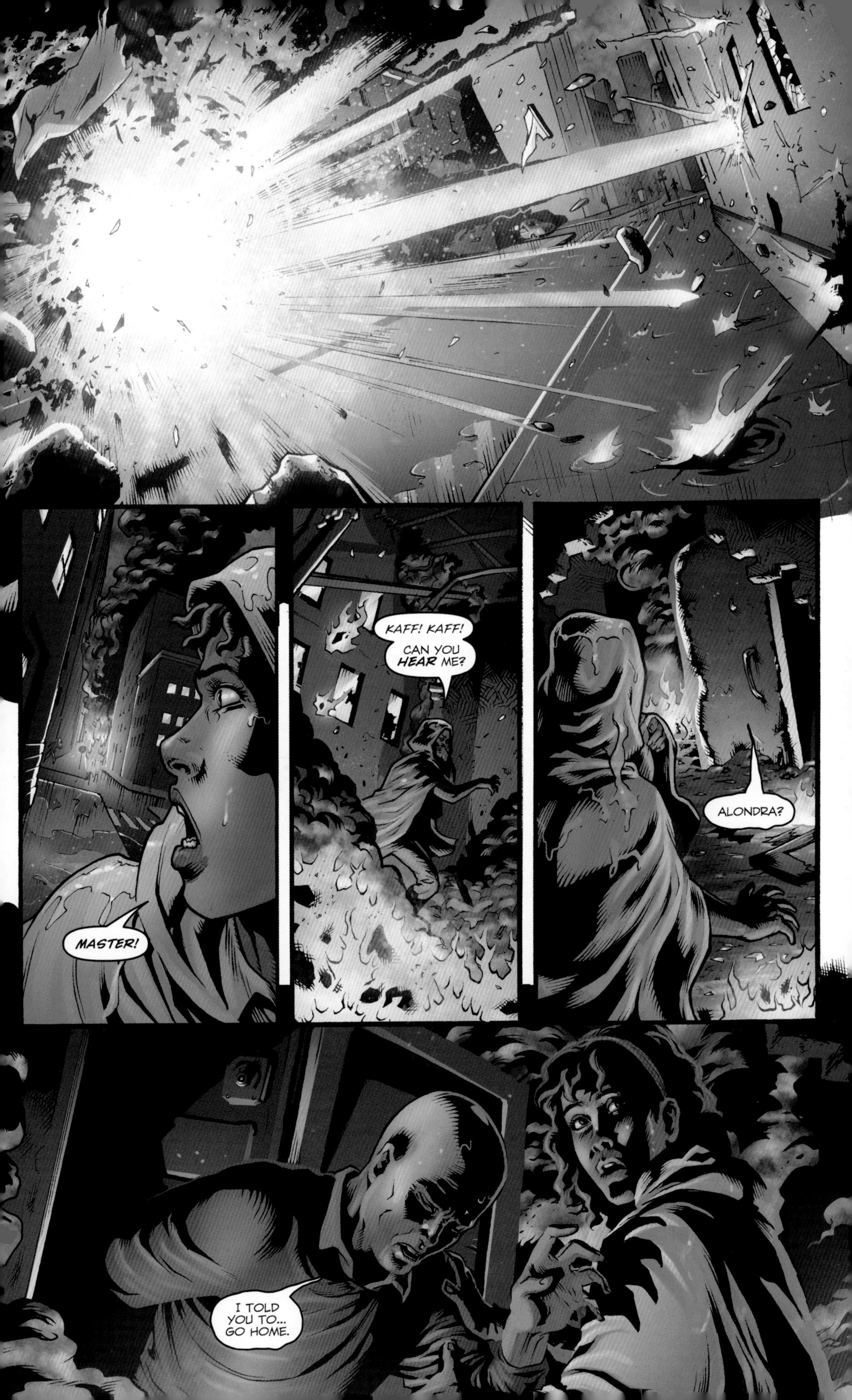
MASTER!
KAFF! KAFF! CAN YOU HEAR ME?
ALONDRA?
I TOLD YOU TO... GO HOME.

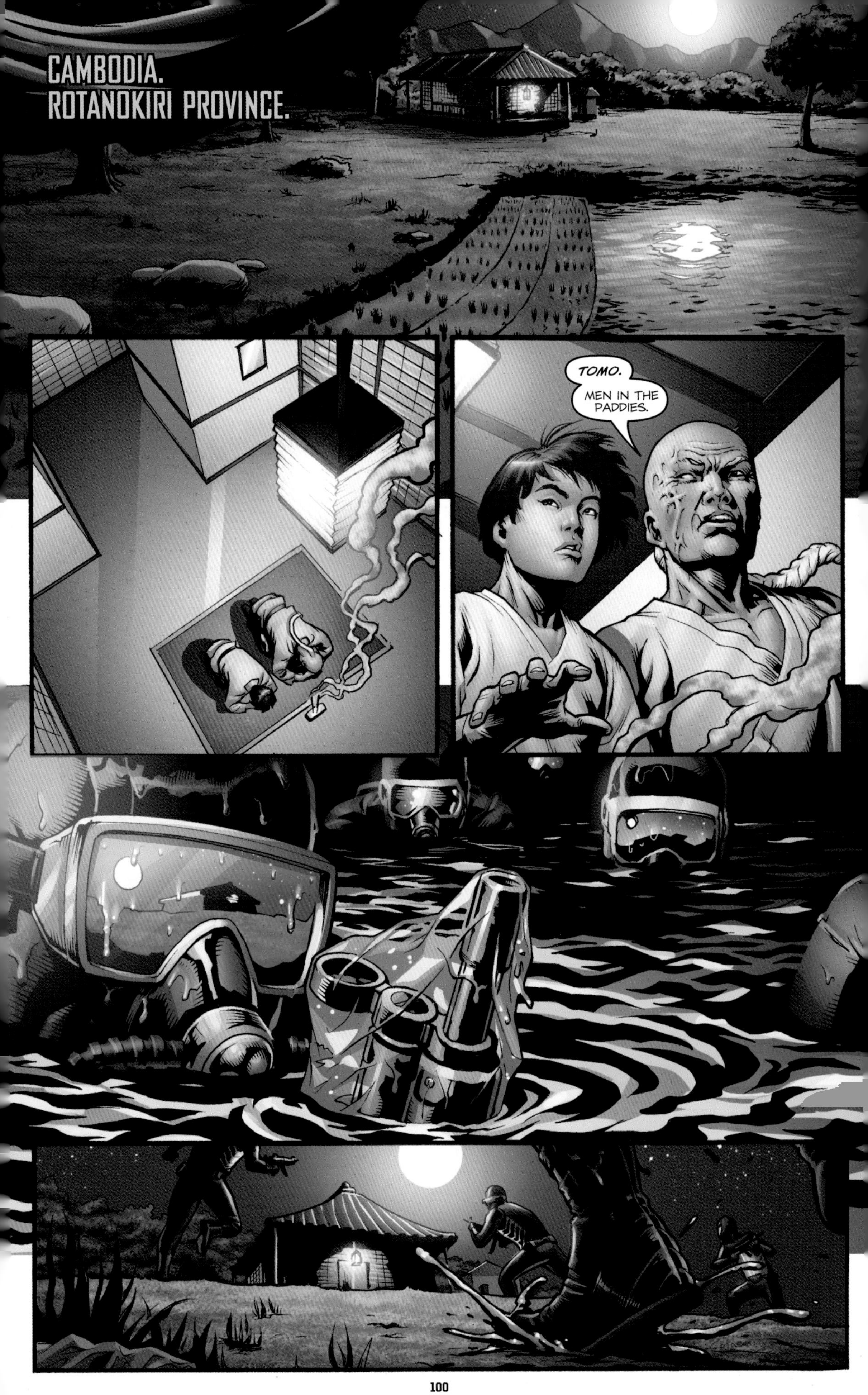

CAMBODIA.
ROTANOKIRI PROVINCE.
TOMO.
MEN IN THE PADDIES.

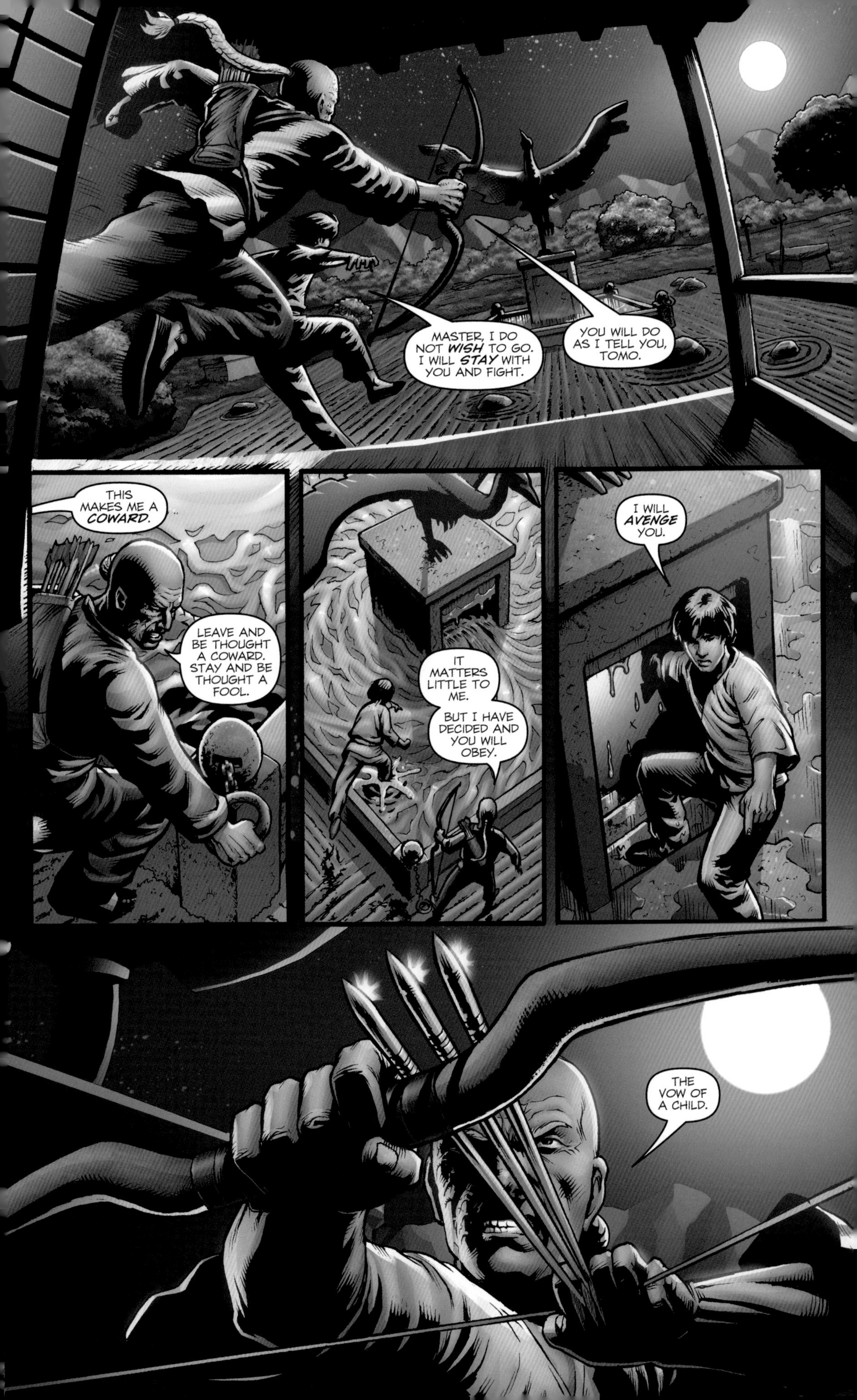
MASTER, I DO NOT WISH TO GO. I WILL STAY WITH YOU AND FIGHT.
YOU WILL DO AS I TELL YOU, TOMO.
THIS MAKES ME A COWARD.
LEAVE AND BE THOUGHT A COWARD. STAY AND BE THOUGHT A FOOL.
IT MATTERS LITTLE TO ME.
BUT I HAVE DECIDED AND YOU WILL OBEY.
I WILL AVENGE YOU.
THE VOW OF A CHILD.

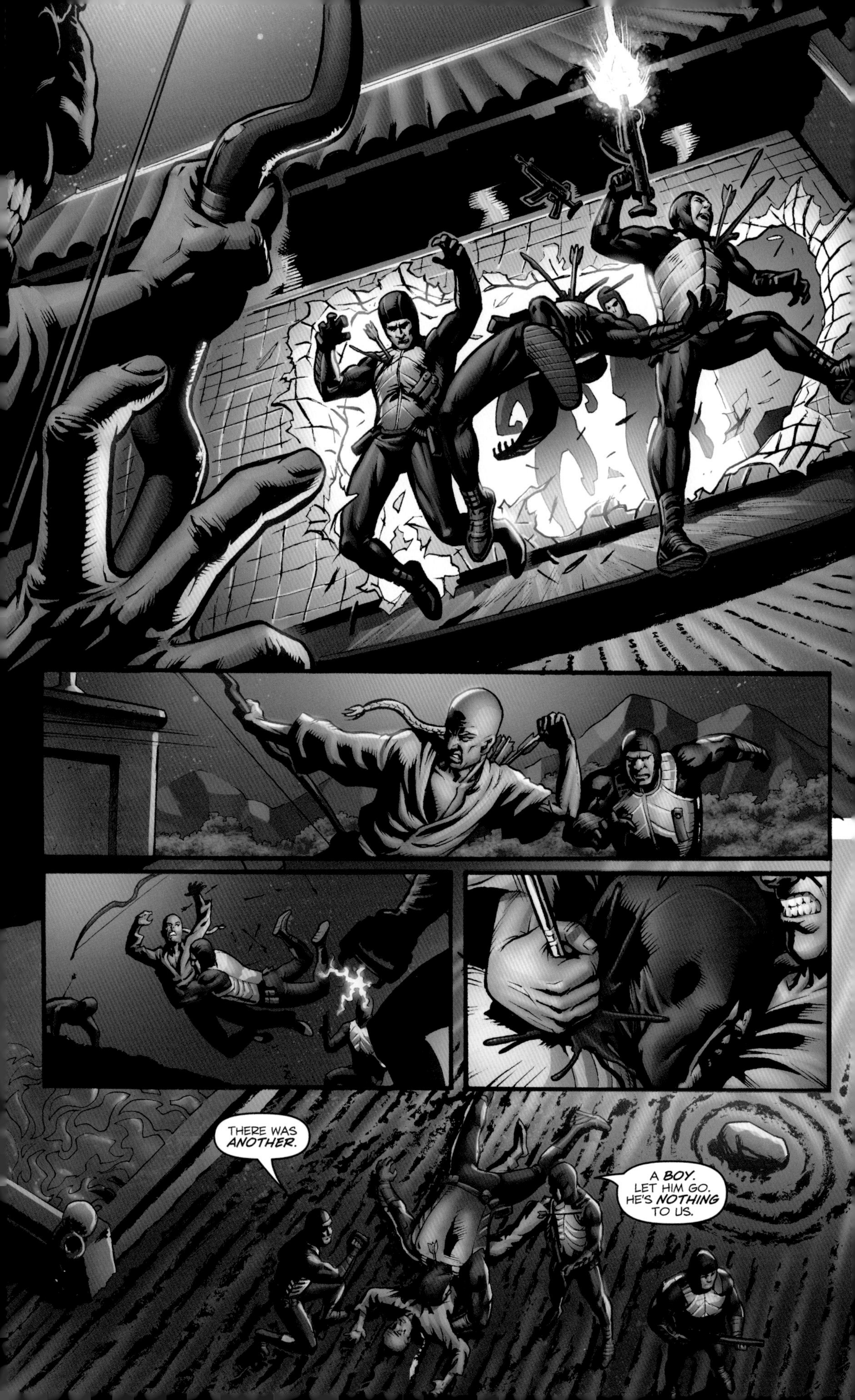

THERE WAS ANOTHER.
A BOY. LET HIM GO. HE'S NOTHING TO US.

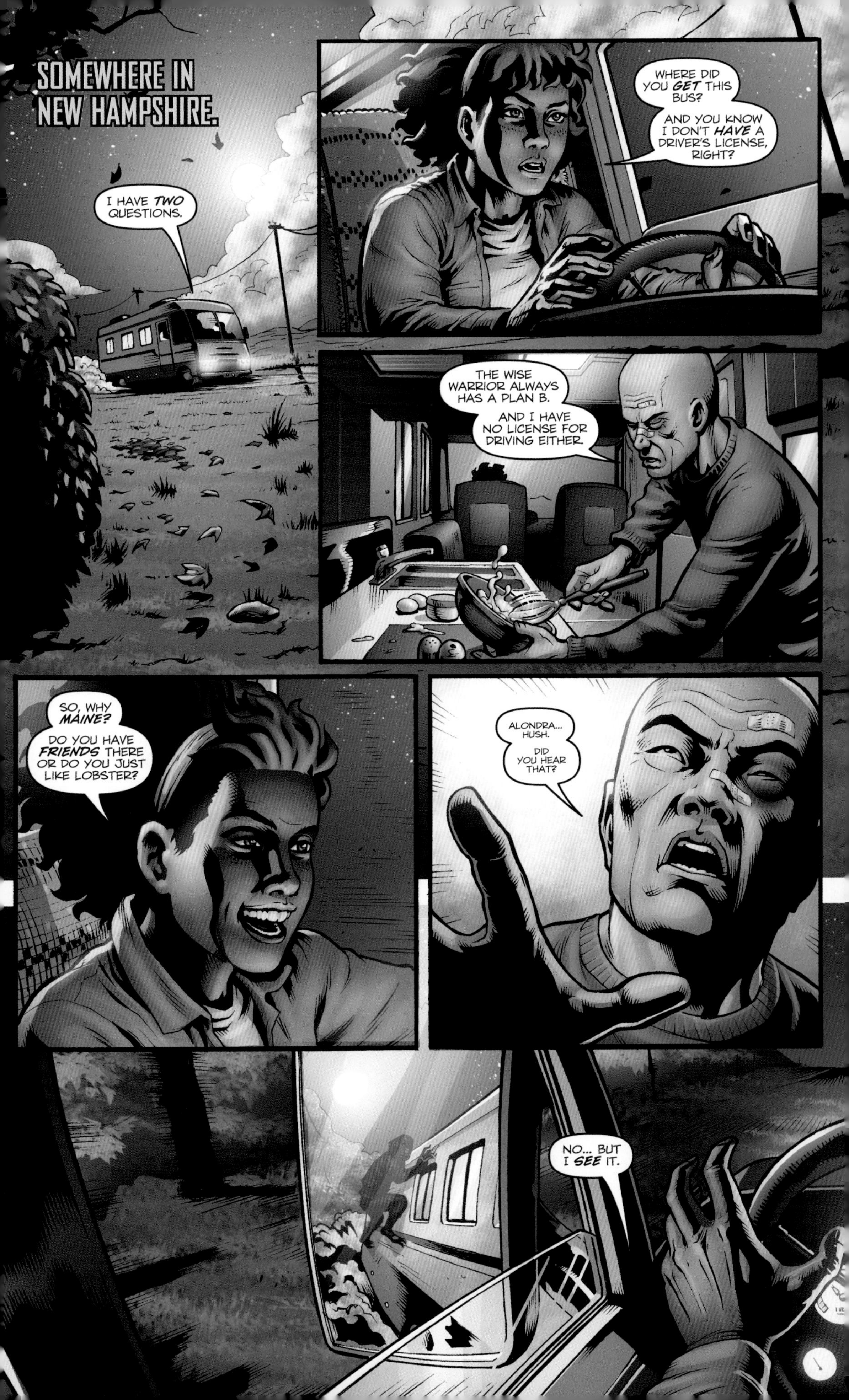
SOMEWHERE IN NEW HAMPSHIRE.
I HAVE TWO QUESTIONS.
WHERE DID YOU GET THIS BUS?
AND YOU KNOW I DON'T HAVE A DRIVER'S LICENSE, RIGHT?
THE WISE WARRIOR ALWAYS HAS A PLAN B.
AND I HAVE NO LICENSE FOR DRIVING EITHER.
SO, WHY MAINE?
DO YOU HAVE FRIENDS THERE OR DO YOU JUST LIKE LOBSTER?
ALONDRA... HUSH.
DID YOU HEAR THAT?
NO... BUT I SEE IT.

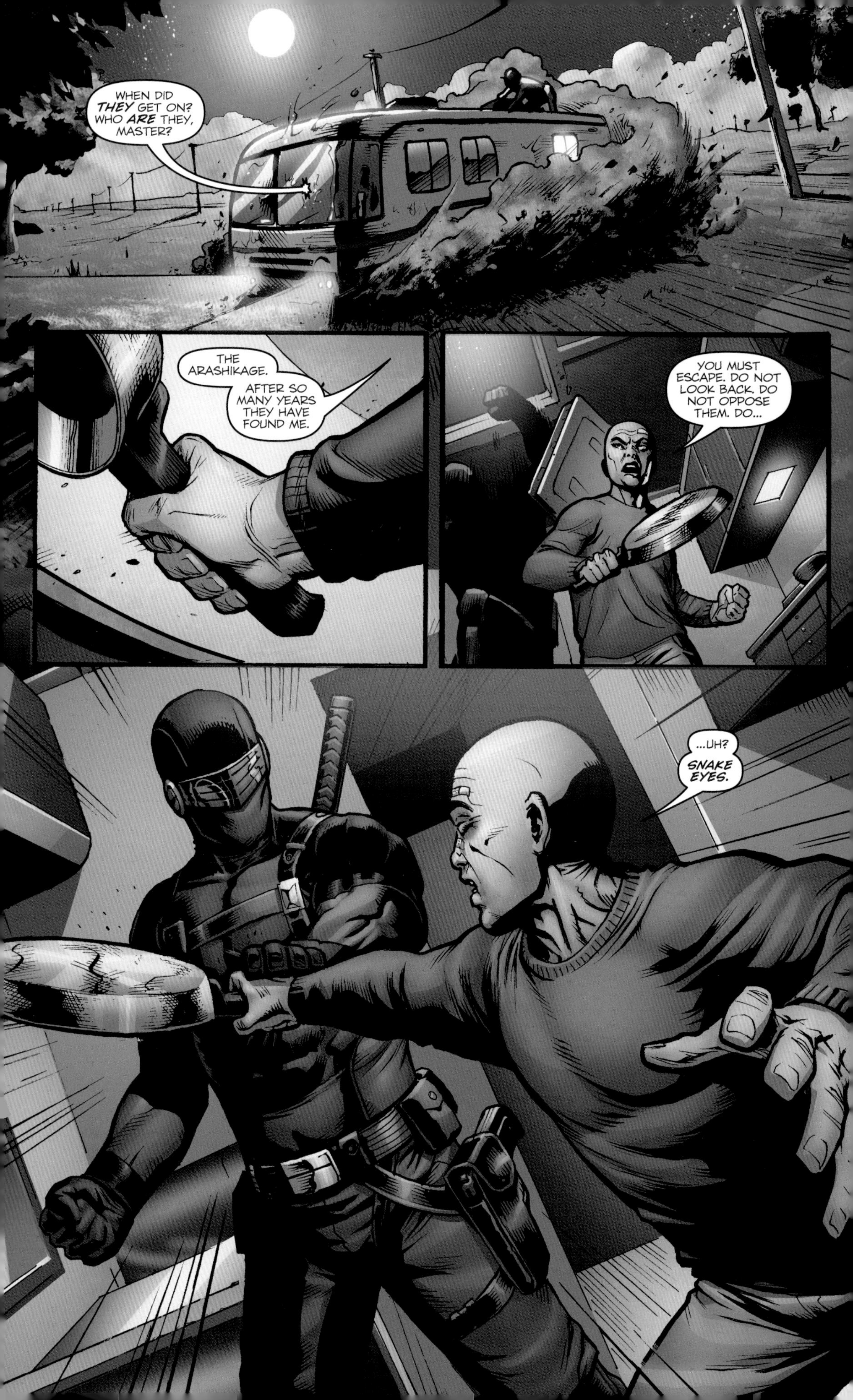
WHEN DID THEY GET ON? WHO ARE THEY, MASTER?
THE ARASHIKAGE.
AFTER SO MANY YEARS THEY HAVE FOUND ME.
YOU MUST ESCAPE. DO NOT LOOK BACK. DO NOT OPPOSE THEM. DO...
...UH?
SNAKE EYES.

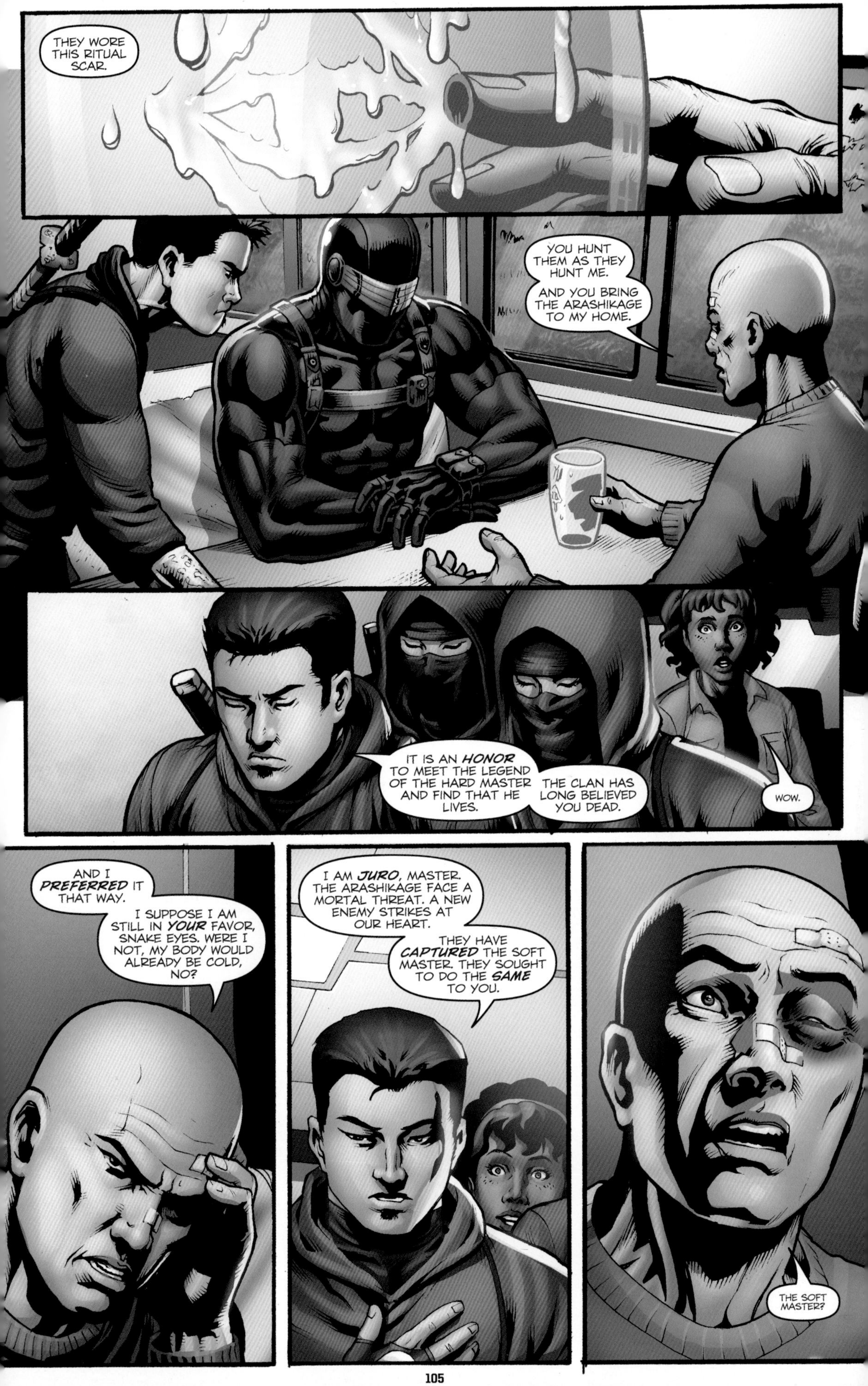
THEY WORE THIS RITUAL SCAR.
YOU HUNT THEM AS THEY HUNT ME.
AND YOU BRING THE ARASHIKAGE TO MY HOME.
IT IS AN *HONOR* TO MEET THE LEGEND OF THE HARD MASTER AND FIND THAT HE LIVES.
THE CLAN HAS LONG BELIEVED YOU DEAD.
WOW.
AND I *PREFERRED* IT THAT WAY.
I SUPPOSE I AM STILL IN *YOUR* FAVOR, SNAKE EYES. WERE I NOT, MY BODY WOULD ALREADY BE COLD, NO?
I AM *JURO*, MASTER. THE ARASHIKAGE FACE A MORTAL THREAT. A NEW ENEMY STRIKES AT OUR HEART.
THEY HAVE *CAPTURED* THE SOFT MASTER. THEY SOUGHT TO DO THE *SAME* TO YOU.
THE SOFT MASTER?

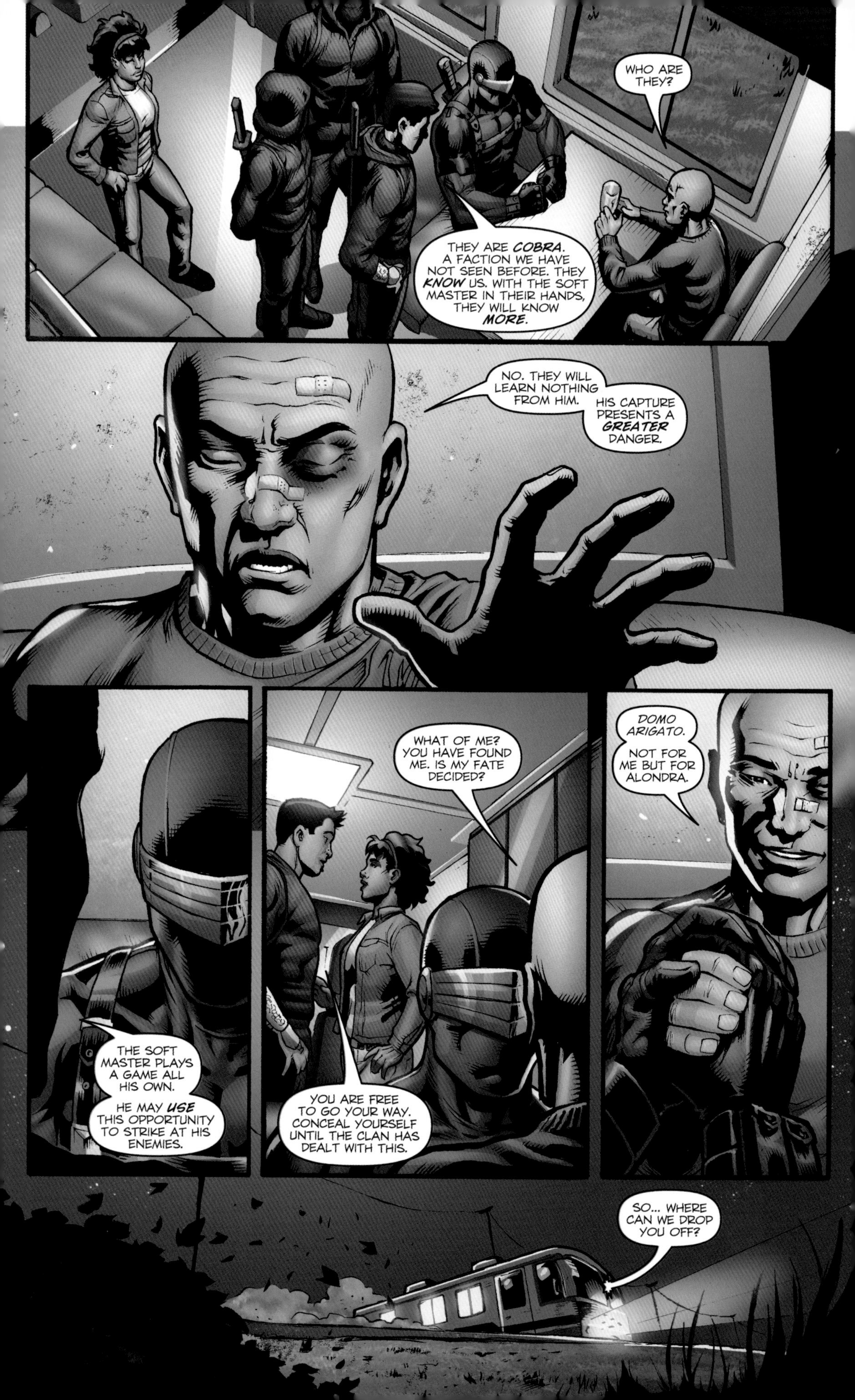
WHO ARE THEY?
THEY ARE COBRA. A FACTION WE HAVE NOT SEEN BEFORE. THEY KNOW US. WITH THE SOFT MASTER IN THEIR HANDS, THEY WILL KNOW MORE.
NO. THEY WILL LEARN NOTHING FROM HIM.
HIS CAPTURE PRESENTS A GREATER DANGER.
THE SOFT MASTER PLAYS A GAME ALL HIS OWN.
HE MAY USE THIS OPPORTUNITY TO STRIKE AT HIS ENEMIES.
WHAT OF ME? YOU HAVE FOUND ME. IS MY FATE DECIDED?
YOU ARE FREE TO GO YOUR WAY. CONCEAL YOURSELF UNTIL THE CLAN HAS DEALT WITH THIS.
DOMO ARIGATO.
NOT FOR ME BUT FOR ALONDRA.
SO... WHERE CAN WE DROP YOU OFF?

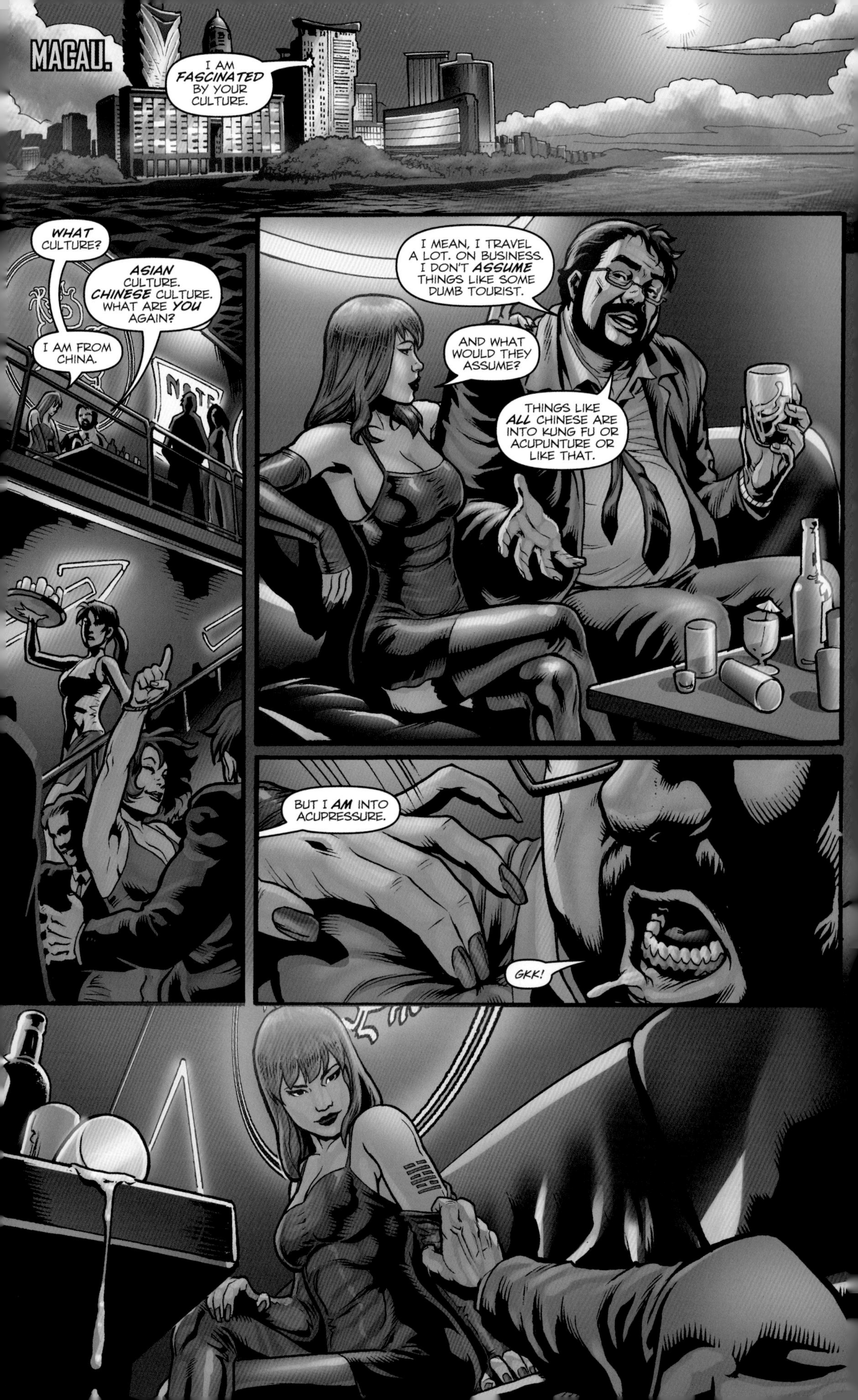
MACAU.
I AM FASCINATED BY YOUR CULTURE.
WHAT CULTURE?
ASIAN CULTURE. CHINESE CULTURE. WHAT ARE YOU AGAIN?
I AM FROM CHINA.
I MEAN, I TRAVEL A LOT. ON BUSINESS. I DON'T ASSUME THINGS LIKE SOME DUMB TOURIST.
AND WHAT WOULD THEY ASSUME?
THINGS LIKE ALL CHINESE ARE INTO KUNG FU OR ACUPUNTURE OR LIKE THAT.
BUT I AM INTO ACUPRESSURE.
GKK!

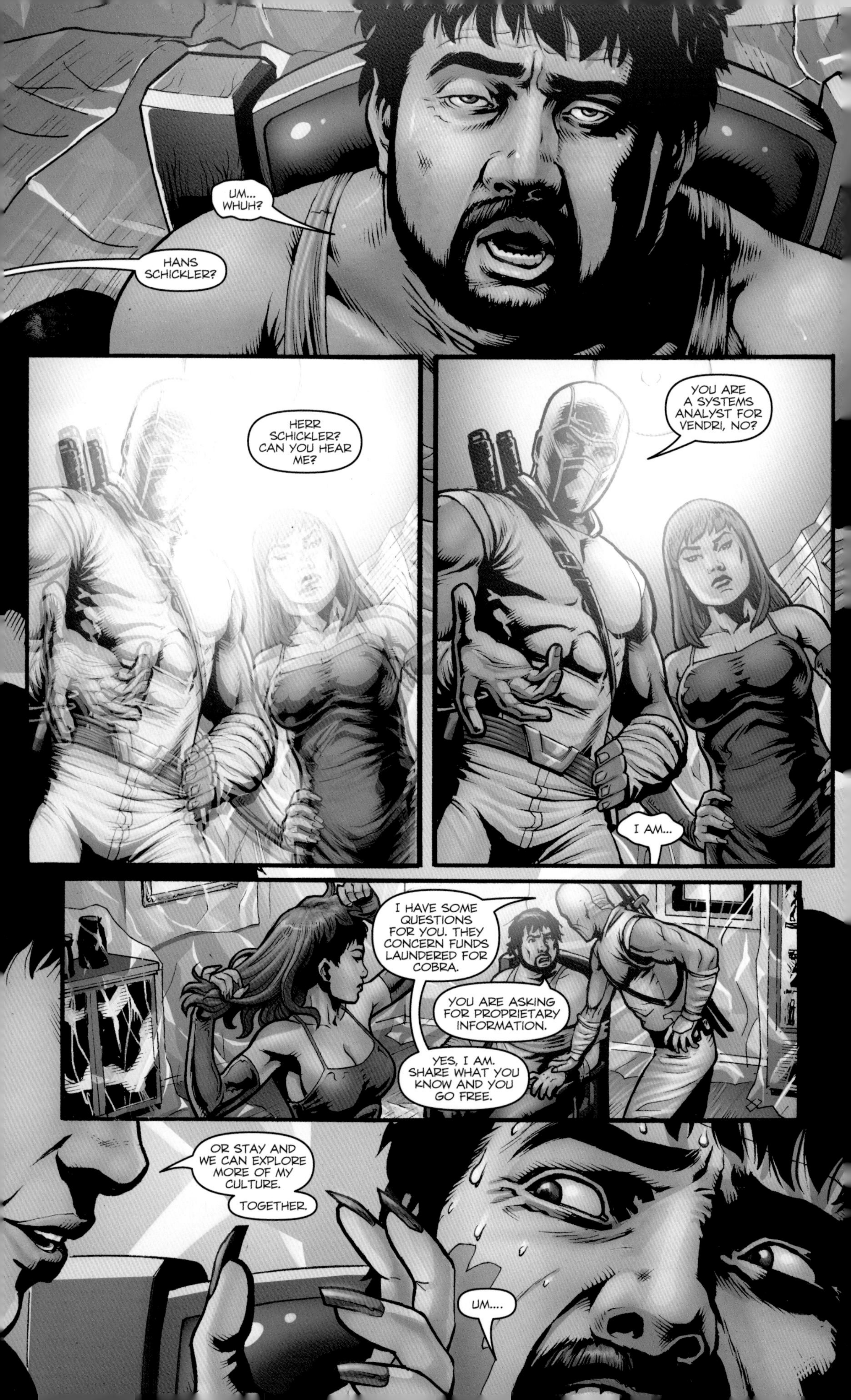
UM... WHUH?
HANS SCHICKLER?
HERR SCHICKLER? CAN YOU HEAR ME?
YOU ARE A SYSTEMS ANALYST FOR VENDRI, NO?
I AM...
I HAVE SOME QUESTIONS FOR YOU. THEY CONCERN FUNDS LAUNDERED FOR COBRA.
YOU ARE ASKING FOR PROPRIETARY INFORMATION.
YES, I AM. SHARE WHAT YOU KNOW AND YOU GO FREE.
OR STAY AND WE CAN EXPLORE MORE OF MY CULTURE.
TOGETHER.
UM....

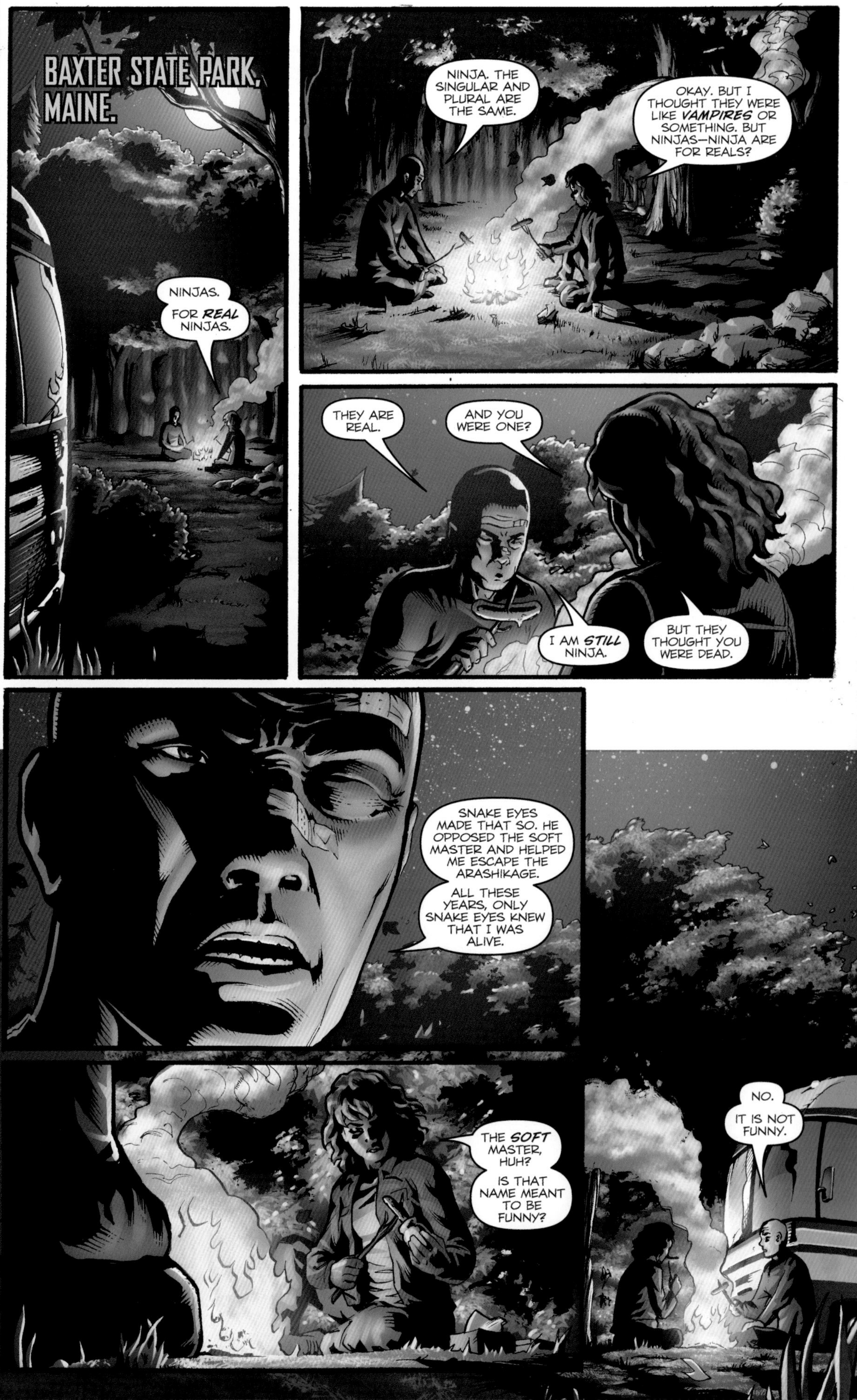
BAXTER STATE PARK, MAINE.
NINJAS.
FOR REAL NINJAS.
NINJA. THE SINGULAR AND PLURAL ARE THE SAME.
OKAY. BUT I THOUGHT THEY WERE LIKE VAMPIRES OR SOMETHING. BUT NINJAS—NINJA ARE FOR REALS?
THEY ARE REAL.
AND YOU WERE ONE?
I AM STILL NINJA.
BUT THEY THOUGHT YOU WERE DEAD.
SNAKE EYES MADE THAT SO. HE OPPOSED THE SOFT MASTER AND HELPED ME ESCAPE THE ARASHIKAGE.
ALL THESE YEARS, ONLY SNAKE EYES KNEW THAT I WAS ALIVE.
THE SOFT MASTER, HUH?
IS THAT NAME MEANT TO BE FUNNY?
NO.
IT IS NOT FUNNY.

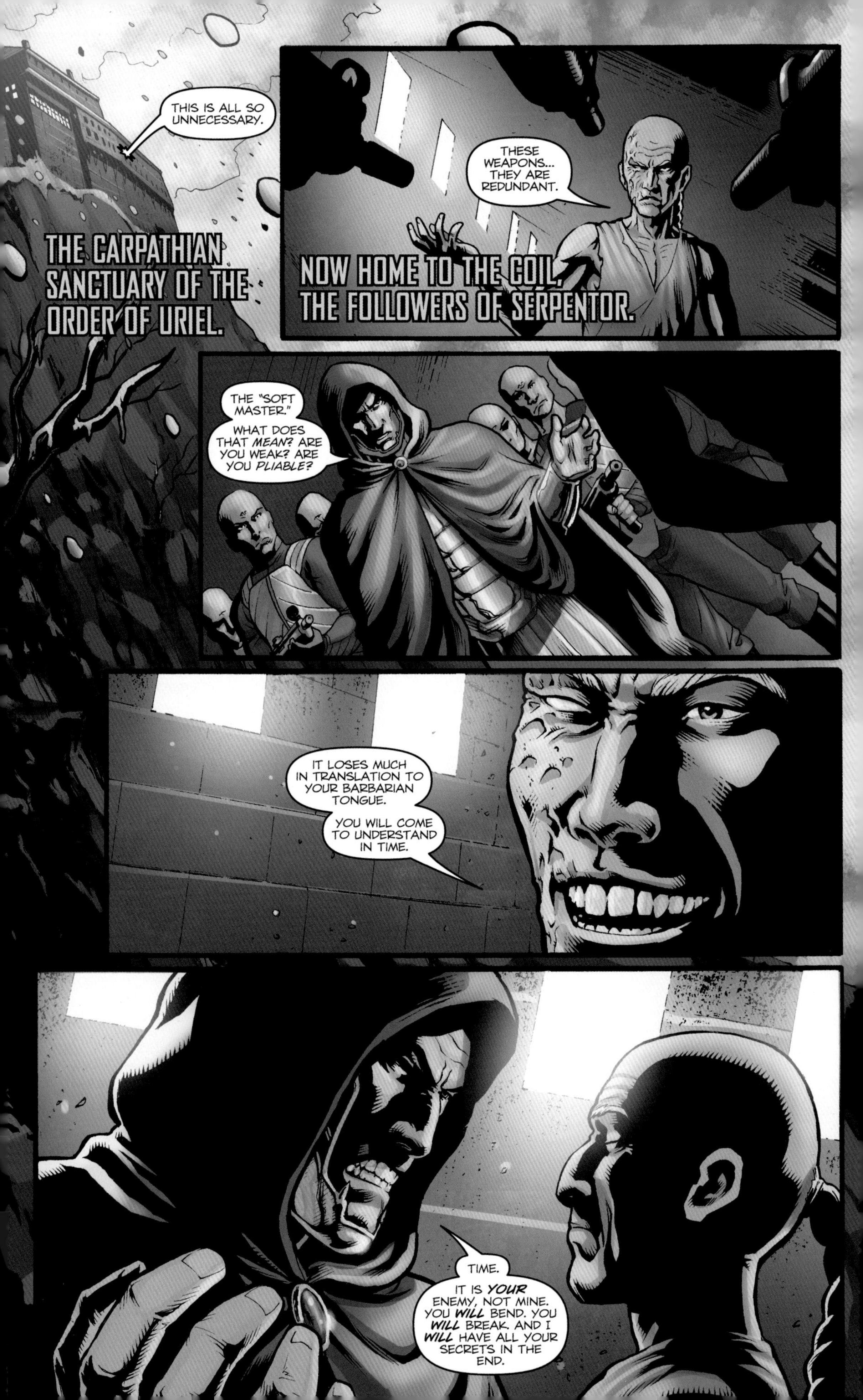
THIS IS ALL SO UNNECESSARY.
THE CARPATHIAN SANCTUARY OF THE ORDER OF URIEL.
THESE WEAPONS... THEY ARE REDUNDANT.
NOW HOME TO THE COIL, THE FOLLOWERS OF SERPENTOR.
THE "SOFT MASTER."
WHAT DOES THAT MEAN? ARE YOU WEAK? ARE YOU PLIABLE?
IT LOSES MUCH IN TRANSLATION TO YOUR BARBARIAN TONGUE.
YOU WILL COME TO UNDERSTAND IN TIME.
TIME.
IT IS YOUR ENEMY, NOT MINE. YOU WILL BEND. YOU WILL BREAK. AND I WILL HAVE ALL YOUR SECRETS IN THE END.

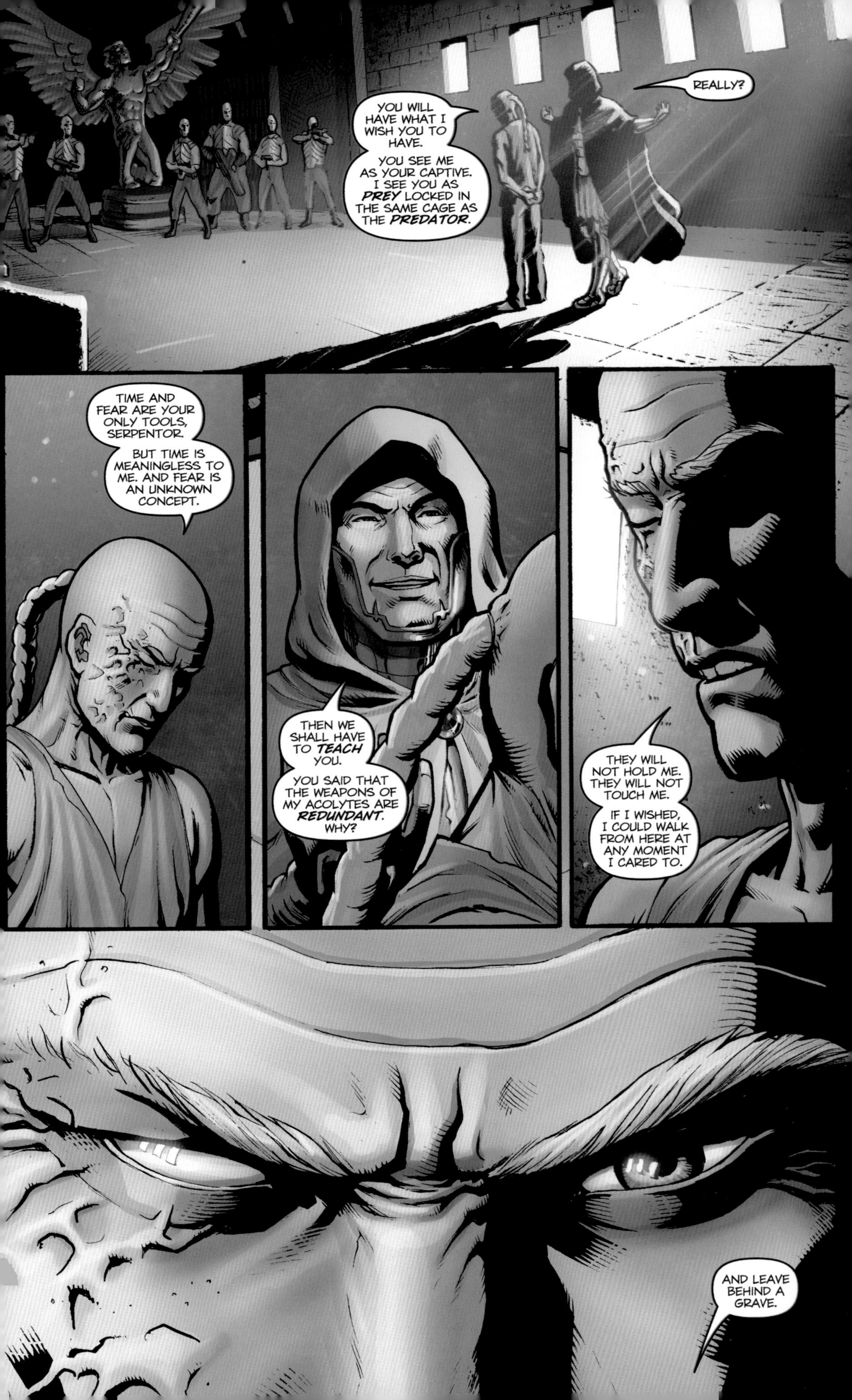
YOU WILL HAVE WHAT I WISH YOU TO HAVE.
YOU SEE ME AS YOUR CAPTIVE. I SEE YOU AS PREY LOCKED IN THE SAME CAGE AS THE PREDATOR.
REALLY?
TIME AND FEAR ARE YOUR ONLY TOOLS, SERPENTOR.
BUT TIME IS MEANINGLESS TO ME. AND FEAR IS AN UNKNOWN CONCEPT.
THEN WE SHALL HAVE TO TEACH YOU.
YOU SAID THAT THE WEAPONS OF MY ACOLYTES ARE REDUNDANT. WHY?
THEY WILL NOT HOLD ME. THEY WILL NOT TOUCH ME.
IF I WISHED, I COULD WALK FROM HERE AT ANY MOMENT I CARED TO.
AND LEAVE BEHIND A GRAVE.

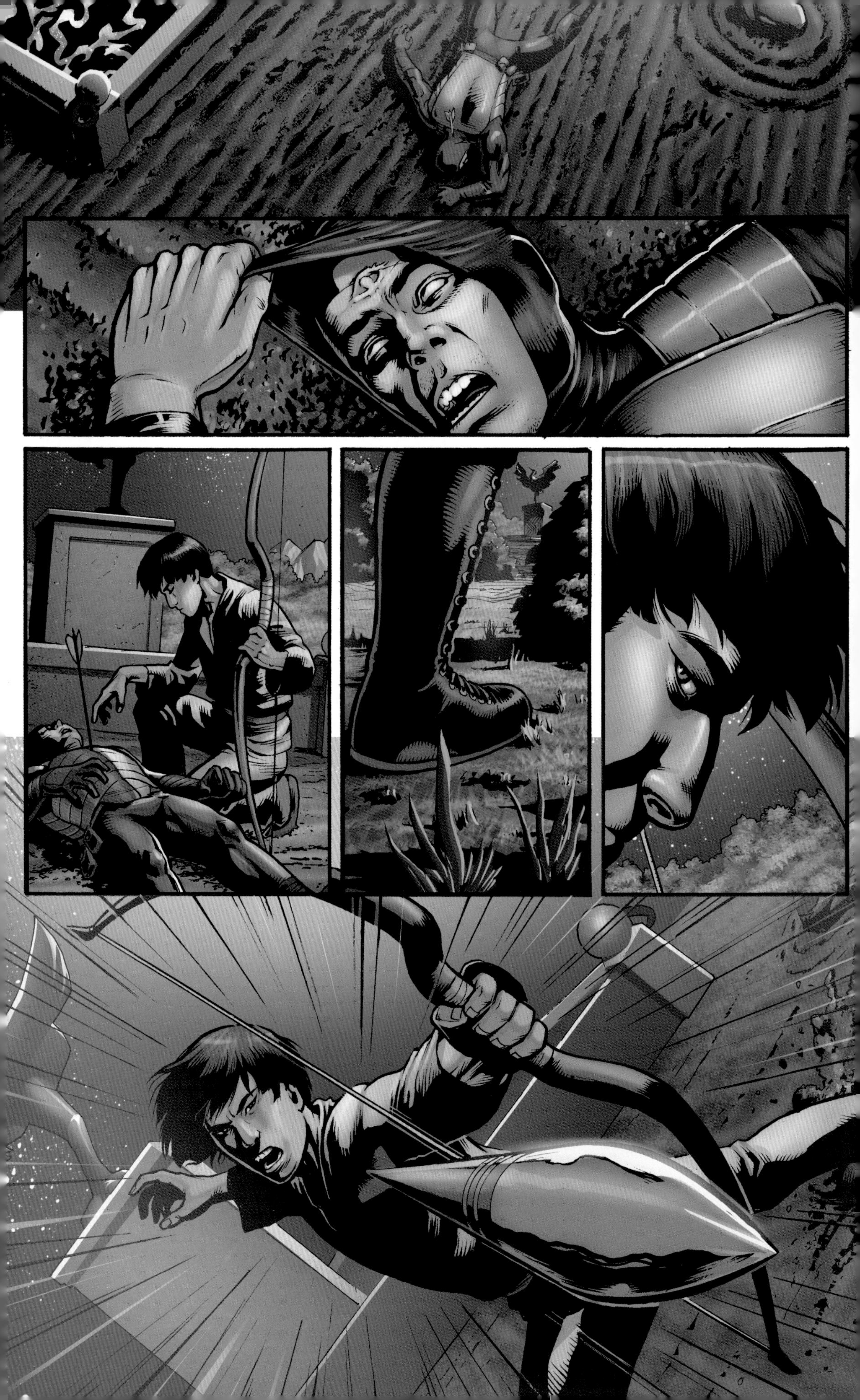

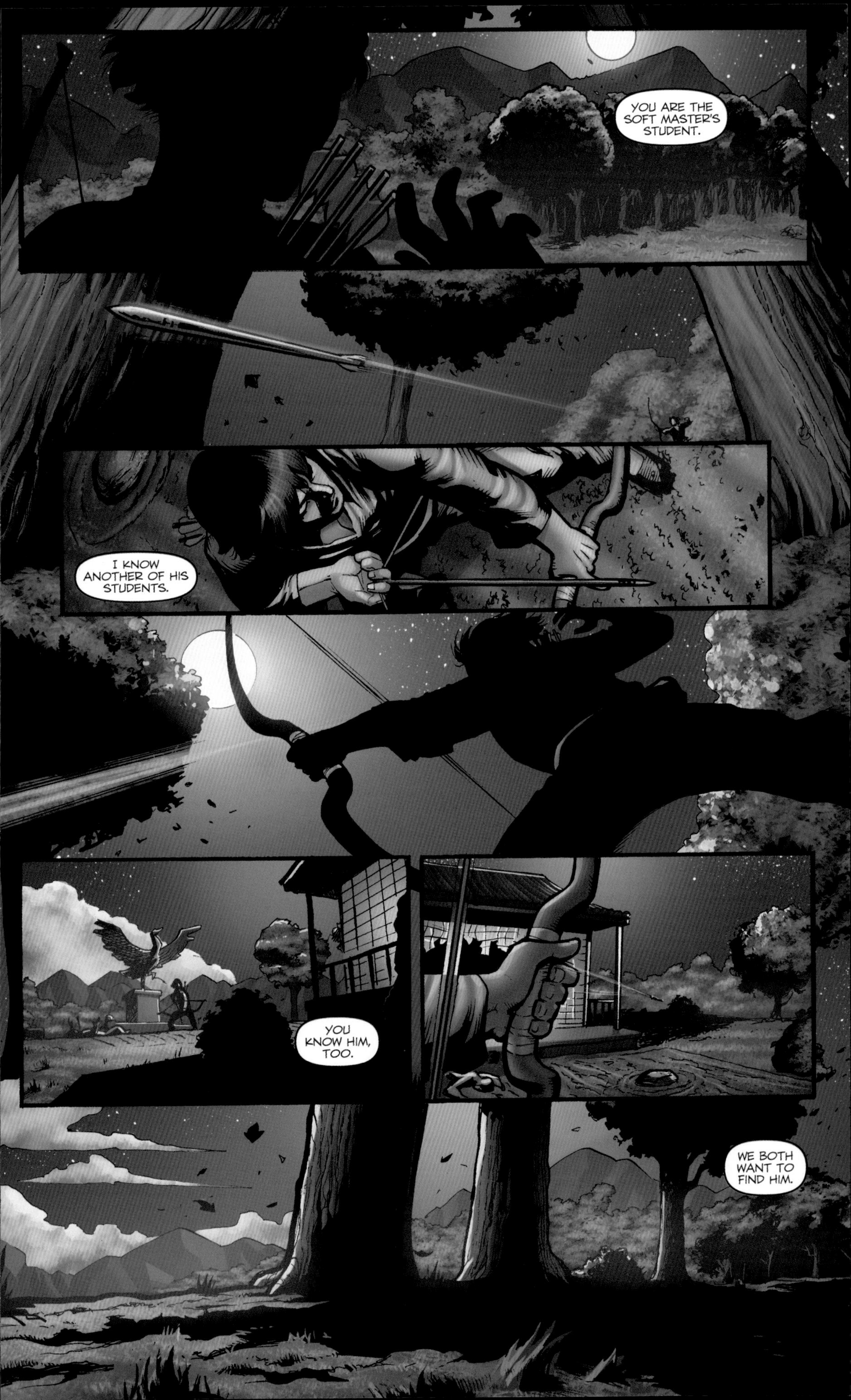
YOU ARE THE SOFT MASTER'S STUDENT.
I KNOW ANOTHER OF HIS STUDENTS.
YOU KNOW HIM, TOO.
WE BOTH WANT TO FIND HIM.

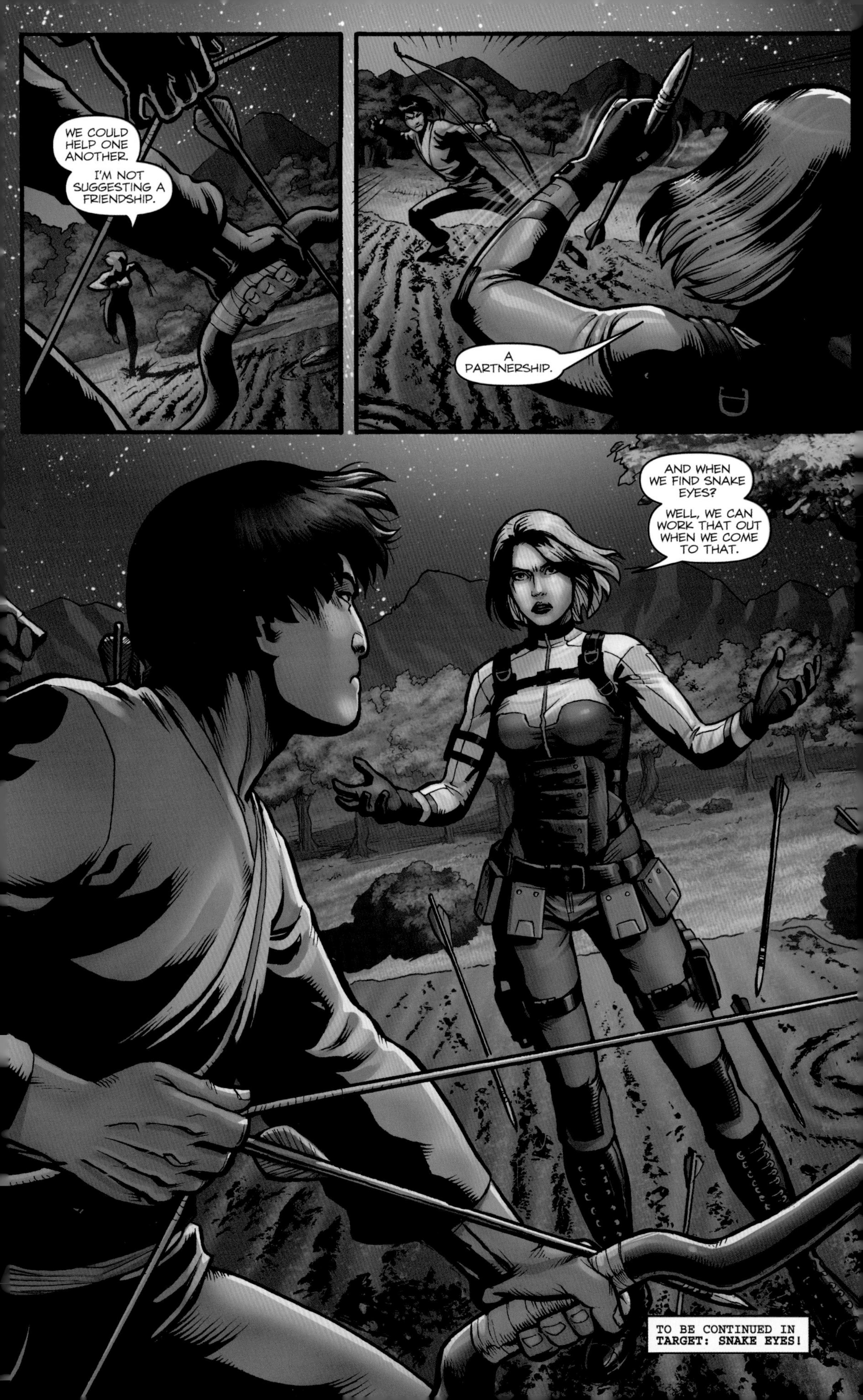
WE COULD HELP ONE ANOTHER.
I'M NOT SUGGESTING A FRIENDSHIP.
A PARTNERSHIP.
AND WHEN WE FIND SNAKE EYES?
WELL, WE CAN WORK THAT OUT WHEN WE COME TO THAT.
TO BE CONTINUED IN TARGET: SNAKE EYES!

Art by **Steve Ellis**

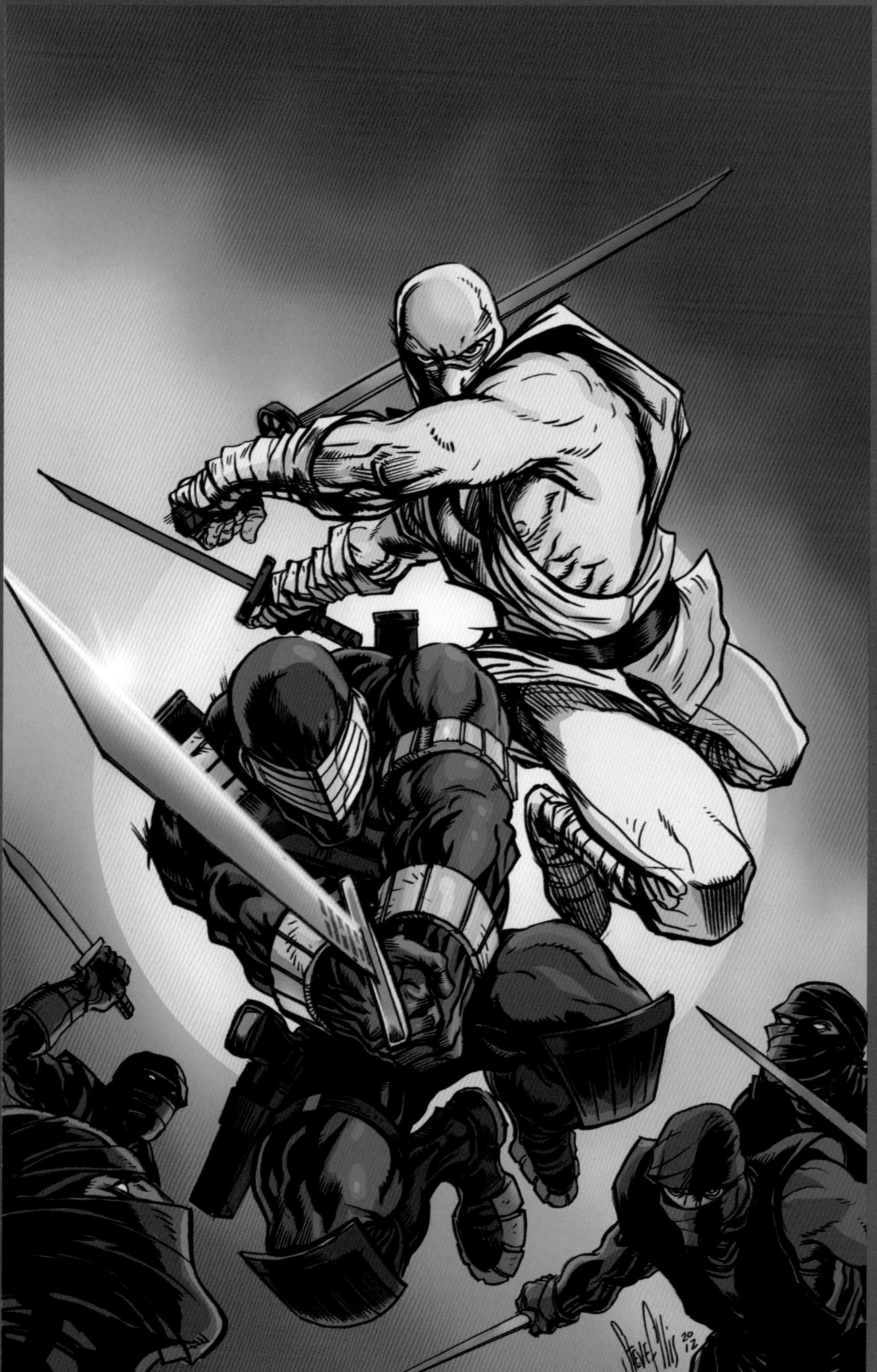
Steve Ellis 2012

Art by **Robert Atkins** | Colors by **Simon Gough**

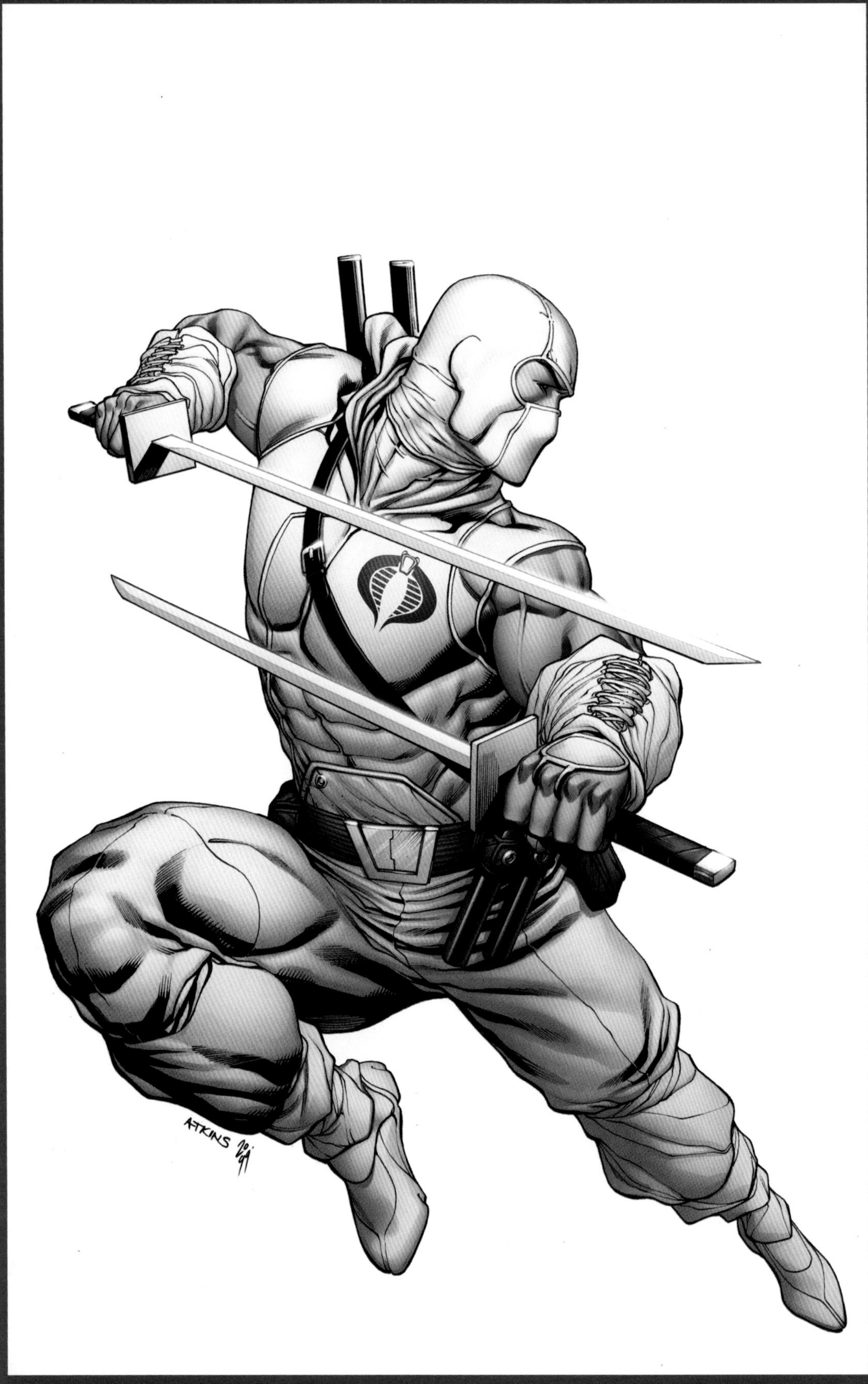
ATKINS

Art by **Robert Atkins** | Colors by **Simon Gough**

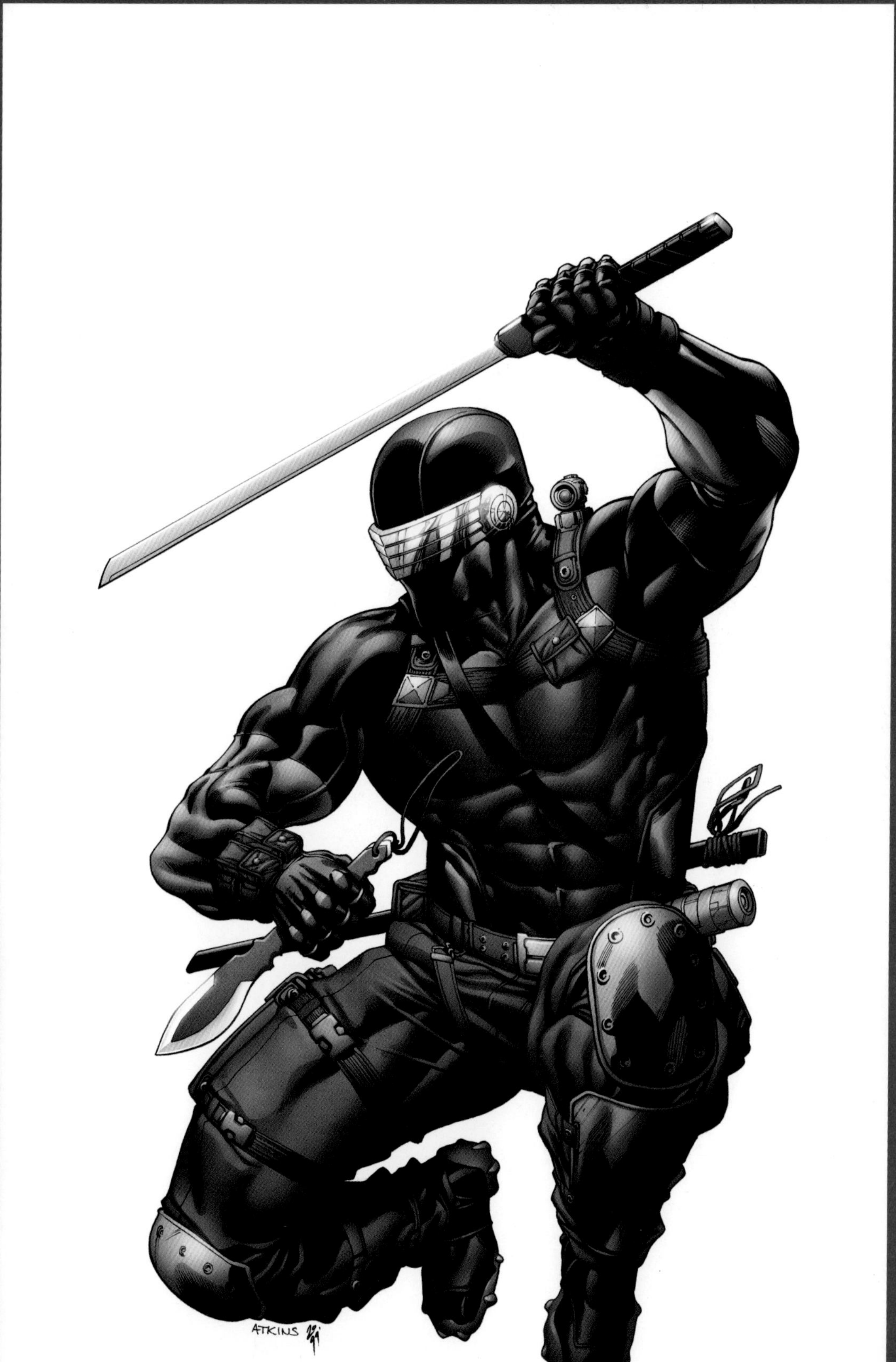
ATKINS

Art by **Andrea Di Vito** | Colors by **Laura Villari**

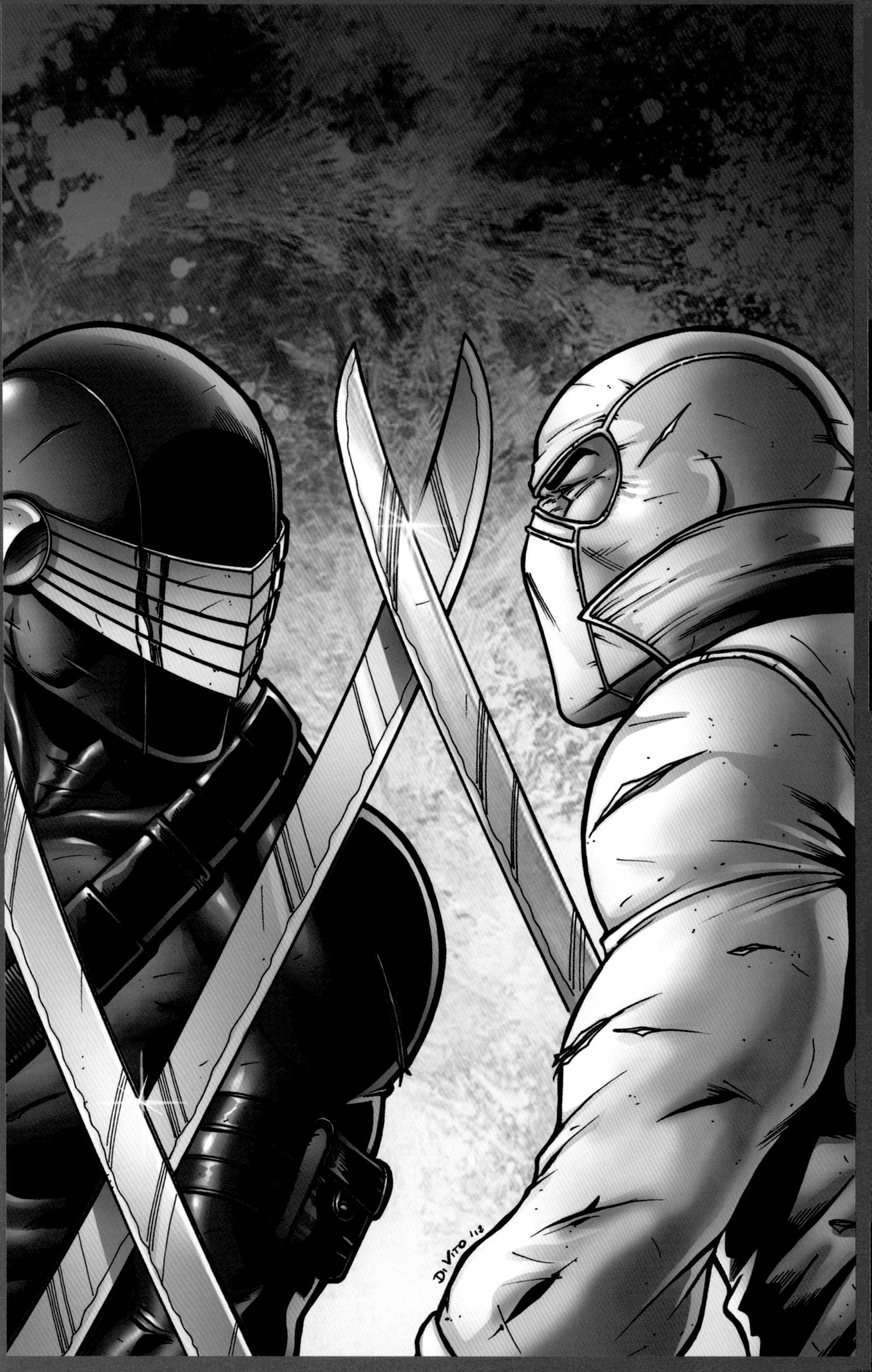

Art by **Lee Ferguson** and **Sal Buscema** | Colors by **Joana Lafuente**

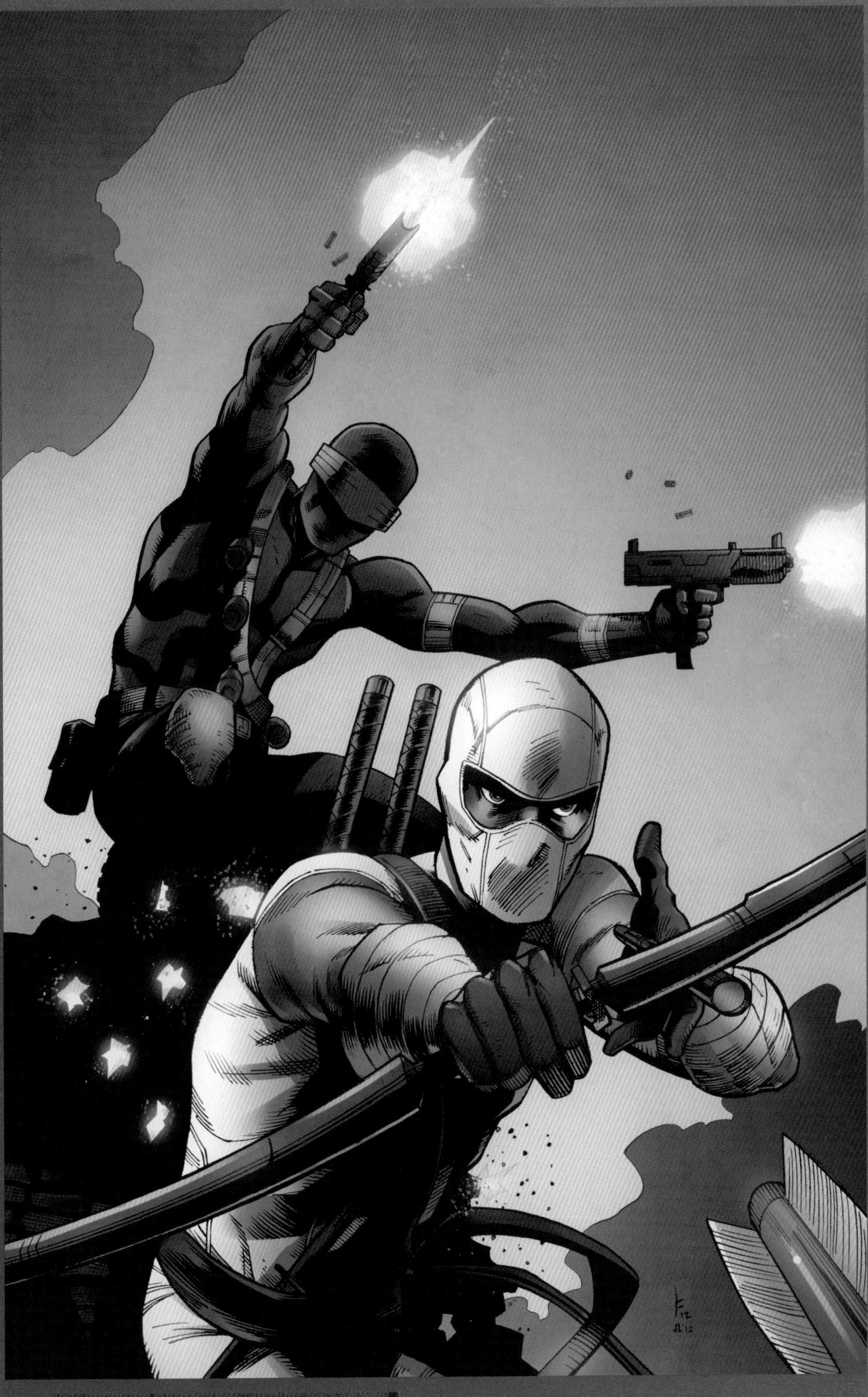

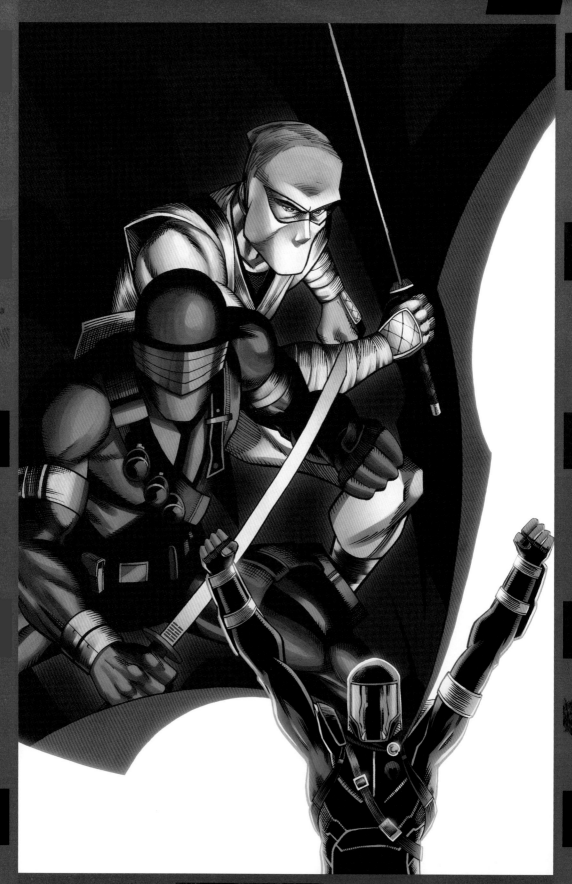

Art by **Alex Cal** | Colors by **J. Aburtov**

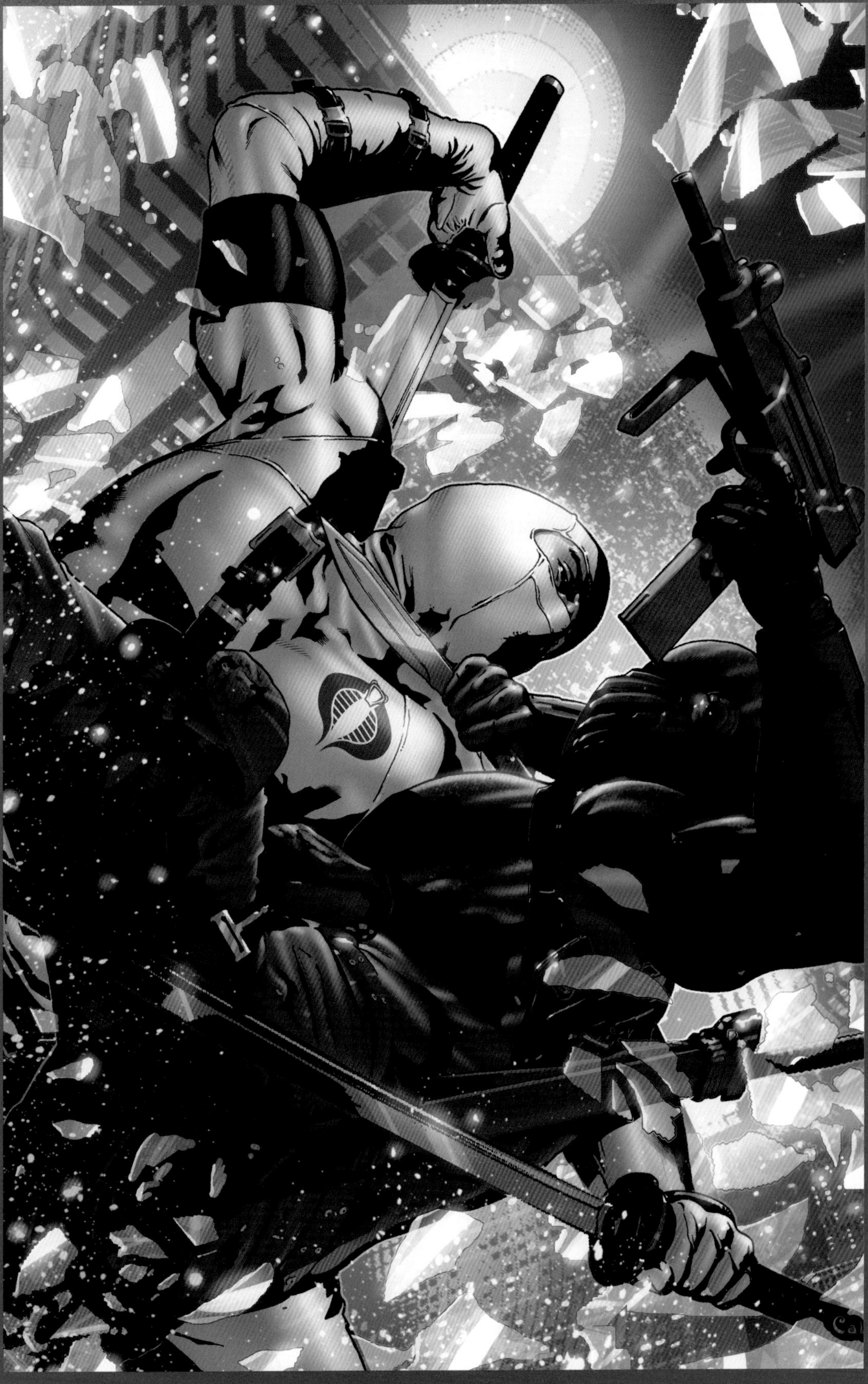

Art by **Robert Atkins** | Colors by **Simon Gough**

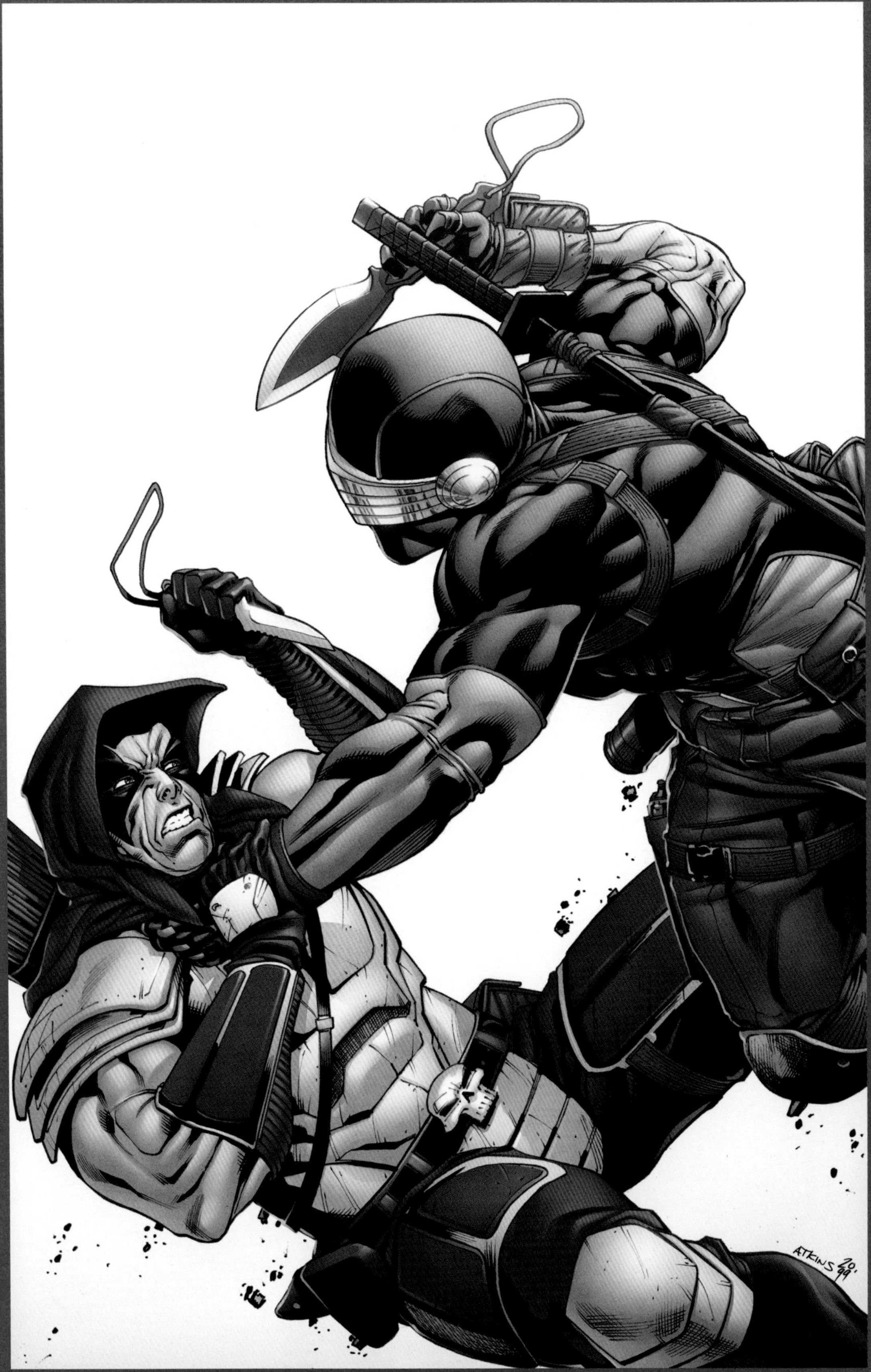

Art by **Kenneth Loh** | Colors by **Joana Lafuente**

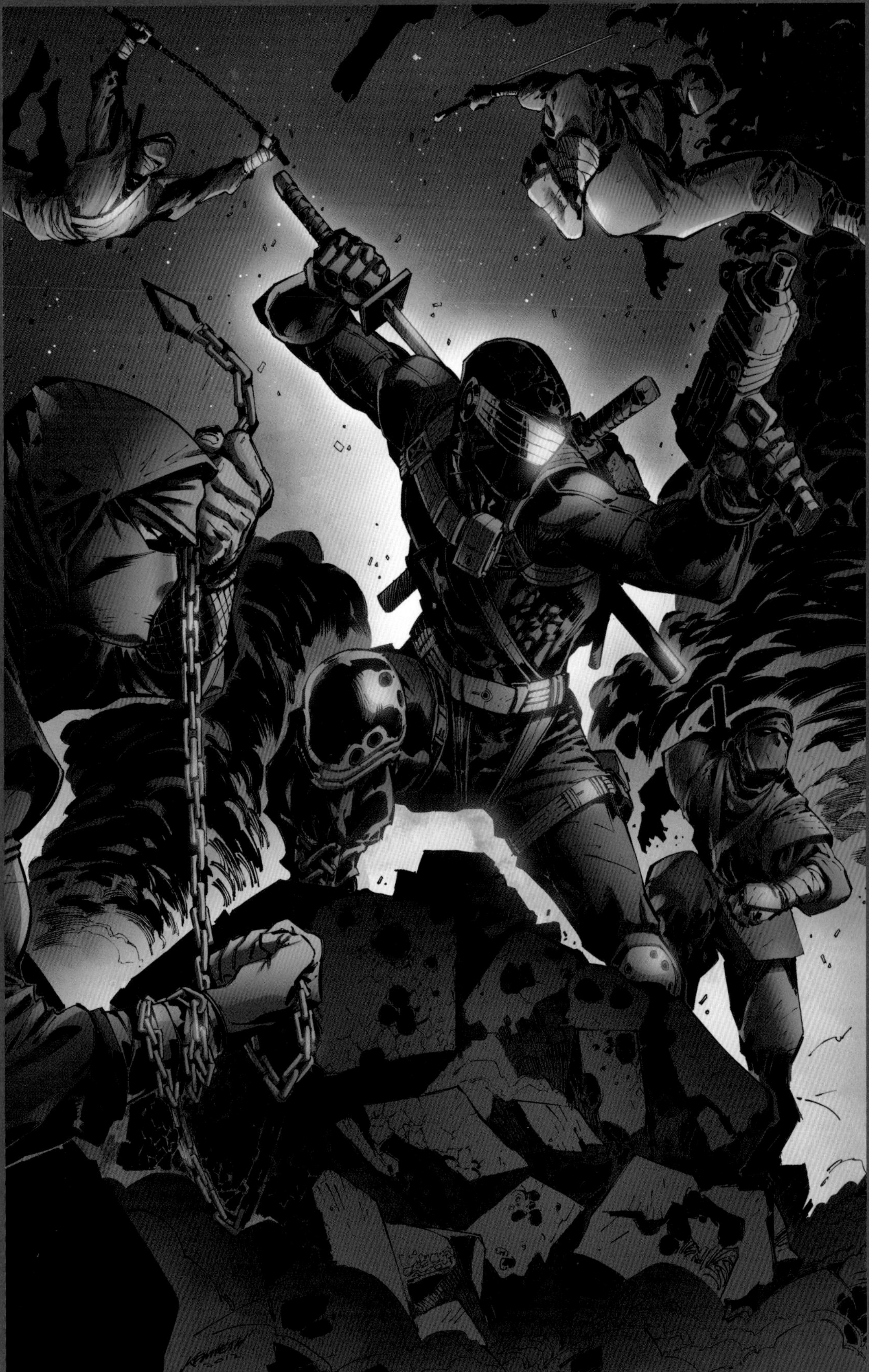

Art by **Robert Atkins** | Colors by **Simon Gough**

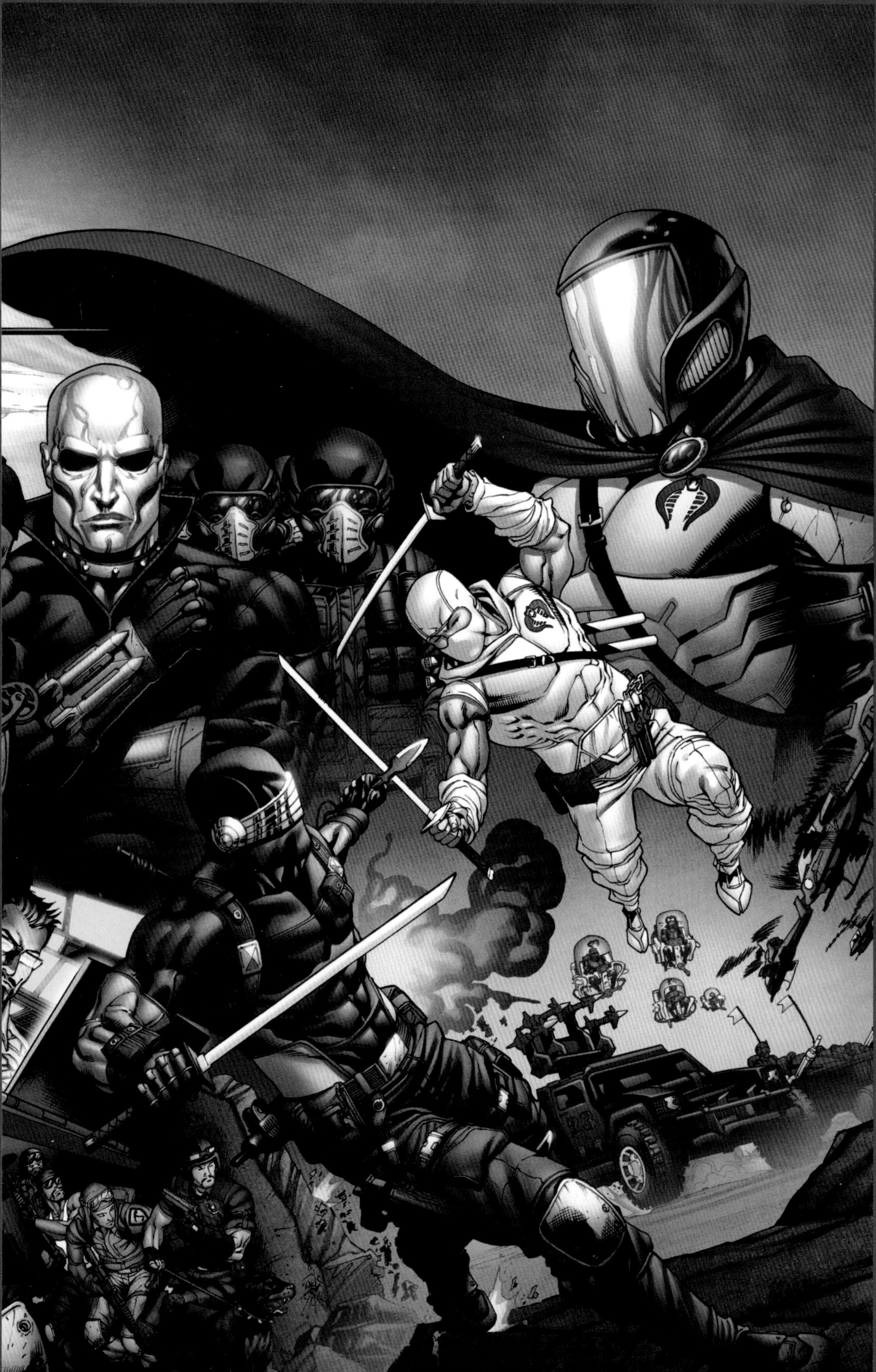